SILENT SCREAM

Also available from *New York Times* bestselling author Karen Harper

South Shores

SHALLOW GRAVE
FALLING DARKNESS
DROWNING TIDES
CHASING SHADOWS

Cold Creek

BROKEN BONDS
FORBIDDEN GROUND
SHATTERED SECRETS

Home Valley Amish

UPON A WINTER'S NIGHT
DARK CROSSINGS (featuring "The Covered Bridge")
FINDING MERCY
RETURN TO GRACE
FALL FROM PRIDE

Novels

DOWN RIVER
DEEP DOWN
THE HIDING PLACE
BELOW THE SURFACE
INFERNO
HURRICANE
DARK ANGEL
DARK HARVEST
DARK ROAD HOME

Visit karenharperauthor.com for more titles.

Look for Karen Harper's next South Shores novel
DARK STORM
coming soon from MIRA Books.

KAREN HARPER

SILENT SCREAM

mira

mira

ISBN-13: 978-0-7783-6983-7

Silent Scream

For questions and comments about the quality of this book, please contact us at
CustomerService@Harlequin.com.

BookClubbish.com

Printed in U.S.A.

I cherish our thirty winters in Naples, Florida.
This novel and the others in the South Shores series
are dedicated to our friends who are still there, full- or part-time.
And as ever to Don for his continued support.

SILENT SCREAM

CHAPTER ONE

Naples, Florida
Sunday, May 22

"Would you stop pacing and looking out the window, sweet-heart?" Nick asked Claire. "You're making me nervous."

"I'm walking the baby," she said and smiled down at their three-month-old son, Trey, in her arms. "Well, I am a bit on edge. I haven't seen my old college roommate for years, and that's quite an offer she's made me. Really, Nick, I'd just retire from my forensic psych work for a while, but this opportunity sounds too intriguing to pass up. Plus, it's nearby—and impor-tant. I've always examined the lives of the deceased, but ones who are thousands of years old in an archaeological dig? Oh, here she is, parking out in front."

She put the baby into his arms. "Give us a second, then bring Trey and Lexi in so Kris can meet them," she told him and pecked a kiss on his cheek.

"I just don't want you two to adopt your old 'women in jeopardy' nickname again," he called after her as she headed for the door.

"That only related to our problems in the old days, and we 'womjeps' are both under control now," she called back to him.

But her heartbeat kicked up. She and Kristen Kane, nickname Kris, had been through hard times together at Florida State as they'd studied, worked jobs and dealt with their disabilities. With her face blindness, Kris had struggled to recognize people, even those close to her, while Claire was desperately trying to navigate a life with narcolepsy and taking powerful drugs to deal with that. If she hadn't, she'd have fallen asleep in class and had terrible nightmares.

She swept open the door before her old friend could ring the bell. "Dr. Kane, I presume! Welcome! So good to see you after all this time!" Claire cried as they hugged each other.

"You still have your great red hair," Kris said as, arm in arm, they walked into the house. "I was hoping so."

"Yep, not going white-haired yet, though I've been through some things that could have done me in."

"So I hear and read, but you know what I mean," Kris told her as they stopped in the tiled foyer while Claire closed the door behind them. "Your unique hair color was how I identified you until I heard your voice. But you know what, my friend? Working with the bog bodies in Denmark—even here—somehow, I can recall their faces and ID them easily. And it isn't just their twisted postures either. Well, you'll see. What a great house," she said, looking around. "But then since you're married to a big-deal criminal lawyer, what would I expect?" she teased. "I haven't found my knight in shining armor yet, but then I've moved around too much. I'm here now though, for the foreseeable future anyway."

"Come sit in here, and I'll introduce my family before we have lunch and get caught up," Claire said, leading the way. "I can't wait to hear about this fascinating dig."

At age thirty-four, Kris looked much the same, maybe with a few new worry lines or squint marks at the outside edges of her blue eyes. Her Florida-girl complexion was a bit paler than Claire recalled. She probably bleached her straight blond hair now, though she still wore it blunt-cut, chin-length with bangs. As ever, Kris looked so serious when she didn't smile. Almost as tall as Claire, who was five-foot-ten, she came across as confident, though for both of them, that confidence had once been a mutual facade to get through tough times. But what a challenge for Kris to not even recall the faces of her family members without other visual clues.

Kristen Kane had thrown herself into a major in forensic archaeology while Claire had stayed with forensic psychology. Kris had a doctorate and studied dead people from the past, ones who no doubt weren't upset if she didn't recognize them.

As Lexi bounced into the room, Claire introduced her six-year-old daughter. "Almost seven in ten months!" the child told Kris. Nick followed, holding the baby whom Kris soon fussed over. Lexi was Claire's child from her first husband, Jace, but little Nicholas Markwood III, whom they called Trey, was hers and Nick's.

"I see Nick is a good catch, looking like a Mr. Mom," Kris said with a little laugh after introductions. She hit Nick's arm lightly with a fist. He just smiled, but Claire felt he still looked every bit the courtroom lawyer with his height of over six feet, erect posture, piercing gray eyes and dark but silvering hair. Kris was studying his face as she always did with someone new.

"I did look up your picture online, Nick, and found one on your law firm's website," she admitted. "I try to do my prep work. I guess Claire explained my prosopagnosia."

"It certainly hasn't slowed you down, Doctor," Nick assured her. "It sounds like you have a fascinating career."

"Important too—really. We learn so much about the present and future by studying the triumphs and tragedies of the past."

"Are you a baby doctor?" Lexi asked, looking up at her. "We

have one now, and Mommy said she wished he'd come to the house."

"No, not that kind of doctor," Kris told her as they sat back down, Nick still holding Trey and Lexi perched on the foot-stool by Claire's chair. "I do try to find out what happened to people sometimes, though—if they got sick or not when they were alive, things like that."

"I heard Mommy say she might help you, and she told Dad that her motto is 'The dead still talk if you know how to listen.' But I don't think you can hear what dead people say unless they are Halloween ghosts and that's all pretend. I do like secrets, though, and I keep them really quiet."

"Well, you have a very bright thinker here," Kris said, turning toward Claire. "I can tell Nick's concerned about what I want to offer, but don't be, either of you. Not a thing to worry about except getting bog mud on yourself, a few mosquito bites and keeping a secret. And, if you accept my offer, both of you must keep our privacy agreement too."

Claire looked at Nick, but thank heavens, he didn't frown or protest, because she wanted desperately to help with this mys-terious dig into the past.

After lunch in the Florida room overlooking their fenced-in pool and backyard, Nick excused himself and went to put Trey down for a nap. He was a great father and stepfather, Claire told Kris, explaining that they were still friends with Lexi's father, Jace, and his fiancée, Brittany.

"I'm so glad to hear that," Kris said, frowning. "I was wonder-ing how you and Jace were doing, sharing your daughter and all after the divorce. Before I saw how great she is today and how happy you are now, I was feeling guilty that I introduced Jace and you. I know you two fell for each other hard and fast, and it seemed so right at the time. Jace isn't like so many of those other handsome flyboys. I always had a soft spot for that derring-do kind of guy myself, though nothing ever came of it."

"When you set us up seems so long ago. Obviously, Jace and I had some great times—and then some bad. But Lexi was the best, and we are sharing her well. He's engaged now. Nick and I know and like his fiancée, and she's good with Lexi. Works at a zoo, so that goes a long way. Even Nick and Jace are friends after some of the tough times we've all been through."

They both looked out in back to see that Nick was now sitting in a lounge chair with some paperwork while Lexi perched by his feet staring at a picture book she had already "read" over and over. Claire was glad they were in the shade because the sun was hot for late May.

But Claire and Kris remained in the glassed-in, air-conditioned room, facing each other in matching rattan swivel basket chairs. At lunch, Kris had talked about her life in Denmark in general, but with Lexi there, she had obviously said little about the ancient bog people her crew had disinterred and studied. But now she leaned forward, elbows propped on her knees, gripping her hands together.

"Claire, you won't believe this amazing local archaeology find until you see it. Not to sound cute, but it is absolutely groundbreaking. Extremely significant, but we've managed to keep it top secret to all but a few in the Florida state government and museum world because support money is a challenge. The site is privately owned, funded and controlled to keep a lid on what we are uncovering there."

Claire sat up straighter. She only nodded at Lexi when she came in and announced she was going to the bathroom before disappearing down the hall.

"Let me just give you an overview," Kris went on, leaning even farther forward. "In Denmark, I've been working with Early Neolithic bodies—Stone Age. Most of the ones we excavated were sixteen to twenty years old at death, so we assumed, and then found evidence that they were either human sacrifices or executed criminals. And that's what got me the job offer here."

Kris's face and voice were so intense, but Claire realized she was holding herself rigid too, hanging on each word.

Kris went on, "But so far none of the bodies in Black Bog nearby show signs of violence or ritual. Claire, archaeological sites are often like crime scenes. You specialize in psychological autopsies where you don't have a body, but still examine the person's life and death to help the police make a determination of the type of death—natural, accidental, suicidal or homicidal."

Riveted, Claire just nodded. She'd recently discovered a shallow grave and the tragedy it had been connected to, but to be able to peer into an ancient grave and solve that death—amazing.

"Have you heard of the Windover Culture?" Kris went on. "The bodies dug up in a bog quite a ways north of here near Disney World in the early 1980s?"

"Yes, but I don't remember details. I know they found Stone Age people there."

"Here too, near Naples in Black Bog. I have been hired to lead the dig team that is excavating a treasure trove of ancient people, and I need you to consult. After all, your expertise of studying the lives of the dead could be invaluable to us. I'll do the science, you put the clues together to psych out how they lived and died. If you'll agree to visit the dig with me, I'll introduce you to the property owners and dig controllers, Andrea and Bradley Vance."

"Bradley Vance? Wasn't he a state senator or something?"

"One and the same, recently retired, so he has some clout around here and in Tallahassee, not to mention an inheritance from his family to finance this, though I think he and his wife have gone through that already. But his wife, Andrea, is even more important. Do you remember my talking about Professor Andrea Carson after you graduated, and I went on for a masters and doctorate?"

"You admired and worked closely with her."

"My mentor, oversaw my dissertation, later my orals. I did some prehistoric Anasazi tribal digs with her out West. I've worked hard for her, and she's brought me along in her impressive wake. A genius, and we'd be working directly with and for her."

"I'll have to convince Nick if it will take a lot of my time."

"Like I said in my letter, you can work three days a week, part-time, if need be, but I—well, I need your help, frankly, figuring these ancient people out. Like I said, for now, it's top secret so we don't get looting or reporters tramping all over, ruining things in that delicate environment of moss, mud, water and peat. Neither you nor Nick—and not even sweet, little Lexi with her secret-keeping—can let on about what you and I are really doing, not until we know enough to go public with this huge find without having outsiders tell us what to do and how to do it. Deal?"

"I will explain to Nick, tell him how much I'd love to do this. When we first got your note right after Trey was born, he said that, after all, what can go wrong when you're dealing with those who are long dead, who have no family members or even enemies to file a lawsuit or cause a problem?"

"Right. I know you've been through a lot, but this is different. Oh, by the way, though the dig is state-of-the-art, I should tell you there are no cell towers close enough to the bog that cell phones work there, so we use two-way radio transmitters to keep in touch with each other on-site. You know, walkie-talkies, our only real concession to nontech. I know from your Clear Path website that you do consulting only online these days, but this will be hands-on. The Vances and I need your help, and it will contribute to the knowledge of all mankind."

Claire nodded. For the first time, she would not be helping living people, but knowledge of the past was important too.

"Think about this, Claire. Black Bog bodies are seven thousand years old but only look two years dead! They were interred before the time of Christ, before the pyramids were built! Yet they're only a bit shriveled. They've been preserved under piles of peat that has tanned their bodies to a dark brown, but you can see their expressions, absolutely what they looked like. Even someone with face blindness is blown away by their individuality and the stories they have to tell."

So passionate, so convincing. Deeply moved, Claire could only nod yet again. Instead of hugging this time, they shook hands.

Later that evening, Claire was ecstatic. Maybe she could have it all—a wonderful family life, an understanding husband she was madly in love with, and a safe and exciting at-least-part-time career. Nick had agreed and had even been intrigued by her consulting offer, which she would actually accept or reject after she visited the Black Bog dig, met the Vances and saw the terms of her contract. Nick, who had worked hard to build his father's criminal law firm and run his South Shores project on the side to help people determine whether the deaths of their loved ones were murders or suicides, had thought that was a good plan.

They had dropped Lexi and Trey off at Claire's sister, Darcy's, house for the early evening, because they were going to help their newlywed friends, Bronco and Nita Gates, clean up the house they had bought for an excellent price with a loan partly financed by Nick. Bronco worked as a security guard at Nick's law firm. Nita was their part-time nanny for Trey and Lexi, and the four adults were close friends.

Though they were still living in an apartment, Bronco and Nita had bought their new house in East Naples, a one-floor stucco painted aqua in a middle-class development just off the Tamiami Trail. The price had been good because the house had been owned by a recently deceased elderly woman who was a hoarder, and it would need a lot of work even after being cleared out. It had been a private sale by the woman's son, Dale Braun, who was a junior partner at Nick's law firm, Markwood, Benton and Chase. The housing development covered a large piece of land where a mansion once stood at the back of the Braun estate.

"Nita loves the color of the house," Claire told Nick as they parked in front. "'The color of the sea,' she says."

"She'll love it a lot more once they get all that stuff hauled out of here, but they're making progress." As they headed for the house, they passed a rented dumpster sitting in the driveway, full of various junk to be thrown out.

"We're here!" Claire called as they knocked, then went in through the unlocked screen door.

Juanita, whom they called Nita, a lovely Mexican-born woman, appeared, wiping her hands on her jeans. "Been digging through so much and sure can use your help," she told them. "I'm in the kitchen area, and Bronco's out back, Nick. There's stuff spilling out of that little shed behind the garage. Don't know how someone could live this way. Does her son have a messy desk at work?"

"No, it's evidently not hereditary," he told her with a smile.

"Go ahead," Claire encouraged him. "I'll pitch in with Nita here."

"Good thing you dressed the part," Nita told Claire as Nick went out back. "That little room off the kitchen is jammed full of stuff, a lot of it piled on top of an old freezer."

"I'll bet that's an electricity hog if it's still plugged in," Claire said.

"Oh, *si*, still running. The way she threw nothing out, bet it's full of old food," Nita said and gestured at the big chest freezer.

"You'll need a team to get that heavy thing out of here. At least you've been making good progress unloading the things on top of it," Claire told her, eyeing the piles of items not only on it but sitting on the floor.

"Wish I'd find some hidden money. Just kidding. I'd give it straight to Mr. Braun. Doesn't pay to do anything illegal in this life, that's for sure. Maybe there's something we can sell round here, though, 'cause Mr. Braun said all of this is ours if we want to use it, if it's not tied direct to him or his family. He's not married though, broke up with his fiancée, a neighbor said. Mr. Braun told Bronco he's looking for another place to live now 'stead of next door since he doesn't have to worry about his elderly bats-in-the-belfry mother anymore. Honest, Claire, that's what he said."

"It doesn't take much looking around here to realize she was eccentric at the least. Maybe she had dementia because that increases the tendency to hoard. Let's keep clearing stuff out."

From atop the old freezer, they lifted and carted out stacks of moldy newspapers and magazines, then two boxes of Christmas decorations, including a big one with a smiling plastic Santa Claus with a frayed extension cord dangling from its innards. Once they had unburied the freezer, which was still humming with power, they unlatched and lifted the heavy lid together. A cloud of moist, stale air wafted up at them.

"Quite the antique," Claire said, fanning her face to see better as they peered into the crowded depths. "Maybe the manufacturer will buy it back as proof their product lasts."

"I'm just hoping there are steaks or lobster in here," Nita said with a nervous laugh. "This house has been quite a treasure hunt."

"Looks mostly like frozen vegetables. Wow, I haven't seen this Birds Eye brand packaging for years. Even though this stuff is frozen, you'd better not eat it. There must be an expiration date on this," she said picking up a package of rock-hard frozen broccoli and scanning it. "With the piles of things on the lid, she obviously didn't get in here much and not for years. What a waste, so sad."

While Nita rooted around at the other end of the long freezer, Claire moved a large opaque plastic bag that looked as if it might contain whole strawberries. And under that, as if she'd unearthed her from her icy tomb, the frozen face of a young woman stared upward with her eyes and mouth wide open as if in shock or horror.

CHAPTER TWO

Their screams brought Nick and Bronco running.

Nita leaned against the wall, her hands covering her face, while Claire steadied herself, gripping the open freezer and staring into it. This reminded her of standing by her mother's casket with her sister beside her. Darcy had been crying, Claire trying to hang on to sanity just before they'd closed the lid.

"Claire, what?" Nick's voice jolted her back to reality.

Nita threw herself into Bronco's arms. Claire pointed and cried, "There! A dead woman—frozen!"

Nick peered down and gasped. "She's real," he whispered and pulled Claire hard against him. "Nita, do you know who this is? Bronco, take a look. I'm going to call the police and the medical examiner."

Nita took another look and Bronco peered inside. Shaking her head and trembling, Nita whispered, "Never seen her." Pressing her hands over her mouth, she started to cry again.

"Me neither," Bronco muttered and pulled Nita back into his arms. "She is—was—kinda young. Boss, this gonna mean trouble for us in our new house, even if we're still in our old apartment for now?"

"Just for a little while if we handle this right," he said, digging his phone out of his jeans pocket and thumbing in numbers. He put one hand on Claire's shoulder as she continued to stare down at the frozen face.

"Yes, an emergency," he said into the phone. "This is attorney Nicholas Markwood. We have discovered a dead body in a newly purchased house that's been empty for about two weeks since the death of its previous owner. No—it's not the previous owner's body. We don't need a squad but send officers—I'm requesting Detective Ken Jensen, if he's available, and the ME. Yes, I know. I promise you we won't move or touch anything, though we did open the freezer where we found her."

He gave them the address, then took a photo of the woman in the freezer using a flash. Claire looked down at the woman again, her features lit by that sudden jab of light: maybe late twenties, a pretty blonde, staring up at them through boxes of frozen vegetables and clear-wrap packages of chicken breasts. How absurd. How horrible.

"You took that picture to ask around who she is, boss?" Bronco asked. Big and burly as he was, he was trembling too. "Won't the police do that?"

"Probably. But since this house was recently owned by Dale Braun, one of the firm's junior partners, he may be questioned and I may be too, so I'll keep this photo. Sadly, I'm always thinking like a criminal lawyer—plan ahead for every contingent."

"Yeah, I know who he is from checking him in at my guard post," Bronco said. "A real go-getter, comes early, stays late. He's a handsome dude, acts like it too."

"Oh, *that* junior partner," Claire said. "The one who always seems dressed up and doesn't have a dark hair out of place. Since this was his mother's house, it ties to him and so to the firm. And Nita and my fingerprints are all over that stupid freezer."

"You both have a rational explanation and no ties to this corpse," Nick assured them. "I just wish she didn't have her eyes and mouth open like that. And I hope it's not just her head without a body."

Nita said, "It makes this house feel—well, not good now—kind of not ours."

"They'll clear it out good as new," Bronco insisted. "Hey, I hear a siren already."

"Me too," Nick said, pulling Claire away with him as Bronco and Nita followed. They waited in the small cluttered living room. It was paramedics who pulled up in front, but what could they do for a definitely dead and frozen, no doubt murdered, woman?

They saw two police cars and an unmarked vehicle arrive in front too. Nick greeted them at the door with Bronco right behind him. The detective, Ken Jensen, with whom they had worked before, asked an officer to put police tape around the front of the house, and told the paramedics to wait to see if the ME's office brought a van.

"I'm glad you got word that I asked for you, Detective," Nick told the man. They hadn't seen him since the shallow grave case they'd worked six months ago. He shook hands with the tall blond detective, who also greeted Claire.

"I understand why you turned down our department's offer to consult on cases, Claire," Detective Ken Jensen said. "Congrats on the new baby. But here you are discovering a case of your own."

"Not our case, this time," she insisted. "Pure, sad chance." She extended her hand too, then introduced Bronco and Nita as the new homeowners. "None of us know the victim. Nita and I were just clearing things off the top of the freezer while the men worked out back. The previous owner, an elderly woman, was a hoarder—and was evidently unknowingly or knowingly hoarding a very dead, frozen body."

Nick moved his knee against hers to stop her. Damn, he thought, she sounded like she was testifying in court like she had so many times, as a forensic psychologist expert witness to help clarify cause and manner of death. She had real instincts for psyching people out, but he didn't want her any more involved in this than she was, because he was afraid he might have to be. He only hoped there would be no link between the dead woman and his junior partner who had sold Bronco and Nita this house. No—no way, or Dale would have made sure the body wasn't here to be found, though stranger things had happened.

"Sorry, detective, maybe too much too soon," Claire added, her voice sounding steady at last. "Back in my forensic psych mode."

"Well," Detective Jensen said, "if this does become a case that goes to trial, you could be called to testify, but not in that capacity. Let's have a look at the body before the ME gets here. Lead the way."

Bronco went first, holding Nita's hand, then Claire, then Nick and Ken Jensen. The five of them crowded into the small room with the freezer. Frosty air still wafted upward. Jensen looked inside and jerked a bit at the sight.

"She looks like she's shocked and screaming." He said the obvious. "Like she is being attacked right now."

No one said a word while he took several flash pictures with his phone, then used it to call for a crime scene photographer and evidence technicians. He moved them back to the living room and called one of the policemen in. "I see there's a curious neighborhood crowd gathering outside," he told the officer. "Take my phone with this photo and see if anyone can ID this woman. Send the ME in when he or his people get here while I take statements."

They sat on unpacked boxes in the living room, waiting to individually give their statements to Detective Jensen out back in the small Florida room. Nick dug his phone out again and texted Dale Braun, who was not at his house next door, but got no answer back. If it hadn't been a Sunday, he would have called

him at the office. Dale was a dedicated worker, a little hard to
get to know, very bright but not really socially adept for a guy
so good-looking. He was in his early thirties, an upper-range
millennial.

Claire looked stunned. Nita too, even after talking to Jensen. Nick jolted when one of the cops knocked on the door near
where he sat, and Jensen got up to answer it. The detective had
closed the place up and turned the air-conditioning on full blast,
as if to keep the already frozen corpse cold for the ME. With
an assistant, he would dig the body out for a preliminary onsite
investigation before they took the corpse to the Collier County
morgue for an autopsy.

"Hey, Detective Jensen," they heard the officer at the door say
as he handed Jensen's cell phone back. "Got a positive ID of the
deceased from a neighbor lady two doors down, a Mrs. Betty
Richards. Says it's the former fiancée of the guy next door whose
mother owned this house, ah, a Dale Braun, a lawyer no less.
Even knows the name of the victim—Cynthia Lindley. We'll
go next door and see if Dale Braun's there."

Nick's gaze slammed into Claire's. He'd been hoping for more
time to find and question Dale. This would implicate him, pull
the firm into the investigation. The husband, the boyfriend, the
fiancé—always the first one the cops looked at.

"I've been trying to reach Dale Braun," Nick told Jensen.
"He's a junior partner in my law firm. He's not home next door
and not answering his phone."

"But you've seen him recently?"

"At the firm on Friday."

"No kidding, Counselor," Jensen said, jotting that down in
his notes. "Hate to say it, but the plot thickens about who could
have hurt that girl."

"All circumstantial so far, as you know," Nick said. He wanted
to say much more, that Dale Braun seemed like a straight arrow,
though Nick had not known he had a fiancée, let alone a for-

mer one—evidently a missing one. It didn't make sense that
Dale would sell this house if he knew a woman's body was still
in it, knowing he could be tied to it so easily. And where was
Dale and would he show up to work tomorrow morning or at
his house next door before that? No doubt the cops would be
there in both places waiting to question him.

Claire reached out to take his hand. She sat up straighter and
only narrowed her eyes, unlike Nita, who had not stopped crying. Yeah, Claire looked stunned but steady. But then what a
shock to open an old freezer and find a human face staring upward. A pretty face. A face contorted in a silent scream.

With Jensen's permission, Nick took Nita and Bronco home
with them that evening to stay in their guest room rather than
letting them head home to their apartment, in case the police or
the press showed up there. If they were implicated at all—and
he knew they weren't guilty of anything—he'd assign someone
from the firm to represent them—or even take the case on himself. Before he and Claire headed to pick up their kids at Claire's
sister's, he had wanted to get some warnings out of the way.

"No way you can hang around a crime scene," Nick had told
them before they went out to their cars. "But I'll bet you'll get
back in a couple of days." *If people don't stand around staring at the
"death house,"* he did not tell them. "I wish I—or they—could
locate Dale," he went on. "It's going to look like he fled, which
I hope he didn't. He'd better have an airtight alibi."

"You'll defend him if he asks?" Claire asked.

"If he's indicted either I, or at least the firm will, but let's not
jump to conclusions any more than Ken Jensen evidently has.
You just go away from all this with your friend Kris tomorrow,
and Nita can stay with Trey. Bronco, you just do your security
job at the firm tomorrow and don't answer questions from anyone but me when word of this breaks," he said, frowning out
at the neighborhood gawkers. "The newspaper and TV report-

ers will be here soon with a frozen dead woman for a headline. The four of us plus the kids are going to lock ourselves in our house tonight with no comment. That's at least until tomorrow when we see what the ME and Jensen come up with. Everybody got that?"

"Sure, boss, Nita and me are fine with that, right honey?"

"*Si*. I just want our new house back with no more awful surprises," she said and blew her nose.

"Aye, aye, Captain," Claire said to his orders, but he could tell her clever brain was spinning. He hoped she was thinking about visiting the Black Bog dig with her friend tomorrow—dead people, sure, but ones that would cause them no trouble. He'd seen that Claire had not only texted her sister they would be there soon to pick up Lexi and the baby. By borrowing his phone, she'd also taken another look at the picture of the dead woman, Dale Braun's former fiancée whose stare sliced right through you as she opened her mouth to scream and—and then someone killed her.

CHAPTER THREE

"I'll bet you're relieved to be going to the land of the long dead instead of the newly dead. Sorry if that came out wrong," Kris told Claire as she drove them in a Jeep on the Tamiami Trail toward Black Bog. Kris had told Claire their destination was beyond Seminole State Park, east of Blackwater Bay, which was only about a half-hour drive. "I just mean after you had that terrible experience yesterday."

Kris frowned and bit her lower lip hard as if she wanted to say something else, but kept it back. Sometimes Claire wished she didn't read body language. But maybe her friend only regretted she had brought that up after Claire had recounted the horrific find in the freezer, not that it wasn't public knowledge on all the news media this morning, including some national programs.

"It's a joke among the crew," Kris said, still frowning and obviously trying to change the subject, "that we're not far from Mud Bay. We do get 'boggy dirty' on this dig. At least the Everglades runoff from Lake Okeechobee doesn't flow through the bog. It's more solid peat, not water."

"Sounds delightfully muddy anyway. Kris, it's okay to ask

about the woman in the freezer. Honestly, I've been through tough times before."

"I didn't mean to hit you with all that right away. The bodies we deal with are hardly frozen in this South Florida climate but they are frozen in time."

"The TV stations and *Naples Daily News* picked up on the story fast, but I can see why, so I'm glad to 'get out of Dodge' today. Thanks for picking me up at my sister's where—I hope—reporters won't know to find me later. Nick won't escape them at the office, though, especially if Dale Braun shows up there for work this morning."

"Yeah, to no doubt get arrested the moment he does—at least dragged in for questioning. And that poor couple who works for you—to have a picture of their new house and its address all over the news. They'll get ghoulish gawkers, which is exactly why the Black Bog dig is top secret."

"Bronco and Nita have had it tough. They and another couple we know—a tech guy who also works for Nick, and the techie's girlfriend—have been through a lot with us. But let's talk about something cheery—like the bog bodies you've managed to hide from the world so far."

"Claire," Kris said, turning her head briefly toward her, before looking back at the road, "*that*—excuse me for putting it this way—is deadly serious. You'll see why this has to be classified information for now. Carefully read that part of the contract the Vances will offer you. You may even have to lie to people you know. We have to keep the lid on this. I've said it before, but our findings are important to archaeology and mankind. You'll see why when Andrea and I show you around."

"I can't wait, and, believe me, you can trust Nick and me. The others will just know I'm working on a project that's private for now—even chatterbox Lexi."

"She's a doll," Kris said, as she made the westward turn onto an unpaved road which kicked up a trail of dust behind them.

The month of May was early in the rainy season: the sky was a bit gray, and rain clouds threatened. Claire was grateful that Kris seemed so easy to work with. Even when her friend had some serious, almost stressed-out moments, they had always segued easily back into their longtime trust and friendship. Claire sat up straight and pulled her big purse with touch screen tablet and good old pen and paper notebook closer to her legs. She wanted to be prepared in case her iPad didn't work out here. She had to really pay attention, take notes to go over later, since this was foreign territory in more ways than one. She'd taken things pretty easy with work since Trey's birth and wondered if her concentration and stamina would hold up. She'd seldom been in on something as unusual or fascinating as this—lots of dead bodies with totally foreign lives and deaths. And she had the opportunity to psych them out, to bring them back to life in a way.

"I saw that road sign we just passed said we're heading toward Blackwater Bay," she observed. "Is Black Bog along that bay?"

"In the vicinity, but not on the water. You do know the difference between a bog, a fen and a swamp, don't you?"

"I have a feeling I'm going to have a lot to learn here. I know a swamp is standing water and various stages of plant growth. Tell me the rest."

"A fen—which there are so many of in the colder countries of Europe, but some here in the Southern US—is an open body of water on a bog's surface. If there's a fen in a dig, we drain it, as we have here, at least as best we could during the dry seasons, so pray there's not much rain for a while," she said, squinting at the gray sky. "If it rains, we cover what we have and come back another day."

"But this is obviously a bog, not a fen or swamp per se."

"Right. Bogs, which we are mostly dealing with, hold layers of dead plant material often called peat, including rotting sphagnum moss. Sphagnum releases tanning acids that preserve the corpses, almost as if they've been pickled—a gross picture, I admit. Some bogs are as thick as forty feet, but fortunately, Black

Bog is only about twelve feet deep, and we've drained and excavated that down to about eight to ten feet. We have to be very
careful resurrecting bodies and any artifacts, of course."

"Do the bodies damage easily once they're out?"

"No, they're amazingly resilient. The bones are pretty soft
because the acid in peat has leached out a lot of calcium phos-
phate, so the bodies are rubbery and look kind of deflated. But,
Claire, you can see expressions, stubble, eyelashes!

"It would make things so much easier," Kris went on, "if
we could use a GPS finder like we can use over digs on solid
ground, but those things are heavier than a lawn mower and
would sink. You'll see our system of planks laid out in grids over
our finds. You'll have to learn, as we say, to 'walk the plank' to
get a good look at the bodies in their graves before we disinter
them. Enough said, because I'll let Andrea give you the tour.
Brad may be back later, but he had to oversee their art and antique store in Naples this morning. Art For Art's Sake. Funny,
huh? Their real antiques are top secret, but they sell other ones
in stores on both Florida coasts."

"It all sounds totally intriguing. As Lexi likes to say, 'Are we
there yet?'"

"Claire, our work in this place is going to blow your mind."

"Nick, I swear to you, I had no idea there was a body in my
mother's freezer—especially not Cyndi's! Yeah, we had a bad
breakup, but I'll always love her and never would have hurt her!"
Dale Braun protested and threw himself into a chair in front of
Nick's desk.

Nick had finally reached him by phone and told him to come
up to the office the back way, using the janitor's entrance and
stairs. Bronco had met him and led him to Nick's office because
the police were waiting out by his secretary's desk as well as at
the front door of the building. They both knew they had little
time before, at the least, he was taken downtown for questioning.

Nick shoved away from leaning against his desk. He didn't want to seem intimidating, but he wanted the truth from this man in a hurry.

Nick had been pretty hard on Dale this morning, but he needed to get a feel for his employee's emotions as well as the truth about this mess. He wasn't putting this firm out on a limb only to have the branch cut off if this guy had murdered that poor girl.

"Now I've got the law after me," Dale said the obvious behind muffling hands over his mouth. "Damn, that's a great way to say it, right? The law is after the lawyer, and, yes, I know why," he went on as his hands flopped to grasp his knees. "Yeah, I broke up with her, not the other way around, so who knows what she told her friends or family."

"Exactly when was this? I'm sure the ME will soon rule on how long she's been dead and what killed her, but give me the basic time frame and just hope it doesn't sync with what the ME will find on time of death."

"Just over a week ago. Ten days, I guess. Yeah, before last weekend, shortly after my mother's funeral."

"Not at your house or that one, I hope. Dale?" he prompted when the man hesitated. "Just answer questions, don't fume and agonize or it will look like you're making things up as you go."

"Yeah—at my house. But Nick, she's the one who was angry, not me. Will the firm stand by me, defend me if it comes to that? I did not kill her and sure as hell didn't stash her in my demented mother's freezer just after she died."

"We'll stand by you, but you're going to have to cooperate with the police. I'll be there with you for your statement. You know the drill. Just stick to the facts, offer nothing extra and, as my forensic psych wife would counsel, look the detective in the eye and don't fidget all over the place. Dale," he said, leaning down to grip the man's shoulder, "we not only defend strangers but our own here. The firm is like a family too."

"Thank God," he said and exhaled hard. He seemed to deflate with relief.

"I'll need your complete statement, of course, but you're going to have to go with Detective Jensen before he knocks my office door down. I'm sure he wanted to question you before you lawyered up, but this is our territory."

"Your sticking by me will carry weight, yours and this firm's reputation," he said in a raspy voice, but he shook his head as if trying to convince himself. Nick didn't like how strung out Dale looked, with bloodshot eyes and dark circles under them when he had supposedly been away to relax and hadn't been hit with all this until about an hour ago, though of course—hopefully—it was a shock. So why hadn't the guy been sleeping and decompressing this weekend? Had his decision to break up with Cyndi done that to him or was he tormented by something more recent?

"I'll invite the detective in," Nick said, heading for the door. "He'll probably insist on our going to the station. But he can't arrest and hold you for anything—can he?" he asked, turning back. "Like your fingerprints on that old freezer?"

"Of course, I've been all over that house for years, even recently before the sale to Bronco and Nita was finalized. Nick, my mother had stage four dementia, so who knew what she would have said if she was alive. She still thought my German great-uncle was alive and living in his big manor at the rear of the estate. She'd get everything confused.

"Anyway," he plunged on, "I'm sure I left DNA if—if they find that was the—the crime scene. Not just where she was hidden but where she was murdered as well. I just hope to hell she wasn't put in there alive. I mean, you said it looked like she was screaming."

A whole string of questions popped into Nick's head such as who else had keys to the place, but he'd save that all until later. Right now they had to cooperate with the police—and eventually, he feared, with the prosecuting attorneys of Collier County.

"Nick, if I touched that freezer, it was long ago," Dale repeated, circling back to that, maybe overexplaining. "I was hop-

ing Bronco and his wife would get it out of there—just because
it's so heavy, I mean. Obviously, I would not have stashed my
ex-girlfriend—"

"Your former fiancée. Keep everything straight."

"Right. I would never have put her body there, then sold the
house. Damn, my head hurts with all this," he said, gripping
his skull in his hands again. "Too much so soon after learning
she's dead. I did love her…but it just wasn't going to work out."

Why not? Nick wanted to demand, but that too would come
later. He wished he didn't empathize with Dale so much but he
understood emotional devastation. Fear. The powerful way a
woman could change everything in life, one way or the other.
He hesitated with his hand on the doorknob, because he sensed
something else was coming.

"I just wanted to get away this weekend, get over her. Nick,
she was just too grasping, self-centered, wanted too many big
things too fast. She knew my family had money, though I told
her my great-uncle didn't leave me much except that deserted
old mansion that's in ruins. I plan to tear down what little of
it's left, but demolition costs big bucks. Listen, I thought Cyndi
went to Georgia to stay with her brother's family for a while—
that is, I assumed—"

"Assume nothing. You're rambling. Sit up straight. Don't put
your hands over your mouth and mumble. I'm opening this
door to let the detective in, and we'll face him together. And
you know damn well not to offer so much—blurt things out
like this, no matter how devastated or emotional you are. Self-
preservation time, Dale. Answer questions, tell the truth, but
no more than that."

He came back to his desk, squeezed Dale's shoulder, went over
and opened the door.

Claire was really glad to have Kris here as friend and support.
One look at the setup at Black Bog made her realize she should
assume nothing and take in everything. Her senses went on

alert. She felt the quickening breeze brush her skin. She heard the screech of a gull overhead and the distant roar of an alligator—or was that thunder? Darn, she hadn't thought of gators or being near a bog if there was a lightning storm. She gripped her purse as she got out of the Jeep.

The first surprise was how finished, even formal, everything looked. She'd almost imagined tents, but after all, Kris had said the Vances lived here, and they were obviously wealthy.

On one side of the gated entry road stood a small guard house, where a guy in khaki shorts waved at Kris and opened the gate. The entire acreage was fenced with a see-through wire barrier. To the left on the narrow entry lane, an elevated new-looking one-story house with a wooden deck all around it and a large, screened-in porch in back dominated the area. Two vehicles, one a small truck, the other a black BMW, similar to Nick's, were parked under the first floor which was elevated in typical South Florida storm-surge style. But a storm would be a catastrophe for a bog this close to the water.

"That's where the Vances live now," Kris told her, pointing to the house. "It's so shady in here the house only gets sun for a couple of hours around noon. You should have seen their other place, really gorgeous. Had a pool, right on the beach, you know, one of those places on Gordon Drive in Port Royal. It just shows you how dedicated they are to this project that they have that place up for sale. They are funding this Black Bog effort and that takes big bucks."

The other main edifice was really a collection of buildings. Elevated walkways connected them, one of which reminded her of a long dock, reaching out into what looked like swampland guarded by twisted ficus trees with overhanging branches. That sprawling building had several air conditioners humming.

"The forest primeval, right?" Kris said as she led Claire toward the large spread-out wooden building. "That's the path to

Black Bog, but we'll talk to Andrea first, and she'll give you the tour if you're still interested in the assignment."

"So the Vances actually live here all the time?"

"They do now—total dedication to this project. There is a staff restroom and shower over there," she said pointing at a small building on the edge of the sprawl.

They stopped at a door under an overhang of roof that had printed letters A VANCE on it. Claire saw there was a slot for a pass card. Kris knocked.

"I saw on the cameras you're here, Kris," came a sharp voice through the door. "In more ways than one, bring her in!"

CHAPTER FOUR

First with preliminary questions in his office, then at the police station, Nick sat with Dale, who had finally pulled himself together to face the barrage of questions from Ken Jensen. Dale left with the knowledge he'd be interrogated again soon. Nick drove him back to the office rather than taking him home where, no doubt, gawkers at the least and the press at the most awaited.

Nick told Dale to just lock himself in his office for a while to defuse. The younger secretaries and paralegals always fussed over him and eyed him, but today were standing clear.

Nick knew he had work waiting, and he wasn't expecting any word from Claire until at least the afternoon. What a day so far!

His tech genius Hector—called Heck—Munez was camped out on a chair by Nick's secretary's desk. "More chaos than usual," Nick told Heck, who followed him in. Nick dropped his briefcase and closed the door behind them. Heck kept the firm up on various online activity, so this visit wasn't really unusual.

"If it's good news, let's hear it," Nick said. "Bad—save it."

"The firm gonna defend him?"

"If it comes to that, absolutely. He would not have left Cynthia Lindley's body on his mother's property to be found. We don't hire idiots in this firm and that includes you, so what have you got?"

"Facial recognition technology."

Nick sank into the chair behind his desk and put his feet up, tilting back. He closed his eyes for a moment and pinched his nose with thumb and finger. "That's a good one. What about it? Claire is with a friend right now from her college days—they're just hanging out for a while," he added, wishing he didn't have to hold things back from people he trusted. "Anyway, this woman has what is commonly called 'face blindness,' which I guess isn't common, though some famous people have it. Her facial recognition is nil—*nada*."

"Heard of it. I'll look it up. Maybe this technology could help someone like her someday. See, I got a chance to moonlight, make some extra money with a company that's into—*way* into—producing facial recognition software and then selling it. I could work on the production part. It's big business and getting bigger. For example, companies like high-end stores use face prints to ID their top customers when they walk in so the staff can greet them and serve them better. The thing is, I could work for this company in a consulting capacity to produce even better technology."

When it rained, it poured, Nick thought. Claire and now Heck, both eager to branch out, but he could see why. Amazing possibilities abounded lately.

"I'd like to take this side gig, boss. But the thing is, they're gonna need legal help on all this too, 'cause, of course, there will be pushback on it, privacy violation and all that. But I need your permission and your advice."

"How are the faces recognized?"

Heck sat even farther forward. "Boss, I swear, it's the wave of the future. So a scanner picks up a face it's programmed to recognize, and immediately the owner of the scanner gets data on his screen or phone as to who the person is, their preferences, maybe their financial past, stuff like that."

"Whew!" he said, lifting his feet off the desk and sitting up straight in his leather swivel chair. "What next?"

"Yeah, but this is already here, and we ought to get in on it. Nothing like learning from the present to see the future."

"There is nothing like looking at the past to see the present and future better," Andrea Vance told Claire once they'd been introduced and everyone was seated at a round conference table with laptop stations.

Looking at all the advanced tech gear made Claire realize the touch screen tablet she'd brought was almost primitive. Funny to be using such technology to record information on primitive people who probably didn't even have an alphabet.

"You come very highly recommended and trusted by my indispensable bog forewoman here," Andrea said, and Claire noted a little smile between the two.

Andrea had brown hair with wisps of silver worn loose around a serious face. Next to Claire's five-feet-ten, she was short at about five-two, but she seemed tall—in command, charismatic. Her handshake was very strong, almost too strong. The former archaeology professor was sturdy looking, and her commanding voice projected well. She wore immaculate white running shoes, and Claire saw she had several spare pairs of them as well as white jeans and blouses on a rack nearby. So much white with so much bog and peat and mud? Perhaps the elements didn't dare sully Andrea Vance.

"I'm sorry Bradley isn't here to meet you, but he will be tomorrow if you choose to come back and help us," Andrea went on. "I hear you have a young family, so if we can have you for at least twenty hours a week here for starters, that will be most helpful. Flexible hours are fine, although when we uncover a new find and bring it—him or her or them—up, we really would need your presence and expertise on-site so you can view them both in situ and in the labs."

She glanced at Kris, then reached behind on her desk to produce a document, one with at least ten pages stapled together. "I understand you are married to a criminal lawyer who knows his way in and out of these silly clauses, but please read the privacy section carefully. I am sure you will find the hourly salary section to your liking."

"Yes. I understand," Claire assured her as Andrea slid the contract toward her. Knowing she and Nick would have to go over it thoroughly, Claire slid it into her bag.

"I found it ironic," Andrea said with a nod, "that you discovered that local shallow grave that made all the newscasts several months ago, when we had you on our radar to help us examine these graves. Kris and I saw it as a sort of sign you would be perfect to help with our exhumations here."

A young woman came in with coffee and doughnuts, each one frosted with vanilla icing and decorated with a chocolate BB on it, no less, but Claire could sense Kris and Andrea were in a hurry to take her on the tour of Black Bog. She nearly burned her mouth on the coffee, but its temperature didn't seem to bother Andrea or Kris a bit.

"First, let me give you an idea of what we are speaking of here when we say bog bodies," Andrea said, standing after they finished their food. She gestured them through a door in the corner behind her desk, a door Claire had not noticed, but then Nick had a private back "escape door" as he called it in his office. Criminal lawyers always had enemies as well as friends by the nature of their careers.

They walked into a room that reminded Claire of a bunker. Under stark ceiling lights, surrounded by gray concrete walls, she saw wide filing cabinets with drawers lining both sides of the long narrow room. The metal file drawers were labeled with things like Young Man with Tooth Gap, Woman with Broken

Wrist, Woman with Medicine in Stomach. The drawers seemed to stretch on and on, maybe thirty at least, some with no labels.

"My!" was all Claire managed.

"Each drawer is climate controlled and infused with nitrogen for preservation," Andrea said.

She pulled out the Woman with Medicine drawer, and there lay a leathery-looking corpse with totally recognizable arthritic hands with each swollen knuckle visible. Claire's eyes widened and she sucked in a breath.

The facial features looked skewed and a bit smashed, but the face—even eyelashes—were visible. The head had hair that stuck out from a flat round cap made of some sort of plant, maybe palm tree fiber. For one moment, Claire's thoughts flashed to opening the freezer, to seeing the female body there, though, thank heavens, this ancient woman's eyes and mouth were closed. But for millennia she had been frowning as if in consternation or pain.

Claire had to struggle to find her voice. Her gaze was riveted to the body, nearly naked but for a sort of apron that curved around her knees she had bent up to her chest in fetal fashion. "Medicine in her stomach? But—"

"Oh, yes," Andrea said. "We always check the contents of the stomach for clues of diet, location, illness. She had quickly chewed—not well—elderberries and willow bark, which contain some of the same alleviants as are in our aspirin today."

"The thing is," Kris spoke for the first time in a while, "we've found that in quite a few of them—as if they are drugging themselves, hoping to head off pain for something—or preparing for some terrible rite or ritual."

Claire's head snapped up and around toward her friend. "Not such as being buried alive?" she asked. "Those stakes and that crude rope with her. Was she—staked down?"

"I told you, Andrea," Kris said, "Claire will help to solve crimes. She's worth the training and the salary."

"Then let's show her the pièce de résistance," Andrea said,

without answering her question either. She turned toward Claire with an avid look in her clear brown eyes as she slowly closed the drawer. "I refer to the brains of the Black Bog people, like those in the Windover cemetery up near Titusville. We remove, study and store their brains in a freezer, which later will be more completely examined and maybe someday, somehow—probed and, well, the results uploaded to our database."

Claire nodded, trying to take in each new bombshell. But it was the word "freezer" that made her own brain ache.

"So how was school today, Lex?" Jace asked his daughter as he drove her home from school Tuesday afternoon.

He picked her up that one day each week for some sort of adventure or treat. He also took her on occasional weekend jaunts. The school knew their schedule, but he still went inside to pick her up in the office. A good precautionary practice, he figured, since his daughter had been abducted, and by someone posing as him. Once he and Brit were married and he had better than a bachelor pad, it was agreed he'd have her for longer periods sometimes.

"School was good. When I told Miss Gerald my dad was going to marry a lady who works at a zoo, she said not to tell everybody right now so they get all excited, but maybe we can take a visit there someday. Her favorite animal is butterflies, but she likes all kinds."

"Great," he said, wishing they weren't behind one of the big yellow Collier County school buses, since it would make frequent stops. "Brit will be excited about that, and she'll understand why it has to be a secret for now. Don't want to get kids so excited they can't pay attention in school."

"I think there are too many secrets around here."

"Really? I thought you liked secrets."

"Well, if they don't take Mommy away into the swamp with bodies."

"Whoa! What? Your mother is certainly not going into any swamp with bodies."

"I heard so—buried ones you dig up."

"No, honey. You're just mixing that up with something that happened earlier and turned out bad, but now everything is okay."

"Well, when I went to the bathroom at home I heard them talking, her and that arch lady, Kris Kane."

"Kristen Kane? Your mother's old friend, the archaeologist? I thought she was living in Europe."

As Lexi chattered on about Mommy's friend from the old days when Mommy went to school, then veered into the names of her own best friends, Jace's mind spun back. He remembered that Kris, who had fixed him up with Claire, had a problem recalling faces. She'd told him once with his blond hair, blue eyes and muscular physique that he should have been a Viking from the days of yore. That's how she'd said she remembered who he was—"the Viking guy from the days of yore that used to sail in their dragon ships." Funny, how over the years when he flew fighter jets in combat over desert sands or the big passenger 747s over the Pacific, he'd sometimes thought of that.

"So, Daddy, did you have a good day? You always ask me, so I should ask you too. And I know we will both have really good days when you marry Brit, and I get to be a flower girl at your wedding, 'cause I'm good at that after doing it when Mommy married Nick and Nita married Bronco."

"Yeah, honey, I had a good day flying my little airplane and spraying crops," he said with a sigh. But he didn't tell her that he and his pilot friend Mitch were considering something in addition to that undercover gig for the government, something far more dangerous but damned exciting. It was in his blood, his fictional Viking blood, but he hadn't told Brit yet.

He was almost scared to before the wedding, or she might just call it off. She didn't even like the fact that some of the local drug smugglers he helped to get arrested might want to shut him down. It had happened in Tennessee where a drug dealing cartel had brought down a Stingray plane like his with a drone, and the pilot had burned to death in the wreckage. But yeah, maybe there *were* a lot of secrets around here, because no way was he telling Brit about a pilot's death or even what his challenging new career could mean.

CHAPTER FIVE

Andrea Vance led Claire and Kris into another back room, a smaller one this time. It was evidently a lab with large electron microscopes and other instruments Claire could not name. Several suitcase-sized silver metal freezers sat on a tile countertop.

Misty, icy air wafted out of the state-of-the-art freezer Andrea opened. Claire stepped back as Andrea pulled out a plastic tray, placed it carefully on the counter and removed its lid. Within were four small divided compartments, each holding a single gray-brown shrunken brain next to a laminated white card labeled with neat printing.

"These are the brains of the first four inhabitants we excavated from Black Bog," Andrea said, her voice almost reverent. "If only we could learn what once passed through these convoluted lobes." She paused a moment, then went on, "After removing these for study and preservation, we put the top of the skulls back on and pull up any skin, replacing any hair we can. Some of the heads have plant fiber hats we can replace. Textiles come out great at first but then shrivel, even if kept wet. With the textiles, we can use polymer coating to keep them looking fresh but not with the brains. Since their brains do not speak to us, we need you, Claire, to examine what is buried with the bodies as well as the inhabitants' body language. In short, we need you to pick the brains without psyching them out."

"I'm amazed they are only as large as baseballs, though they remind me more of big walnuts," Claire marveled, looking even closer at them. There was a faint odor, something like formaldehyde.

"Shrunk over the centuries to about one fourth their size," Andrea said. "Their DNA is intact, however. But, as I said, perhaps you can glean some of their thoughts and memories, just as you would with a living—or newly deceased—person from observation of their bodies and, in this case, burials."

Kris put in, "Perhaps someday, some brilliant techie will find a way to extract what is in there. For now that's where you come in, though we can contribute some hypotheses too. Let's go out to the burial site—ritual site, accident site, execution site—it may be all of the above."

"Yes, let's go on out to the bog," Andrea said, recapping the tray and replacing it in the freezer where Claire saw two other trays of ancient brains were stored. With a nod and intense stare at Claire, she added, "Yes, we need your expertise, your intuition, your opinions and judgments to go beyond what archaeology and science can surmise or prove, and that is a great deal. We'll just give you a glimpse of our work today, but I must tell you there are some puzzling and strange burials here in Black Bog, and we are totally dedicated to getting answers one way or the other."

"Detective Jensen's not the only one who needs more answers from you," Nick told Dale as they drove from the sheriff's office back toward the law office after Dale had been interrogated a second time. "At least they didn't detain or arrest you, but that search warrant for your house and office—taking your electronics too—when they've already fine-tooth combed your mother's house means you are definitely a prime person of interest."

"I know—I know!" Dale said, raking his hands through his hair. "But do you think for one minute that a trained criminal lawyer—even one in his twenties—would be stupid enough to put someone he murdered—someone he was linked to—in his mother's freezer right next door to his own house? I'm not crazy or suicidal!"

The usually calm, stoic man generally kept his hair neatly upswept with some kind of gel product and was careful about his looks and clothes. But since getting in the passenger seat, he had raked his hair into clumps and had dried gel all over his hands and now his trousers.

"So, let me ask a question they didn't," Nick said, not willing to back off until he had more answers. He had the worst feeling a clock was ticking, that time was of the essence. "You told both me and Jensen that you last saw Cyndi alive over two weeks ago."

"That's right. So?"

"So—have you ever seen that old Alfred Hitchcock movie, *Psycho*? Or the *Bates Motel* TV series?"

"Nick, nobody got slashed in the shower, and I'm not some nutcase who dresses like my dead mother to kill an attractive woman so her son doesn't go after her!"

"Granted. But three weeks ago your mother was still alive. Still in her house. Could your mother have resented Cyndi, the woman you were enamored with, sleeping with, as you admitted to Detective Jensen? You said your mother had dementia and didn't like Cyndi. Your mother is so recently deceased that the timeline would work."

"You go for the jugular, don't you? You're supposed to be helping me, not incriminating an old woman I recently buried!"

"Yeah, I go for the jugular," he said, hitting the brakes for a red light and lots of traffic. "How do you think I got so many of my clients off on murder one charges? You damn well know your defense team, if it comes to that, will need to cover every possibility that will pop into Jensen's or the prosecutor's devious brains."

"I know, I know!" he said, putting his head in his hands and messing up his hair even more. "And now they used that warrant to search my place, my office, my online history, even though I've got nothing to hide except a few gambling debts at the Seminole Casino."

"Which might have made a fiancée angry with you, and an argument ensued, things got physical—an accident occurred and you didn't know how to hide a body fast."

"Hell, Nick! Whose side are you on?"

"I've just learned to think like the enemy—psych them out."

"Wish you'd leave that to your wife. Well, not really," he added with such a huge sigh it seemed to deflate him. "Nick, I've seen you interrogate others, but lay off! I wanted to go into law to help the accused, not be the accused. But Cyndi—it's horrible that someone killed her, and I don't know why, let alone who. Like I told Jensen, I really cared for her, even though I knew we wouldn't work out. And what I and my defense team—if it comes to that—need to do, is figure out not only who hated her, but who wanted to set me up as—as her possible killer."

"We may have to shake the trees for other persons of interest. Look, we'll go in the back way at the firm in case the media is still hanging around. Duck down when we pull in. Why don't you phone Bronco at the front desk to be sure we'll have a clear path to get upstairs? You get back in your office, see if the tech team took anything other than your laptop. Then brainstorm for every—I said *every*, including your mother's—possible motive people might have for harming Cynthia Lindley and then having the nerve and access to put her in that freezer. I don't know why the ME's cause of death report is taking so long, but it has to be imminent."

"Maybe it's taking so long," Dale said, his voice shaky, "for that very reason, that she was frozen in death."

Claire stared out at the grid of planks that neatly dissected the part of Black Bog the team was digging in today. Andrea said, "Kris, tell her what you can at this point. I need to talk to the dig team. Be right back."

Claire asked Kris, "'Everything you can at this point' means until I sign the contract and can actually get close to one of these digs—graves?"

"I told you this is all top secret. So, anyway," she said, pointing, "what do you think of the site at first glance?"

"This setting seems like something out of Edgar Allan Poe. Remember how I told you my mother used to read to us all the time after my dad deserted us and she became a recluse? The dark water and peat here, the sun creeping through the heavy foliage over that ancient, open grave…"

"Better stick with calling it a dig site. I've got to admit I feel that way too, if I stand back objectively—which I seldom do. Wetlands archaeology, this site especially, reminds me of those terrifying Dead Marshes from the *Lord of the Rings* books and movies. But, the thing is, my friend," she said, putting a hand on Claire's shoulder as they walked on the boardwalk that stretched out over the bog, "you just have to shut that out. We need to bring these ancient people back to life, so to speak. We can usually discover cause of death, but we need you to weigh in on what they might have been like in life. You can't question them, but you can observe and theorize. Now watch where you step on the planks, and if you come back tomorrow as part of the team, I'll show you the latest excavations and exhumations up close.

"And," Kris added with a swat at a mosquito, "these voracious buggers are the monsters of this bog, though we fog for mosquitoes a lot. Sorry, I forgot to spray you before we came out. That funny smell out here comes from several camphor pots we have way back in the trees. It helps keep the mosquitoes away, but the smell is pretty acrid."

They stepped out on a pair of planks which shuddered slightly under their weight, but held firm, supported by two-by-fours Claire could see were pounded into the base of the bog.

Kris pointed outward as two men and one woman, all on their knees on a wooden platform, peered into a five-foot-square hole about fifteen feet away. Near them rested the tools of their trade. Shovels, trowels, brushes, cameras, clipboards and plastic sheeting were things Claire could recognize from here. Standing behind her team, hand propped on her knees, Andrea leaned over, looking down too, blocking Kris and Claire's view. Around the digging trio lay slivers of peat they had been slicing and scooping away to get to the corpse.

"We shall call this one 'Hunter.'" Andrea's words floated to Claire as she and the team still stared down in apparent awe. "He looks to be quite muscular and still holds his knife. He's dressed in some kind of pelt. And—look—another body must be close, because there's a hand as if reaching out toward him. Be especially careful if there are other bodies nearby. I've never seen one that close. I've got to tell Bradley. He should be here for this!"

She pulled her two-way radio out of her shirt pocket, then turned and looked at Claire through the gray, shifting shadows. She nodded as if to say, *By tomorrow you could be here with us.*

But suddenly this scene seemed so staged, so perfect a lure, for who would not want to get a better look into that grave with the ancient hunter and someone else's outstretched hand?

Even as Andrea put her transceiver to her ear and began to talk, Claire thought about the words from the Robert Louis Stevenson poem, ones she could not quite recall, but went something like, "Home is the hunter, home from the hill." Above all, she realized she had to talk to Nick about this significant but strange place the moment they were both home.

★ ★ ★

Nick was exhausted and hungry, so he'd asked his secretary to send out for a sandwich, and it awaited him on his desk. He hadn't even thought about food for a while. Dale had been in a waiting room here until the police techs were finished with his office, and they had just handed it back.

On his desk phone console, he hit the number of the secretary who worked with two of the junior partners, including Dale. "Tracey, Nick here. Be sure Dale gets another laptop, because I'll bet they took his."

"Will do. Has he—well, has he been indicted or what? He just stormed into his office and shut the door."

"Not yet and we hope never. Keep an eye on him, since he's upset."

"I guess so. He looks like he's been through the wringer. We'll take care of him."

Though Nick had an open-door policy with the firm's part-ners and employees, he was going to close his door to call Claire. Surely, she was out of bog land by now, though he wasn't sure if there were cell towers out that deep in the wilds. He checked his voice mail and texts. Nothing yet, except one from Jace say-ing he had picked up Lexi from school as he and Claire had ar-ranged. Nick decided she'd call when she could and he shouldn't seem to be checking up on her if she was with the staff there.

Though his mouth was full of his sandwich, at a knock on his office door, he called out "Enter!" He was expecting his secre-tary, even Dale again.

It was Bronco, looking jumpy and pale.

"Sorry to bother you again, Boss, but Nita called to say a couple of reporters knocked on our apartment door for a state-ment. She said no but one filmed her at the door. So they got us staked out both at our new house and old apartment. Nita—she's real upset."

"As soon as I can talk to Claire, it might be good for you both to pack a bag and stay a couple days with us. It would be good to have Nita right there at the house for the kids anyway, especially if Claire takes that part-time consulting job."

"Oh, yeah. What's that all about?"

"Consulting for some people who need help at a job site. Bronco, calm Nita down and tell her everything will be fine."

"She don't think so, boss. Doesn't want to live there anymore. I—I think she believes the place might be—kind of haunted."

"But we know better than that, right? I'll work on it as soon as I hear from Claire. If you need to go home early, go."

Cuddling little Trey in her arms, Claire paced at home. Jace had let Lexi call her to say they were at the zoo with Brit but he'd have her home in plenty of time for bed. "We're hunting for the funniest monkey and the tallest giraffe," he had told her, "now that we've seen Brit and the big cats."

Now Claire's thoughts quickly returned to her own day. She wanted to convince Nick she should take the job. It was only the secrecy that bothered her, but she understood that too. After all, Nick had to keep a lot at work private. Jace was flying on classified government missions, not only to spray for bugs, but to pinpoint the locations of criminals through an undercover Stingray program that hunted down and traced cell phones—another sort of bug. Many things in life had to be top secret. As long as she could share *some* of what was going on at Black Bog with Nick, surely nothing could go wrong, even though she'd have to lie to some people about what she was doing.

Little Trey went beautifully, innocently to sleep on her shoulder, so she went to put him in his crib. How eerie it was to think that those long-dead human beings lying in the bog had also once had people they loved and needed and had children to protect. No doubt they had people they hated too, problems they tried to solve. And she had picked up on the fact that Kris had said the people in Black Bog were not only being exhumed but might have been executed. Since Claire had worked with murder and suicide cases before, was that why they really wanted her?

She began to pace again, in and out of Trey's nursery, back toward the front door. Nick might be late because of the mess with Dale Braun, so she hated to bother him at work. But she needed his coolheaded advice, not that she'd seen anything really amiss at Black Bog. It was just that one look Andrea had given her. Claire had psyched out that the woman was used to getting what she wanted. And herself? Yes, she wanted to jump in—graves and all—with both feet.

CHAPTER SIX

"I don't think we should put off setting a date and planning our wedding any longer," Jace told Brit when he picked her up after taking Lexi home. "We've weathered some bad times, but let's forge ahead."

As he pulled out into traffic, she turned toward him in the passenger seat, bending her left leg to face him despite her seat belt. "You do bring up the most important things at the craziest, least romantic times, flyboy. But actually, that would make me happy too—not to mention our little flower girl."

"Yeah, she's psyched. But I want it for us, not Lexi. I know it's pretty soon after losing your father, but—"

"But he would have been very happy for us. And if we can somehow get my dear brother *in* the wedding party rather than playing his violin, that will suit me."

"I'd ask Mitch to be best man."

"I can hardly ask Claire to stand up with me, however close we've become. Just wouldn't do to have your ex up there with you again while you say your vows. But what triggered this all of a sudden, if it wasn't Lexi?"

"I don't want to let you down or lose you," he said, hitting the steering wheel with his left fist. "I can see how the other big cat keeper looks at you. Don't want him or some other guy swooping in."

"Swooping in? Says a guy whose nickname is Hawk! Don't be silly. I'm wearing your engagement ring, and everyone knows we're a couple—a couple in love, sharing everything, right?"

"Absolutely. Affirmative that," he insisted, though guilt bit at him again that he hadn't told her about his new, dangerous job opportunity. "Now I'm gonna pull in to this grocery store, because I need to seal this with a *looong* kiss. I admit this wasn't the most romantic place to bring it up, and neither is this parking lot, but we'll make up for that, I promise."

Before he could pull over, they got stopped not only at a red light but by a long funeral procession. Life could be short, he told himself, gripping the steering wheel and wondering if she was thinking the same thing.

The truth was, part of the reason he'd decided they should get married soon was that who knew how long either of them had. Not only was he hesitant to tell her about the dangers of hurricane flying, but what he was doing now was getting even more lethal.

Once the funeral procession passed, he pulled into the grocery store parking lot and drove into the back row under a tree to get some shade. He killed the motor and undid his seat belt while she unsnapped hers. They hugged hard over the console between them and kissed deep and long until a couple of teenage boys walked by and hooted.

As they broke their embrace and he honked the horn to make the boys move on, he felt like both a rat and a coward. He had dodged her question about why he wanted to speed things up. He'd almost worked up the nerve to tell her he was considering a dangerous assignment, one that would serve the public good. Surely, she'd understand—but would she? She'd lost so much recently, he could picture her going ballistic over this.

Mitch had talked to him about signing on with him to become a hurricane hunter, flying into the eye of deadly storms for the National Oceanic and Atmospheric Administration. Mitch had even kidded about changing his nickname from Hawk to Hunter.

Jace almost blurted it out, but he didn't want to argue either about the hazards of that career or have her insist he turn it down because he could be instantly on call if the weather was bad. And he'd need special training again. But he wanted more excitement in his life, he needed more than what he was doing, more than loving her, and she wouldn't understand that.

"So because of his weapon, clothing and muscular build, they named their newest find Hunter," Claire told Nick in another gush of words after he got home and sat on the couch to read through the Black Bog contract. She'd put out wine, crackers and cheese on the coffee table for him while she put Lexi in bed. The child had been tired and full of a chicken nugget dinner when Jace brought her home, so she had conked out already, and Trey had not awakened for a feeding yet.

After being filled in on the latest about Dale's questioning at the sheriff's office, Claire had tried to keep calm as she told Nick about the day she'd had at Black Bog. She realized how excited she was to share what she'd seen—and convince him she should take the job.

"Very professional, very complete," Nick told her, tossing the contract on the coffee table while she sat beside him on the couch. "Of course, like all legal documents, it benefits the creator more than the signer, but it looks solid enough, and the pay per hour is excellent. I just hope the secrecy clauses will be passé soon, and they can release some of this to the public."

"But you do see why? In a way, they're sitting on a powder keg if some of this information were to get out."

"True, and we've had enough of getting things blown up

in front of us. But I think, since this is really part-time, it will work out."

"Especially if we have Nita on-site here to help with Trey and Lexi. I'm all for your idea of letting them live here for a while until things calm down after finding that poor woman's body."

"Which I'd like more information on, so I told my secretary and assistant to call me here if the ME releases cause of death tonight. Meanwhile, Mrs. Markwood, what's your strategy to keep your new endeavor secret from our inquisitive daughter, let alone everyone else?"

"The cover story will be that a fairly new business is hiring me part-time to interview prospective employees. They are developing a new product they don't wish to discuss right now. Not a lie, not quite the truth, but, after all, I've advised other companies on hiring tactics, so—"

Nick's phone on the coffee table sounded with the music from a lawyer TV show, then a clickety-click she'd always thought of as his brain working. Oh, darn, after seeing those shrunken brains today, maybe she had brains on the brain.

He snatched it up. "Nick here." She was sitting so close to him she could hear what the voice on the other end was saying. She recognized the woman's voice as his secretary, Cheryl.

"Nick, I was about ready to go home when the ME's office called about information on the death of Cynthia Lindley. She had some bad bruising on her arms and legs, especially her neck, though those were hardly cause of death. She was fully clothed. Of course, she was frozen solid, but cause of death was strangulation. Her hyoid bone was fractured. We'll have a fax of the entire report tomorrow a.m."

"Thanks, Cheryl," Nick said, and punched off. "Did you hear that?"

"I admit I did."

"So, conclusions, my fave forensic psych?"

"Whoever killed her and lifted her into that freezer was strong—not some old woman."

"Good point. Unless the murderer had help. I'm thinking that supposedly one third of female deaths where the hyoid bone at the front base of the neck is broken is from rough sex—temporarily cutting off the oxygen for a higher high, and then it all goes wrong."

"Really? So there's another piece of evidence that could point to Dale."

"I wouldn't figure the guy's that type, very controlled, but then still waters run deep. Anything else that comes to mind?"

"The person hated or feared her enough to kill her, yet had feelings for her—didn't just dump her body somewhere, even kind of arranged her clothing and body for the freezer. But then, he or she perhaps opened the victim's eyes and her mouth in that silent scream—but why?"

"Feared her. Never thought of that. She might have known something secret and she said she'd tell. Blackmail?"

"Unfortunately, until we somehow look into her life, the possibilities are endless," she admitted.

"*We?* If you sign that contract and don't intend to put Lexi and Trey up for adoption, no way you're on this case. Yes, I know we decided to have Nita here for a while to help. You will be busy enough, even though I would love your help. And the one thing I don't like about your lucrative Black Bog contract is that your cell phone won't work there if I need you—or if the kids do."

"I will only be part-time there and won't stay for entire days. Meanwhile, I predict, leader of all you command, Mr. Brilliant Mind, Senior Partner of Markwood, Benton and Chase, that you will need my skills—at least my opinions—before this is all said and done. I intend to sign this Black Bog contract now, but I also signed on to help you through thick and thin, through hell and high water, or whatever we vowed, and we've managed to survive all that."

He hugged her hard, pulled her down onto the couch and then lay beside her. "I don't know what I'd do without you in all kinds of ways. I love you, sweetheart, and always will. As obsessed as I—you too—get with our projects and endeavors, it's our family and our marriage that matter most. I run that law firm that seems like a little town and try to help people on the sly through South Shores, but you're at the heart of everything. I know we don't want to upstage Jace and Brit, whenever they finally set a wedding date, but I think it's about time for us to plan that long-delayed wedding reception we've talked about. We can have it at the country club I never use. What do you think?"

"I think it's a great idea—perfect. With a shotgun wedding in another country where we only had Lexi at the ceremony, we owe that much to our friends and family—and ourselves. Life goes by fast, things happen. That's one truth that hit me at Black Bog today. Let's do it!"

Tears stung her eyes. She tried to blink them back, but they clung to her lashes. "I never thought things could be so perfect—that I could be so happy," she got out before he crushed her to him in a commanding and possessive hug.

"There's another contract we are going to celebrate tonight," he said, sitting up and pulling her into his arms as he stood. "No better place to plan a celebration than in bed."

"But you said you were hungry."

"Mostly for you. Lexi's out like a light, Trey's quiet. This way, my love."

He actually carried her out of the Florida room and down the hall to their bedroom. He lay her on the bed and, standing over her, began to strip off his shirt and pants.

"I feel like we're newlyweds again," she said, pulling off her top and wiggling out of her shorts. "And we'll soon have Nita and Bronco around, and they really are just married. Then there's Jace and Brit, thinking of—"

"Enough," he told her as he pushed her back on the bed and

lay naked beside her. "Too much thinking. Let's just go with feeling for now."

And they did.

CHAPTER SEVEN

Despite how tired Claire was after last night, adrenaline poured through her. Taking her signed contract, she drove to Black Bog and was welcomed by Kris and Andrea. Kris gave her a two-way radio transmitter and a quick lesson in using it.

"Obviously, only for on-site communications," Kris explained while Andrea nodded. "Numbers for each staff member are pasted here on the back. Your cell phone will work when you get about four miles back toward town."

Soon Bradley Vance joined them for what must be the daily hot coffee and BB-decorated doughnut ritual.

"Damn glad you're on board!" he told her, shaking her hand with an overly firm grip that almost made her wince. He was an imposing man, with premature white hair over a broad fore-head, sharp blue eyes and a healthy-looking tan. "We need to ID our precious finds from all sorts of angles, and psychology is one key way. More of our brand of great women's intuition around here doesn't hurt either," he added with a nod at Andrea.

"Which reminds me that I wanted to ask," Claire said. "So far, what has been the percentage of men you've found in bog burials compared to women—or even children?"

"No children," Brad—Kris had said to call him either Brad or Senator—told her. "At least not easily discernible ones, depending on where you draw the line on children versus adolescents. I mean, no doubt by our standards, these people died young, but it seems to be an adult cemetery. One theory is that a burial bog was a magical place where people communicated with the dead, so young children weren't allowed to be part of that. It was perhaps a frightening place, a netherworld, so they buried children elsewhere. That's one reason you're on the staff now, to look for clues, draw conclusions and present us with hypotheses."

"I understand. I can't wait to get started."

Andrea said, "Then let's begin with the final exhumation of the man we've dubbed 'Hunter.' And then follow that outstretched hand we've uncovered to see why someone would be interred so close to him—unusual. Black Bog's secrets await, so let's go."

Nick had a ridiculously busy day ahead, but he'd scheduled Heck into a 9:00 a.m. appointment, or he figured he wouldn't get to him at all. The guy had been invaluable over the years. He could find about anything online and stayed up with the huge tech curve for Nick and for the firm. After all they'd been through together, Heck was as much friend and family as employee.

Waiting for the familiar knock on his door, Nick stared at the lengthy ME's report which had been faxed to them this morning, since the firm was now on the record as attorneys for Dale Braun.

Although the bruises on the female victim's body, he read, skimming partway down, *were consistent with the subject being manually restrained and possibly held down, there is no evidence of sexual activity, no rape, no bruising in the genital area.* Nick looked even lower in the long report. It had been difficult to establish time of death because the timing for the frozen state of the corpse could interrupt and throw off the estimation of time for rigor mortis.

There were no drugs in the subject's system. There were, however, the remains of a steak dinner with salad and baked potato and red wine, but no unusually high alcohol readings.

The open mouth and open eyes did not indicate the victim had been placed in the freezer alive. In the ME's best estimate, the mouth and eyes had been deliberately opened before the body was frozen, though that assumption could be contested.

Nick sighed. Everything could be—maybe would be—contested if it came to an arrest and a trial. But what had really caused the death of Cynthia Lindley, or, that is, what had led up to it? They knew how she had died. But the why, that was the thing. And, yes, Claire was right. He could use her help on this, as long as she was not taking risks.

He heard Heck's usual three quick raps on the open door. "Enter!"

"Morning, boss." He ambled in and sat down as if neither of them had a care in the world. "Word is you're busy on a big case, so I can make this quick."

"First, how is Gina liking med school and living in Miami?" Nick asked about Heck's girlfriend.

"Likes it, especially the big Cuban population there, almost like home, she said. When I told her about this face recognition stuff, she said she'd recently considered being one of those artists who does facial reconstruction—you know, with clay after measuring a skull. I didn't even know she had art talent. Crazy, huh?"

"Maybe not. She's been worried about the expense and length of med school, and that would mean she wouldn't go after that medical degree. So explain a bit more about facial recognition technology in case I want to talk to the senior partners about possibly getting involved with your idea for a sideline career."

"Just learned the Russians are deploying it to spy on their own citizens, so it's far-reaching, developing fast. Moscow has a network of around 170,000 surveillance cameras across the city to ID criminals and boost security. That's way beyond what I was telling you about high-end stores using it. This facial recognition tech was designed by a Russian startup called N-Tech Lab, Ltd. It cross-references images from a database against those captured by cameras at entrances to buildings."

"Big brother is watching you, in other words. I'd like to think that's just Russia, but it's coming here, I'll bet. I do know that even our more advanced allies are jumping in with both feet. I read that the UK uses so-called CCTV cameras too, maybe as many as 70,000 across their nation."

Heck nodded, scooting to the edge of his seat. "I knew that too. Boss, it's as scary as it sounds, that a government can find and arrest criminals that way. So why not the good guys too, so-called enemies of the state, or just a guy who criticizes them? I'm sure the Russians don't want us getting ahead of them in this or even catching up."

"You're right. A different kind of terrorist, the ones running the country."

"There's even an app called FindFace that was a big hit in Russia last year. Really accurate, this technology is going to take our world by storm, and this company that wants me will be in on that. *Caramba,* the competition is really cutthroat as well as cutting edge. It will be just to consult—kind of like Bronco said Claire's agreed to do for some startup company. And like I said, they're gonna need legal help 'cause there's lots of folks gunning against this new invasion of privacy."

"So that's where the firm would come in," Nick said. "I'm all for this, Heck—someone like you involved who knows the possible dangers if this isn't reined in, as long as—like I told Claire about her consulting—it's safe, and you still have time for what you were hired for here. And by cutthroat, you don't mean Russia could reach out here to try to harm American tech firms whom they see as competition in this software?"

"I don't think so," Heck said with a shrug. "No one said that, and my work would be pretty hush-hush."

"Someone like that friend of Claire's might be able to benefit from face recognition technology down the road, so keep that in mind."

His mind darted to last night with Claire in bed. His beautiful wife, under him, on him in the dark of their bedroom where he couldn't see the expression on her face, but he knew what it was. Trust. Joy. Ecstasy, and—

"So what do you think about someone from this startup company, FindFace, contacting you, boss? I'll go ahead and sign on to work with them then."

"Oh, yeah," Nick said, jumping back to reality. "Sounds good, at least to explore our options. Meanwhile, I need some help on this current murder case that involves Dale Braun. Look into anything you can find online about the victim, Cynthia Lindley from Atlanta. History, social media presence, whatever. Dig up anything you can."

"It's kind of funny that you call this walking the plank," Claire told Kris as they followed Andrea out to the site where the team had uncovered "Hunter" yesterday. To Claire's surprise, Brad Vance had not come along, so had he no curiosity about a new find, or did he just leave all of that up to Andrea? No doubt, there were business matters he must oversee here, but he'd given no indication he wouldn't come out with them. She would ask Kris later, because she didn't want to overstep or seem too curious in front of Andrea about the living here—just the dead.

Kris tried to prep her for what she would see. She explained they had slowly, carefully dug out more of Hunter's body, then had placed plastic sheeting over the site until today, in case of rain, so she'd be there for the retrieval of the body.

Everyone hovering at the site looked up and stood when she joined them. Andrea made introductions. "Just first names for now, and you can get to know each other later. Kind of like when we excavate a new grave site, right, gang, then figure out what we've found?"

Claire nodded and said hello to the same team she had seen here yesterday. The two men—Doug and Aaron—seemed young, maybe grad students. Yi Ling was a beautiful woman with sleek black hair held back from her face by a cord. She had also covered it with a net, no doubt to keep from dropping foreign objects, even strands of hair, into the graves. They were all obviously anxious to keep at their work. After short greetings where Andrea introduced Claire as "part of the brain trust," they eagerly bent back over the site.

Claire steadied herself for the first glimpse of Hunter. Kris braced her by her upper arm as they and Andrea looked in over the heads of the excavation team.

Although she'd seen the bog bodies in lab drawers inside, Claire jolted. Unreal, but so real. All tanned to a dark brown, yet amazingly preserved with chin-length hair, beard stubble, even a facial expression, which was one of grief or maybe pain. At being buried here? Alive? What had he been thinking when he died or was laid to rest? He hardly looked at peace—had violence been involved?

She also noted the hand attached to a wrist from a nearby, still bog-covered corpse, indeed reaching out toward Hunter. Beseeching him for something? Begging? Could their closeness be just coincidence or was there some relationship, shared feelings or a unity in death? Andrea had said it was unusual for two bodies to be so close. Though not quite touching, they seemed connected somehow. After all, Hunter's tormented face had been turned toward that other body for eons. And it was a small hand, a delicate hand. A woman, perhaps his wife. Claire hoped this wasn't a culture where a wife was forcefully interred with her powerful mate before her time. As shriveled as Hunter looked, he evoked strength.

Andrea, Kris and Claire stood back on the wooden platform

which held the tools for excavation. The team struggled to slowly, carefully slide a plastic sheet down and under the man's body.

Claire whispered to Kris, "He won't slip deeper, will he?"

"They've already shored up the peat under him, or otherwise, yes. Everywhere off the platform and planks, it's like a swamp that can swallow a person. That's why we have to be careful where we walk, and never get off the supports. We found one modern body that seems to have fallen in and gotten sucked down, suffocated. A corpse maybe from the late 1800s or early 1900s. So never, never come out here alone. If you fall in, you can be gone in no time—I'm sure a terrible death."

Claire saw Andrea shudder. "When I was young," she said quietly, still watching her team work, "I saw a movie set in Africa where the villain was horribly sucked down to his death in a swamp. It took me a lot of courage—and the desire to resurrect this people and their culture—to walk out here at first. Brad still avoids it, because he did fall in once, and I had to run for help to pull him out or I would have gone down too. I laid tree limbs for him to hang on to until I brought help. But, the truth is, he's had claustrophobia from a young age, so that was double horrible for him."

That explained his absence, Claire thought. The three of them watched intently as the team lifted the man's body by the plastic sheet, then laid him nearly at their feet in a space on the platform.

Claire stared wide-eyed. Centuries old but he could have been disinterred from a merely historic, not prehistoric grave. Although not this close-up, she'd seen an exhumation of a murder victim once, but this...

She could tell he had been an imposing man with big shoulders. His face was smashed a bit sideways by the long weight of water, mud and peat, but he still seemed—well, he must have been handsome with that strong nose, high cheekbones and firm chin. One foot was shod with a sort of laced leather shoe, the other bare. His toenails were visible. In his right hand, Hunter clenched a double-edged dagger as if he would never let it go.

His only other garb besides the one crude shoe was the animal pelt wrapped around him—no, it was more than one. They were crudely stitched together to hide his body, chest to thighs.

Andrea broke the awed silence. "I wonder how someone this strong, and apparently young, died. He looks—I know this sounds insane—healthy."

Claire cleared her throat. She wasn't sure her voice would even come out at first. "I observe the same. Amazingly, he seems to evoke a personality. Have you seen others buried with a dagger?"

Andrea answered, "Not like that one. Only scraping knives with plant residue still on their dull edges. But nothing this apparently special, this—commanding."

Claire noted they were all having trouble finding words. In a glint of light, she could see that Hunter's dagger was etched with some sort of design, though peat now filled the cracks to make the surface one dark blur. It was not metal but some sort of stone.

She asked, "Do we know what kind of animal pelts those are? If it's a rare or special animal, that could mean high status, which his dagger suggests."

Without looking up, Doug answered, "Short hair. Probably white-tailed deer. Doubt if they had the means to kill bears or panthers."

When Claire finally glanced away, she noted that Kris had narrowed her eyes and kept frowning at Hunter's face as if forcing herself to remember it. She had claimed to be able to recall ancient faces, but she could just be memorizing his build or clothes as she had in college days. Claire sensed something else was also bothering her, so she looked where Kris was staring—at the part of the pelt over his chest.

"Is there blood on that deer skin?" Claire asked, getting carefully on her knees to lean closer to the body. "I know the pelt is dark because of bog and tanning acids, but I see blotches. Maybe blood on his garment is a status thing too, because blood means so much in many cultures, especially in sacred and spiritual matters. Wouldn't it be something if we could figure out some of their religious beliefs—if they had any?"

"Let's get him inside and do our usual exams," Andrea's voice cut in. "I'm sure Brad is waiting to see what we found, and he oversees artifacts like that dagger."

When Kris stepped forward to take the fourth corner of the plastic and the team lifted the body, the pelt slipped off his chest. Despite the brown skin and curly hair, they saw where the blood had come from—much more of it.

Everyone gasped. At first Claire thought Hunter had been stabbed, but then she saw his heart was missing and long-dried blood bathed his entire chest and torso. She cried out as though she'd been hit in the gut, but Kris's scream drowned that out, echoing over Black Bog.

CHAPTER EIGHT

The circle of the living stared aghast at the murdered dead.

"Never seen that before," Aaron said, sounding breathless. "Man! A sacrifice or an execution? And he holds that dagger, though it could have been put in his hand after."

Andrea, her voice very quiet, said, "That may not be the murder weapon but a sort of marker of his occupation or even his social standing. Let's get him inside, then the three of you come back out and work on whoever has—had—that hand that's reaching out toward him. Careful now. Let's go."

Claire followed the strange procession. She felt as if they were going to a funeral. Her thoughts came fast and hard. Were they in a section of the bog where criminals had been buried? What about the woman next to him—if it was a woman? As many people as she had advised, as many cases as she had worked to understand and help the living, this one was starting to obsess her.

Inside, the team laid Hunter on a stainless steel table that reminded Claire of the one she'd seen in the Collier County morgue. They kept the pelt, now askew, over his hips and, under bright lights, bent closer to examine his ravaged chest. Even now his hand had not released his dagger, as if he still needed it for protection.

Andrea called Brad on an intercom system which Claire had noted as well as the various security cameras. Then Andrea put on some sort of protective glasses. They must magnify, because her eyes looked huge. "When you go out again, be certain Hunter's heart wasn't anywhere in the excavated site," she told the team.

"We'll look again while we disinter the woman," Yi Ling said, "unless it's a small man or a child. Should we bring a surgeon in for an opinion of what—what was used to cut into Hunter like that?"

"No outsiders!" Brad's voice boomed from behind them as he came in. "Claire is the last of this team until I say otherwise."

His tone of voice and assumption of authority surprised Claire, who figured Andrea had the last word on excavations here. As if the dig team wanted no problems from Brad, the three of them hustled back outside, though Claire noted that Yi Ling turned to smile back at Brad.

"Any further observations, Kris, Claire?" Andrea asked, pulling on latex gloves.

Claire said, "You've found no other burials with people maimed, maybe punished or executed? And that dagger—you said nothing else but crude knives have been found."

Andrea nodded as she reached out with gloved hands to try to take the dagger from Hunter's hand. Claire held her breath, almost wanting to ask Andrea to leave it alone. He'd held it all these centuries, and it had meant something to him.

"There!" Andrea said, wresting it away and lifting it toward the overhead light to study it.

"I can't wait to clean this and see what it reveals—to hold it," Brad said, making Claire want to speak out again to tell them it wasn't really theirs. She not only pitied this ancient man, but, strangely, wanted to protect him.

Kris's gaze met Claire's over the corpse as Andrea placed the dagger in a metal tray and handed it to Brad. "Bog and blood clings," she said, "but the blood doesn't mean he hurt himself. People don't tear out their own hearts, except emotionally, and that's where you'll come in on this, Claire."

Claire hoped Brad would let them look at the dagger closer, even before it was cleaned, but, with another quick glance at the corpse, he took the artifact from the room.

"Unbelievable!" Nick told Claire that night as she described her first working day at Black Bog. He sat at a kitchen bar stool while she put the dinner plates in the dishwasher. He had gotten home late; Lexi and Trey were both in bed, and he'd kissed Lexi good-night and stood over Trey's crib for a while before joining Claire in the kitchen. "I'm just grateful you were in an archaeology lab and not a modern morgue."

"I'm certainly going right to work for the Vances. I'm anxious to know if that next body—pretty sure it's a woman's—will have met with violence too."

"I hate to bring this up now when I'd rather be relaxing, but I have sicced Heck on the frozen-woman case to figure out what Cynthia Lindley was like before she died. We need to find who could have hated her enough to kill her, who would have known where to find her—and known where to store or hide her body."

"Heck always turns something up."

"I've also got to have Dale give me his version of Cyndi's life and character, and I'd like to have him over here for dinner for that. You could listen too—not take notes, not seem to interrogate him, but I'd like another set of ears, not a lawyer's. And you do come at a reasonable price."

"Right. Your love and life. Your lovemaking, your son..."

Claire's voice drifted off. Did Hunter once have a son? A wife? Did someone wait for him to come home with deer meat, with a warm pelt for their bed? What went so wrong that he—

"Sweetheart, I said is that okay? I know it puts more work on you."

"I'm honored you asked, and you know I love to be included. Yes, of course, as soon as you need to pursue that—him. Dale still could be involved, right?"

Claire's phone on the counter rang. She walked over and glanced at it. "It's Brit," she said. "Hope nothing's happened to Jace, doing all that flying, just when things are looking good for them."

"I know you still worry about him," Nick said.

"Of course I do. Lexi would be devastated if something happened to him," she said as she slid the phone icon upward to answer it. "Brit, Claire here."

"Hi, Claire. I know it's late, but Jace and I were having a celebration dinner, and we wanted to tell you and Nick something before you hear it elsewhere. We've set a date for the wedding, Saturday, August eleventh. Now don't get your hopes up that Lexi's going to have another new baby to fuss over, because it's not a shotgun wedding except I may have held one to his head so he'd set a date. Of course, we want you two as guests and Lexi as flower girl."

"Congratulations from both of us—and, of course, from Lexi. No problem with setting a date, since you're both ready."

"It will be a small wedding, though I'm not sure we'll be able to take a honeymoon then with Jace's flying demands—well, my work with the animals too."

They chatted a moment more, then said goodbye. Claire explained to Nick, though he'd picked up on this end of the conversation.

"So, that's good news," he said, smiling. "Let's have that private reception of ours sooner than that. I called the Orange Grove Country Club today and we can have the Blue Room there this Sunday afternoon. Nothing huge, no formal invitations, just our friends, including the almost newlyweds. I suppose you'd better explain to them we had this more or less set up, so Brit doesn't think we're stealing their thunder."

"That's great about our belated reception," she told him, but she turned quickly back to wiping down the sink area. "She'll understand. I'll let them know tomorrow." As she wrung out the dish rag, she glanced at her face in the window over the sink. Daylight was almost gone, and the lower pane of glass had become a dark mirror.

Jace had rushed his proposal to her years ago. They had rushed their wedding. It had almost been an elopement. A whirlwind romance that had too soon become regrets and separations—but at least they had Lexi. With his long international flights, she and Jace had spent too much time apart. She had tried to hide her narcolepsy from him. Too late, she'd tried to reach out to him to mend things…

The memory of that hand reaching toward Hunter in the bog leaped at her. A woman he'd loved and lost or left?

She jumped as Nick appeared in the window reflection behind her and put his hands on her shoulders.

"Are you all right, sweetheart? You said you like Brit and think they are good for each other—and for Lexi."

She turned toward him and into his embrace, pressing her cheek against his chest where she could hear his heart beating. "Of course they are, despite being risk takers, both of them. Jace on the hunt for bad guys, Brit protecting her beloved endangered animals."

Wishing that long-gone Hunter didn't make her think of Jace, she put her arms around Nick's waist and held hard.

At the firm the next morning, Nick kept thinking about Claire's reaction to her ex-husband's coming marriage. He hoped she was just worried about things working out well when she had to share Lexi with him and Brit for longer periods, not that she was somehow sad or reluctant he was remarrying.

And, as fascinating as her work at Black Bog was, he could already feel it was consuming her thoughts. Well, he told himself as he sat down at his full-of-work desk, that was always the way Claire was, full-steam ahead, and he recognized that workaholic drive in himself. What was that saying about birds of a feather flocking together?

He heard a man's raised voice outside, one he couldn't place, then his secretary Cheryl's steady reply, higher pitched than usual. "Sir, I don't know how you got past our security desk, but you cannot just go into Counselor Braun's office. No, I will not tell you which it is, and I am calling security."

Nick jumped up and headed for the door. He'd told Bronco he could come in late today because he and Nita were moving in with him and Claire for a few days. Was a police officer out here, ready to arrest Dale? Why hadn't Detective Jensen advised him of that?

He yanked the door the rest of the way open. It wasn't Jensen, not a police officer or anyone he knew. It was a red-bearded man, stocky and bald, dressed in jeans and a leather jacket over a long-sleeved flannel plaid shirt—totally un-Naples, especially this time of year. At least at first glance, Nick thought the guy wasn't armed.

"May I help you, sir? I'm Nick Markwood, senior partner here."

"I'm looking for that bastard rat lawyer works here, kilt my sister. She said he works here."

Nick almost blurted out Cyndi Lindley's name, but that might be construed as admission Dale killed her.

"No one in this firm killed anyone, but am I to assume you are Cynthia Lindley's brother from Georgia?"

"The same. Drove down here straight from Zebulon, an hour south of Atlanta. Got a call from the county coroner, so I'm here to claim her body. Never met her so-called intended before he dumped her, but I got more'n words for him!"

"Please come into my office and calm down. Cheryl, we won't need security, but bring in some coffee for—your name, sir?"

"Tanner Linschwartz. It's her real last name too, but she was hell bent on getting away from her former life, out of Zebulon where she was hostessing in the Down Home Restaurant. Gone first to Atlanta and ended up here, seating people in some fancy restaurant, where she musta met her killer."

"Step inside," Nick coaxed again, gesturing toward his open office door. Finally, the man's angry stance relaxed a bit; his shoulders drooped and his fists uncurled. It was totally understandable that he'd be exhausted and on edge. Vengeful too, so Nick had to watch that. Seemingly calmer now, the man shuffled past Nick into his office.

"Cheryl, I'll leave the door open. Get hold of Bronco and have him wait out here. And," he whispered, "tell Dale to clear out for now, go somewhere nearby, and I'll call him when the coast is clear."

Visibly shaken, though she'd been through a lot around there, Cheryl nodded and jumped up to head for Dale's office just down the hall.

"Very sorry for your loss, Tanner," Nick told the man and sat down in the chair next to him. "You'll take her back to Georgia for a funeral?"

"Going to get her cremated here, then spread her ashes on the beach, in the waves. She'd've liked that, even said so once, so I'll honor that."

"It's unusual for someone as young as your sister—"

"Near on thirty."

"Yes, but to think about dying, to plan for her funeral."

"She was scairt of someone, and now I know who, and got a big score to settle with him. She said he might just be playing her along, that he was going places, maybe where he wouldn't want to take her. Ten to one he kilt her and put her in his dead momma's freezer till he could toss her in the swamp or somewhere. Well, I'm gonna be sure he gets caught for killing her, or if not, pays the price for what he done."

"So," Nick said, realizing he should also tell Cheryl to call Detective Jensen, "tell me about why your sister came to Naples, what she was like. As I said, I'm sorry for the loss of such a lovely, and no doubt ambitious, person."

"She shoulda stayed to home and married Will MacBride, not go gallivanting off to parts unknown."

"So Will MacBride was pretty sad or upset she left?"

"Can't blame him. Childhood sweethearts and all that. She gave him his ring back. I was damn ticked off too."

This man was right on the surface, coming in here with threats and admitting a motive for being angry with his sister, though he didn't seem the type to think of putting her in anybody's freezer. But then there was this Will MacBride and what was he thinking when he heard about Cyndi?

Hell, who really knew what anyone was thinking or was capable of in the heat of passion? He wished this case and Claire's new endeavor could just be calm, objective business. Like she had said last night about that Black Bog body they were calling Hunter, didn't the poor prehistoric guy's chest wounds seem symbolic of life in general? Didn't some things just tear your heart out?

CHAPTER NINE

Claire thought the arm that was slowly being uncovered by the dig team was definitely stretched out toward where Hunter had been buried. She grew impatient at the slow going as they were barely to the body's elbow, so she went back inside again.

She had been given a desk in the corner of Kris's small office. Its single, long window had a view of the bog, that is of the twisted-trunk ficus trees that surrounded it. She tried to put things out of mind and get familiar with their online system of linked laptops, but the dig kept calling to her.

By standing up to look out the window, she could see Kris still waiting, so she prepared to head back out.

She passed Andrea's office down the hall. The door was open and lights on. No Andrea. Brad was in there, though he had a separate lab area, not really an office. He was not seated but was bending over Andrea's chair, stiff armed on her desk, looking closely at her large laptop screen. At a quick glance, Claire thought a series of ancient tools or utensils were on the screen.

He must have heard or sensed her presence, because he closed the screen and turned around just as Claire started to move on.

"Hey, going back out?" he called to her.

So he knew she had come in. She went back a few steps. "I think they'll have reached the second body soon, so I'd like to be there for that. Are you going out too?" She knew the answer to that, but wondered what he would say. His claustrophobia and reluctance to be on scene outside obviously wasn't a secret around here.

He came a couple of steps closer and jammed his hands in his jeans pockets, almost as if he were a kid caught at something. "As you'll see, I don't do much of the field work. My bag is PR. Contracts. Especially funding. Actually, I have claustrophobia, so I don't like to see or even think about someone being closed in the dark heavy ground that long."

"I can understand," she said, edging away, though he came closer to the door. "So, are you able to look at the photos they take?"

"I look at the bodies once they're in the lab."

"One more thing, if you don't mind. Do you prefer being called Brad, Bradley or Senator by the staff, as I've heard all three."

"I answer to each and any," he said with a shrug and a sheepish smile as he leaned against the frame of Andrea's office door. His body language was so unlike the take-charge former Florida senator as she'd pictured him. Had she caught him at something when he was looking at Andrea's screen? "Calling me Brad is fine. So, I know who your husband is, and see you two have had your problems with the law."

That was a strange way to word that, she thought. "Only because we had some unscrupulous people trying to harm us. And then, of course, finding the body in the freezer, which gave the media a field day recently. That was pretty horrible."

"I hope they're right that poor woman was already dead when someone stuck her in there. Talk about claustrophobic nightmares…"

Claire almost asked him if he had such nightmares, but she was probing and presuming too much. Yet she could not believe that Brad wasn't curious enough about a new, unusual discovery in the bog to go out and at least take a look, which she intended to do right now. The grave, after all, was being opened, not closed, though she had to admit those huge, heavy ficus trees with their twisted trunks and roots seemed to press in on the entire area.

"I'd best go back out, Brad," she told him and walked away.

She was relieved that he had seemed not only friendly but honest. And it made her feel good he had admitted knowing Nick—at least who he was, though she hoped his mention of their public troubles wouldn't cause trouble here in this supersecret environment. But then she had not been hired here to psych out the living—just the dead.

It was late morning by the time Detective Ken Jensen responded to Nick's call about Tanner Linschwartz having left his law office and heading to the ME's morgue to take possession of his sister's body. Nick sat him in the same chair Tanner had recently vacated. Nick thought he had settled Tanner down, maybe even convinced him that Dale had really cared for Cyndi but had just realized their marriage would not work out. Since she was a hostess at a tony restaurant in town, Tanner had to admit she could have met someone there who had hurt her, especially since he'd said, "Yeah, she was a man magnet everywhere she went."

Great, just great, Nick thought, in growing frustration. That probably meant lots of possible perps to check out—all of which he conveyed to Jensen right away. He also explained that Bronco and Nita Gates would be at their house for a few days if he needed further statements from them.

"Hey," Jensen said, finally looking up from scribbling notes, "maybe you and Claire can take me in too so we don't have to keep meeting like this." His expression hovered between a grin and a grimace.

Nick told him, "I hope you're not focusing on Bronco and

Nita. I know you and I have a silent agreement not to tell each other how to do our jobs, but shouldn't you focus on this new loose cannon from Georgia? He's volatile and aching for a confrontation at the least."

"I warned the ME's office after your secretary called and have an officer there, but I can understand why he's distraught. He sounds like a real Georgia good old boy with a touch of redneck in him. Thanks for defusing him here a bit—though I'm sure you were thinking he'd sidetrack me off focusing on your junior partner. Irate brother finds sister at Dale's house, they have a fight, he chokes her, stashes her body next door in a freezer to make it look like Dale did it."

Nick decided to ignore that. "Tanner told me Cyndi had big dreams about moving up in the world," he told Jensen. "She dumped a repairman boyfriend named Will MacBride, and if he's anything like his buddy Tanner, he should be a person of interest. Evidently Zebulon is just a long day's drive from here. Since Cyndi worked her way first to Atlanta and then to Naples, other men she's met along the way might need looking into. She was a magnet for men, as Tanner put it."

"Gotcha. By the way, Nick, as I've said before, if Claire ever wants to work part-time, the department could use a forensic psych. Seriously, I like her, trust her. Keep it in mind, okay?"

"She's working part-time as a business consultant. With the new baby, that's enough, at least for now."

"Sure, I understand. If she did facial reconstruction models, we'd have a full-time job for her, but I get you want her working somewhere private where she can keep out of the trouble you two seem to find. See you soon, Nick," Jensen said, leaning over so they could shake hands. "Hopefully not in court."

Claire thought the extended arm and hand of the next body looked as if she—or he—had wanted to touch Hunter, or even shake hands, but who knew what their customs of greeting were.

The team had excavated one shoulder, but to everyone's surprise, the corpse was not turned toward Hunter. Rather the body lay flat on her or his back with the other shoulder and arm evidently reaching out in the opposite direction.

Doug said, "If this burial wasn't centuries before Christ, I'd say it's almost posed like someone on a cross. 'For all this His anger is not turned away, but His hand is stretched out still.'"

"Another Bible verse?" Yi Ling asked as she carefully brushed bog from the arm and Doug kept picking at tiny hardened clumps of peat with what looked like a dental pick. "Claire, Doug is our walking, talking quote man of Bible verses. What was that one you use to warn people not to get off the planks and into the bog?"

"Oh, the one from *Jeremiah*?" he asked.

"I think so," Yi Ling said. "I'm afraid it fits even more now that we've learned Hunter was executed or at least—what's that word Andrea used? Eviscerated?"

"I don't mean to interrupt," Claire said, "but that's a possibility too—that Hunter was an honored man so they kept his heart when he died." She sighed. "But then, I think they would have done a better job of removing it. So what's the Bible verse, Doug?"

"Okay," he said. "Jeremiah wasn't called 'the weeping prophet' for nothing. That section goes, 'Your close friends have set upon you, and prevailed against you; your feet have sunk in the mire, and they have turned away again.'"

"That possibly fits here," Claire said, surprised her voice was shaky. "Not only the sunk-in-mire part but the idea that Hunter's own friends might have turned against him. But for what?"

Yi Ling said, "How and what and why—that's the name of the game around here. Well, we give you the evidence, and you come up with the answers, that's your thing here, Claire."

"Wish I did have answers instead of just more questions." She realized she was trembling. Was she just excited to see what they would turn up here, had her awkward encounter with Brad shaken her—or was it because she felt so bad for Hunter? Ridiculous to get emotionally involved with a millennia-long dead man.

"Someone should go get Andrea," Yi Ling said, without looking up again. "She always likes to be here when we uncover the body itself. It's her tradition to name each person, and I hate to just summon her on the walkie-talkie for something this important."

"I can go," Claire volunteered, "but I didn't see her in her office. I just saw Brad."

"I think," Aaron put in, "she's back in the room with the brains. As for the senator, he never likes to come out where we're working."

And now she knew why, Claire thought, as she carefully walked the planks back toward the main walkway and the building. Stopping for a moment, she glanced back at the trio of archaeologists. Even though Yi Ling was so petite, she held her own with the men. Kris had said that Yi Ling, last name Chung, was Chinese, a graduate of Peking University. She had written Andrea for the opportunity to study with her, then had stayed on.

Claire walked toward the building. Even in late morning, with the sun pretty much overhead, the heavy limbs and leaves of the ficus trees made it feel darkish here. Besides, clouds had covered the sun, and she thought she even heard a rumble of distant thunder out over the gulf.

She went in the bog access entryway and walked down the hall toward Andrea's lab. The door was closed, so she knocked.

"Who?" Andrea called out.

"It's Claire. The team would like you outside since they are close to the body."

"Step in a minute."

Claire opened the door and went in. On a screen, many times magnified, was an image of Hunter's dagger, at least one side of it. For the first time, Claire could see that it was flint, carefully chipped to a sharp blade and point—and it had some kind of pattern carved in the hilt.

"Surely, that isn't some sort of writing," Claire said as she squinted to study the strange shapes.

"An attempt at artwork, I think, but I can't tell of what. The game he hunted maybe—abstract, of course," Andrea said with a shrug.

"Stick figures. People?"

"Some sort of message from the grave. This blow-up of it could blow up the world of archaeology," she added in an awed voice as she continued to stare at the image.

"The motto for my Clear Path website has been 'The dead still talk if you know how to listen.' That's true here too."

"I remember that, from when I was researching you," she admitted.

"In this case, the motto should be 'The dead still talk if you know how to see,'" Claire said.

Andrea finally looked her way. "Somehow, some way, we will get the answers from these bog people and then be able to share all we've learned and found with others. I will do anything it takes to accomplish that as my life's work!"

Staring back at the intense woman, Claire nodded. What else was there to say, at least right now, but for one thing. "Are there photos of the other side of the dagger?"

"This is the decorated side. Well, time to study this later." She turned off her projector. "Let's go outside and see who was reaching out to poor, mutilated Hunter, just the way we would love to reach out to all these poor, buried, long-lost souls."

"You might know it started to rain right then," Claire told Nick that evening when they finally had both Trey and Lexi asleep and their guests, Bronco and Nita, had gone up to their bedroom. "And just when they were ready to uncover the next body. Their policy is to just cover what they have and get back to it tomorrow—if it isn't raining then. Andrea was as disappointed as I was. The trees that edge the bog protected us for a while, but then dripped water on us too, so that was that."

"It's like a treasure hunt, isn't it?" Nick asked as he added another name to the guest list for their Sunday afternoon reception. The club was providing the catering, so things were going smoothly. Claire would extend the invitation to friends by phone tomorrow before she went to work. Nick would ask his staff at the firm.

"Yes, a treasure hunt's a good analogy," she admitted. "I never thought I would get so involved with long-dead people, though that's exactly what I've been hired to do."

"It's a good thing you're doing that part-time, because I think you can use a break already. Today will be your last day there until Monday, so we can drop by the club and check out the room, talk to the staff. I was at a function there, but it was a couple of years ago—pre-Claire."

"Sounds good. Let's do that in the morning because Kris is going with me to dress shops in the afternoon, probably to get an outfit for herself too, since I invited her. Lexi loves her dress from Nita and Bronco's wedding, so she'll wear that. Sorry for the fashion commentary. Any more word on poor Cynthia's brother? From what you said, he sounds like a loose cannon."

"Since I've been able to informally depose him, he's Jensen's problem now, but, yeah, he bears watching. I assume he'll be busy with her cremation tomorrow or whenever they release the body to him. Sad to think that beautiful woman will become ashes in the wind and water."

Blinking back tears, Claire nodded and reached out to cover Nick's hand with hers.

CHAPTER TEN

Under their big umbrella in the steady, gentle rain, Claire held Nick's arm as they went into the Orange Grove Country Club. They had been invited to look over the facilities for their much-belated wedding reception. Despite all Nick had to do at the office, he was planning to go in late. At least this off-and-on rainy weather was supposed to clear up soon.

"If it wasn't for this umbrella, I could still carry you over the threshold," he teased as he opened the door for her. He shook out the umbrella and left it with the others on a rack.

"I'm happy to say your toting me into our bedroom now and then is quite enough. Besides, it wouldn't do to have the man of the house and my favorite lawyer-at-large hurt his back two days before our party."

They were greeted by Mary Ann Manning, special occasions director, who showed them the Blue Room they had reserved. It had adequate seating for forty as well as one long buffet table and several other tables scattered throughout the area.

"The Blue Room comes with the air-conditioned, glassed-in verandah which runs along the side," Mary Ann told them, with a sweep of her hand at the long space outside which also had chairs and small tables. "In good weather, we open the sliding doors, and it becomes one large room. We could do that, put the cake and food in here, then let your guests go either in or out. We have special laminated glass on this long window to cut the UV rays. Even golf balls hitting the glass won't make it shatter," she said with a little laugh. "And, as you can see, there is a lovely view of the eighteenth green and the orange grove surrounding the area."

"I read there's been a dispute over the property lines," Nick said.

"I'm afraid so. The original orchard owners are demanding an exorbitant price for the small amount of extra land we want to lengthen the practice driving range. I'm afraid they have even pulled some dirty tricks, like smashing rotten oranges on some of the greens, even stuffing them in the holes. Someone has lobbed oranges at foursomes out by the seventh and eighth holes. But slightly higher tech, someone has buzzed golfers with a drone. The grove owners have denied doing that. Dare I say we could use some legal advice on how best to proceed?"

Nick turned and smiled at the dark-haired woman. "Dare I say, I could recommend someone to help in exchange for all the help you're giving us here? It would have to be a junior partner right now, but the senior partners ultimately oversee everything."

"I'll tell our board," she said with a nod. "Now, please, both of you, explain how you would like things laid out on the verandah, and our caterers will have everything, including that belated wedding cake, ready for your guests at four on your big day."

As they spent a half hour with her, Claire realized how excited she was over all this. As much as she loved being married to Nick, their wedding had been a nightmare, forced on them by their sworn enemy. But this would all make up for it, choosing a cake, buying a dress...

"I said I've got to run, sweetheart," Nick told her and pecked a kiss on her cheek as he walked her to her car, since they'd driven separately. "Have a good time at lunch and dress shopping with Kris."

"Will do. And I'll text you or leave you a message if we get the call that the rain has let up enough that the team will be ready to disinter the second body in Hunter's grave—their grave, I mean. It's custom that everyone's there for that—except for Senator Vance—unless there is some real conflict."

Conflict. Was there some sort of unspoken conflict she was picking up between the senator and Andrea, or was she just reading too much into it?

Nick gave her another quick kiss before she got in her car. "You do realize," he said, leaning down with the umbrella still in his hand to open the car door for her, "that if someone overheard us talking graves and bodies, they would either think we were nuts or call the cops. See you, amateur archaeologist."

"You look great in that!" Kris assured Claire as they met in the mirrored central aisle between their separate dressing rooms in Talbot's at the Waterside Shops in Naples. "The color goes really well with your red hair. Good thing I'm not color-blind. Being face blind is bad enough," she added with a sigh.

"I know, but you do beautifully, handling it. Now, look at this. I love the cut out pattern on the shoulders and back neckline." Claire tried to get her back on track and she turned to glance in the mirror again. "I have the perfect earrings and necklace for this light green. Do you think I'd need matching shoes or just white or beige?"

"Either light color. I think I'm going with the pink-and-navy suit, but probably won't wear the jacket to the reception."

"This kind of grabs my hips in back," Claire said, still turning. "I'm going out to see if I should go up one size, because the bust is a wee bit tight too. I guess that's what having a baby does to you. I was so much younger when Lexi came along."

Since the saleswoman who had been helping them was ring-ing up a customer, Claire went to the well-lit rack by the front window to check for a larger size in the same dress. And found herself staring through the glass at someone who was looking in. The other person seemed to startle, stared, then turned quickly away and hurried off.

Hadn't she seen that same person more than once walking past the restaurant window earlier? They'd had lunch at Brio's before starting their shopping.

The surprise of it made Claire's heartbeat kick up. Was that a man or a woman? A Tampa Bay Buccaneers baseball cap and big sunglasses hid the forehead and eyes, but she could see chin-length hair. That mustache looked fake. What *did* that person look like? It made her feel she was face blind too and sympathized with Kris even more.

As for clothing, the person wore loose slacks and a pullover, both in black. Well, what did it matter if someone dressed weird? she scolded herself and went back in to the dressing rooms.

"Lucky you, to find that," Kris greeted her. She'd changed back into her casual clothes. "If I go up a size, I have no excuse of a new baby. Which reminds me, we never found a body of a bog woman who was pregnant or had just given birth, so I was hypothesizing that they seemed to survive childbirth—sturdy women. I'm sure in general they got enough exercise. Yet so many of them seemed to chew those natural painkillers."

"Don't so much as say the word *killers*," Claire said from under the dress as she pulled it up over her head.

She pictured again the person looking through the windows. Well, so what? Didn't lots of people window-shop? Maybe the person was eccentric or mentally off or homeless and just roved the shopping center.

"By the way," she added, "I noticed the rain has stopped outside."

"Hope at Black Bog too. Can't wait to see Hunter's companion."

Claire almost told her about the person peering into the store, one she couldn't even identify by sex. That made her wonder if the body in the bog they would see next was a female.

"Look," she said, trying to keep her mind on the present, "this dress fits much better."

"You know," Kris said as they finally gathered their purchases, "I never have trouble recalling what someone wears. So why the curse of the face blindness?"

Claire took her arm. "Do you think you can recall the bog faces so well because you recognize them by their clothing or the position of their bodies?"

"It can't be by the artifacts with them, because Andrea always takes those to study right away, and that's one thing the senator is totally intrigued by. But as for your psyching out my coping mechanisms, why is my best longtime friend a sort of shrink, even if a forensic one?" Kris said with a mock sigh, looking upward.

They bought their outfits and were heading out toward a shoe store in the open-air mall when Kris's cell phone and Claire's rang almost at the same time. "Oh-oh," Kris said, as she produced hers from her pants pocket. "I—we—may have to head for the bog."

Kris took the call fast. Claire could hear Andrea's voice on the other end as she dug her phone out of her purse. "I'm in town so I could call you. Surely the rain stopped at the bog too. I'm heading there and expect to see you there quickly." They both had their cars, and Claire skimmed the parking lot for hers just two rows over from Kris's.

And there, staring at her then moving quickly away, was that androgynous person again. Were she and Kris—or just one of them—being followed? But by whom and why? It was probably just a random thing and they had to get going. Her past had made her paranoid. She didn't want to alarm Kris, but if that person appeared again, she'd point him or her out.

"Let's go," Kris said, punching off, as Claire took her own

phone call. Hers was from Yi Ling from the dig team who was also heading for the bog.

"Are you coming out, even though you're not scheduled?" Yi Ling asked excitedly. "I think you're right that it's a woman. The rain has quit, and we're going to excavate around her right away. I swear she has breasts. And maybe there's a string of bodies there, linked somehow."

"We're on our way," Claire told her even as Kris jumped in her car.

"Follow me, okay?" Kris called to her as she rolled her window down.

"After you drive around to my car!" Claire called back as she began to cut through cars in the next rows. She had no intention of meeting that person—where had he or she disappeared to? Surely Nick wouldn't assign someone to keep an eye on her for safety's sake. It must be coincidence, but she'd learned long ago to expect no such thing—especially if you dabbled in danger like finding a body in a freezer.

A peek inside her car showed no one in the back seat, nothing disturbed. She put the box with her new dress on the passenger side. Should she show Nick her dress, or surprise him, like a bride at her wedding?

Oh, no. That's right! Dale Braun was coming for dinner tonight—and for a conversational interrogation she was supposed to assess right along with Nick's observations. So she couldn't stay at Black Bog too long. She'd promised Nick she'd help, and family still had to come first.

But she was so certain, so hopeful after all that she'd been through, that her life was all—well, almost—normal now.

Jace waited for his Stingray contact and friend, Mitch Blakeman, at the huge door of the hangar at the Marco Island Airport just as Mitch was taxiing off the runway toward him. Jace watched as "Falcon," a former Marine pilot, shut down the single-engine so-called crop dusting plane inside and walked to meet him. They had both been in the local skies lately, spraying for insect pests, including Zika virus mosquitoes. But the equipment in their planes actually allowed them to troll for drug runners' locations by tracking their cell phones. Huge stashes of drugs were supposed to be coming in from Mexico. Since a recent murder of a Stingray pilot in California, their job had become a lot more tense.

"Sometimes I feel we're on a par with the Wright brothers, in the small old planes—sitting ducks," Jace called to Mitch, with a glance back at the single-engine propeller aircraft that passed for what local farmers would use. "I'm homesick for a fighter jet and some speed. How about you?"

"Yeah, a baseball hat instead of a helmet's not really my style," Mitch said as he fell into step with Jace, twisting and nearly wadding up his billed cap. Even as they passed through the small airport, they kept their aviator sunglasses on. "So, have you done any more thinking about my proposal to fly for the hurricane hunters? A WC-130 turboprop plane sounds good to me, even though it's not a jet. Those big babies fly right through the eyewall of the storm, so the excitement's sure there, all in a day's work. Besides, like I said, there are signs the bad boys running drugs into Southwest Florida might be onto us. Time to face a storm instead. So, did you tell your Brittany yet?"

"Not yet. Got formally engaged, though, and set a date. Finally gave her a ring. We've had each other's back for a while, and I'd appreciate it if you'd be my best man."

"I'm honored," Mitch said, shaking his hand, then clapping him on the shoulder as they emerged from the small airport terminal. They sat at a picnic table on the other side of a fence from the runway. "I think we're both ready to move on to new careers—new lives. But will Brittany be okay with the new gig? I mean, our current flights can be dangerous if our cover gets blown, but eleven-hour-long flights into insane winds while being responsible for a crew of up to sixteen people…"

"Yeah. On the other hand, I miss flying five hundred people over the Pacific. But you know, I have a friend named Bronco whose new wife went ballistic when he kept something back from her—"

"Are you nuts? You mean you proposed to Brittany but didn't tell her—ask her—about flying into hurricanes?"

"Keep it down," Jace whispered as a man and wife with two small kids walked past them into the airport. "We're going to a wedding reception—my ex's, no less—and Brit will be all emotional over that, so I'll bring it up when we're alone after."

Mitch heaved a sigh that seemed to deflate his always rigid military posture. He was lanky whereas Jace was more solidly built. Mitch slumped a bit, elbows on knees, staring at the grass. The sun on his close-cropped light blond hair made it seem to glow.

"I've got to tell you something else," Mitch said. "About our current gig—about that California pilot an explosive drone shot out of the sky. His girlfriend was with him. I didn't learn that right away—didn't read the papers from there. But just out of curiosity, I looked it up online yesterday."

"Damn! Yeah, I'd better get out of Stingray. More than once Brit wanted to go up with me, and I said later she could. Listen, I figure once we change jobs we can get an article in the paper to announce, not that we're leaving Stingray, but that two local guys are now consulting and flying full-time to protect the entire state from hurricane dangers. Okay, Mitch?"

"Yeah, yeah. I'm in."

"Doubly terrible what happened. I don't want to run or be a coward. I've risked my life plenty of times for the right reason, but I'm not going to endanger Brit—or let my chance at happiness go."

"I wish I had someone. I'm tired of going home to an empty

house after missions. Like I said, I'd be honored to be your best man, and I'm taking what you said as a yes for your becoming a hurricane hunter with me. Otherwise, protocol would have to make me move on without you so we wouldn't be seen together where the drug boys could spot us—so, hell," he said, turning his head to look at Jace again. "Here we are like sitting ducks at the airport we fly out of, on the chance that someone wants to knock us off. My marine sergeant would have killed me himself in the old days for something stupid like this—hoo-ya, man!"

They smacked raised hands. As Claire had said to tease him in the old days, Jace told Mitch, "Pilots of a feather fly together. And know what? I think I might just have the girl for you, a sharp blonde I knew years ago in college—no, I never dated her, so don't look at me like that, but she did introduce me to my ex, Claire. Thing is though she's into digging up bodies."

"What in the…"

"She's an archaeologist. You look up, she looks down. Tell you more if you meet me at Snook Inn. Let's go get a brew to toast our new careers, and I'll explain. For once, my man, you're buying."

Claire and Kris both ignored the fact they were going to get their clothes bog-mud dirty. Even the raised planks they walked were water-and peat-speckled. Although the rain had stopped, drops of water peppered them from sodden leaves when the wind blew. But the plastic tarp that had been over the dig site had kept the grave quite dry. Doug, Aaron and Yi Ling were in their usual positions, half in and half out of the grave. Andrea was bending over them, somehow in another immaculate white outfit, even her shoes.

"Oh, I see what you mean!" Claire cried as she sidled closer to get a better angle. "Yes, that arm must be a woman's, and I see the swell of her breast."

"And," Kris said, "her flat-on-her-back position and that other raised shoulder do indicate her other arm must be stretched out."

Andrea said, "Obviously she and Hunter were somehow related, and not just in death. Claire, a challenge for you to discern and hypothesize how. Is that— Is she wearing a pelt? Perhaps she was Hunter's wife."

"Yeah, a pelt," Aaron said, "though it's so muddy it's hard to tell. But I can see she has shoes still on her feet that look as if they might be deer hide—kind of shaped like modern bedroom slippers."

Claire's back and neck ached from leaning forward by the time they uncovered the woman's face. She looked—well, young. Strangely, still pretty yet either she had died distressed or the weight of the bog had distorted her features.

"Look," Claire cried. "That leather thong or whatever it is. Those stones and shells on it. It must be a necklace that came off her neck! Some smashed shells but those must have been pretty, polished stone."

"I see it," Andrea said. "I'm going to radio Brad and tell him we have another important artifact. We'll treat it carefully and analyze it thoroughly. Put it in one of your plastic packages— carefully so it doesn't come apart any more—and hand it to me, Yi Ling."

Despite the peat and mud obscuring some of the stones and shells, Claire thought it must be a real work of prehistoric art. But then, Andrea was probably the kind that had to clean it first, study it and label it before coming to that conclusion.

"All of you know I name each of our finds." Andrea's sharp voice cut into Claire's agonizing. "It's their welcome to this modern world, sort of a naming ceremony. I am naming this one Reaching Woman."

Aren't all women reaching for something? Claire thought. But when such a rare artifact was found, didn't Andrea usually name the body after the artifact versus the body's position? The early bodies she had seen were Woman with Mirror, Woman with Medicine in Stomach. Why not Woman with Necklace here? It must be because Andrea valued, above all, the relationship among these three people, and psyching that out was now Claire's assignment—and burden. All this seemed not just fascinating but almost sacred to her, and perhaps it did to Andrea too.

As they excavated Reaching Woman's head and torso carefully, Claire asked, "She's all there, isn't she? I mean, not like Hunter with his chest hollowed out?"

Without looking up, Aaron said, "I can tell she's all here, not caved in like Hunter, so—"

But he stopped in midthought. Yi Ling gave a grunt that sounded as if she'd been punched in the stomach. "Damn!" Doug said. "Do you believe it? What are we in here, murderer's row—or murdered row?"

"What is it?" Andrea demanded, leaning closer.

Claire saw there was a large slit in the bodice of the woman's clothing. The poor thing's heart might be there, but it had a flint dagger much like Hunter's in it, protruding upward from the left side of her chest.

CHAPTER ELEVEN

Claire was dying to tell Nick all about the second executed or murdered person they'd uncovered today at Black Bog. But he came in late, and she couldn't unload all that on him while helping Nita prepare dinner. Besides, their guest Dale Braun pulled into their driveway just a few minutes after Nick.

"Bronco and I are gonna eat our fajitas out in the gazebo," Nita told Claire. "I'll check on Trey now and then, and we'll feed Lexi, give you three time to talk."

She lowered her voice though Nick and Dale were out in the Florida room having a martini—Claire's idea to get Dale to relax a bit so he might be more conversational. Their goal tonight, besides assuring him as a coworker and client that the firm was working hard for him, was to learn as much as they could about Cyndi and their relationship. Nick had said that if Cyndi was anything like her brother, she'd been as different from Dale in background and personality as day and night.

"Lexi will love eating out with you two," Claire told Nita. "Just be sure she's got mosquito spray on her. Those little nasties are out early this year."

"Oh, *si*, all three of us get sprayed, even though Bronco always says he's too orn'ry to get bites. You know, Claire, helping with your family—kinda being a part of it," she said, turning away from the stove, "it really makes me want children even more."

Claire put her hand on Nita's arm. "You will have them, my friend. So sorry your plans took a hit when we found the body in the freezer."

Nita sniffed back tears. "It must have been so awful for her— Cyndi. I—I swear she was screaming, but it was a silent scream with no one to help."

Because, Claire almost said, whatever sort of person Cyndi was, whatever Dale or her brother or anyone else said about her, she was a woman who was in danger. Such a sad, too common story even in this modern world. And then there was Reaching Woman, newly born from the bog but stabbed in the heart. Both that ancient female and Cyndi had needed someone to reach out to them, and Dale Braun had let Cyndi go. She just prayed he hadn't hurt her more than that.

"Delicious food," Dale said, wiping salsa off his mouth. "If I'd known Nita was a great cook, I'd have reduced the price of their house and had her deliver a meal now and then. But, yeah, I'm out of there as soon as possible, a decision I made way before the—the tragedy. Gonna move way downtown, I think, turn into metro man and let somebody else sell the houses on the land I inherited, now that my mother's gone too. But I'm not even staying there now."

Nick said, "I asked this yesterday, but you haven't seen Cyndi's brother, Tanner, have you? At least he hasn't been back to the office."

"No, but that's one big reason I'm staying in the hotel downtown right now. I don't need him cornering me somewhere, especially after what you said. I'm hoping the guy scatters Cyndi's ashes on the beach and heads north. Tanner is just one more piece of proof I never should have fallen for her."

"Nick, I forgot to ask," Claire said. "What does Tanner look like?"

"Big and burly. Shaved head. Not to stereotype but a typical good-old Southern boy."

Definitely not, she thought, the person who might have been stalking her or Kris. Claire realized this was not the time to think about it, but she couldn't forget that person watching, perhaps following her. It wasn't coincidence and she wanted to tell Nick, but that, like her news of the new bog body, would have to wait. Besides, all she needed was him thinking she should stay home all the time.

"I've seen pictures of Tanner," Dale said, rolling his eyes. "The guy was standing in front of the courthouse in their Georgia hometown with a statue of Jefferson Davis and the Stars and Bars flag flying behind him."

"Oh, great," Nick said, frowning and shaking his head. "So what else made you decide to call off the engagement? I consider you to be a pretty discerning, careful guy, so why did you fall for her in the first place?"

"Infatuation, I guess. Well, it—she—kind of swept me away. Obviously, she's—she was—beautiful, so feminine, flirty. She seemed needy, looked up to me, all that."

Claire just nodded whenever he glanced her way. She intended to let Nick guide this conversation, but he'd asked her to weigh in if she saw a good opening to learn more. All she could sense so far was that Dale was suddenly more nervous, almost stuttering, but that was understandable. Still, she wasn't in total agreement with Nick that his junior partner had to be innocent.

In the awkward silence, Claire said, "I'll bet there was some incident that made you realize the two of you were from different backgrounds."

"Yeah, no kidding. I ignored that at first and shouldn't have. Two things. We double-dated with one of the other junior partners—it was Brent Atkins, Nick—and that night it hit me that

Cyndi had no knowledge or interest in things, like—well, even current events, let alone culture, beyond Hollywood personalities. She thought the Kardashians were the royalty of America. I don't mean to sound like a snob, but I am ambitious in my important and damn serious profession. She could hardly talk about something else over dinner besides what someone at the next table was wearing."

"I understand," Nick put in.

"Of course, she was ambitious too in her own way—just not my way. I know," Dale rushed on, gripping his hands together so hard his fingers went white, "here we're both from the deep, deep South, but her small-town Georgia background just didn't mesh with mine. I finally came to my senses that night—the double date."

There was a long pause. He stared at his hands, then folded his arms over his chest as if to hide or protect himself, classic "I'm guilty" body language. And his reference to "that night." Was that also the night he broke it off with her?

"We know this is so hard, Dale," Claire assured him, leaning slightly forward. "That night you told her your engagement was off—when was that?"

"I told Detective Jensen and Nick it was just before my mother died."

"Then she was seen after that, surely," Nick put in. "You even told Jensen that Cyndi went to say goodbye to your mother."

"Right. Mother didn't like her, so that would have been good news. That is, if Mother didn't think she was someone else."

"You mean she might have thought Cyndi was someone else because of her dementia?" Claire prompted.

"Right. The thing is," he plunged on after taking a breath, "you know, that double-date night Cyndi even made a couple of comments about her family once owning slaves way back. She said she could 'use a couple of those.' Just a joke, I guess, but enlightening and objectionable. Politics—I learned not to go there with her. That's what I meant by saying I realized—too late—it just wouldn't work out."

He sighed, almost seeming to deflate, still gripping himself with crossed arms as if trying to hold himself up. "Besides all that, when I showed her the old ruined mansion my great-uncle had built when he fled here from Germany just after World War II, she said she absolutely wanted a place like that—maybe rebuild our home right there. She thought my heritage was great—probably thought I was rich too—even though I've tried to keep that low key."

Nick visibly startled. "You mean that ruined mansion is still in the picture, still a concern?"

"Wait," Claire said, hoping to head off Nick's frustration. "I'm evidently missing something here. You own a ruined mansion? And you've tried to keep your German ancestor low key because they fled Germany?"

"Yeah. Right near the end of World War II. It's all water over the dam—way past, so I shouldn't even bring it up. But here's the thing. My great-uncle, Wilhelm Braun, who went by the name Will Braun here, came from Germany with a lot of money near the end of the war."

"Go on," Nick prompted when he hesitated.

Dale nodded, and plunged on talking fast as if he had to get it all out. "So Uncle Will, like many others, was trying to establish himself as a solid citizen here, because he had been a Nazi, pretty top ranking. The name of the game in Uncle Will's life was to bury the past, though I knew nothing about this until after he died. See, after World War II, many of Hitler's elite SS fled to South America, but Will came to South Florida, a less settled place in the 1940s. He was wily—knew not to go where the others went and could be found, not safety in numbers but safety in being a loner."

Nick looked riveted. Dale paused and took a huge breath. Claire nodded. She knew there had to be more coming.

"As I said, Uncle Will had money," Dale went on, frowning. "He built a sort of Southern plantation on his large estate, the land on which I now have a house, where my mother lived and where Bronco and Nita bought their dream home."

He cleared his throat, hunched over with his elbows on the table and rested his chin on the heels of his hands, almost as if he'd like to gag himself, though he kept talking.

"What's left of the mansion sits at the far back of the properties that were built on the site after Uncle Will died. Of course, it was a family secret he'd been a Nazi, in favor with Hitler, high up. It's amazing he escaped arrest and a trial when the Americans and Russians came crashing into Berlin and rounded up war criminals. He was just plain lucky that no Nazi hunters tracked him down later."

Claire said, "Of course, all that is safe with us. He's long gone. The sins of the fathers—and great-uncles—should not be visited upon the children."

He nodded. "Before he died twenty plus years ago, he told me never to call his fortune dirty or tainted money. I didn't but I'm sure it was *Reich* money."

Silence reigned for a moment. Blood money, Claire would have called it, but she didn't want to stifle these revelations now. But how could any of this tie into Cyndi's murder? Could someone have known about Dale's family's Nazi ties and tried to frame him for a murder, using poor Cyndi as the sacrificial lamb? No, she was reading too much in here, creating fiction instead of finding facts.

"So he'd worked closely with Hitler?" Nick asked. He cleared his throat. He looked and sounded stunned.

"Yes, but there's more," Dale admitted. "My last name— his last name, Braun. Uncle Will was related to Hitler through marriage."

Claire's mind raced again. "But isn't it true Hitler only married right before he and his bride killed themselves so the Allied forces wouldn't take them alive?"

Dale nodded, kept nodding. "See, I shouldn't have shared all that with Cyndi. You no doubt see it for what it was—something to be hidden. To her it meant fame—she thought I should write a book, make a big deal of it to get publicity, TV interviews, a movie contract, and she'd be right there with me in the limelight."

Nick just kept nodding, so Claire said, "Tell us how he was related to Hitler's wife."

"So here's the deal," Dale said, sitting up straight at last. "My great-uncle was the brother of the father of Hitler's longtime mistress Eva Braun whom *Der Führer* married just three days before their deaths. Cyndi wanted to use that connection to make hay, as she put it, wanted me to rebuild and open up the Braun mansion to the public, give it back its German name. Frankly, I was appalled, saw her for what she was. I told her not to go out there to see the place but then caught her there. But damn it, I didn't kill her, though I guess this would give Detective Jensen and his cohorts a lot more ammo. I'm not an idiot. I realize my wanting to stop her stupid ideas is another motive for murder."

He put his forehead in his hands, staring down at his empty plate. "I'm just telling you two this now—that seeing that side of her hurt and infuriated me, and I threatened her not to exploit my family's legacy. I told her it was over, but—I repeat," he said, looking up at Nick and then Claire, "I did—not—kill—her!"

"But maybe she told someone else about your family," Claire whispered. "Which, I suppose might mean someone could try to blackmail you. Have you ever felt or noticed you were being followed?"

He shook his head. "I just want to be proud of my name— make my name my own," Dale said with a sniff as Nick reached across the corner of the table to put a hand on his shoulder. "I don't want it dragged through the mud, fame as she put it, a curse as I thought of it. I am not my great-uncle even if I'm stuck with the remnants of his haunted mansion—well, not haunted, except all this haunts me."

"I can see why," Claire said. "You're like an innocent bystander in someone else's wreck. So Cyndi went out to see the remnants of the mansion without your permission or knowledge at some point, then maybe even again later, maybe the day she was killed. Have there ever been vagrants or just nosy people there? You said it's not well known but..."

"A lot of area people used to know about the place, but—I think—not its sordid past. I suppose it was once a real attraction on Halloween. The place has been vandalized more than once. I hate it myself—can't bear to go there. But if you want to see it, I'll take you. In broad daylight."

"Why didn't you just have the rest of it torn down?" Nick asked.

"Did you ever check out the price of having anything razed and hauled away? Besides, I have to admit, as much as the place feels like the corpse of a family curse sometimes, there's just something about it that whispers 'hands off!'"

Nick said, "How about tomorrow morning? We need to get a take on this, then consider telling Jensen about it before he learns some other way. Sorry, but he should even know about the Hitler and Eva Braun connections, because it may all come out anyway. Was there any way Cyndi could have known you were well-to-do and come on to you for your money at first?"

"I don't think she knew, not at first," he said, looking and sounding hurt. "The houses Mother and I lived in are middle-class at best, though I took Cyndi out to good restaurants, took her on a one-week cruise."

Rising, Nick said, "I think this is important. Claire. You aren't working Saturday morning, are you?"

"Not scheduled, but—you know—on call if something else turns up. But this is important too, and I want to go with you."

"Right. Dale, we'll meet at your house and go together to take a look at the ruins of the place. What did you say its original name was?"

"In German, *Verdrehte Baume.* It means Twisted Trees."

Claire pictured the ancient trees surrounding Black Bog. Twisted trunks like the twisted lives of the living and the dead.

Later, they both walked Dale out to his car in the driveway. Nick was grateful that they had managed to settle him down over dessert. Dale had even asked to speak with Bronco and Nita. He'd thanked Nita for the excellent meal and tried to reassure them that their house and neighborhood would survive the scandal. He even offered them some money to help furnish the house, but Nick could tell that Bronco, and especially Nita, were reluctant to accept—or to even move in there. But just wait, Nick thought, until they tried to resell a place where a woman's body had been stashed, though the cops and forensic techs had found no evidence she'd been strangled there too.

"Oh, the full moon's out," Claire said. "The clear sky gives me hope the rain will stay away for a while. And look at the reflection of it on your car."

But it wasn't that. The silvery dust on the dark trunk, top, hood and front windshield glittered coldly.

"Dew?" Nick asked, as if to himself. "I smell ashes. Maybe someone had a barbeque or backyard fire, and it blew over here…"

Dale pulled out his car keys and with the other hand took a long swipe of the stuff on the top of his car's hood. "It *is* ashes," he said, smelling, then trying to look at his hand in the semidarkness. "Heavy here, but not on the driveway or grass."

Nick heard Claire gasp. It hit him then too, even as Dale seemed to realize what this might be. The poor guy sank to his knees in the grass and put his head in his hands. Bronco, who must have been watching from the house, ran out. "Boss, what's that stuff? It smells ashy."

Nick ordered, "Everyone, back into the house. Now! Dale, don't wipe that off your hand until we get a sample. Bronco, turn on the porch light and keep an eye out the window. Everybody, move!"

Bronco helped Dale to his feet. Claire seized Nick's hand as they ran inside. Nick told her, "Got to call Detective Jensen. This may be a trick or some kind of threat. Maybe Cyndi's brother couldn't find Dale, but could find us—and then found Dale. Maybe a very bitter brother didn't scatter his dead sister's ashes in the Gulf of Mexico after all."

CHAPTER TWELVE

Claire perched on her vanity stool in the steamed-up bathroom as Nick took a shower that night. Although he hadn't let on until Dale left, he was steamed up in another way, and Claire was trying to calm him down. So unlike him, he'd been on a tirade and hadn't quit. His voice echoed from behind the frosted-glass shower door. It was nearly midnight. She'd taken her narcolepsy meds but felt dead on her feet. Jensen and his forensic evidence team had finally left with most of the ashes, which a rising breeze had not pulled away. At least it hadn't rained.

"Nick," she tried another tactic, "at least the police now have another suspect besides Dale. If those ashes could be Cyndi's, that leads to Tanner. If he does something that crazy, he might have lost his temper at his sister for something else. Maybe he didn't just recently arrive from Georgia."

"Yeah, but put her in a freezer in a house he knew nothing about? I'll bet Tanner has an alibi that he was in good old Zebulon when Cyndi was killed—even though they can't quite pinpoint when she died. But there is her wronged, one-time Georgia fiancé who could be looked at too. Jensen said those could well have been human ashes, not my specialty," Nick went on as his voice echoed above the pounding of the water.

"Then as for Dale," he added, "the man's a bright lawyer, for heaven's sake, and he let his hots for an icy blonde—no pun intended—do his thinking for him? I'll bet the moment she opened her mouth, he should have moved on, but she was probably only too glad to open her legs for him too. I swear Dale could have hired someone to dump those ashes when none of us were looking out front, so the assumption would be it was good-old-boy Tanner or an accomplice. Actually, I hope Tanner has an alibi that leaks like a sieve—if the cops can find him. For all we know, he's bound for Georgia again."

"Nick, this isn't like you. Calm down. If the ashes are human— are Cyndi's, if they can even tell—they will focus on Tanner or, like you said, maybe her dumped fiancé back in Georgia. Still, I think your loyalty to a junior partner can only go so far if you really think he's guilty of murder."

"Damn, but I've gotten guilty people off before. Early ignorance. Overly stupid ambition. Everyone deserves a defense and from time to time I've been too good at that. But I'm not going to court for Dale if he killed that girl and stuck her in his mother's freezer, then got someone to dump ashes on his car to implicate her redneck brother. Dale could be thinking there's no way people would believe he's that dumb, whereas Tanner is. Reverse psychology, right, Mrs. Markwood?"

"You're tired. You're going in circles. You need a good night's sleep. And so do I."

"I can just see myself or one of the partners in court arguing this case we'd like to keep low-key because it involves the reputation of the firm. Oh no, Your Honor, we are not just defending Dale Braun because he's tied to Markwood, Benton and Chase. Yes, as well as possibly losing his temper at the victim, or being afraid she'd embarrass him and ruin his career path, yes, he could also have been afraid she was going to blow the Braun family secret wide open. Oh, is that another member of the international press coming in with their cameras to cover this trial because of the Nazi connection, Your Honor? Yes, that's right, the defendant's property was inherited from and belonged to a high-ranking Nazi who was even related to the defendant through marriage and to Hitler's wife—and furthermore, Your Honor—"

"Nick, stop it! It will work out. If you become certain he's guilty, there surely are alternatives to defending him, to putting the firm on the line."

The shower stopped. His shadow moved behind the frosted glass. The door slid open. His hand reached out for his towel. That reminded her—who else, she thought, was Reaching Woman trying to touch or beg from on her other side in that grave? Claire had left a message on Kris's phone that she could not come out to the bog Saturday morning but would stop by that afternoon unless it was raining, so answers must surely be coming.

"Sorry to carry on like that," Nick said as he stepped out with the towel wrapped around his waist. "This whole thing is really getting to me. I'm afraid I can't see the forest for the twisted trees. And I see I've created our very own sauna." He wiped a circle on the foggy mirror so he could see his face in it. He frowned at himself, then ran a comb through his hair. "Thanks for listening and bringing me back down to earth, sweetheart. It could be worse—we've been through worse. What is it you wanted to tell me when I went off like that? With Dale, the ashes, then Jensen, today's been a mess."

"I just wanted to tell you that the second bog body I've seen disinterred is a young female whom Andrea has named Reaching Woman. Talk about needing a murder trial—she was stabbed in the chest."

He stopped combing his wet hair and turned to her, eyes wide. "And the first body had its heart hacked out. More tragic proof that murder is as old as mankind."

"Murder or an execution. I've got to examine everything in that bog grave for answers. And, I imagine, if these two somehow-related people were executed—I surmise for a common crime—they did not have a brave attorney to stand up for them. What you do is important, Nick."

She almost told him about their strange stalker—but that could just be coincidence and he already had enough to keep him awake tonight when he—she too—desperately needed sleep. If she or Kris spotted that man or woman again, she'd tell him. Maybe she and Kris could split up in a safe place and see if the person stuck with one or the other of them.

Nick threw his comb down, came over and pulled her to her feet. He hugged her hard to him. "It's just—I know I said we've been through worse—but I'm scared, Claire. Dale is scared too—I get that—but this whole thing just doesn't feel right. I think this mess is going to get worse, so after we check out the 'Twisted Tree' Nazi ruins, that's it for your being involved with this case unless it's totally online research, and Heck can cover that."

"You said he's really busy right now, with his new sideline— facial recognition technology, of all things." She realized again that she and Kris could use some of that—but their stalker seemed almost faceless and sexless.

Nick went on, "You just stay with ancient crimes, and I'll try to handle this one, and with a lot more self-control than I showed just now. It's a blessing I have you to listen, to care. Don't know what I'd do without you."

"So what were you doing up so early?" Nick asked Claire with a yawn as he backed them out of their garage the next morning. They were heading for the neighborhood where Dale lived, where Nita and Bronco had bought their house—and where they were going to see the ruins of the Twisted Trees mansion.

"Doing internet research," she told him. She waved again to

Nita and Lexi at the front door, feeling a bit sad. After all, she should be the one standing there on a Saturday morning with her children, not Nita. Maybe she was trying to do too much, getting too involved with outside challenges.

"You mean Googling more about bog people?" he asked.

"Actually, at first I was reading some about former Senator Bradley Vance. He and Andrea have an art and antiques store downtown on 5th Avenue and one on upscale Las Olas Boulevard in Fort Lauderdale, you know. But I spent most of my time reading about Nazis living in the US."

"Whoa! That can't be common. I mean most of them would be really old or dead by now."

"You're right, most are probably dead, like Dale's great-uncle. But I learned there could be hundreds alive still. The Simon Wiesenthal Center hunts them down. They recently found one living undercover for years in Minnesota. Anyway, research has found that people without a conscience have less stress and may live longer than we would expect."

"It's going to be bad enough that Dale's great-uncle is dead, let alone if he was still living. Damn, I wish this case would just go away so I could go back to defending people I believe are innocent and you could—"

"Right. So I could go back to dealing with ancient executed people, not recently frozen ones."

"Look, there's Dale pacing in his driveway," Nick said and they pulled up by the curb when they arrived. "At least his stress proves he has a conscience, right?"

When he rolled the window down, Dale asked, "How about I just get in your car? We'll drive a little ways back in and walk the rest of the way."

"Sure," Nick said and hit the door locks open so Dale could climb in the back. "Good to see that there's no one hanging around Bronco's place, waiting for them to show up to question or bother."

"Not now. Betty Richards, down the street—she knows everyone else's business—told me that several people have been by just to gawk and take pictures, look in the windows, stuff like that."

"Oh no," Claire said. "We've all been trying to assure Nita that wouldn't happen anymore. Mrs. Richards is the one who ID'd Cyndi to the police, so I hope Nita doesn't phone her to see how things are going."

Beyond the intersecting streets of the housing development, screened by those invasive melaleuca trees and several ficus like the ones surrounding the bog, Dale directed them to an overgrown lane that bent back out of sight. Nick felt closed in already. He could just imagine the trees around the bog Claire had described, but he thrust that thought away.

"Let's leave the car here and just walk," Dale said. "It's rained, and we don't want to get bogged down."

At the word *bogged*, Nick caught Claire's narrow gaze. Sometimes he could almost read her mind, but not now. Was she thinking there might be a body bog back here? Probably not. That this Nazi connection could screw things up for Dale?

He took her arm as they followed Dale back through the twisted trees for which the mansion had no doubt been named.

His eyes still heavy with sleep, Jace rolled over in bed at his apartment and reached out for Brit. And got nothing but pillow and twisted sheets.

He propped himself up on one elbow. The bathroom door was open but the light wasn't on and he heard no sounds of movement anywhere. But hadn't some sound awakened him? Oh, he did hear banging around in the kitchen. And smelled something great—or was that a burning odor?

He got up, wearing only his shorts, and tiptoed toward the kitchen. Yes, some serious banging of pots and pans—and crying?

"Brit, honey?" he said as he peeked into his apartment's small galley kitchen. "What in the..." was all he got out before he took in the sight of scrambled eggs—or maybe an omelet—all over the tile floor.

"Trying not to get burned, I spilled it and got so mad that I threw it," she choked out and burst into tears. "I was—was trying to make you breakfast in bed. And, it slipped. I'd just like to scream, to break things. I want things to go so well, and I just keep losing it when they don't. You've got cold feet, don't you—about the wedding?" she demanded with the empty skillet still in her hand. "I can tell you're upset, and I am too!" she insisted, her voice rising as she choked out sobs again.

Man, had he been that transparent? And in her state of mind, she looked as if she'd like to brain him with that skillet. He might have fought the damn Taliban, but he'd take them over this right now.

"Put that down. I'll help you clean up, honey. No, I don't have cold feet, not for that."

She put the skillet down on the stove, not too carefully, and threw the mitt into it. "What then?"

"I need to tell you something I was scared to."

"Another woman?" her voice rose to a near screech. He started toward her now that she wasn't armed, but he slipped barefooted in the egg mess. He went down on one knee, would have fallen flat, but she grabbed him, held him up.

"No way," he insisted. "It's just I—I've been offered a job that I really want to take but there is some danger involved. It's with Mitch, flying for a good cause, gathering data about hurricanes to save lives, but I thought you might have a fit if I took it."

She helped him get up, then grabbed a dishcloth to wipe the eggs off his knee and shin. "Jason Britten, I will have a fit if you *don't* tell me things, not if you do. You think my working with big feral cats after my father was killed by one isn't scary, isn't dangerous? I may not like a new job for you, but I know you're sick of flying little planes. Besides, I finally pried it out of you that the drug cartels could want to harm Stingray pilots like you and Mitch, so I've been worried about that as it is. Tell me, then help me clean up this mess, and let's eat some toast and juice and go back to bed—and not just to talk. I love you, Jace, and we're a team," she said throwing her arms around him. "So no more secrets!"

"So how secret is this place, really?" Nick asked Dale as they plunged through the thick screen of trees. Claire just kept quiet, studying Dale, trying to take it all in, ignoring even the low whine of mosquitoes.

"I know some people stumble on it, then tell others. Years ago, the cover story was that the owner was a German industrialist whose factory had been bombed out in World War II, and he just wanted to leave a devastated country. After my great-uncle died, my parents lived in it for a while, but it was too damned big— obviously," he added as they got their first look at the ruined structure.

It was a silhouette against the trees, yet its strong cedar bones still stood. Claire gasped. She could see where a grand staircase had been and the doorways, even some rooms. No windows remained; some plants grew inside as if the place had a green beard. The roof, like a moss-covered toupee had partly caved in near the chimney which had obviously served several large hearths. Most of a garage or stables still stood.

"There was a fire in the mid–1980s," Dale explained. "Hurricane Andrew in 1992 did the rest. Then water damage, critters, some vagrants… It would be exorbitant to repair or replace, even to tear down. I just pay the property taxes out of my trust fund."

They walked through deep sawgrass that grasped their pant legs as if in a feeble attempt to keep them away. Claire had pictured that the place would have been brick, but it must have been mostly wood. Several crows flew out from under the shattered roof, cawing at them as if screaming, "Away! Away!"

"It must have been grand," she said.

"I hardly remember it that way, and remember him only from pictures. I burned his photo album as soon as my mother died. He actually dared to have photos of his 'grand days,' as he put it. SS uniforms, swastikas, like huge black spiders on blood red flags. But especially when my mother's dementia increased, she had either inked out the face of Eva Braun in the photos or actually cut them out. Said she wanted to kill Eva—well, just a figure of speech, born of dementia, and anger, of course, because Eva was long dead."

Claire's gaze slammed into Nick's. A revelation hit Claire hard, a crazy leap of logic, but who knew? When she'd researched Nazis this morning, she'd seen a picture of the blonde, pretty Eva Braun. Her smile in the photo had been so sweet and sincere, innocent. Hitler's fiancée, later briefly his wife, was hardly screaming—but—but she looked a lot like Cyndi. Could an old woman with dementia who'd hated Hitler's wife have mistaken Cyndi for her and, elderly or not, had rage and strength enough to—

"Look!" Nick interrupted her agonizing as he pointed toward the desolate mansion. "There's a blonde woman over there in the trees watching us."

CHAPTER THIRTEEN

For one moment, Claire feared the woman watching them might be lifting a rifle, but it was a camera with a telephoto lens. Still, Nick pulled her behind him.

"Hello!" Dale called out. "Can we help you? You're trespassing, you know."

"It's obviously not lived in," the woman shouted back and came out of the trees. "But still such a beautiful place. I can explain why I'm here."

Claire breathed out hard. The woman was dressed in jeans and a long-sleeved navy shirt, probably to keep mosquitoes at bay. Her clothes were tight fitting, even belted. She was probably in her fifties, much too tan for safety's sake these days, with a heart-shaped face framed by hair so blond it looked white. She was extremely slender—gaunt, really. And she walked with the slightest hint of a limp.

"May I ask who you are?" Dale went on as she came closer and stopped about ten feet from the three of them. "I'm the owner here."

"Then you must be a descendant of the German man. I couldn't learn a lot from the county property records."

"Yes, I—"

"The Nazi. You realize that makes this site even more important and unique than if it were just built and owned by a wealthy early landowner."

Dale looked speechless and shaken. His worst nightmare, Nick's too, would be for it to get out that Dale had a relative tied to Hitler. Talk about prejudicing a jury and causing a media circus. They'd been through that trauma before.

"I'm Marian James with the Endangered Properties Committee—not the same as the county historical society. We're into historic preservation, though, and—sorry to say—I took a phone call about nine days ago from the poor woman who was murdered, your former fiancée, Cyndi Lindley."

Dale gasped. "Why would she call you?"

"She wanted to let me know about the great history of this place and invited me out here. She said it could lead to magazine articles, news stories, even television promotion for our group. Well, I was away and when I returned and got her phone message at the office, I learned she was dead—murdered—and...frozen."

Nick said, "But I'm sure you understand that Mr. Braun needs some privacy at this time. For himself and this property."

"Oh, yes," Ms. James plunged on. "Please accept my deepest sympathy on your loss, though I read in the paper she was your *former* fiancée. But I'm hoping you'll still want this story told. Why, ties to the Nazis and Hitler just a couple of miles from the Everglades—what a story. It will echo far beyond Naples. Our efforts are well endowed by some wealthy individuals, and they could help you turn this place into a protected historic area or at least have a historical plaque here. So sad that this house has died," she added as she came slowly closer, "and Cyndi cared about it, and now she's dead too."

"The publicity—not at this time," Dale said, almost stammering. "I—I may sell."

"What a pity. But one more thing," she said, not retreating

one step when Dale tried to move past her. "Cyndi mentioned over the phone that she thought someone might be following her, trying to scare her. I just tell you that—and would be willing to testify—if the police wonder who could have harmed her. I could also tell she was heartbroken and really angry about something."

Claire doubted most people could get that much from a recorded message when there was no real conversation. Was this woman to be trusted? Had she actually talked to Cyndi, maybe met with her in Cyndi's attempt either to get publicity for herself or even to find a way to blackmail Dale? What Marian James had just said could be taken two different ways. If Cyndi had a stalker, that could help to clear Dale of suspicion. But if Cyndi was angry over their breakup, it could suggest she confronted Dale and he, accidentally or not, strangled her sometime within the last nine days. If this woman was telling the truth.

Nick said, "Where did you park to walk way in here, Ms. James? And what a coincidence you're here the same time we are. If you have further comments or observations, please make them to me, Nick Markwood, Dale's attorney at Markwood, Benton and Chase," he said, pulling his card out of his billfold.

Claire's thoughts still rampaged. Indeed they had not seen her car, though she was now telling Nick a friend dropped her off and would be back soon. And was it mere chance she showed up here when they did? The more she studied this woman the more she thought she could be the person who had followed her and Kris.

Still, she knew she was getting too suspicious of absolutely everyone. She was even having a tough time liking or trusting Dale as well as Ben Vance, and he was her employer and a well-respected former senator, not that politicians were ever to be trusted.

Marian James started to walk away, then turned back. "I really should call the police with all this. If I told them about poor

Cyndi's stalker—if she was right about that—it could change the way some people always blame the man in the victim's life, so I'm sure that could be a help to you. I see in the newspaper and TV photos she was very pretty. Maybe she attracted a stranger who killed her instead of someone else close to her."

Claire could tell Nick had a comeback, but he kept quiet. With a nod at the still stunned Dale and a narrow-eyed look at Nick and Claire, she turned and walked away, yes, with just the slightest hitch in her step, not really a limp. As she disappeared behind the twisted trunks of the ficus trees, Claire thought it was almost like a ghost vanishing, but this one would no doubt materialize again and could spell real trouble for Dale if he didn't cooperate with the Endangered Properties Committee.

Nick told Claire he didn't want to leave Dale right now. He wanted to calm him down and plan a strategy if Marian James went public with her story. So Claire drove Nick's car home from Dale's house and Dale would drop him off later. Besides, she knew Nick wanted to look around Dale's place since the police had searched it.

At home, she spent an hour with Lexi and Trey—"How long before a little baby can finally talk, Mommy?" her daughter had asked—then grabbed a sandwich and headed for Black Bog. What a help it was to have Nita tend the children and Bronco as extra security. Claire was in a hurry now, as Kris had left a message that they were getting close to uncovering the next body.

She kept her eyes on the road as her thoughts pounded her again. Nick didn't want her anywhere near Dale's case, but psyching things out was in her blood. Cyndi Lindley was emerging as a clever, greedy person, not entirely sympathetic, despite having been murdered. Claire had already checked the woman's Facebook page and had gone way back through the pictures— mostly of herself, pouting sexily, some in a skimpy swimsuit— real bait for voyeurs, so maybe she *had* attracted a stalker. Why hadn't Dale gotten turned off if he'd checked her page—or had he just gotten turned on by it? Also, there were a few pictures from two years ago that showed Cyndi with her beefy first fiancé, a real bruiser. She planned to show those to Nick to see if he could get Detective Jensen to look into that angle.

She was so wrapped up in thoughts she almost missed the turnoff toward Black Bog. She hit the brakes, and the car behind her—following much too close—honked and roared around. Claire slowed on the narrow approach road.

The guard at the gate opened it electronically and waved her on through. It would have been good to have such security to protect the Twisted Trees mansion, she thought, as she pulled into a parking place next to Kris's Jeep.

Claire was tempted to run, not even stopping to ditch her big purse, but the planks bounced and she slowed. They had said they didn't want her or any of the team to take their own photos, except for the official ones Doug shot, so she reluctantly put her phone away, thinking again of Marian James's expensive camera at the Twisted Trees mansion.

Nick had assured Dale he'd get a stop on the photos with a threat of illegal trespassing if necessary. And despite the fact it was a Saturday, he'd already called a junior partner to get on contacting Ms. James and her so-called committee immediately. He said he hadn't warned her on the property because that might have made her quickly disperse or publish her photos.

Out of breath, Claire joined the dig team and leaned closer to see.

"Bog body number three," Andrea told her, looking up, then into the grave again. "I've named him Leader—more formal than Chief or Boss. He commands attention and respect."

"He's tall," she said, "or maybe it's just that he's not curled up like the others. And he's dressed well. That robe has some sort of faded stripes. And look at that polished stone bracelet around his wrist. It reminds me of the necklace on Reaching Woman. Whatever happened to that? I'd like to study it."

"All the artifacts are specially cleaned, handled and stored," Andrea told her. "As for the stripes on his garment, berry juice dye and beautifully done. It's obvious that he was an important person—but who and why, Claire. That's your bailiwick."

"What's that in his hand?" Claire asked as the three diggers carefully removed more peat from his head so they could un-cover his face.

"Some sort of rod or staff," Kris said. "Maybe symbolic."

"It's carved," Doug said. It was hard to hear him because he was bent low in the grave. "We found some other items with him, but we've already sent them inside."

Still awed, Claire whispered, "The staff and robe are no doubt symbols of his office, his importance. But what is his relation to the executed pair? At least he doesn't seem to be stabbed or worse—his heart's not cut out, is it?"

"He's apparently intact," Yi Ling said. "Even dead and buried and muck-covered, he still has an aura of power or knowledge."

"I hope he wasn't judge and executioner of the other two," Claire said. "But then, why would he be buried near them, espe-cially if his death is a natural one? And Reaching Woman seems to be stretching her arm toward him, as her other one was to-ward Hunter. Maybe caught somehow between the two men."

"You're right," Kris said. "If he's a kind of judge that sen-tenced both of them to death, why be buried with them? Maybe Reaching Woman is meant to be begging for mercy, something like that. Leader stands, the other two have bent knees. But all that's what we hope you can figure out, Claire."

Everyone went silent as Doug, Yi Ling and Aaron brushed away the last bits of centuries-old peat and soil from Leader's face. His eyes were wide open. At least his mouth was closed—stern, firm—no hint of terror or a scream. Did his open eyes mean his people meant for him to be looking at the other two, looking into the future, or into the land of the dead which the bog represented?

Claire suddenly felt overwhelmed with all she was expected to theorize. She was trembling uncontrollably as if she were freezing when the day was warm. It scared her even more to realize something else: Leader couldn't help but remind her of Nick.

Dale was still shaken, and Nick couldn't calm him down. He had looked around Dale's house from which the police had confiscated items and fingerprinted a lot of places, leaving graphite powder Dale had not cleaned up.

"I think you need to stay here for a while and calm down. Maybe take a nap, clean up the remnants of the police search," Nick told him when Dale came out of the bathroom for the fourth time. His stomach must be really upset too. The guy was falling apart. Guilt? Fear? Suppressed anger? Damn, he wished he had Claire here to read the signs.

Nick went on, "I called Bronco to come get me so you can stay here for a while. Maybe you shouldn't drive right now."

"I don't like to be here anymore. I'll head back to my temp place downtown. At least Bronco knows how to get here, huh? Nick, I'm sorry that he and Nita are going through this. Cyndi is kind of haunting me from the grave—from her ashes, that is— telling that woman all about my background, which my family did a good job hiding."

"I've put things in motion to muzzle her for now. Maybe one of the heavy hitter donors she mentioned will want to buy Twisted Trees from you. Just be careful if you drive, okay? And if your secret about who built the mansion goes public, don't act like you've been trying to hide it. Say you just didn't have the time to restore the place. You can't go anywhere now or it would look bad, but after we see this through—and no one's made a move to arrest you—you might want to clear out of the entire area."

"Nick," he said, grabbing his arm as they saw Bronco pull up in front, "just don't throw me to the dogs. I didn't kill Cyndi!"

"Then just be sure you level with me and your defense team. Maybe you won't even be indicted or arrested. But this Hitler connection is a big deal if it gets out, especially since Cyndi wanted to use it to get attention, money, revenge—something. And you didn't want that."

"So a second motive for my strangling her? Damn that 'Endangered Properties' woman! I wish she'd just disappear."

"Be careful what you wish for," Nick warned. He squeezed Dale's shoulder and headed out to the car as he heard Dale close the door firmly behind him. He worried for a moment he should go back in, but he didn't think Dale, even distraught, was either a flight—or a suicide—risk.

"Hey, boss," Bronco greeted him, getting out of the car and coming around to the passenger side. "Thought I might have to come in for you. When I told Nita where I was going, she got all shook again." A thin, sprightly woman was coming down the sidewalk tugging at her short-legged, perky-looking Chihuahua on a bright red leash that matched the dog's collar. She had a slight limp, but it wasn't slowing down her speed.

"Oh, is Dale moving back in?" she asked them. "It's all so sad. I'm Betty—live right over there three doors away, the one who identified the poor dead woman for the police from her photo. Why, I've told the other neighbors and the newspaper people it was terrible to see her all frozen with her mouth open like that."

Even without Claire, Nick knew he could nail this woman's character exactly. But rather than brushing her off, what could he learn?

"We're friends of Dale's," Nick told her as the little dog looked up at its mistress with the curiosity that Nick suddenly felt too. "And that was such a help to the police that you could quickly identify Dale's friend."

"Yes, well, she and Dale were tight, if you know what I mean," she said with a nod of her white, curly head. "But really, I was friends with his mother, Lucinda—Lucy, I called her. She had him quite late in life, you know—could have been his grand-mother age-wise. The Brauns lived quietly, but she said they had money, and that Cyndi was a gold digger, because she probably knew the truth about their wealth—mostly land wealth."

"I guess it's always good to know the truth," Nick said with a nod at Bronco who nodded back. "So you knew Dale's mother well?"

"Years, lots of talk time, especially after she was widowed, like me. I really regretted it when she started to get so terribly confused with dementia. It changed her from a sweet person to a crabby one, even nasty sometimes."

"That's very sad. So maybe that's why she really didn't like Cyndi—it was just her personality with dementia."

"That and, I think Cyndi reminded her of someone she didn't like, someone who gave the Braun family a bad name or a bad time. I think," she said, lowering her voice and leaning closer, "Cyndi reminded Lucy of a woman who had ruined the fam-ily, because she said that woman was in with the Nazis. I mean, who thinks about the Nazis anymore?"

"Did Lucy ever mention Hitler?"

"The more she lost common sense, the more she seemed to go back in time. Yes, she mentioned Hitler. I told her he was dead and gone. But she not only thought Dale's father was still alive, but Dale's great-uncle too, the one who came from Ger-many and built that mansion that's in ruins."

She dropped her voice to such a whisper that Nick almost had to read her lips. She was much shorter than him, so he leaned closer. "But the one Lucy really blamed was some rela-tive named Eva."

"Really?" Nick asked as Bronco stopped leaning against his car and stood up straighter.

"Yes, it was a bit confusing, but it was a woman she hated.

Anyhow, Lucy thought Cyndi looked like or acted like—I don't quite know—this Eva, and that's another reason she didn't approve of poor Dale's fiancée. Why, I recall those awful days of World War II when I was young. I put things together since Lucy's last name was Braun, but she explained the Eva Braun connection to me anyway. I wish Lucy hadn't been so out of touch before she knew that Dale was splitting up with that gold digger. Why, a nice, hardworking young man like Dale ought to be married, don't you think? Just not to some gold digger!"

Nick didn't know what to think and with a nod and a "thanks for all your insights, nice to meet you" headed for the car. Claire would have known how to get more out of this woman, but he could bring her in later if evidence led to the possibility that an old woman with dementia could have strangled a much younger, stronger Cyndi—thinking she was Eva—and somehow lifted her into that freezer.

CHAPTER FOURTEEN

That evening Bronco took Nita out to dinner, so for the first time in a few days, it was just the family at the table. Claire had held Trey in her lap to feed him, burped and walked with him, then had laid him down to sleep. Sprawled on the sofa, Lexi was reading a book on butterflies because her teacher, Miss Gerald, had shown the class her butterfly collection, though Lexi didn't like that they were "dead and stuck with pins."

"Finally, peace and quiet," Claire told Nick as she slipped back into her chair across from him to eat her dessert.

"Quiet anyway," he said, finishing the rest of his wine.

"Why are we whispering?"

"'Little pitchers have big ears,' to quote my mother."

"Meaning?"

"Meaning," he said, reaching across the table for her hand while she met him halfway, ignoring her caramel flan, "I need to tell you I got a call from Ken Jensen before you got home. Private, so I didn't bring it up before Nita and Bronco left, but not private from you."

"He had the ashes tested? Were they Cyndi's or just fake?"

"Unfortunately, the lab can't tell—meaning he'd tell us if he knew. It turns out DNA is destroyed during cremation."

"Darn. So that ashes-on-Dale's-car threat does not necessarily point to Cyndi's brother Tanner."

"Could, but doesn't. Here's the kicker. I couldn't figure out why Jensen didn't pursue not only Tanner but also Cyndi's former fiancé. But he admitted, when I pressed him on it, that he was calling from Atlanta and he'd been to Zebulon. He said neither Tanner nor Cyndi's once-upon-a-time high school sweetheart are currently in what he called 'scenic' Zebulon where he went to interview them. Tanner, of course, could still be here, but maybe the former boyfriend is too. Jensen said he would never have divulged that except he'd learned both men were volatile, and we should tell Dale to be extra careful."

"And he meant, I'll bet—nice guy that Jensen really is—that we should be careful too. Whoever put those ashes on Dale's car did it in our driveway."

"I don't think that was aimed at us. But it does worry me if Dale's being followed." He nodded and heaved a heavy sigh. "Let me put things away here, while you get Madame Butterfly over there in bed. Bronco and Nita won't be out long, and he's got instincts like a guard dog, so I'll hate to see them go. Maybe we should keep them around a little longer. Nita won't mind. And tomorrow's our big day to finally celebrate our marriage with friends and family."

They clasped hands together tighter over the table. "I'm so looking forward to it," she said. "Despite complications sometimes, I've never been happier."

"Me too," Nick said and blew her a kiss, a promise she knew he would make good on tonight—tomorrow—all their days together. She'd once thought she was happy married to Jace, yet that had gone all wrong. But had Reaching Woman reached out to the wrong man at first? And then paid some sort of terrible price—her life?

★ ★ ★

Sunday morning, while Bronco and Nita went to mass—Nita was praying hard for the Virgin Mary to cleanse and bless their new house—Claire and Nick took their children to join Darcy's family at their church.

Nothing like a real family day from beginning to end, Claire thought. Besides, she got to show off Trey to people she had known when she used to attend here with Darcy, and Lexi was only too happy to see her cousin and almost-sister, Jilly. Drew, Darcy and Steve's son, now seven, who thought it was beneath him to have to put up with two younger girls, was the only one who fidgeted at all.

Claire had not realized there was going to be a full water baptism at the beginning of the service or she would have explained it to Lexi. Especially when the pastor lifted the person from the water tank behind the altar, she herself felt as riveted as Lexi was at his words:

"And from the *Book of Romans*, I say to you these words, 'Buried in death, but raised to walk in newness of life.'"

"What does that really mean, Mommy?" Lexi asked in a stage whisper.

"I'll explain later. It means the person is choosing a new life."

But after church, even after Claire tried to explain to Lexi about changing a former life to make a new beginning, those words haunted her. The Black Bog bodies had been buried in death—two of them a violent death—but had now been raised from the grave. The bodies, if not the people, had a new life, to be studied, probed and puzzled over.

In a way, Claire agonized, the three ancient people she knew best and would get to know more would not let her go as if they walked beside her, clung to her, especially Reaching Woman. She surely had meant something to both Hunter and Leader. She was trapped between them, stretching out her hands to both, asking for something. Yet had one of them ordered her death or taken her life?

Why? What had she done to them? Or what, as so many times in history and even in modern life, had the men of her society done to her?

Later, as Claire dressed for the reception, fastening the double strand of pearls Nick had given her around her neck, she thought of Reaching Woman's broken necklace of smooth polished stones and shells. She would have to ask to see it after it was cleaned. She knew an examination of the woman's wounds might reveal if the dagger that had killed her had been similar to the one Hunter held. She would like to see and touch those, to really feel items they had used and treasured.

"Claire, you ready, sweetheart?" Nick's voice broke into her thoughts. "Time to go. Nita's got Trey ready, and Lexi's driving everyone crazy. Oh, yeah, and Jace just called, because Brittany had a problem with that pregnant lioness at the zoo, but they'll be there later."

"Coming," she told him, shaking off her almost-visions of long-dead people. She reached for him to keep him close a moment and to kiss him. "Yes, I'm ready."

Claire had sent Bronco and Nita ahead with potted orchids for the buffet table and the one with the cake, while their country club hostess, Mary Ann, had brought in other plants and decorations. The Blue Room entrance led to the glassed-in verandah where everything was set up.

Nick lifted Lexi so she could see what was written on the large, one layer cake: Never Too Late to Celebrate Love. The only other thing on the table with the cake, plates and napkins was a large crystal bowl of pink punch. A coffee urn and bottles of wine were set up on an open bar at the end of the verandah, staffed by a bartender from the country club.

"That means love for all of us, right, not just grownups?" Lexi asked, pointing at the cake. "Even Trey?"

"Especially you and Trey," Nick told her as Claire blinked back tears of joy. The cake—in more ways than one—was beautiful, with elaborately scrolled words and iced orchid flowers to carry out the theme.

"Well, where is everybody?" Lexi asked as Nick put her down. "Mommy, will you save Jilly and me good corner pieces with lots of frosting?"

"Yes, but we'll cut the cake later," Claire told her, straightening the child's taffeta puff sleeves. "We are going to have nice, polite talks with our guests, then they can have the food from the buffet table, and the cake and ice cream will come last."

"Pretty much like a birthday party," Lexi said with a nod as she scampered over to Nita who was seated and holding the sleeping baby on her lap.

To Lexi's chagrin, the earliest guests were Nick's law partners and staff. Claire was glad to share time with them under these relaxed circumstances. She hadn't seen Nick's longtime secretary, Cheryl, for quite a while and had a good chat with her before taking her place in the informal reception line.

She and Nick stood near the verandah door to greet guests. The noise level rose: chatter, laughter. It felt so good.

Heck came in with Gina, home for the weekend from medical school in Miami. Claire hugged her while Nick and Heck huddled for a moment in a lull. "How are things?" she whispered to Gina. She still looked as beautiful as when they'd first met her in Cuba, though the lack of sleep was showing.

"Tough, but that's good. My Spanish really helps me in the clinic, though I know I got—have—a too-strong accent in English. Anyhow, it's great to be helping others too," Gina told her.

She pulled Claire a bit aside and lowered her voice. "Please tell Nick I'm worried about Heck. He's so set on this extra facial recognition firm consulting job. But he finally admitted there's a lot of competition to control that technology in the future—big money, political power. And another firm—I had to pry this out of him—is playing tough ball."

"Hardball? Meaning what?"

"There's a rogue firm—not the one Heck trusts—well, the brakes on one guy's car who wanted the job Heck is up for got tampered with and he had a wreck—who knows what's next? Cutthroat competition, very bad, especially if it is aimed at my man. Like he always say, *Caramba*!"

"I'll tell Nick, and he can talk with him. Maybe he's telling him that right now."

Speaking of being in trouble, Claire thought, here came Dale, looking sporty as usual but nervous. He kept fooling with his pocket handkerchief and shifting his weight from one foot to the other.

"Glad you came," Claire heard Nick tell him as Gina snared Heck and headed for the bar. Claire joined Nick and Dale. "You have a lot of people in this room who support you," Nick tried to assure him with a nod.

"And a lot who still look at me like 'There's the guy who might have killed that girl.'"

"I know it's difficult to keep your chin up," Claire told him. "But it's important for how it looks—and for how it feels for you too."

"I keep worrying about how it's going to look if that Marian James woman blabs about my heritage on top of everything else. And she hinted she's got wealthy, important backers. Look, sorry," he added with a shrug. "You've both been great to me, and I don't mean to darken this occasion. Congrats to you both on a great marriage and two darling kids. I'd love to get there someday—you know what I mean."

As if that had summoned Lexi, she came over, dragging Nita who still held Trey. "You said you wanted to show him off, Claire," Nita said. "He's a magnet and being so very good."

"It's 'cause he's sleeping," Lexi put in. "When he's awake, Nita, you know he's not always good, but I am."

Claire's gaze met Nita's. Lexi had not shown a bit of jealousy before, so they'd have to work on that. Claire took Trey in her arms and he stirred. So beautiful, so innocent.

Soon others arrived including Darcy, Steve, Drew and Jilly, who could barely stand still until she saw Lexi across the room and ran to meet her. Hugs all around. Steve and Nick talked off to the side, then Nick showed them the family table Claire had staked out.

Kris arrived in her new outfit she'd bought recently. "Thanks for including me," she told them.

"Of course," Nick said and gave her a quick, one-armed hug. "After all, you've known Claire longer than anybody here except her sister."

"I don't do crowds well," she whispered. "But I will recognize your kids. Oh, dear," she added as she looked across the room. "There are two little girls over there, but I'm guessing Lexi's the one on the left."

"You are right," Claire told her. "Just remember the taffeta dress with puff sleeves. The other little girl is her cousin Jilly, the closest she has to a sister."

"At least so far, but you never know for the future," Nick put in with a little laugh and a waggle of his eyebrows as he put his finger in Trey's fist when the baby stirred awake at last.

Claire and Kris both laughed. "Wish I had that problem—a man who loved me making innuendos," Kris said. "You know, Nick, Claire and I used to kid about us being 'womjeps,' women in jeopardy. I think we've both found our niche, though I admit a good man is hard to find."

With Trey still in her arms, Claire took Kris over to meet Heck and Gina, then came back to Nick when Jace and a beaming Brittany came in. It made Claire's day to see both of them so happy, and she hoped things worked out better for them than it had for her and Jace, who kissed her cheek for the first time in ages.

"He's just so darling," Brit told Claire as she cooed "hi-there-handsome" to Trey, who thought she looked pretty interesting too. Claire let Brit hold the baby.

"She never says that to me," Jace deadpanned.

"Lexi's been waiting for you," Claire said. "See if you can keep her from going into her flower-girl mode this afternoon and sticking her finger in the icing before we cut the cake."

"Speaking of the birds and the bees—which we weren't," Jace told them, "I see Kris Kane is here. Do you know if she's seeing anyone? I don't like to play matchmaker, but I have a friend who would like to meet her."

"She just said she wished she had someone. I think her face blindness has held her back in the men department, plus how dedicated she is to her work. You know, Jace, she always picked you out because she thought you looked like a Viking—her focus on the buried past coming out there. But I'm sure she'd be interested. Sounds perfect."

"Yeah, well, he's a pilot too, and I know that can cause problems."

"Sometimes," Claire said.

Nick cleared his throat almost in unison with Brit. Claire realized she and Jace had been having an intense, two-way talk. She pulled her gaze away from him and glanced at the huge window behind the cake table. Because the trees of the orange grove beyond were thick and dark green, the window made a muted mirror. And there she was, with her hands lifted slightly toward not only Jace but the taller Nick. Reaching Woman flashed through her mind again, caught somehow between Hunter and Leader.

"Enjoy, you two," Nick said to Jace and Brit in the sudden lull as Brit handed Trey back to Claire. "Get something to eat and talk to Kris. She really doesn't know anyone here but us and

Lexi. And there's a great view, Jace, out the window to watch the golfers on the eighteenth green."

"Sure, good," Jace said, seeming suddenly uneasy as Brit took his arm and they moved away.

"Let's circulate, get something to eat, then cut the cake," Claire said, turning away to look at it again.

"You're a poet and don't know it," Nick said with a groan at his own words. "But most importantly, above all else, you are my beloved wife and Lexi and Trey's mother."

"I love you, Nick," she said, turning back to face him and reaching out to touch his arm. "You are so strong and support-ive—and—and understanding."

"Not always."

"I mean we've had some tough times, but things are differ-ent now."

"Good," said the man of many, well-chosen words. "Good."

As they started away from the cake table, Claire heard a boom and a strange crackling sound. Her ears popped. Trey started to cry. Oh, where was Lexi?

The long, high window behind the cake and buffet table seemed to explode, not shatter, but blast into a thousand ugly glass cobweb pieces which rained down onto the floor in thumb-sized shards.

The bottles behind the small bar shook. Shelves holding them broke, dropped in a second round of shrieking noise. The bar-tender ducked, then fled crunching glass.

The noise, the impact, several screams—people hit the floor. Nick grabbed Claire, still holding Trey and rolled them under the white folds of the skirt of the cake table. They huddled there, shaking, waiting for what came next. But nothing but people's screams, cries and questions.

A golf ball against the glass? Was someone shooting? A bomb blast somewhere outside or sonic boom? She realized just a min-ute or so had passed.

"Stay here with Trey!" Nick told Claire. "I'll get Lexi." Keeping low, he rolled out and scrambled away, crunching glass.

Claire cuddled Trey close as his cries went to sucking sobs, his little voice blending with other shrieks. She was tempted to crawl out and find Lexi herself. Where were Darcy and her family?

She peered out to see fleeing feet and bodies on the floor. Was that blood in front of her? It glittered in the sunlight pouring through without the safety glass.

She gasped. She was looking at globs of white icing stained by red punch that had exploded onto the floor with bits of broken glass in it.

Claire opened her mouth to scream, but no sound came out.

CHAPTER FIFTEEN

Nick's fear fast became fury. The place looked like a small war zone, with those who hadn't fled huddled—hurt?—on the floor. He saw Jace and Gina had protected Lexi with their bodies. Kris, Bronco and Nita, all sprawled on the floor amidst glittering glass, were looking around, stunned. The hot, humid outside air slammed into him. The safety glass had crackled into circular, fine-line pieces, and some parts had shattered into a storm of shards.

He saw Jace's cheek was cut and bleeding. Lexi was wailing. Gina, God bless her, was pressing a napkin against Jace's cheek, then Kris took over.

"Who else is hurt?" Gina cried.

Nick echoed her in a louder voice, "Anybody else hurt or cut? We have someone to help here!"

Jace held the napkin to his cheek and, one-armed, handed Lexi to Nick who took a quick look at her, then tugged her toward the ruined cake table.

"Dad, my ears hurt! Too loud a bad noise! Why did the window break?"

No time for all that, and who had answers? "You'll be all right, sweetie. I'll put you with Mommy and Trey out in the hall."

The hell with *Never Too Late to Celebrate Love*, Nick thought when he saw the shattered cake. Some damn idiot must have lobbed a huge rock against the window. Surely a golf ball didn't do all this. Hadn't the hostess told them this window was unbreakable?

Still on her knees under the cake table, rocking their son in her arms, Claire reached out for Lexi, but Nick hauled the child past them into the hall. "Stay right here!" he ordered. "I'll bring Mommy and Trey, and you can keep them from crying."

Lexi immediately stopped sobbing and nodded. The kid had some of her gutsy mother in her. Shaking, her cheeks wet with tears and her pretty dress a mess with some sort of food, Lexi sat up straight in an armchair. Nick darted back in for Claire, lifting her to her feet.

"I hope there's no follow-up to that," he muttered.

Cheryl appeared. "Nick, how can I help?"

"I think the bartender ran for help, but be sure they called 9-1-1 and the police. Detective Ken Jensen if he's available."

"Oh, and I think Dale's left arm might have broken when he hit the floor," she told him. "Heck's girlfriend is tying it up for him."

She darted off. Poor Dale. Poor all of them. Claire looked both stricken and angry. Nick led her out to the chair where Lexi perched and sat her down next to her.

"Darcy and her family?" Claire asked, cuddling Trey tight as she pulled Lexi against her.

"Huddled in a corner. I'll get them."

Several others came out, looking dazed, covered with food and drinks and those tiny shards of glass, though no one else looked bloodied. Jace must have been hit by flying broken glass from the bar, not this window stuff. Nick turned to go back in when their hostess, Mary Ann, came running down the hall toward him.

"A drone!" she cried, out of breath. "I would have come in earlier, but we thought we could spot who was flying it. A drone with an explosive on it, but it didn't detonate, we think—fell below to the patio after it hit the window. Damn that Lavell bunch who own the grove! I've called the squad and the police. Is anyone in there hurt?"

"At least one broken arm, one cut."

She tore inside with Nick. She started to make her rounds of the people who were getting up to brush off glass and food, and she was soon joined by two other club workers, both men who likely worked in the office. They were asking everyone if they were okay and explaining, commiserating.

Though it must not have even been ten minutes since the attack, Nick could hear the screech of a siren—more than one—coming closer. His eyes filled with tears as he surveyed the ruin of the verandah, now an open-air room. At least Steve and Darcy looked all right and were comforting their kids. Their boy Drew looked more shook than Jilly. Nick gestured for them to come out into the hall.

"A drone!" Nick told them as they hurried toward him. "The club hostess said the family that owned the grove has harassed golfers with a drone before and this one went on attack, probably not aimed at us."

Once everyone cleared the room and were checked out by the paramedics, Nick went to the verandah entry again and looked in. The room had been roped off by the staff and stood vacant now except for a worker getting ready to board up the long, open space with plywood sheets. Hot, humid air still swept in, smothering the air-conditioning. He realized he was wet with sweat, and his heart was still thundering in his chest.

But what he was really seeing in his head were the drones that his arch enemy had sent to spy on him and Claire when they first knew each other. The bastard was dead now, but this seemed a nightmare from the past. And what if, despite what he had just told Steve and Darcy, this drone was not sent by the grove owner, but had targeted him or those he loved? Had the explosive been meant to go off and not just threaten?

To Claire's disappointment, Ken Jensen was not back from his business trip, and a Sergeant O'Brien was in charge of the chaotic scene and questioning the many witnesses—or targets. The afternoon and evening she had so hoped would go well was a catastrophe. At least people were not seriously hurt but for Dale's broken arm the medics had tended to, though he needed to go to the hospital to have it set and get a cast. The first responders had also tended some cuts—Jace's was the worst. Everyone had ruined clothing from exploding food at the buffet table or bottles at the bar that made them look as if they'd been in a food fight. People kept picking little pieces of glass out of their hair and clothes.

When Claire finally went to use the bathroom, she saw her red hair had reddish icing in it, like coagulated blood. She took wet paper towels and tried to pick and wash it out even though that plastered her hair to her scalp. Her head hurt, her eyes ached from crying. This was agony on many levels, but it was fast turning to fury.

At least Nita and Bronco had taken Trey and Lexi home. Claire went back out into the office Sergeant O'Brien was using to talk to witnesses before he let them leave. Nick and Claire had said goodbye to each guest, apologizing, though no one blamed them.

"So counselor," Sergeant O'Brien, thin and tall with a shaved head, said to Nick, "hated to save you till last but was hoping what I learned from the others might turn up a motive we could discuss."

"And did it?"

"Some things have come up, but I don't want to go into specifics until I hand this information over to Detective Jensen when he returns."

Claire said, "It will be easier to put that window and the room back together than to salvage our special day."

She sniffed hard to hold back more tears. Hadn't she cried enough? This wasn't like her. She had to regain control. Nick reached for her hand and held it.

"I'm sorry for your—the loss of your celebration," O'Brien said. "But the thing is, there was an explosive head on that drone."

Nick squeezed her hand so hard she winced. "Which obviously did not detonate," Nick said.

"Luckily for all of you, it didn't. Our forensic team disarmed it and took it to the lab to see if it was a dud or malfunctioned. We already have a search warrant for the grove owners' house and property. The, ah, Lavell family," he said, glancing down at his notebook, "the original property owners who've been harassing the club over the price of extra land. If it was Lavell, stupid of him to use a drone, since he's used them before around here, and it can probably be traced to him."

"*If* it was him," Nick muttered. "I'd like to think so. Then he could be locked up, and we won't have to look for worse, more personal motives."

Claire recalled Nick saying the same about why Dale could not have killed Cyndi. Who would do something as obvious—especially a trained, bright lawyer—as putting his former fiancée he'd just strangled in his mother's freezer, then let the new owners in to clean the house? Could the grove owners be that stupid, take that risk? And eons ago, would Hunter have stabbed Reaching Woman with a hunting knife that looked just like his own? She had to ask Andrea to see those artifacts they guarded so closely.

She and Nick answered the sergeant's questions and went over the guest list with him. "No, I don't have a pending case where I've received threats," Nick told him in answer to the next question. "Of course, there can always be disgruntled former clients or, usually, those our firm beat in court."

"Mrs. Markwood," the sergeant said, turning to her, "any possible suspects who could be trying to warn or hurt you?"

"There have been times I would have said so, but nothing I know of that's current."

"Then my report is complete for Detective Jensen," he said, snapping his small notebook closed. "I can tell you this much to ease your minds. There are two possible targets besides the country club itself, just my observation, but this will all immediately be handed over to him."

Two possible targets besides the club? Those words echoed through the wall of Claire's anger and exhaustion. That made three total possibilities? Well, thank the Lord, as this man had said, for once it wasn't them. But who then?

"Sad to think that everything got ruined," Claire said to Nick over, of all things, the comfort of hot chocolate on that warm evening. Their kitchen clock said ten, and they'd finally gotten Lexi to sleep. Trey had gone back to his crib with hardly a peep. Ah, to sleep like a baby. She prayed neither of her children would inherit her narcolepsy.

"At least no one was killed or maimed, if that was the intent," she went on, sounding so weary to herself. "Or maybe that was meant as a warning—that the explosive was a dud this time, but look out next."

"Not a dud, I'll bet, but didn't detonate. That grove owner must be a nutcase."

"Nick, I'm angry. Everything seemed so perfect, but I guess we've never had that. Oh, forgot to tell you, Bronco said he's going to stay up all night, sleep on the couch in the Florida room, prowl around. Poor Nita with that body in the freezer at her home—then we get ashes on a car, and someone explodes our party..."

"Two other possible targets in the group besides the poor country club that idiot keeps harassing. Let's check on our dynamic duo of kids again, then go to bed. In the morning, things will seem more—well, better, if the aftermath of this publicity and your working with ancient bodies can be called normal."

Before they could get up, Nick's cell phone sounded—the hard-driving music from the original but now defunct TV series *Law and Order*.

"Nick Markwood here." He listened for a moment, then mouthed to her, "Ken Jensen."

"Yes, okay," Nick said. "Tomorrow morning we'll wait for you here. Seven a.m., then. Drive carefully, detective, and keep your eyes out for drones, especially when you get into Naples. You probably know more than we do about who that damned thing was aiming at, because we sure can't figure it out."

CHAPTER SIXTEEN

Nick kept pacing while Claire fixed more coffee and set out ba-
gels for Ken Jensen.

"I'd forgotten today's Memorial Day," she told him, "and you
won't have to go in to work. Nothing seems real right now—a
big blur. I ignored my herbal stimulants and took my hard-
hitting meds to get through this interview and handle the bad
memories of yesterday."

"I know, sweetheart. Hard-hitting stamina is what we both
need. At least Jensen's been straight with us before. I trust him,
and I think he trusts us. Hey, there he is, pulling into the driveway in an unmarked car, right on time. I wonder if he even went
home last night after driving back from Georgia."

Nick greeted him and brought him into the kitchen. He was
grateful to be able to trust this man, though he had no doubt
that his job would take precedence over any friendship the three
of them had built.

"Thanks, Claire," Jensen said as he sat down with them at their
kitchen table, and she put a steaming mug of coffee in front of
him. "Could smell the coffee when I hit the door. Wish I could
mainline caffeine into my veins right now."

"I know what you mean," she said. "We're running on adrenaline and anger."

"So how was Zebulon, Georgia?" Nick asked. He knew they'd soon move on to the country club mess, but he hoped Jensen had found out something to incriminate Cyndi's brother or first fiancé to take the heat off Dale.

"Scenic, if you like to see the Stars and Bars still flying over the old courthouse and statues of Confederate generals. Let's just say the two Southern gentlemen of interest were gone with the wind and haven't been back home for a while, and no one knows where they've gone to grieve for Cyndi's death. Yeah, they're in the mix of suspects for ashes on cars and even drone attacks—and maybe murder one—so I hope we can find them hanging out around here.

"But to business, because I need your help," Jensen went on. "Once again, welcome to the law enforcement club. I got the info on the interviews from O'Brien about the incident," he said as he paused to down some coffee. Nick leaned forward, his chin in his hand; Claire clasped her hands in her lap. Jensen did not have a notebook as O'Brien had. How could he look so awake and seem so sharp after driving back from Georgia?

"Okay," he said, looking from one of them to the other, "here's the nitty-gritty. There was an explosive on that drone, and not one damned fingerprint. The lab guys think either the explosive was not set to go off, or the pin was jostled in flight or when it hit the window."

"If their assumption's right," Nick said, "maybe the drone was a threat rather than attempted murder—so far."

"Maybe."

Claire said, "Sergeant O'Brien admitted that there were two people in the room who might have been targets, and, for once, we think, it wasn't us. Can you share what you know with us— to help us—to let us help?"

"Forewarned is forearmed, right?" he said, looking from one

of them to the other. "I agree. But first—sorry, you two—but looking at your track record for attracting trouble, I need to ask you both again. Has anything other than Dale Braun's fiancée's murder come up in your lives lately—anyone who could be out to get you? Anything at all suspicious, unusual, out of order?"

Nick shook his head. "Not even volatile legal cases, though I'll have a look back at the files we've always kept on possible explosive situations—sorry to use the word *explosive*—that we've kept at the firm for years for that very reason."

"Good. Let me know. Claire? Any new dangerous assignments or kooks you're working with lately with your Clear Path online site or in general?"

"I am on a part-time assignment but nothing unusual there," she told him, feeling like a total liar the way she'd worded that. Then it hit her. That person who had seemed to be watching her and Kris...in the rush and chaos, she hadn't even told Nick, and if she blurted that out now he'd have a fit. But she had to share it.

"There was something minor I haven't even had time to mention to Nick yet—didn't think it was much, but it was strange. It happened when I was shopping late last week with my old friend Kris Kane—who was at the party."

"Right. The archaeologist. She insisted there was nothing strange going on in her life."

Claire sat up straighter. Of course Kris would say that to hide top-secret Black Bog. She hoped Nick didn't decide to breech her contract, but he only shifted in his seat and said nothing. "Yes," she said. "Anyhow, when the two of us were shopping at the Waterside Shops on the Trail, I noticed a person who might have been following us and mentioned it to Kris."

Nick sniffed in a big breath of frustration but didn't interrupt.

"Description?" Jensen said, taking another long drink of coffee, then finally producing a notebook and pen.

"Kind of difficult to say, because I couldn't actually tell if it

was a man or a woman. Loose, nondescript black clothes. Baseball cap pulled low. Big dark sunglasses. Thin."

"Did this person approach you or Ms. Kane?"

"No, but when I went out of the dressing room to a clothing rack, he or she was staring close through the window. We
saw the same person when we went to our cars but he/she just
walked away, and we left in a hurry."

"Duly noted, but then both of you are attractive ladies. Besides, that shopping area had some shoplifters lately, stupid ones
who stick out like sore thumbs but we just haven't nabbed them
yet. Let me know if either of you see that person again."

Nick added, "And perhaps let your husband know too. So,
Ken, can you tell us who the two guests at our reception were
who might have been targets or had some link to a drone or
whatever Sergeant O'Brien was alluding to?"

"Sure, because I want your help to find out more, maybe
things you and Claire can get out of them the police couldn't.
Both seemed to be holding back on naming specific suspects we
could talk to. I was surprised you didn't know because you've
been quite close to both of the people who consider they could
be in some danger—Jason Britten and Hector Munez."

Jace was annoyed that Mitch was late when he joined him
at the back corner table of the Skillets Sunrise Café on Airport
Road in Naples. They both liked the place, partly for the food,
partly for the sounds of planes flying over from the airport just
down the road. Frowning, Jace looked at his watch—7:30 a.m.
Damn, even frowning hurt the cut on his face.

"We've got to stop meeting like this," Mitch told Jace with
an exaggerated waggle of his eyebrows.

"Very funny. I am starting to feel like we're hiding out,
though. You think that drone attack I told you about could
have been meant for me?"

Mitch slid into the booth opposite Jace, who had positioned

himself so he could see the restaurant. Let his former superior in the Stingray program look at the damn boring wall. He only hoped he could convince him of what he'd already set in motion. Mitch thought he held all the cards, but they were about to become equals in their next endeavor—he hoped.

"Sorry I'm late," Mitch said. "Before I got your text about the drone attack—and the friend you want to set me up with—I was out like a light last night."

"Yeah, well, we're both going to be out for good if we don't pull off this change of occupation and let whoever might be targeting us know we're out of Stingray. Not only me, but you could be next on a hit list."

"Yeah, especially if you lead the hit man of some drug czar we've been following to me at this restaurant. I took a roundabout way and watched to see if I was being tailed like you suggested. But, really, sorry everyone went through that attack—and thank God no one was seriously hurt."

"I didn't text this but a junior lawyer from Markwood's law firm did get a broken arm when he fell to the floor in an awkward position."

"Not the guy suspected of killing and freezing that woman?"

"You got it, sad to say."

"How's that rather obvious cut on your cheek? You texted you were going into an all night ER for stitches."

"Fourteen of them. The only good thing was Brit was there to hold my hand. Hope I don't look like Frankenstein's monster when I get this bandage off." But maybe, Jace thought, it would add to what Kris Kane had kidded was his "*Top Gun* and Viking allure."

"So," Mitch went on, "you're thinking you could have been the target, because of the connection to the Stingray pilot killed by a drone in California? Tell me about this secret plan to let our enemies know to lay off—and tell me about this Kris Kane you mentioned."

"Okay, but something else first," he said, leaning closer across the table and lowering his voice despite the restaurant's buzz of voices. He stopped talking entirely when the waitress came to fill their coffee cups and said she'd be right back. "I've got a reporter from *The Naples Daily News* joining me in about a half hour—or us, if you agree to my plan. If not, I'll go solo with it."

"You're getting desperate," Mitch said, leaning forward and keeping his voice down.

"I'm getting real. I've got a daughter and a fiancée here, and I'll have to steer clear of both of them if I don't get some life insurance—make sure that explosive drone wasn't meant for me or else make sure they're not in the next line of fire. You know those drug boys don't mind wiping out related lives as a warning to others. So, yeah, I think a newspaper interview I mentioned before is the way to go—life insurance. We are now flying hurricane hunter planes as full-time work…yada, yada, yada…"

"Hell, we can't let on about Stingray to a newspaper, even if we're getting out of it."

"Would you just listen for once? Here's all the reporter—and anyone out to get us—needs to know. We are just retired Iraq war veterans who have been battling the Zika virus and citrus crop pests and blight, but now we have both been accepted to the government team that flies into hurricanes to save lives. It's our new career, and we're dedicated to that effort. The reporter already liked that slant."

"But do we think a public story like that will—well, will fly?"

"See, that makes us community good guys, heroes again. I'm hoping, if the drug cartel we've been spying on realizes that we're not living in the shadows but are public faces, they'll lay off. Otherwise, they'd have public opinion and the press after whoever harmed us, as well as the police on their backs."

"Okay, got to hand it to you," he said with a sigh that made his usual erect posture and square shoulders slump. "Sounds like a plan, flyboy, and I'll hang in as your wingman, even though I don't like the 'coincidence' of the California Stingray pilot and his death by drone. But what if this reporter really wants to talk to you because you were at the site of the country club drone attack? Bet they do a story on that today or tomorrow."

"They did today, but it was all about harassment of the golf club by the owner of the grove. The article had some interviews with golfers he's bothered when they were on the course. The guy, Lavell, was arrested but posted bond already. He's got to have a screw loose to use rotten oranges and drones to harass the players and club."

Their waitress came back, all bright-eyed, which annoyed Jace. However exhausted and nervous he was, Brit had been all chatty this morning too, talking about how sad it was for Claire and Nick to have their reception ruined, how they had to be sure it didn't happen to them. Of course, she had no clue that he could have been a target of that damned drone, but he supposed he had to level with her about that. She was going to have a fit if he said she should move out and avoid him until he was sure the coast was clear of more deadly drones.

They each got their second jolt of java, then ordered pancakes and eggs. "So," Mitch said, looking at the cute waitress as she sashayed away, "I repeat, tell me more about this lady you talked to about meeting me. If this local media blitz of yours doesn't work, I don't want to endanger her."

"See, now you're starting to think like me. I passed you off as a vet who just never had time to settle down, not that you were a local kingpin of secret ops."

"Okay. What's she like?"

"Kristen—goes by Kris—is probably about five-foot-five, around age thirty, good-looking. Much more petite than my ex, Claire, who's a friend of hers from way back. Educated and well traveled. An archaeologist, though I think she's just working with one of her former professors right now as a consultant—

something like that. She did say to tell you she has a problem though and—"

"I knew it. Twice divorced? Actually hates men? Has three legs?"

Jace ignored that. Their food came. "Well?" Mitch demanded.

"She has what's called face blindness, which simply means she can't recall faces enough to remember who is who, so she looks for signs like hair color, clothing, voice recognition, stuff like that."

"Wow. Never heard of it. Tough lady if she copes with that but has done well in life," Mitch admitted as they tucked into their food. "Wonder what she'll remember about my face."

"That it has a smart mouth and roving eyes. Claire says Kris is very bright," Jace went on while he poured maple syrup on his pancake stack. "Of course, if she puts up with you after one date, I'd have to question that."

"Very funny."

"You want me to set something up?"

"Just get me her number and ask if I can call her, okay?"

"I just happen to have her number here," he said and dug out a business card Kris had given him. Yeah, he'd remembered right, he thought as he handed it over. Kristen Kane, Educational Archaeological Consultant.

"If this works out," Mitch added with a little laugh while he studied the card, "maybe we could double-date. Sorry if I sound like I'm fifteen. It's been a while for me since I met a lady I really cared about. And I won't do more than phone her yet in case we're targets."

"Sounds good. We both need something good, right? Maybe wait to call her, though, until we see if our job-change declaration goes public. Hey, I think I see the reporter," he said, squinting past Mitch toward the restaurant entrance. "At least he was willing to meet with us on Memorial Day. He's got a camera too. We ready to really step out into the light with this?"

"It's a gamble we don't tick off the drug boys this way too, but I'm thinking it's the lesser of two evils. If we pose outside for a photo," he added as Jace half rose and gestured to the man, "let's just be sure there are no damn drones in the sky."

CHAPTER SEVENTEEN

Claire had Nick's breakfast ready when he came into the kitchen the next morning. She perched across the table from him and waited at least until he drank his orange juice.

"Nick, if Jace is being watched or targeted somehow, probably because of his Stingray flights, he shouldn't be anywhere near Lexi right now. Actually, he should steer clear of Brit, too, until this whole thing is solved and settled."

He put his juice glass down and narrowed his eyes at her. "Nor should he be near you or this house."

"Right, but he's not going to take any of that well, at least not to stop seeing Lexi. And just when the two of us were getting along better. Tomorrow's his day to pick her up after school and take her to the zoo or on some adventure. But surely he'll see we'll have to cancel that."

"Explaining it to Lexi will be just as hard."

"She's been through a lot because of us, and I'd just die if she was ever abducted or hurt again. She'll freak out if I try to tell her that her father's in danger. Jace is going to have to go along with us—say he's busy, something. Maybe he can say he had to leave to be a hurricane hunter early, since Brit says that's in his plans."

She thought again of the Hunter of old. What was his relationship to Reaching Woman who had lain beside him all those centuries? Or was she tied somehow to Leader—or to both of them and that had led to her terrible fate?

"Earthman Nick Markwood calling spaced-out wife Claire. I said I have to take my coffee and go, sweetheart. Since Lexi's not down yet, kiss her for me before Bronco drops her off at school. I told him to come into the office late, hang around here a little longer. If you feel you need to call Jace, go ahead, but if he's being targeted, his phone could be bugged. How about I call him from the office?"

"Yes, all right. Then let me know somehow as I'm not going out to the bog until about two. This morning I'll spend time with Trey. I plan to catch Brad Vance this afternoon since he seems to be the keeper of the keys to view the artifacts from the graves."

"Sounds like a plan—one of them," he said in a teasing voice, obviously trying to lighten her mood. As if they had not a care in the world, he tossed his keys in the air and caught them in a quick move behind his back, though he was in full lawyer dress mode: striped tie, cufflinks, power watch, suitcoat over his arm and newspaper under it. "Don't you just wonder," he said as he leaned down to kiss her goodbye, "what archaeologists would think of us and our artifacts if we were buried with our favorite toys?"

She nodded but didn't answer. Had Leader with his striped robe and staff and dagger chosen to be buried with those items or had they been selected by someone else so he would have them for his life-in-death in the bog? She would never really know, but somehow she was going to dig deep into all their lives and present the Vances—and eventually the world—with the very best theory she could figure out.

Thank heavens Jace agreed with them about not seeing Lexi right now, Nick thought as he hung up his office phone after a short, intense talk with him. Nick's phone had protection on it to scan for bugs or third-party eavesdropping. Jace was taking measures, he said, to end any relationship he'd had with the Stingray program. And he didn't have to worry his contact wouldn't take it well because the guy he referred to only as "his wingman" was also taking a new job as a hurricane hunter.

"As a matter of fact, check *The Naples Daily News* for a feature article announcing that to the world," Jace had said. "Life insurance, though I'll give it a little time before coming near Lexi or you guys again. But you and Claire have to promise to explain to her that it wasn't my choice—without upsetting her. Easier said than done with that kid, I know, but Claire's not a psych major for nothing."

Nick wanted to call Claire right away to assure her Jace would stay away, but *would* that assure her? No, it would make her sad, and not only because Lexi couldn't see Jace. Nick knew Claire still cared for her first husband, though he didn't worry about that. Not too much, that is, especially now that Jace had Brit.

A knock on his door jerked him back to reality. Cheryl stuck her head in. What would he do without her? She was almost old enough to be his mother and sometimes treated him that way, but he gladly kept her on and would miss her when she retired. Besides, she was a link to his father. She'd been a temp here at the firm when his father had died so terribly. After law school, when he'd tried to fill his father's very big, empty shoes, she had guided him through more than one complication of taking over the law practice.

"Is Heck here?" he asked.

"On his way." She came clear over to his desk. "You doing okay after that chaos yesterday?"

"Not really, but one foot ahead of the other. I'm grateful you and the staff weren't hurt—but for Dale."

"Not an omen for his situation, I hope. He's living in fear the police could arrest him any day. It did hurt me to see you and

Claire suffering. You've both been through a lot. Oh, Dale called a while ago and insists he's coming in soon, even though you told him to rest. I understand he needs to keep busy."

"Yeah, I get that too. Speaking of which, Madame Secretary, I promised Detective Jensen that I would look through our files to see if there were any loose cannons from past cases who might hold a grudge against me or the firm. I can think of a few but I don't want to miss anything."

"You want me to look in my spare time—ha, ha—or just pull case files for you?"

"All of the above."

"How far back, Nick?"

"I'd say ten, fifteen years. I can't believe someone wouldn't act on a serious grudge by now if the firm or I let them down."

"Got it. Got your back too," she said, heading away. "Don't know what you'd do without me," she teased.

"You know me too well!" he called after her as she went out, but she popped right back in. He was expecting another rejoinder, but she said, "Hector Munez here to see you, Attorney Markwood."

Heck came in without the usual swagger. He looked as if he hadn't slept either.

"Sorry, boss, but I drove Gina back to Miami, and we left at four in the morning. Just got back. Hated to leave her there, but she's adjusting. Can't say I am without her."

"No more bruises or hard knocks after that mess yesterday?"

"Only that I still worry I'll lose her—to some guy, some med student or doctor over there. Anyway, I know what you want."

"Tell me then. What did you tell Sergeant O'Brien that made him put you on the possible hit list for that drone? Something with that new facial recognition deal?"

"Yeah, *caramba*. I had no idea what I was getting into, the cutthroat part of it. Facial recognition is about to become the next big thing in security software. There's ways to hack into digital devices and locations and the like with fingerprints, eye or voice recognition, but facial is a lot harder to fake. Whoever controls facial rec tech is gonna be filthy rich—big, big bucks. So maybe sharks are circling to scare away or knock off people who could help their competition."

"So dirty play competition is of concern? And someone has figured out you're good—and might go with a particular firm?"

"And maybe trying to scare me off. Or kill me and anybody nearby who might have a clue why. So sorry to tell you all this, that I might be a sitting bird on a wire."

"I think the phrase is a sitting duck, Heck. But I get that this is going to lead to new frontiers of privacy laws."

He nodded, kept nodding. "That's why I told you about it in the first place, plus I wanted your okay to be part-time with them. But I'm feeling scared, boss, real scared. I'd rather live off Gina's doctor salary someday than have a lot of money and be in someone's crossover hairs."

Nick didn't correct his English this time. He knew damn well what his friend meant. And he knew he'd give up this law practice and his covert South Shores investigations—all of it— to protect the ones he loved.

Claire had two goals at Black Bog that afternoon. One, to view the bodies, especially the faces, of the three who had shared the latest excavated grave. Second, to get a close look at the artifacts which had been buried with each person, and which had been taken quickly away for cleaning and preservation. She thought it was rather sad that those items which had been with them so long should be separated from them now.

She felt much more relaxed and grounded after a morning holding and playing with Trey. He was getting so responsive, and despite the fact he was only a little over three months old, developing a personality.

"Hope today's been better," she greeted Kris as she went to

her own corner desk and laptop in their shared office. "No sore spots or bruises from the shock yesterday, I hope?"

"I'm fine. And I won't even say your party was a blast," she said and hugged her, while Claire gave a dramatic groan. After all, Claire thought, what was there to do but plunge ahead and be grateful for the support of friends and family who had—for the most part—not been hurt.

"So," Claire said, putting her purse in a drawer and turning on her laptop, "think you'll hear from Jace's pilot friend?"

"Don't know, but it will be interesting. I need something like that, an interest in a live man instead of the other kind. What's that motto on your website, 'The dead still talk if you know how to listen'?"

"And I'm hoping they do, especially around here. I'm going to ask Andrea for a close look at the new trio. Want to come along? And then—what's the protocol for getting a glimpse of the artifacts from Brad?"

Kris didn't answer at first. Had she even heard that last question?

"He does huge blow-up photos of each one," she finally said. "Of course, he'll let you study those."

"But not see the items themselves?"

"They're precious, priceless, and it's not good to handle them, so much as breathe on them, once they're cleaned."

Claire sank into her swivel chair and rotated it to face Kris. "So I can view them only on my laptop screen?"

"On his. It's like he's keeper of the keys for the artifacts, though I can see why."

Claire felt deflated and a bit frustrated. Brad didn't go out to the digs, had claustrophobia and guarded the artifacts even from the team? Well, everyone had their odd habits and quirks. And she should talk. She understood how important, how consuming it could be to protect precious things and precious people.

"So," Kris cut into her agonizing, "let's go to Andrea and take a look at our three somehow related bog people. You can ask Brad to view the artifacts later. Maybe we can get a theory on these unusual bodies before they dig up any more."

Nick was scanning some of the files Cheryl had brought him when his desk intercom rang. Cheryl said, "Bronco called from his post downstairs. Another most interesting person is insisting on seeing you."

"Tanner Linschwartz again or another guy from Georgia? Call Jensen and tell him before Bronco even passes them into the lobby. We might need security."

"No, it's a very irate woman who is throwing her weight around—which isn't much. I took a look at her on the security camera down there. A Ms. Marian James from a local group called the Endangered Properties Committee. And she says if you don't back off, she's going go public with your obstruction of rights and sue Dale and the firm."

"Actually, I've been expecting something from her. Is Dale here?"

"He came in about a half hour ago, and I hear he's on pain pills and not looking good."

"Keep him in his office and have Bronco escort her immediately and politely all the way to my office, then hold my calls."

CHAPTER EIGHTEEN

"I want to really get started with my study of the Hunter, Reaching Woman and Leader today," Claire told Andrea and Kris as they walked through Andrea's office to the back room that stored the bog bodies in deep drawers. "If I can just study these remains and the artifacts, I believe I can come up with a hypothesis and then consult with all of you."

Andrea didn't so much as blink at her saying she wanted to study the artifacts, so perhaps she'd be more of an ally than Kris in getting Brad to show her those.

Although Claire had been present at the disinterment of all three bodies, she steeled herself as Andrea opened the first drawer, now marked Hunter of Trio.

There was no gut-wrenching smell as Claire had learned to associate with a coroner's office, just an earthy odor. Hunter was still partly covered with the tarp he had been carried in, curled up almost as if he were kneeling. Even under the bright blue tarp, Claire could see his chest was hollowed out.

"We'll be working on examining him tomorrow," Andrea

told her. "After a thorough outer examination, we'll remove all three brains for study, then reconstruct head and hair."

The pelt Hunter had worn for centuries was matted with peat and blotches of blood, but Claire could still tell it was animal hair. She noted it might have been made extraheavy, two-layered, up around his big shoulders. Had someone lovingly sewn it that way to keep him warm in the winter? Or to buffer something heavy he carried over his shoulders? But it appeared to have been pulled awry when someone had stabbed him, stolen his heart and life.

"Was his heart found in the grave?" Claire asked.

"The team looked around carefully," Andrea said. "They found only that dagger in his hand, encrusted with either peat or blood. Brad's examination of it will let us know soon."

"If there is blood on the dagger," Claire said, "Brad won't wash it off, will he?"

"Eventually. What does it matter? We can't type their blood."

As accommodating as she had started out, Andrea seemed in a hurry now, even on edge. Claire wondered if she'd overstepped. To answer the questions they had hired her for, surely they knew she had to probe.

"Could I see the other side of his face?" she asked, shifting her position so their shadows from the bright overhead lights didn't obscure him.

"Of course," Andrea said and slowly lifted the top of the tarp away.

Claire moved around Kris to look at the other side of Hunter's face she could not see from this angle. The right side was somewhat smashed but this left side had fared better.

"Oh," she cried, "he has a slashed cheek! I mean a scar, long and deep, not new. Well, definitely not new."

Both women gathered close and edged her out to see it themselves. It reminded her so much—too much, as if it were some awful omen—of the cut on Jace's face.

★ ★ ★

"So you can get an article in the paper, but I can't!" Marian James shouted and threw a copy of today's *The Naples Daily
News* on Nick's desk.

He had asked both Bronco and Cheryl to stay, and they sat
against the wall in the back of the room by his bookcases.

"Please sit down, Ms. James, and we will talk rather than
shout," Nick told her, ignoring the newspaper at first. She must
be referring to the article about the drone attack at the country club.

She sat, perched ramrod stiff on the edge of her chair. He slid
the paper closer. Where had he put his own copy of it? He'd left
the house with it. Too damned distracted. Maybe it was still in
the car. He'd read it in a hurry, not much of it at that.

He glanced down at it again, a small article, thank heavens,
including a picture taken of the shattered window from the
eighteenth green. At least there were no photos of the sad chaos
inside the verandah. And, he thought, at least the article didn't
include a guest list and only quoted the club hostess. Nothing
about Jace's or Dale's specific injuries, no other interviews except a brief comment by Sergeant O'Brien.

But in the second section that had slid out from under the
front page was an article he hadn't seen. Jace, face bandage and
all, and—oh, yeah—he was with his pilot friend, Mitch Blakeman. They were both smiling in front of the nose of a jet at the
Naples Airport. Local Vets to Hunt New Enemy—Hurricanes,
the headline read. He and Claire had been so intent on the drone
article, they hadn't looked beyond.

He had to tear his attention away from that back to the irate
woman, but at least she seemed to have calmed down a bit.

"Despite what Cynthia Lindley told you before her death,
Ms. James," Nick said, trying to steady his voice, "access to information and legal entry to the grounds of the Twisted Trees
mansion was not hers to give. Mr. Braun has every right to

keep those ruins and information about their long dead original owner private."

"It's living history! I'm sure we could find a buyer for the property if he doesn't want to share it with the public. As I said, our committee is not some fly-by-night organization but a well-funded one with some influential people on its board. And the German-Nazi connection makes the Braun mansion all the more important and valuable. Why, that's of international concern. People have a right to know!"

"Perhaps at a later time. I congratulate you on your admirable efforts but—"

"What if there are artifacts there? This could even go into the realm of the state government control at the least, national interest at most. Magazines like *The Smithsonian* and *National Geographic* would be all over this, provide funding for reclamation and restoration of the site. And why is that carriage house or servants' quarters or whatever it is boarded up and fairly intact when the rest of the place is in shambles?"

Nick had to admit that this woman did raise some interesting questions. He had no answer for that. Did Dale?

"I know Mr. Braun has problems of his own right now," she went on in a calmer tone, "but please put this to him again, or I will have to bring more pressure to bear—and publicity. Yes, I know you said you'd insist I was trespassing when I took those photos. But since I'd earlier been invited by Mr. Braun's fiancée—"

"Former fiancée, not a family member, and now, sadly, deceased."

Marian James shot to her feet so fast, behind her, Bronco stood too. "I have a recording of the woman's phone call to me! I know the timing is bad for this, but time is of the essence for derelict buildings, just as it is for murder suspects like your client. Please inform him he needs to cooperate with what will be very generous offers. On the other hand, I can at least let the media know that I had a call from a soon-to-be dead woman and have every right to share what she told me. I will, however, think that over for exactly one week before I act. I assure you, I and my committee will be in touch, but perhaps you will want to be in touch with me first."

She seized the newspaper from his desk and made a fast exit with Bronco right behind her, hopefully to be sure she didn't try to get to Dale.

Cheryl closed the door behind them and leaned against it as if to block the woman out. "Do you want Heck to research her and her committee, Nick?"

"He's got enough on his mind. I'll have Claire check things out with me looking over her shoulder. I'm starting to think I might have missed something at Twisted Trees. But we have enough to do around here. Once you're certain she's gone, send Dale back in if he feels up to it," he told her. "And even if he doesn't."

Claire stared down at the next drawer Andrea pulled out. It was labeled Reaching Woman of Trio.

"Her pelt is the same kind as that on Hunter, don't you think?" she asked. "Do other bodies have deer pelt clothing?"

"No, more woven plant material, similar to Leader's robe," Kris said.

At least she was getting steadier and more used to seeing these naturally mummified bodies. Her voice wasn't shaking right now, nor was she trembling, and her stomach wasn't twisted in knots. She was simply left with the feeling of awe—and fierce determination.

"We'll examine the crude thong stitching on both of the similar deer pelts, but that even looks the same," Andrea observed.

"Like Hunter, she has her legs drawn up," Claire said, "as if she were kneeling—or cold."

Kris added, "Or trying to protect herself from that knife thrust—almost a praying position, if they prayed."

"Or one of deference or submission," Claire said. "Maybe she was begging for mercy. Shouldn't that knife have been left in place until she was further examined? I see it's been removed."

"A key artifact to be studied and preserved," Andrea recited her usual mantra.

In other words, Claire thought, although Andrea was the trained archaeologist here, Brad ruled on that. Dare she question him on his tactics to get his hands on those precious items so quickly? Perhaps since he could not bear to see people enclosed in their graves, he was especially eager to oversee his part of this work. Besides the dagger being gone, what had appeared to be polished stones on a necklace spilled off a broken thong from around the woman's neck was missing too. She knew better than to ask, but she planned to face Brad over that. Especially if the stone beads matched the bracelet Leader had worn.

"Let's just be certain again that her heart is there," Andrea said, frowning. "Hunter's chest was so carved out, but I'm sure her heart is intact, even if she was stabbed in it."

Kris shined a light she wore around her neck. It reminded Claire to ask for one of those little flashlights. Andrea carefully lifted the hem of the stiff garment from the woman's bent knees.

All three of them peered up the woman's skirt. Claire gasped. Kris grunted as if she'd been struck, and Andrea swore. Reaching Woman's chest had not been cut open, although she had indeed been stabbed in it. But a second heart, stony, hard and dark—but unmistakable—lay upon her shriveled thighs.

CHAPTER NINETEEN

"All right, what's up?" Brit demanded. "Jace, why are we parking at a police station? Something else about the drone attack? What's going on?"

"I wanted to get you here before I explained. Insurance for you and for us," he said, killing the engine and unhooking his seat belt. He turned toward her so she wouldn't have to see only the bandaged side of his face. He didn't want to remind her of that attack or scare her more than he had to.

"I figured you wouldn't like it—would refuse," he explained, reaching out to cup her shoulder with one hand. It was more to steady himself than her. "Nick has set all this up, but I asked him to. I'm going in to talk to Detective Jensen while an officer drives you to our apartment and waits until you pack your things, then follows you while you drive your car to your mother's house. Brit, you have got to stay with her, or at least somewhere else, until I'm sure I'm clear of whoever sent that damn drone. If both of us moved and I'm the target, they'd find us again."

"Whoa! Who would find us? You think that drone was sent to scare—or even kill—you? I figured Nick must be the target.

You mean because of Stingray, like—like some criminal found out you're trying to nail drug smugglers?"

"That's not exactly top secret anymore. I can't take the chance that you'd be hurt, if I'm the target. If they try again, you or anyone else could be—well, collateral damage."

"So we're going to be apart for how long? What about our wedding plans? Oh—you think because the Markwoods' reception was hit..."

"Yeah, maybe. We can't take that chance."

"Don't you think that write-up in the paper about you and Mitch moving on from supposedly crop and mosquito spraying to mere hurricanes is enough to keep the bad boys at bay?"

"I'm sorry, honey," he said, gripping her hands in his as she turned even more toward him. "I screwed up, miscalculated. See, there was a Stingray pilot in California who was targeted by a drone—in his plane. It crashed and he died. For all Mitch and I know, a drone's the latest calling card of the Mexican drug mafia instead of a quick bullet in the head by some hit man or enforcer. I just can't take a chance you'd be hurt."

"Or you would be. But for how long? Can we even talk?"

"I figure I can call your mother, and she can give you the phone."

"Oh, really, like I'm six years old? And I call you how? Send smoke signals? Use poor Claire as a go-between? I know darn well you still care for her, and she'd do it for you, even if it endangered her."

"Not that now, honey. I'm just trying to do what will keep you safe."

She started to cry. "So this Detective Jensen agrees you might be the target?"

"He doesn't know—we don't know. There are other possibilities, including, as you heard, that the family who owns the orange grove wants more money for an extra piece of land. But that's too obvious."

She pulled one hand free and wiped tears from her face. "Just like it's too obvious that Dale Braun would have strangled then frozen that poor girl, like she was stored chicken on ice to be devoured later. Someone running and ruining our lives from afar is horrible. I hate it, but I don't hate you. So okay, we'll be apart, for a little while."

"I hate grilling you on this with all you're going through right now, Dale," Nick told him as they sat in Nick's interview chairs at the small table away from his desk. He was trying to trust this junior partner—his client—but there was something strange going on.

"I understand," Dale told him. He rested his cast on the table; in general, he looked like the walking wounded. "I wish Marian James hadn't turned up right now with everything else falling in on me. I can remember my dad quoting some Shakespeare play— 'Thus do all things conspire against us,' something like that."

"I'm sure Claire's heard of it, but I do know the feeling. So, help me out with a couple of questions I have about the Twisted Trees estate. Why is what Claire called the carriage house, which I'm sure was used for a garage, so intact-looking compared to the rest of the mansion?"

Dale shrugged, then winced from the movement. "The hurricane that ripped the roof off didn't touch that. Sturdier built maybe or lower to the ground. Dad used to say that was fate, like there was some sort of reverse curse on that part of the place, after its history."

"I'm not following now. Explain what he meant."

Dale heaved a huge sigh. "Sorry if I don't make sense. These pain pills are making me a little spacey. He meant—I found out from my mother years later, because she was bitter and talked more once she had dementia—that's where my great-uncle kept his German mistress."

Nick sat up and leaned forward. "No kidding? In a garage?"

"There's an apartment on the second floor, above where the cars were kept. That's all I'd need is that woman and her committee getting a look inside there. It's been sealed up for years, like a time capsule or a tomb. Mother said there's Nazi regalia in there, things that no one needs to see, but she couldn't bring herself to clean it out—well, you know she was a hoarder. Now that there's pressure to see it or sell it, I've got to get in there and pack things up, clean it out, but—hell, Nick—I was told not to when I was young and just haven't been able to get up the nerve to do it."

"You're right about checking it out, maybe clearing it out. I can always claim attorney privilege if we find strange things in there, so how about I go with you? Bronco too, to keep a watch for us outside. So your great-uncle brought not a wife but a mistress with him when he fled the Third Reich in its darkest days? She's obviously long gone—dead, or did she return to Germany after the war? And why didn't he marry her?"

"Don't know, but no, he didn't bring a wife to Florida when he fled. She had died before the end of the war, some American B-17 bombing raid, so I overheard once." Dale grimaced as he attempted another shrug. "I suppose it might have been secret because, in past times, a mistress was something you hid. And why didn't he marry her? Don't know that either."

"Yeah, you'd think with no wife, she'd be mistress in the big house, especially one so private and plush."

"I've thought about trying to get answers, going through the place, but it just seemed—well, as both my parents used to say, *verboten*."

"Yeah," Nick said. "When I found my father dead with his gun in his hands and half his head gone, no one wanted me to talk about it or pursue it, to prove there was no way he would have committed suicide. But I did and eventually proved it was murder. Then I finally stopped the man behind it."

"I heard," Dale said. "I'm sorry it—it haunted you like this haunts me. But I guess I'm finally ready to have answers, even if they are terrible ones. Okay, before Ms. James and her cabal of secret sponsors push us more, let's take a look at what's been locked up there for decades."

Claire had waited in the hall outside Brad Vance's office for a good ten minutes after he'd said on the in-house phone she could come to see the artifacts. She was excited, pacing. She must have misunderstood that she couldn't see them. He had opened his door a crack to say that he would be a little longer on the phone with what must be an inside-the-grounds call, then closed it again.

She scolded herself for being tempted to put her ear to the door to see if she could make out anything he was saying, but all she'd need was to get booted out of there for eavesdropping.

The muted sounds of his deep voice stopped inside. Brad opened the door. She realized that he must have some way to call out of there when no one else did. Or did he have some private line to their house nearby and linked in to that? But no way she was going to pursue that question and seem nosy. She'd just ask Kris later. Her target was getting to see those artifacts. He motioned her in, and she went, her eyes skimming the room for any of the precious grave finds he might have out to study.

But his examination table under bright lights was bare. The huge computer monitor she'd seen him looking at before was lighted but blank. An even larger screen, one that would have been good for watching movies, was suspended from the ceiling, also blank. No, there was a small caption at the bottom of it: Trio Exhibit.

"I don't usually keep myself shut in here—open door policy," he said as he sat on a high rotating stool and gestured for her to sit in the other one about three feet from him. "In general, I don't like closed rooms or doors."

She sat and put her feet on the round rail beneath. "I've worked with people who have claustrophobia," she told him. "It often, as I'm sure you know, stems from a particular frightening incident in childhood that is internalized in an older adult who suffers from that malady too."

"I've looked into it more than once," he admitted. "I just live with it, but that's right, you're a psych major—which is why Andrea and Kris thought you could help. So—to the artifacts. I have them blown up here twenty times their size for comparative study."

Her hopes fell. He was still going to have her looking at pictures, not the real items. How much should she protest? He was obviously the man with power behind Andrea's archaeological throne.

But she was intrigued by what was on the screen: two daggers, no peat or blood on them, evidently chipped out of flint. One was no doubt Hunter's and one the murder weapon that had been in Reaching Woman's heart. So strange, but at the moment, Claire felt as if something pierced her chest with pain. She scolded herself, for she'd always been too empathetic with those who were hurting. But of a long-dead people, buried for centuries in a bog?

"I suppose you heard," she said, "we found what we believe is Hunter's heart nestled on Reaching Woman's thighs."

"Andrea told me just a few minutes ago. She's hoping you can posit the meaning of that. Punitive? Ritualistic? Sexual? Religious?"

"Just think how we might say today, 'She had his heart.' I need time—and clues, like from a close look at the artifacts—to try to figure that out."

"So, okay," he said, turning his attention back to the screen as if he did not want to discuss that bizarre find further or her subtle plea to see the real items. "Both daggers are made of chert, not flint. Chert is a lot more lustrous than flint and a bit stronger. A mixture of chalcedony, quartz and silica, probably from microfossils—even bacteria—over the ages. The greenish tinge may come from eons of alga or moss being pressed together. Like flint, striking a chert dagger against another stone can start a fire, so the dagger could be doubly useful, for instance to cook meat a hunter brought home."

"Do you mind if I take notes?"

"Sure, but I'll keep any photos in my control for now. So you can see why I cleaned the bog mud and blood off these weapons."

"Chert does have a certain luster to it. Can those kinds of stones be found locally, or do you think they had to trade for them?"

"I'd say they came from somewhere north, but did they trade for them or come from there themselves? So many questions to answer, puzzles to solve."

"If Andrea and her team have turned up other daggers, utensils and the like, were any of them of those substances?" she asked.

"No. Much more, let's say, plebian, but nothing this valuable and useful. Of course, there is the fact Hunter's dagger seemed to have carvings on it."

"As did Leader's staff of office or whatever it is. Do you have slides of those?"

"Of course, but let's stick to these right now."

Claire jumped as a high voice came from right behind her: "Brad, I have what you wanted— Oh, so sorry. I did not see you had someone here. Hello, Claire."

"Hi, Yi Ling."

"No problem. I will come back later," she said, frowning.

Yi Ling had nothing in her hands. Claire read that the young woman was used to just walking in there and was rather put out that Claire had been there with Brad. It had seemed to her earlier that the digging trio reported only to Andrea, but she must be mistaken. She sensed strange vibes that bounced between Senator Vance and this petite woman who nearly scurried from the room.

"Anyway," he went on, after clearing his throat, "we've found flint that would chip away, even wooden utensils, some with sharks' teeth embedded in them to give them bite, so to speak." He turned and smiled at her, as if he'd made a joke. His teeth, especially for a man of his age, were—well, telegenic. White and even. Large.

"Could I actually see the woman's broken necklace and Leader's bracelet, at least?" she asked, looking down at her notes to break the tension between them. She didn't know why she felt so nervous near him. He had even left the door open, so they weren't really alone.

"Locked up in a safe for now. Let's stick with these high-resolution photos." He moved the slides along, showing what looked like big bone needles, maybe a leather drumhead, a small clamshell cup and a turtle shell that might have been a mixing bowl.

"There," he said, sounding strangely triumphant as a slide appeared which showed cleaned stones with thongs through their drill holes, though the longer one—Reaching Woman's broken necklace—had its polished stones separate and laid out side-by-side.

"Agate is the material for these," Brad told her. "Lovely patterns called banding, though these are not fine enough examples to be classed as gemstones. A rough surface here and there, because their tools were so primitive. Nothing carved on any of them, though the mud stuck in some of the crevasses made it look that way at first."

"I was hoping so."

"There is carving on Leader's staff, which I'll show you next, and that is a mystery. Nothing recognizable to modern eyes, though maybe you can copy the lines and discern some pattern—primitive writing, even."

"Wouldn't that be a bombshell?"

"Speaking of that, I—we—need you to be very certain that you are not being followed or somehow targeted, after that attack on your event at the country club. If something else happens like that, I'm afraid you might need to withdraw from this project. Kris tried to explain it all away, but, as you know, secrecy is of the utmost importance to us here until we are ready to go public with all this."

"I told the detectives it was not aimed at me, though, of course, my husband has a career which has some fallout at times."

"Yes, I should think so. Having been in politics, I can sympathize. I made a lot of friends, and, unfortunately, a few enemies too."

"And despite the fact that it was our event, other people attended besides us, and the country club itself is under a sort of attack by a neighbor."

"Yes, so I gathered from Kris and the newspaper article. Just wanted to be clear that you must bow out if there is any question of your being a chink in our armor, so to speak, a break in the dam of privacy and secrecy here."

"I'm aware of the concerns, Senator Vance, really."

"Good," he said with a decisive nod and what she considered to be a forced smile as he brought up the slide of the cleaned and lighted staff. Claire was disappointed. There were some carvings on it but they seemed only decorative. She'd glimpsed the staff briefly, but hadn't there been more, or had the mud and peat just made it look that way? The other side of the staff was amazingly similar but with more peat clinging to it.

"Let me run you through some earlier photos of artifacts," he said after she'd taken some notes without further comment. "Nothing as grand as the ones found with our trio, that's for certain."

Claire nodded, but what was for certain around here? She could fully grasp their need for secrecy with the outside world until they had a chance to study everything, but she had the strangest sensation that there were other secrets being kept around here too.

CHAPTER TWENTY

"So is Daddy just too busy for me right now?" Lexi asked Claire when she tried to tell her Jace couldn't pick her up after school tomorrow and might not come over to see her for a little while. She was sitting on Lexi's bed, trying to tuck her in, though the child kept throwing the covers off.

"It's just that he's changing jobs." Claire tried another tack.

"Then doesn't he get a little vacation between them? Or does he just want to spend time with Brit now 'cause he loves her more."

"No, sweetheart. He will always love you, whether or not Brit is in his life. The way he loves Brit will be like a husband and wife, but you are special, his only and very best girl."

Leaning down, she hugged Lexi closer. "I don't know," the child said with crossed arms and a big sniff, "'cause I heard him say Brit was his girl."

Claire knew she was doing a bad job of explaining this, but what to say? Nice to have all those psych classes years ago and a darned diploma on her wall, but she was failing miserably counseling her own daughter. The problem was she felt protective of both Lexi and Jace in this situation. Her heart went out to both of them…both of them…again she saw that horrid heart cradled in Reaching Woman's thighs.

She shook her head to clear that dreadful picture. "You know grownups have problems sometimes," she told her daughter. "But it doesn't mean that you are not dearly, dearly loved, and Daddy will make it up to you when he can."

"Can you pick me up at school instead?"

"You must ride the bus like usual. Okay? Hey, how about we have mac and cheese tomorrow night and make dinner together? I have to go see the people I'm helping tomorrow afternoon."

"Mac and cheese is okay, but I'm kind of sad. I want to call Daddy and tell him."

"We'll call him later—sometime. Lexi, he's feeling bad too, and he can't help some things right now."

"Sometimes I wish my 'maginary friend would come back, but I think she died."

Claire held her even closer. "Don't say that. Remember, you finally let her go off on a trip, but you don't have to let Daddy go. You know Dad Nick loves you too," she said, evoking Nick as Lexi had come to refer to him.

"It is funny to have two dads and you had both of them for husbands, right, Mom?"

"It happens, my dear girl. You know, I think I'll just stay right here until you go to sleep."

Feeling exhausted and overwhelmed—and so inadequate— Claire turned off the bedside table lamp and stretched out beside her. And found herself wondering if Reaching Woman had loved both of the men she had slept beside in the bog, almost for eternity.

"I didn't know where you were until I looked in on Lexi," Nick said later that night while she reheated supper for him. "Sorry to wake you up."

He hadn't wanted to get home late, but he had. Too much time spent on current cases after he'd sent Dale home early.

"Yeah, I conked out having a heart-to-heart with Lexi about why she can't see Jace for a while. I did a lousy job of it, I'm afraid."

"I don't mean to put this on you when you're tired, but maybe tomorrow, as soon as possible, I'm hoping you can do me—and Dale—a favor. I know you'd once started to research Cyndi Lindley and were on her Facebook page, but if you could turn up anything else about her online, it might help. Her phone call to Marian James is causing a mess. The woman has given me and Dale one week to let her release her photos and info on Twisted Trees or she's going to publicize the phone call, and that won't help Dale. Frankly, I'm hoping you can find something else to cast doubts on Cyndi being responsible or trustworthy. If Dale didn't kill her, we have to come up with who she got in with who could have. And Tanner and her ex-fiancé might not be enough."

"Back to proving the gold digger and getting-in-over-her-head angle? I agree the Nazi connection could blow things wide open for Dale again," she said, putting his plate of spaghetti before him and pouring him a glass of red wine.

"Yeah," he said with a sigh. "If it comes out Dale and two other generations of his family wanted Twisted Trees and the Nazi connection kept secret, that provides another motive for him murdering Cyndi, either to keep her quiet or in anger for her already going public with Marian James. Dale and I are going to take a look in that well-preserved garage–carriage house on the mansion property tomorrow. Dale says his great-uncle kept a mistress in an upstairs apartment there, one he brought from Germany, but why not in the big house if there was no wife in the way?"

"I can't believe all that. A German mistress, probably swastika wallpaper in the garage apartment. 'Curiouser and curiouser,' said Alice in Wonderland."

"You and your mother's literary quotes. I'll take Bronco along to Twisted Trees for security's sake."

"In other words," she said, sitting up straighter, "I can do the online research, but not go with you to help solve the riddle of what's there? Nick, that's exactly what I'm being paid big bucks to do at Black Bog, find and prove a theory—on-site. I want to go with you to look around there."

"I know you're busy. And I'm not sure that it's entirely safe."

"So I'll be stuck looking at my laptop in the den?" she asked, her voice rising as she jumped up. "We used to be a team!"

He could tell she was tired, right on the edge of one of her narcoleptic meltdowns.

"At least," she went on, facing the sink with her hand propping her up, "I'm allowed to theorize about age-old corpses, where little me can't get hurt. Maybe there's some way I can do all that online instead of actually being there, seeing so much as historic artifacts."

"What? Claire, you've been through enough, and you have responsibilities," he said, getting up too and turning her toward him.

"I sure do! And one of them is to be partners with you, not like some secondary secretary, kept in a corner, hiding behind a laptop. Brad Vance won't let me see the real artifacts and you want me to stay in a gilded cage, a padded room!"

"Okay, okay. I'm sorry. Of course, I can use your expertise at Twisted Trees. You want to go with us to check the place out, that's fine," he said, holding up both hands as if she had drawn a gun on him and demanded his money or his life.

That night, thrusting aside the blackness of sleep, Claire climbed out of her grave and went to open a drawer to get more sleeping meds. But in the drawer lay a woman reaching out to her, a woman between two men.

"I feel I know you," she whispered to the woman. "Did you love them both?"

The woman nodded. "Caught between," she said. "Caught between and died for both. An affair of the heart, so I kept one."

Claire walked down the hall to Leader's office and took his dagger off the desk. She went back and clawed through the necklaces she kept inside the drawer. Where was that one with the polished stones, all broken now, broken…

She put one necklace around her neck and then another, another. One from Hunter years ago, one from Leader just last month. They weighed her down so much. Was she choking under the huge weight of the bog above her? Were they strangling her or stabbing her? She reached out and knocked the dagger away, no not the dagger, but something else…

"Claire. Claire, sweetheart, what is it? Why are you up?"

Her vision cleared. She stared into the dark mirror over the dresser. Nick was here, out of bed, holding her by the shoulders, pulling her to him. Leader was in the mirror, but Hunter was gone.

"Claire, it's all right. You haven't had a narcoleptic nightmare for a long time. Maybe you missed your meds."

She collapsed into his arms, holding tight.

"But why all the necklaces?" he asked.

"Don't know," she said, shaking. "Some dream, like you said. Maybe a nightmare."

"Here, let's take them off, put them back," he said, lifting them in one bunch from her neck and over her mussed head. "Maybe, my love, you were planning to go out on the town without me."

"Can't recall, but not that. Lexi—I should check on her."

"I'll look in on her. Here, back to bed."

He started to lead her that way but jolted and looked down into the grave—no, down at the floor. "What's that?" he asked, stooping to retrieve a dagger—no, of course it wasn't that. "Oh," he said, "the letter opener from my desk. You or Lexi must have brought it in, but I didn't see it here earlier."

She went back to bed, but she couldn't recall bringing the letter opener in here. Someone had taken it away, locked it up.

Under the sheet he pulled over her, she felt around her neck. No necklaces now, none broken or twisted. But how much that letter opener looked like a glowing, greenish dagger.

Early the next morning, when the sun was barely up, though Nick had wanted her to stay home in bed, Claire made sure she took her meds and went with him and Bronco to pick up Dale at his apartment and head for Twisted Tree. They stopped at his house and waited while he went inside to get a ring of keys his mother had once told him had unlocked all the doors in the mansion. If only it would unlock its secrets.

The doors to the main house were long gone, but one key on the ring would open the door to the standing building, Dale had said. But they'd have to pry off boards securing the single entryway first since the garage doors themselves had long been broken and would not lift.

Dale with his broken arm was no help, but Bronco and Nick pulled off the old boards with the claw part of two hammers. Dale handed the key ring to Nick, who tried key after key on the rusted lock of the door, until one worked. But it still took Bronco banging his shoulder against the door to get it open.

"Dusty in there," were Bronco's last words to them as they filed in and he went back to his vantage point under a crooked tree to be sure they weren't surprised or disturbed. They could hear him sneezing as they went single file inside.

The dust of decades made all three of them sneeze too and their eyes water. *"Heil Hitler,"* Dale muttered when they came across the first of several dust-covered, framed pictures of the long-dead dictator even on the wall of the small entry room. No wonder his parents had made sure this place stayed boarded up.

"Don't joke," Nick told him. "Damn, look at this!" he marveled as he dusted off the glass of the eight-by-ten color photo with his shirttail. It was of Hitler again—signed by him as simply *Adolph*. "Your great-uncle must have been a fanatic, but I guess many were."

"You don't think your great-uncle's mistress was also in love with Hitler?" Claire asked. "Or maybe that madman just thought everyone loved him and signed pictures that way, even for his SS friends like your great-uncle."

They stepped out of this small entry room into what was, no doubt, a garage large enough for three cars. An old Esso gas can, a few extra tires, nothing unusual. Whatever vehicles had been parked here were as long gone as any human inhabitants.

"Looks like the stairs to the apartment above are over there," Dale said, pointing with his good arm.

Claire could tell this was a tremendous strain on him, but then, her heart was pounding, and she reached out to hold Nick's arm. She had to be strong here, for she was the one who had insisted on coming along.

Dale led the way upstairs. The steps creaked in the best tradition of a haunted house. Another door blocked their way at the top of the flight. Dale tried the knob. Nick leaned forward to help. "Locked," Nick said. "Try your other keys, or we'll break it in."

Claire watched while the men fumbled with more keys. Then she recalled she had worn the small, bright flashlight around her neck which she'd admired on Kris and now had one of her own. She leaned around between the two men to shine it on the keys and the lock.

"I think that one worked," Dale muttered. Nick shoved, and the door opened. Claire squealed as a bat dove out and whipped past them.

"And it isn't even Halloween," Nick muttered, but no one laughed.

Dale went up the last step into a small slant-roofed apartment with two inset dormer windows which were not boarded up but were covered by heavy dark green velvet drapes. Seeing no lamps or lights, Claire pulled one pair of draperies open to reveal a set of sheer tattered curtains.

Wan morning sun streamed through them, half lace, half spider webs. The sagging, torn mattress on the narrow bed was full of mice, which jumped to the floor and skittered away. An armchair, a table, a sunken settee and a single shelf of books, all frosted with gray dust, completed the bedroom apartment, though the doors to an empty closet and a small bathroom with a claw-footed tub stood open.

Two things on the wall over the bed they simply gaped at. A red-and-white Nazi flag with a black swastika. And a framed photo of Hitler with a smiling, pretty blonde woman.

Dale gasped. "But that's my great-uncle's mistress!" he whispered. "I saw one picture of her before Mother ripped it up. She was standing with my uncle on the grounds here, not really smiling, looking sad. So she must have known Hitler, since they're in this picture together. Ha— Mother missed that one. But who knows what's still in the piles of stuff in her house Nita and Bronco said they'd get rid of? After that cursed freezer, no one went through any more items, though the police gave things a once-over, looking for blood or proof that Cyndi's murder happened on the premises—which they didn't find, couldn't prove. Surely she wasn't killed there."

Claire studied Dale's face instead of the photograph. He was so nervous yet defiant, talking too much as guilty people often did, but then that didn't mean he was guilty. She reached out with a tissue from her pocket to gently dust the photo. "Look," she said, leaning closer between the two men. "Along the bottom, near the frame. They've signed it to each other, 'Eva,' and over here, 'Adolph.'"

Dale looked stunned.

"Her name—the mistress—was Gretchen, not Eva."

"So this can't be your uncle's mistress," Nick said, his voice shaky. "Maybe your great-uncle knew Eva before he fled Germany. Are you sure the picture of him you saw once with Hitler's Eva wasn't taken in Germany?"

"No way—the picture I saw was taken here."

"But this can't be your uncle's mistress," Nick repeated. "I had Heck check out Eva Braun. He showed me a couple of pictures of her. The ones here are of her for sure, but Hitler finally married his mistress just a couple of days before they both committed suicide in a bunker in Berlin. Their burned bodies were found later by the Russians, who insisted the teeth in the charred remains matched."

"Yeah," Dale muttered, leaning his shoulder against the wall as if he just couldn't stand on his own anymore. "And we've seen—I think—how powdery bodies are when they get burned up to ashes."

"Unless she had a twin," Nick went on, "that picture, like the others in this place, are absolutely of Eva Braun herself, so they surely can't be your great-uncle's mistress. Or—or can they?"

CHAPTER TWENTY-ONE

Dale sounded more panicked than ever to Claire. "We've got to hide or destroy this stuff and get out of here!"

"Calm down," Nick told him, putting a hand on his uninjured arm. "This is priceless and important. I don't mean to sound like I'm on Marian James's side, but you can't just destroy amazing history like this."

"But you're my lawyer, my friend! I own all this now, and, like you said, we don't need all this hitting the media or the police so they think I was out to stop Cyndi to cover this up. I wasn't. I just wanted to get rid of— I mean, get her out of my life."

While the men continued to argue, Claire moved away and peeked in the bathroom. The tub had brown stains. The small mirror over the basin was dust-shrouded and cracked. The toilet lid had a crocheted cover, yellow with age, which seemed to fit with the cobwebs all over this place.

While Nick tried to calm Dale, she sidled around to peer in the closet. Lots of old wire hangers, nothing else.

She moved on and bent to read the titles of the ten or so books on the single shelf. Every title was in German, but one book looked like a ledger. She slid it out and blew it off. Inside was page after page of large, loopy handwriting, all in German.

She flipped through it, fanning dust so she sneezed again. She noted little drawings here and there. She closed the book and stuck it in the waist of her jeans in back, then settled her shirt over it.

"I have every right just to burn this place down," Dale was saying. "If that was Eva Braun in the picture here with Uncle Will, that could mean she visited here! People would be crawling all over this place. Nick, no way I can allow that, especially with the police looking for motives I could be hiding. And I don't need to be labeled some neo-Nazi in this mess of my life!"

"Let's lock up here, you go back to your apartment and think this through, unless you'd rather come into the firm with me today. We'll make a plan. Maybe you can donate these photographs anonymously, if we can just hold Marian James and her committee off for a while. You've obviously mixed up what you remember the mistress looked like with photos of Eva."

"All right. It was a couple of years ago when I saw that picture, so that must be it. But if Eva died with Hitler, she can't have visited here. I—my memory—I'm just confused. Then, maybe my great-uncle or his mistress just brought photos of Hitler and Eva here when he fled. I am taking your advice, leaning on you, Nick."

He turned to look at Claire. "And you, too, Claire. I'm grateful."

"We'll get to the truth," she told him.

He nodded, but she could sense he did not like the way she'd worded that.

Shortly after, they watched Bronco drive Dale away to his apartment as they still sat parked in their car on the street between Dale's house and Bronco and Nita's new one.

Nick said, "We're going to have to talk Bronco and Nita

into coming back to their house to clear out whatever's inside. Maybe we can help. We need proof that the mistress was not Eva Braun, and Dale's mother has lots of things stashed inside to look through."

"But I have a theory," she told him, sitting forward to pull out the notebook from the waistband of her jeans. "Nick, don't get upset, but I thought I'd better rescue this. It was wedged between what looked like some novels in German. I don't trust Dale not to go back inside and clear everything out, maybe destroy things. What if his great-uncle or his mistress wrote this?"

"Can you tell who that belonged to?" he asked, leaning closer.

"I can't read German, but surely we can find someone who can. Also," she said, pointing, "every so often, there are little sketches, and even they might tell a story. Like knowledge about the Black Bog people, this can rewrite history. Oh, look! A few of these entries are signed."

"By whom? Let me see."

She carefully turned pages and pointed to a signature: *Eva.*

"But that's impossible if Eva Braun's burned body was found. Unless this diary was written earlier and just brought here by Dale's great-uncle—if this signature is by Eva Braun."

"Remember, their bodies were found and burned by Hitler's enemy, the Russians. And are we even believing them these days? Maybe the Russians didn't want to admit they couldn't find her body. Here's my theory— Oh, who is that?" she cried, startling as a thin old lady with a dog on a leash knocked on their passenger-side window and waved.

"Close and hide that and stay put," he said, opening his driver's-side car door. He got out and shut it behind him.

Since the windows were up, Claire strained to catch the conversation.

"I saw Mr. Bronco Gates, the man who bought the house, was with you," the woman was saying. "Will they be moving back in after cleaning out poor Lucy's clutter?"

Ah, Claire thought, that must be Betty Richards, the woman who had identified Cyndi's frozen face and then talked to Nick later about Dale's mother. She hadn't met her, but there seemed to be something familiar about her.

She went on, "I take it the police haven't proved a thing against poor Dale, so I am happy for that, but then who hurt that poor woman? Well, I just want to tell you, Mr. Markwood, if Dale ever does go to trial, you can call on me to testify that Cyndi was not a nice person, you know, very rude to Dale's mother, not that she cared for that tart."

"I'm sorry to hear they didn't get along. Was there a specific instance you can recall that really showed that?"

"Why, more than one. I overheard Cyndi tell her she shouldn't live like a heathen—that was the very word she used. All her clutter should go out in the trash, Cyndi claimed, and then Lucy told her she was trash and she should be thrown out of Dale's life. Oh, is that your wife? Hello," she said louder with a smile and a wave through the glass. Claire was tempted to get out but she stayed put. Since Nick had evidently not wanted her in on this conversation she just waved and smiled, though it was getting warm in there with the windows up.

Claire waved back a second time to be certain the woman had seen her through the reflections on the glass. A busybody and perhaps a loose cannon, but she made a mental note to suggest to Nick that she talk to the woman sometime, maybe if she came with Nita to start weeding through decades of possessions again.

The woman finally walked away with her dog—actually, back to her house the way she had come, so was she really going for a walk, or had she spotted them and just wanted an excuse to talk to Nick? With her own mother and then in several of Nick's cases recently, eccentric, elderly women had inadvertently helped to solve problems. Was there something in the water in South Florida that produced Florida characters, only some of whom could be trusted?

Nick got back in, started the motor and air conditioner and drove away while they assessed "nosy Betty." But he pulled into Sugden Park off US 41 and parked where they could see the lake.

"This was where we had a picnic before we left for St. Augustine the first time we worked together," Claire said. "We are definitely not here for you to try to hire me this time, though, I believe, I have a piece of rare evidence here—evidence for something. Want to sit at a picnic table and let the view calm us down?"

"No, psych major. I'll leave the A/C on and we'll sit in here guarding that prime piece of evidence until you explain to me your theory about that diary or whatever it is. I'm going to leave the doors locked. Tell me—show me again—what you've found."

"Found and stolen. Well, let's say borrowed. I hope you'll be willing to defend me if Dale eventually brings charges," she said with a little laugh. They both unhooked their safety belts and leaned closer over the console, shoulder to shoulder. "Look, this Eva drew little doodle-like pictures, and they translate well."

She turned to the page that had caught her eye. It was laid out like a cartoon in three blocks. To the left in the first drawing, two figures clung together—one with a black, brushy mustache—crying tears yet smiling. They were sharing a bed. In the middle drawing the man waved to the woman as she boarded a crudely drawn airplane. The woman looked pregnant. In the picture on the right, the woman was alone reading a newspaper and crying so hard that—well, evidently, real tears had blurred that drawing and the words beneath. And a tiny baby was floating in a cloud drawn overhead, as if it were in the sky. Or in heaven.

They were both silent as Claire flipped through the other pages, but no other drawings seemed as important. Sketched egrets on a lawn under a twisted tree, like those which grew on the mansion grounds. A woman alone with open but empty arms.

And, at the very end of the book, the last page, though there were others left blank, a drawing of a woman drinking something and then that woman on a bed—maybe the single bed in the garage apartment—with her arms crossed over her chest and what looked like a framed picture clutched to her chest.

When Nick spoke, Claire was so into her racing thoughts that she jumped.

"She could be cradling that picture that's over the bed." He ignored his cell phone when it sounded. "What is your interpretation of all this?"

"Too early to tell, but, for some reason, Hitler must have sent Eva Braun away before he died."

"But the Russians found two burned bodies."

"But like I asked before, do you believe that? Staging that would be easy enough, just kill and burn some innocent bystander or pull one out of the ruins of Berlin. But Hitler and Eva must have thought she was pregnant with his child, and the so-called *Fuhrer* wanted his heir to live. To come back to Germany in triumph someday when all was lost at that earlier time? I know this sounds crazy, but I've been theorizing that Reaching Woman might have been married—belonged somehow—to one of the men she was entombed with, but became pregnant by the other. But back to Eva Braun. Perhaps the baby died—a miscarriage, something. When she lost Hitler and her heir, she killed herself in that apartment. Maybe Dale's uncle had been ordered to hide and protect her and then he had to bury her. Nick, we've got to get this translated, carefully, privately."

"But it's Dale's property."

"And he'd no doubt like to destroy it. This Hitler's heir possibility is more of a bombshell than simply Eva escaping and some other woman taking her place in a suicide pact so that two burned bodies would be found. Do you think Dale could have killed Cyndi? Maybe she was pressing about getting in to see what we saw today. Maybe she was even blackmailing him about his Hitler connection, however distant and long past. Maybe he knows more about all this than he's telling. Can we get this diary locked in the safe at the firm and have someone who can read it come there?"

He heaved a huge sigh that seemed to deflate him.

"Nick, I can take this on myself. I took the journal while you two were talking. I didn't tell you until later—all true. So I can claim I'm the one who had it translated before telling you what it said. You know, I'm pretty sure Kris could wade through this. She had some high school German, and I think she picked up more when she lived in Europe those early years on digs."

"If you can trust her."

"Of course. I'd better. And she obviously knows how to keep a secret, with all her work at Black Bog."

She kept silent a moment, watching Nick agonize over this dilemma. Brad Vance had strongly questioned her own pledge to keep the work there secret, had even said she might have to withdraw from her contract if she was targeted with more publicity. But she didn't have to go public with this. If she and Kris could verify her theory, surely this diary could be handed over to historians, or even the government, anonymously.

But this was so important—as key, in a way, as the discoveries at Black Bog. She held her breath.

"All right, ask Kris if she can come to the office tonight to have a look at this when everyone's gone. But we'll at least have to tell Dale what she finds."

"Isn't there some moral law about something being so important for history—for the knowledge of all mankind—that what someone owns really belongs to humanity?"

"I'll look into it. Sounds like international law to me, not my forte, though, sometimes lately, I'm not sure what is. Damned if I want to defend a man who has been sitting on this for years, and who had motive, means and opportunity to murder a woman. But we're in deep, sweetheart, and getting deeper. I'm sorry I wanted to keep you out of this."

"Apology accepted. We're better working together on things, have been since we first sat at that picnic table over there, and you offered me a job—and I found a new life."

They kissed, then refastened their seat belts before he drove them back out to the highway. Of course, she thought, getting in deep and deeper had caused them problems before, but together they would work through this, like resurrecting human ashes from the bombed-out ruins of Berlin years ago or bodies in a South Florida bog days ago.

CHAPTER TWENTY-TWO

After Lexi was in bed that night—and had been reassured again that Jace loved her—Claire took a shower, then hovered over her laptop. She wanted to do more research on Eva Braun, but she was looking into Cynthia Lindley again for Nick.

"Bingo!" she cried after she'd gone down many a rabbit trail, rereading parts of the woman's Facebook page, then finding Cyndi on LinkedIn, talking about "her dream job." *I think I will be a fabulous salesperson for luxury real estate, here in beautiful Naples! I will soon have some high-class backing from a member of a committee that preserves historic sights, maybe more than one influential sponsor!*

No doubt she was referring to Marian James, but more than one backer? So was Marian lying that she only received Cyndi's recorded phone message and could not respond? Or was Cyndi lying here?

And—amazing! Pictures accompanied the post that had to be of the overgrown lawn at Twisted Trees with ficus trees and more distant palms in the background, though the ruined mansion was not in the picture. The next photo showed Cyndi standing in front of a large modern mansion with palm trees. Behind her, on the lush lawn was a for sale sign. The implication was there, though it was a lie. The Twisted Tree grounds hardly had that stunning home on it.

And the picture looked like a very good selfie, maybe one made with a selfie stick or one of those new little drones that took photographs, obviously a drone much smaller than the one that had crashed into the country club window.

In the photo, Cyndi stood in front of the sign. She had positioned herself perfectly to block out the name of the Realtor and the phone number, so there was no way to follow up to see if she had managed to get a job somewhere, which Claire doubted. No one had evidently come forward when she was murdered to say she'd worked for a particular firm—unless Ken Jensen was not telling them everything.

Or perhaps Marian had lied and had actually talked to Cyndi instead of just receiving her recorded message. Had Cyndi bargained with Marian to get an in with a posh real estate office here in town for the promise of help with her access to Twisted Trees? Or was this all just an egotistical lie from Cyndi, pie in the sky to build herself up? The woman was starting to sound more and more unbalanced and aggressive.

She ran to get Nick.

Claire did not go to Black Bog the next day, but stayed home with Trey and tried to bolster Nita's self-confidence. She had agreed to move back into her and Bronco's house for the coming weekend to clean the place out. That way, Bronco wouldn't be working and could be there to help, and Nick and Claire could pitch in some too. Until then, Claire had Black Bog work she could do at home, namely going through her voluminous handwritten notes, trying to puzzle out a theory about the trio. Also, she, Nick and Kris were going to meet at the law offices tonight after the staff left to take a look at what they were calling *Eva's Diary*.

Trey was asleep in his bassinet in the shade on the back patio table next to her while she searched for even more about Cyndi online. Nick had been astounded at what she'd found last night, though they'd decided not to blindly call any of the dozens of local real estate firms. He planned to call Ken Jensen to see if his team had turned up these clues, but she knew Nick was dragging his feet. No way he wanted her work to be more admired by the police department so they'd try to hire her as a forensic psychologist.

Today, Claire was looking under both the dead woman's names, her real one, Cynthia Linschwartz, and her chosen but evidently not legal name, Cynthia Lindley.

So what else had the woman been willing to lie about? Nick had been amazed and ecstatic last night that Claire had found what must be a mention of Marian James. He had agreed with her questions: was Marian lying about whether the two women had made contact? Had something gone awry in the meeting and Cyndi ended up dead?

But now, it seemed both lines of research had come to a dead end. Maybe Heck could take this further as he was better at online detecting than she'd ever be. If Heck's dream job to work for a facial recognition tech team—the rec tech team, as he called it—was too dangerous, maybe he could be the one to consult with the Naples police. As for her, it was time to turn her thoughts to theories, based on facts, of course, about the trio in the Black Bog grave.

But Trey picked that very moment to wake up and fuss. She fed him a bottle and walked around the pool, holding him against her shoulder. Could there have been a child involved in the trio's lives? If there had been a love triangle between Reaching Woman and the two men, whose baby had she carried? Who belonged to whom, if their culture had recognized some form of marriage? The woman's deerskin clothing matched Hunter's, so had she fallen for Leader when her man was out hunting? But the broken necklace was more like Leader's bracelet. Or had she been

Leader's mate, then had fallen for Hunter and so it was decreed she would be dressed like him and die with him as punishment?

But how and why had Leader died and been interred with them? Could it have been natural causes and so, with his eyes wide open, his people had honored him to lie with the woman he loved? But why did Hunter's executed body lie there too and why was his heart with the woman's body?

She jolted when Nita's voice came close. "Want me to take him for a while, so you can work?"

"I'm thinking while I walk."

"Okay. I will go back to making lists. I thought at first to keep some of the furniture in the house at least, but now I don't know."

"Did you sleep some, Nita?" she asked as her friend turned away to go back inside.

She shook her head and shrugged. "Some, I guess. Claire, I'll go back there, help everyone by cleaning that place out, looking for things—clues—like you said. But her face frozen in that silent scream still scares me. At least the freezer will be gone soon."

"I understand. It still scares me too," Claire said, wishing she could share with Nita how the trio of bog faces, especially the woman's, haunted her. And Leader's open eyes, as if he wanted a last glimpse of the woman he was buried next to, while she reached out toward him and the executed Hunter, who had paid with his life for some terrible deed or act.

"We both need to be brave and find answers," Claire told her friend. Nita, of course, thought she meant about their house a hoarder had left littered with a lifetime of things. But she meant so much more.

"I can't believe you brought Lexi even if it's not a school night," Nick whispered to Claire as they got set up in his office to have Kris look at the German diary.

"She needs to be with us now that she's upset about not see-

ing Jace. Besides, she'll be content looking up butterfly pictures
and information for a two-minute talk she has to give in school
about her favorite animal."

"Yeah, but that has to be her horse, Scout. As soon as I can,
I'll take her over to the stable stall we rented. Ever since she fell
in love with that little dude when we were hiding out in Michigan, it's been like therapy for her to be near him and ride him."

"Right, but she talked her teacher into letting her mention
two animals, so butterflies are in also. Ms. Gerald is ecstatic
someone else cares about butterflies. I think she's a real fanatic."

"Nice they have that connection," Nick told her. "So, Kris,
how much German did you have?"

"Three years in high school until I came to my senses. A very
hard language with huge, long nouns. But I was glad I could
speak it later and came to like it. Speaking of Hitler as she does
here, it was amazing how he screamed his speeches, and an entire nation followed a man like that."

"Can you tell what the writer's attitude toward him is—was?"
Nick asked, sitting on her other side.

"She adored him. She says she wanted to bear his prince—
and then—right here, see," she said, pointing to the page with
the telltale crude pictures. "She says she's pregnant, but he says
she has to leave him to save their child if the fatherland falls."

Nick and Claire stared wide-eyed and speechless and at each
other.

"Something here," Kris said, frowning at the loopy, cursive
penmanship, "about how they could not stay together, despite
their death vow, because if they were taken or killed, the baby,
Hitler's heir, could be too."

"Worrying about the baby but not her—except as the child's
mother?" Claire asked.

"Not sure. There's so much here, frenzied thoughts, on and
on. Strange, isn't it?" she said, finally looking off into the distance
and blinking back tears. "Here I've found a man who wants to

date me—and I him. Mitch sounded so great on the phone, so steady, even when he explained that he had some things to settle before he could ask me out and it wasn't another woman." The corners of her mouth lifted in a wistful smile.

"Then I saw him in the newspaper," she went on, "good-looking, macho—and read that article about him taking yet another dangerous job, and I understood. One has to follow one's passions no matter what the strictures or sacrifices. That's what's going on in this sad, trapped, pitiful woman's life, Eva Braun," she whispered, looking down at the diary again.

Nick shifted position, and Claire said, "I'm wondering if that conflict is ageless. That maybe the ancient people we've been studying had exactly that sort of conflict."

"If so," Kris said, refocusing and frowning, "it didn't go well for them, did it? Well, let me skim through the rest of this and see what else I can figure out."

Though Claire continued to sit beside Kris, Nick, bless him, instead of hovering, went over to talk to Lexi and look at her butterfly pictures on the laptop screen. He had set it up so that she could use his printer to get pictures of "the prettiest ten of them."

"What else?" Claire prompted as Kris seemed to puzzle overlong at the last pages of increasingly shaky scribbles in the diary.

"You don't need to speak German to see it," Kris told her, pointing at a page Claire leaned over. "You had to take a handwriting analysis course in your forensic tech studies, didn't you?"

"Yes, and I still have my notes from the class."

"Well, see how Eva's handwriting is degrading here? See this squiggle like she might have dropped off to sleep more than once? And she says she's depressed. Life is not worth living since there is no baby, Hitler's dead and the dream of the *Reich* is gone."

"Does she say the child died?"

"I don't know," she said as Nick came quickly back when he saw them whispering. "It's like—like it just vanished inside her, she says."

"Like a false pregnancy or phantom pregnancy?"

"Maybe. I think it's technically called a hysterical pregnancy—Weird term, huh?"

Nick said, "Maybe she felt guilty she'd misled Hitler about the baby. Maybe she actually wished she'd stayed to die with him."

Squinting at the page, Kris nodded. "She keeps repeating this defiant phrase over and over—see here: '*Wir Schaffen das!*' That means 'We can do it!'"

"But do what?" Nick asked.

"She evidently asked—begged," Kris said, "her guardian here in Florida from Hitler's *Schutzstaffel* staff—his SS elite troops—to get her some poison. The *Fuhrer* had shot himself, but she wanted to take poison. Her contact here said no at first, but now—I mean back then—she thinks he will do it. She must mean so she can commit suicide."

Claire saw Nick startle at that last word. He'd spent years trying to prove his own father had not shot himself. He'd finally done that, made the murderer pay, but the horror of finding his dad dead still haunted him.

"That last drawing," Claire said, "must be how she envisioned her death, maybe how she staged it. See, she's cradling that monster's picture to her breasts, lying on the bed we saw, Nick."

"As Claire told you, Kris," he said, "this all has to be top secret, but I know you understand that."

"I sure do. Secret for secret then."

"Unless this backfires and I get hit with attorney misconduct charges over mishandling this," Nick muttered, almost to himself. "But I hope my client won't see our taking and reading this book as a betrayal. I'm going to level with him."

"Kris, we can't thank you enough," Claire said, giving her a one-armed hug. "It's great to have someone we can trust in this delicate matter."

"No one would believe me anyway," she said with a little shake of her head. "Wish our bog people would have left diaries or drawings, but we'll have to go on body language—one of your strengths, Claire."

"Don't I wish."

"Mommy, do you and Kris want to see my favorite ten butterflies? But I think it's so sad people catch them in nets, and then they die or get cold in a refrigerator till their babies hatch, and they get stuck dead under a picture frame, and then people just study them."

"Ouch," Claire whispered as she got up from the table and Kris handed the diary back to Nick to lock up in his safe. "My darling daughter doesn't know it, but she just nailed what's sad about what we do, Kris."

"That's partly why what we do is a huge secret, even from those we love," Kris whispered back with a quick glance at Nick. "If anyone talks, and Andrea or Senator Vance find out, then we all get to take something like poor Eva's poison pill. Sorry, not funny, but you know what I mean. Sure," Kris said in a loud voice. "I'd love to see your butterfly pictures. I want to see if I can tell them apart."

"This one here is the monarch because he is king," Lexi said, pointing at the bright orange-and-black butterfly. "The men ones are way prettier than the lady ones, which isn't fair."

Claire's thoughts blurred as Lexi displayed picture after picture. She understood why nature tried to hide the females so they would not be attacked since they carried the next generation. The males in charge again, the males like Leader, dressed more grandly than Reaching Woman, although she too had worn beautiful stones on her necklace, very much a match for his broken bracelet. A love gift? A sign of possession?

And like the tragedy of Eva Braun's life, could Reaching Woman have chosen to join the man she loved in death? But if so, was that Hunter or Leader?

CHAPTER TWENTY-THREE

To clear her head, Claire did not go out to the bog on Saturday, but went to the beach. It had been only two weeks since they had found Cyndi's body, but it seemed like an eternity. She had to cut off all her internal diversions: mourning for their ruined reception; the tragedy of Cyndi's murder and Dale's problems; Jace and possibly Heck being in danger.

She wanted to focus only on the Black Bog trio right now.

It wasn't a sunny day, which helped her find a parking place near the big tourist draw of the Naples Pier, shops and restaurants, and one of the longest stretches of sand and waves in the area. Actually, Brad and Andrea Vance's Art for Art's Sake shop was just a block away. Though they were probably both at the bog, maybe she'd pop in to the shop later. But right now she needed solitude and soul-searching, not of her own soul but of Reaching Woman's.

Claire locked her car and, as was her habit, since they'd been through so much, looked around to be sure she wasn't being watched or followed. At least the thin person had not appeared again.

She walked out on the pier, glad there were some strollers and fishermen around. As ever, the pelicans sat on the slanted shingle roofs or rode the waves, hoping to be tossed pieces when the fishermen cleaned their catch.

At the end of the pier, feeling that she was almost walking the waves in the warm wind, she propped her hands on the wooden railing and stared out into the gulf.

She tried to clear her other concerns away, but were there similarities to Reaching Woman's demise in Eva Braun's tragic tale? Even in her own life, caught between Jace and Nick, though she'd made her choice and adored her husband? Or her own parents' tragedy: her father's desertion of their family and her mother's retreating into agoraphobia, buried in books, ignoring the needs of her daughters. But what was the centuries-old story of the trio?

She decided to write a short journal entry from the point of view of each ancient person. Creative writing, but informed by what she knew about the facts of the Black Bog burials. And she wouldn't do that where there were distractions at home or at her office in Black Bog. She would do it right here in the paper notebook stuffed in her purse. She'd channel them in a way from their dark past.

But she heard a rumble of thunder and saw a circle of rain out in the gulf. Well, then, she'd just sit in her car. Let the rain pound down, because, at last, thoughts were pounding in her head.

"You didn't get word they are going to arrest me, did you?" Dale demanded the minute he entered Nick's office and closed the door. "I just got here, and Cheryl said you wanted to see me. Thanks for coming in on a Saturday."

"Nothing yet about an arrest, so calm down. Actually, no news from Detective Jensen is good news. I just need to explain something I've learned about Cyndi which I thought you might be able to throw light on, but something else too about what was in the Twisted Trees apartment. Let's sit over at the table.

"I need to have you trust me on this new turn of events," Nick told him when they were seated. "By the way," he added, "did Bronco drive you here or—"

"Told him I'd drive myself. I'm careful even though I look like a mess and can only use one hand. What's new then?" he asked, leaning forward, then shifting farther back in his seat as if he were afraid to hear.

"Really, two things. For one, Claire has done more research on Cyndi—not Facebook this time, but LinkedIn."

"She spent too damn much time online. Obsessed with social media, like an unreal world she could control when she couldn't control the real one. In her mind, she had a claim to fame, right up there with the Kardashians. Never knew about LinkedIn, but I checked out her Facebook page once with all her sexy pictures. Then I was stupid enough to prefer the real thing. So what did Claire find?"

Claire was right, Nick thought. Dale seemed to put up a buffer of a lot of words sometimes, which she'd said was a tendency of people trying to hide something.

"Do you have any knowledge about Cyndi wanting to be a real estate agent?" Nick asked. "Or that she pursued that as a career here in Naples?"

"Not that she actually did it, though I can recall a couple of times she brought it up. Piece of cake, she thought, showing rich people luxury real estate like houses on Gordon Drive or in Grey Oaks or Pelican Bay."

"But she never worked for a real estate office? There are enough of them around here."

"Not unless she did it secretly."

"I'm just trying to learn who she came in contact with who could have hurt her. We can hardly phone all the Realtors in town and ask if she worked there."

"What's the second thing you have to tell me?" Dale prompted.

"Okay. Eva Braun kept a diary in German, which was wedged in with the few dusty books in the manor house apartment.

Claire and I thought it should be in our possession to inform us and protect you."

"I—I don't read German," he said, gripping his cast in his free hand. The fingers protruding from the cast looked bruised and swollen. "Granted, I heard a lot of it when I was young."

"As your lawyer," Nick went on, "I had someone read the diary. There are several crude drawings too. The gist of it is that Eva Braun and Hitler believed she was pregnant. He sent her away from Germany by plane in the last days of the war, probably right after he married her. She must have come to South Florida with your great-uncle, who had probably sworn to protect her and the child."

"The idea of Hitler's heir is horrible! The child—it's not someone in my family?"

"As best we can tell, there was no child."

"She lied? Or miscarried?"

"Unless she made it up just to get out of Germany before it fell, which we doubt, as she adored Hitler. It might have been that she had false signs of pregnancy, which would be understandable if she—they—desperately wanted a child, and with all the stress they were under at the end. At some point, after she was at Twisted Trees and knew Hitler was dead and there would be no child, she evidently took poison on the bed in the apartment."

"I—I can't believe it! I'll bet she was like—like a holy Madonna to him. I— This is a bigger bombshell than just knowing she lived at Twisted Trees after the war, after she'd lost everything."

Nick nodded. Tears clung to Dale's eyelashes and flew when he blinked. It touched Nick that he could care about Eva, instead of just hate her. He'd have to tell Claire that and ask if he could fake this emotion.

"You have the diary?" Dale asked.

"Locked in a safe place for now."

"And it was there all that time. Dad and Mother should have gone in and destroyed it."

"We're not going to destroy it. We're certainly not going to announce it to the world right now, but since you have not been arrested—"

"Yet."

"They must not have a case against you, and Cyndi's brother and her former fiancé being missing makes it look like they are on the run. So we're just going to wait this out, and I'll try to reason with Marian James and her committee to lay off publishing pictures of the ruined mansion right now. Maybe we can make her a deal to get some coverage later, once Cyndi's murderer is found."

"Nick, if Marian James put two and two together on this—that Eva Braun was here—there would be hell to pay."

"Instead of just attorney's fees, right?" he said, putting his hand on Dale's good shoulder. "You know, as a member of this firm, you have the right to our defense gratis. You did read the fine print in your initial contract, right?"

"I did, but I suppose I'd be better off with an outside firm. That is, people might think you're defending me just because I'm in the family. You know, nepotism so to speak."

"Are you thinking of other representation?"

"No."

"Then my only caveat right now is that I keep Eva's diary locked up so you can truly say you have never seen it, if it comes to that. Back to work, junior partner. I'm buried too."

As Dale left, Nick wished he hadn't put it quite that way. Claire was getting obsessed with the bog bodies she was studying, and he was afraid they had caused her waking nightmare last night. And the Black Bog ancients didn't write diaries to tell how they lived or died.

Sitting in the driver's seat of her car with her open notebook propped up on the steering wheel, Claire stared at the empty sheet of paper.

Then she began to write. For Hunter, she wrote, *I was proud to hunt to help feed my woman and my people, though I had to be gone a lot. Often in danger too. I made traps. I used my dagger. I carried or dragged meat back to our village for the feasts. I gained praise from Leader. I looked up to him. My woman was proud too and happy when I made her a warm garment like mine from the hides of deer. She was my woman but when I came home, I started to see how her eyes followed him. She had a new necklace, made from fine stones like those in his bracelet.*

For Leader, Claire wrote, *Because I was clever and could explain things well in stories and had a good memory, I became the leader of the village, so I never told anyone I had heart pains at times. I sent people to fetch medicinal bark, to catch fish and turtles and to hunt. I decided who could carve well, especially to make my staff of leadership. I accepted the special striped robes that told everyone who I was. I could have any woman I wanted, and I wanted Hunter's mate. I had to be certain that if she had a child, it was mine, so I sent him far away to hunt the elusive panther. I gave him a fine dagger for protection, but I sometimes wished he would not come back. But he did and found my woman and me together. And the pains in my chest and heart hit me as hard as he did.*

For Reaching Woman, Claire wrote, *My father gave me to Hunter, and he was good to me. But then Leader saw me swimming and came to me in the water. He asked for me and I went. Everyone knew. Everyone but Hunter until he came home and found us. Hunter meant to stab Leader, but he cut deep into my chest. The necklace Leader had given me fell away, and I did too. I did not die right away but heard Leader and Hunter mourning me. Leader fell down from grief, because he had lost me and the child. Or did he hate himself for decreeing Hunter's terrible death for my murder? I raised my hands to hold them both when the oth-*

*ers rushed in. And then my love for both and my sadness in death
made everything I ever knew go dark.*

"I can't believe this," Claire whispered to herself as she sat in
her car, and the sun surprised her by slanting in when the rain
was gone. What she had written might or might not be true,
but she felt it strongly, almost as if she had channeled these ancient people's thoughts.

Suddenly, she had to get out of the car. Out of this strange
mood. Out of the tragedy that must have taken three lives. As
fascinating as her work with the bog people was, she had to get
out of this depression and obsession they pulled her into.

She jammed her notebook back in her purse. She'd just take
a walk before she went home in time to meet Lexi's school bus.
She'd take a look at the Vances' shop, maybe pop in to say hello
to whoever staffed it.

She opened the car door and got out. The breeze was fresh,
the sun warm. It was good to be alive, good to be Claire Markwood, living in the twenty-first century.

She glanced once behind her, then looked around, ready to
dive back into the car if she saw anyone suspicious among strolling tourists, bicycles or cars.

Nothing unusual. She locked the car and headed down the street.

CHAPTER TWENTY-FOUR

Claire's reflection on the front window of the Vances' store stared back at her as she studied one of the most attractive displays she'd ever seen. Such interesting items, so beautifully arranged on several velvet-draped levels: an elaborate bird cage, silk flowers, spills of pearl necklaces and small silk-lined jewelry boxes. The wording in a gilded arch over the top of the window read Art for Art's Sake, Antique Jewelry and Bibelots.

"Bibelots?" she whispered. "Do most people know what they are? Do I?"

Her mother would have known not only what that word meant but could probably cite ten historical novels where the word appeared.

Maybe, she thought, the intrigue of that word alone brought some people in—or scared off others. No, shoppers for this elegant, upscale store must know exactly what they wanted.

An old-fashioned bell over her head tinkled when she went in. No other customers right now, just a silver-haired man who must be a salesman. He had a neatly clipped mustache and wore a bow tie with his pinstriped, long-sleeved shirt with cufflinks and a garter on one sleeve. She decided she'd best just say she knew the Vances but not from where.

"Hello," the man called out to her and came closer, still behind the counter near the front display case, which looked old-fashioned with curved glass over display items. Behind that were modern, better-lit cases including some jewelry displays. What she would call antique knick-knacks made up the back three-quarters of the store's front room.

"And how may I help you?" he asked with a smile. "Bibe-lots is my bailiwick, jewelry too, unless it's one of the marked Victorian pieces in this case. In that case," he said with a little smile at his pun, "I will ask our collector's expert and jewelry designer to join us."

"Actually, I don't have a specific item in mind," she told him as her eyes skimmed the amazing array of china, brass, marble, iron and other unique items. "I'm a friend of the Vances and just wanted to pop in to see their store."

"Ah, both busy people. Have you met them through the university—her former work—or his political career?"

"A little of this and that, which is what I see you have on display here."

"Our latest offerings are doing quite well among collectors," he said with a sweep of his arm, leading her toward the second lighted case. "These are all authentic pieces of Victorian mourning jewelry, with miniature photos of the dearly departed hidden within as well as locks of their hair—quite common in that time period. Of course, if you are really among the cognoscenti of any of our offerings, we have other items under lock and key we could share a look at."

He unlocked the black velvet-lined case with the mourning jewelry and reached in to hold up a chain dangling a gold locket with fancy filigree. "See," he said as he clicked the locket open, "a daguerreotype of the widow's deceased husband and a lock of his hair to remember him by."

An involuntary shudder wracked Claire. "Different customs for different times. I hope you don't mind if I just look around."

"Of course not, and I shall tell the Vances—Senator Vance comes in far more often than she—that we were visited by..."

"Claire Markwood."

The velvet curtain to the back room swept open, and a slender woman appeared. "I thought I heard voices. Too much staring at glass Murano beads for now, so I popped out to show a customer our latest historical beadwork..."

"This is Ms. Markwood, Pippa," the man said quickly. "She knows the Vances."

"They're great, aren't they?" she asked as her face lit up. "They've given me the opportunity to design for them. I'm Pippa Lee," she said, extending her hand across the counter. It was a delicate hand, Claire thought as she shook it.

Pippa talked about the art, antiques and jewelry stores in the area and mentioned that the Vances' Fort Lauderdale store by this same name was much larger. "And," she added, "they have a very talented jewelry designer there."

"As we do here," the still nameless salesman put in.

"Thank you, Reggie."

In a way, this woman reminded Claire of her sister—lively, petite, even down to her pixie-like haircut. Pippa the pixie, Claire mused, quite enjoying their chat until Pippa pointed to a small display at the very back of the shop that was labeled in flowing, old-fashioned script: Inspired by the Ancients.

Within lay several large agate bead necklaces and bracelets, not crudely done but with much more polished banded stone in more colors than the ones from the Black Bog graves. Yet they were so reminiscent of the items Claire had glimpsed before Andrea swept them away—and of Brad's slides of the enlarged, priceless items. Her mind raced. Did Brad quickly hide the grave artifacts so they could be copied—or even sold? Too late now, but she should have pursued a glance at whatever this store offered for the so-called cognoscenti. Was that some password to view even more expensive historic jewelry?

"What ancients were the inspiration for these?" Claire asked.

"Just in the *style* of the ancients," Pippa said. "I take inspiration from many cultures, Inca, Egyptian, Celtic, an amalgam. I do these from study sketches and my imagination."

"Oh, I see," Claire said and forced herself to inquire about some of the metal coin banks on display. But her imagination was running rampant. Brad Vance had just become more interesting and yet more mysterious.

"Can I just walk you to your car, boss?" Heck asked, appearing so suddenly in the nearly empty parking lot behind the law firm that Nick startled. He'd been worried about Claire and Kris possibly being followed, but he'd been unable to convince his stubborn wife not to go off by herself today. She'd insisted she needed the "think time." But did he have to start watching himself to see if he was being followed?

"Didn't know you were here," Nick said.

"I called your place, and Nita said you'd come in here, though it's Saturday. You're working late, boss, but didn't want to bother you till you were done. Been sitting over in my car. I just need to bounce an idea off you real fast, if you got a minute."

"For you, my friend, of course. Want to go back in?"

"How 'bout we just sit on that picnic table people eat lunch at sometimes?"

"And breakfast and dinner. Lots going on here as usual."

Heck nodded and slid into the bench across the table from Nick and said, "On second thought, is it okay with you if we don't sit out here, boss? I mean since that drone broke the windows and broke up your party, I been antsy about being in plain sight."

"Let's go back inside then."

They got up, and Nick dug his master key out again. This

whole thing was making him not as much scared as angry. He'd thought he was done looking over his shoulder, but now this. Damn, if someone was after Claire or any of them, he had to be more careful. He'd been thinking too hard to be careful.

He locked the door behind them, and they sat at one of the two small tables Bronco used when he was working security. The one in the front lobby was a lot nicer than this one.

"Tell me," he said to Heck.

"That friend of Claire's—Kris Kane. She has face blindness, right? I heard her explaining some of it and looked it up—formal name is prosopagnosia."

"Right."

"I'm thinking of researching it better, maybe talking to her about it if you or Claire could set that up. And I'm thinking of steering clear of that face recognition tech firm I was interested in. Maybe I could go out on my own in a small way at first—not leaving my consulting job with you. What if I could invent some kind of eyeglasses or something that read people's faces, then with an earpiece informed the wearer of that device who the person approaching them was?"

"Interesting!" Nick told him, leaning closer. "And a real help to someone like Kris. Claire says, as intelligent and successful as she is, her face blindness always held her back, always made her a bit afraid of people. Who knows, maybe that's one reason she works in archaeology, with people who won't be offended, right?"

"Right," he said with a sheepish smile. "So then I'm hoping you could draw up some official resignation letter from this consulting company's job offer. I didn't sign nothing yet. *Caramba*, if I'm the target of what could have been a deadly drone, I think there must be some kind of spy in that organization. Or maybe a competitor who wants to do them and me in. If I make a big deal about declining the offer, maybe it will take me off that hit list—if someone's after me."

"Sounds like a plan, a good one."

"Gotta admit I took the idea from Jace and his pilot friend going public."

"I'll draw the letter up and have Cheryl type it up and see that it's hand delivered Monday morning after you sign it."

"Whew! I'm just gonna lay low till then since I can't see Gina this weekend anyway. She's working in the campus clinic."

"You have this tech firm's address and contact person?" Nick asked, digging out a ballpoint pen. "Good move to examine who might want to hurt you. I'm looking through old cases where someone was disgruntled or worse and blamed me, but nothing so far. Man, I'd like to think Claire and I are out of the line of fire for once."

"Claire, Kris is here!" Nita called to her.

Claire had just changed Trey's diaper when the doorbell rang, but, with him in her arms, she came into the Florida room to greet her friend.

"Want me to take Big Boy?" Nita asked. "I'm glad we put off going over to our house until tomorrow, since Nick went in to work."

Claire knew that Nita was especially glad to put off facing their house until after the freezer was gone. Nick had received per-mission from the police to get rid of it, though they were going to put it in a storehouse in case they arrested a suspect for Cyndi Lindley's murder and wanted to use it as evidence for a trial.

"Sure, thanks, Nita," she said, shifting Trey to her.

"He's a good baby, isn't he?" Kris asked, putting her finger into his hand. When he grasped her finger, she bounced it a bit, and he gurgled in delight. "Can't say I know much about babies," Kris said, studying his face almost wistfully. "Maybe someday."

Claire lowered her voice. "Trey's even better than Lexi was, but she's going through a stage right now. Let's sit down," she said as Nita carried Trey out. "You look happy." Claire wanted to find out what Kris knew about the Vances' store, but she didn't want to break what she sensed was her friend's really good mood.

"I just had a first date with Mitch Blakeman, and it was great."

"Wow! I thought he told you he'd have to call you later to be sure he's not the one that drone was aimed at. He must figure that newspaper article about moving on to hurricane hunting is insurance."

"We did a special ops date, he called it. Low-key. Unexpected. Out of town in a place no one would target for us. Claire, we went—get ready for this—ice skating at the Germaine Arena, where the Florida Everblades hockey team plays! They give ice skating lessons there and have an open rink during Saturdays if the team's not playing and they aren't converting it into a concert venue for the evening."

"You ice skate?"

"I do now. Mitch once lived in Minnesota and he's good. He held me up, if you know what I mean. Holding hands, arm around my waist."

"Oh, that's a riot. An ice skating first date in South Florida when it's near eighty! How romantic."

"I thought so too. And he met me there so we weren't in a car together. He told me he'd have on a bright green shirt so I would know him. Wasn't that kind? I guess I sound like a teenager, but I don't care—except about him."

Her friend looked so starry-eyed that Claire decided to ask her about the Vances' art stores on Monday. She just couldn't bear to change the glow and the near giddiness.

"I'm going to get two glasses of wine, and we're going to drink to that," she told Kris. "Those flyboys can make you fly pretty high!"

She stood and turned to go into the kitchen and saw Nick had come in. He was just standing there, listening to them. What she'd just said—she hoped he didn't take it wrong.

"Glad you're home," she said, trying not to sound nervous. "Kris was just telling me she had a first date with Mitch."

"Great!" He gave Kris a wave, then lowered his voice so only Claire could hear. "Sure got to watch out for those flyboys."

Even when Claire told Nick about her day writing short entries to psych out bog people and checking out the Vances' shop, there was an unspoken icy chill in the air. He said no more to her about Heck's idea to invent his own facial recognition solution, though he had asked Kris if she'd be on board to help him test it out, and she'd happily agreed. Surely, Nick didn't think his own wife was still in love with Jace, Claire agonized. Tension between them made her want to scream. Rather than just go to bed uneasy or hardly speaking, she decided to clear the air.

"Nick, it's just that I feel bad for Jace lately. Not seeing Lexi. More or less separated from Brit against their wishes when they were planning a wedding."

"I know. Don't worry, I'm just tired."

"And overworked. And worrying about Dale, because you're afraid he's guilty. I'm sorry if I upset you," she said, walking behind him and wrapping her arms around his waist. He was wearing only the shorts he slept in and, wearing only a silk nightgown herself, she could feel each tight muscle in his back.

He turned in her arms and hugged her hard to him. "I know I get overpossessive," he whispered, burying his mouth in her hair. "I've nearly lost you more than once, and I worry. Now that we're a family—I honestly don't want you to just stay home but—well, I guess I do, but you shouldn't. You're talented, you're helping people. Honestly, sweetheart, I'm proud of you, but I just can't stand the idea of your being hurt again."

"Understood. Nick, we'll see all this through just as we have bad times before. I was really shook at our belated wedding reception being blown up—like it was an omen—but we persevere, don't we? Our love makes us strong and—"

He had just put his hands down to cup her bottom and pull her even tighter against him when his cell phone on the dresser rang.

"I'll ignore it," he said. "I need you."

"But with everything that's going on…just check the caller ID, and I'll be right over there in bed."

"No, I'm not letting you go," he said and, clamping her to him, he moved them a couple of steps to the dresser to lean over the phone.

"Damn," he muttered. "It's Detective Jensen."

She clung to him as he took the call. She could clearly hear every word.

"Nick Markwood here. What's up, detective?"

"Counselor Markwood, I thought I should inform you that your client Dale Braun is under arrest for a woman's murder."

Nick's grip on her tightened. "The murder of Cynthia Lindley?"

"That may come, but this is for the murder of Marian James. Murder and arson of his own property. We are at the site of the Twisted Trees mansion, and it's damn dark as pitch out here, except for the headlights of fire trucks and police cars and the remnants of the fire. It was Dale who ID'd the deceased. Somehow she was trapped inside the garage, knocked out, I don't know—flames or smoke inhalation. She's badly burned and definitely dead. ME is on the way."

"And so am I," Nick said and punched off.

Claire held him even tighter for a moment. "I'm going too. I'll knock on Nita and Bronco's door and tell them."

They scrambled for their clothes, for calm, for courage.

CHAPTER TWENTY-FIVE

Nick and Claire hardly needed their flashlights by the time they approached the ruins of Twisted Trees mansion. They'd left their car in the same spot as when they'd been there in the daylight, then walked around a police barrier a little farther on. Through the hulking line of trees ahead, flashing light bars from at least six police cars lit a lurid scene while blinding white beams of light from two fire trucks slashed the smoking rubble.

They held hands, helping each other over the rough ground. Wet leaves smacked their faces, so they bent low under the boughs of the ficus trees. The smell of smoke bit deep into their lungs and clung to their clothes. They walked up to the barrier of yellow plastic Crime Scene Do Not Enter tape.

Nick told the officer who hurried toward them, "Detective Jensen called me. Nick Markwood, Dale Braun's attorney."

"They're both over there," he said, pointing. "Watch where you walk. Fire hoses all over. No fireplugs here, so they used what little water was stored on the trucks. The bay's too far to get water from."

He lifted the tape for them, and they ducked under. How different the grounds and the ruined mansion looked at night, especially with the garish lights. Nick thought of a movie trailer he'd caught Lexi watching of a zombie movie, *Night of the Living Dead*.

People's shadows loomed huge. Hot spots still flickered from the rubble of the skeletal two-story garage and apartment. The pulsating red-blue-white strobes from the police vehicles made everything look as if it would burst into flame again.

They turned off their flashlights and stopped gripping each other's hands as they approached a dark unmarked car with Jensen standing next to it. Nick saw Dale was in the back seat; Jensen had the front passenger door open and one foot in the car, talking to him. An officer stood nearby as if guarding Dale. When Dale spotted them, he held up his wrists, either in greeting or to show Nick he was handcuffed. Nick noted his hair was a mess, his face cut and bruised, his shirt torn.

"Counselor. Claire," Jensen said, looking surprised to see her. "I read him his rights."

"Detective Jensen," Nick said, and they shook hands.

Nick leaned down into the open car door. "Sit tight, Dale. No comments right now. We'll get you out on bail." Turning back to Jensen, he asked, "Why is he cut up and bruised? I'm sure he didn't resist arrest."

"That happened before we got here," Jensen said with a lift of his eyebrows Nick could not quite decode.

Dale shouted, "It's my property! I had no idea she was up there—trespassing again. I tried to pull her out of the rubble when I saw her after the upper floor collapsed, but she was unconscious or dead by that point! No comment?" he went on, ignoring Nick's raised hand for silence. His voice broke. "My only comment so far is I didn't kill her either. Yeah, I set the fire, but I also called it in. Someone's trying to frame me, and it's costing people's lives and mine too! She had to be unconscious in there or she would have run out—at least have screamed or pounded on the door or window. The smoke wasn't that bad at first to knock her out."

"I said, hold it for now," Nick said, bending down to look at Dale. "I'll be with you when you make your statement. Anything you say can be used against you—remember that, counselor."

Jensen closed the car door and the hovering officer stepped closer. "Over there," he said, pointing, "under that tarp is Marian James's body. As I said, Dale ID'd her, though we found her burned purse and camera near where Dale says he found her body, and both items had her ID too. Hope the camera's not too melted to access its photos. That place burned hot. Arson investigators might find an accelerant."

"You do see a pattern here," Nick said, trying to steady his voice. "However shaken he is right now, Dale Braun would not set himself up so obviously to kill two women and have the sites of their deaths and or bodies linked to him. He would not have called the fire department, but let it burn and be miles away."

"I get all that. It makes him look good that he hauled her body out, right? But why did he torch the place? Was he also in a struggle with her beforehand? Will there be any DNA under her nails or even in her body after that conflagration? One victim, frozen, one burned to death? Nick, I can't possibly let him walk this time until we do an investigation. He could be a flight risk. Or a serial killer."

"Hardly. I just hope the judge is fair enough to keep the bail bond reasonable. Can I see the body?"

"Photos of it later. You beat the ME here. The evidence techs haven't even had time to sift through things—too damned hot."

It annoyed Nick that what popped into his head was not only that things were getting too hot, but that Claire had been upset lately that Bradley Vance had shared only pictures of the bog artifacts with her, not the originals.

"Then can you tell us what you know of the scene?" Nick asked. "I need to tell you that Dale took us through the apartment above the garage two days ago. Marian James could have broken in to try to see it for herself as it's pretty much all that's left of the historic old mansion. I can testify to the fact she was trespassing here the day we visited, so no doubt again tonight."

"News flash, Nick. Whether or not the deceased—who was evidently trapped in a burning, arson-set building—invited herself here or was invited, she was incinerated, and your client admits he started the fire. Both his alibis have holes leaking like crazy, and however good a criminal defense attorney you are, I'm betting you can't dam up those holes."

"Granted, arson is a criminal act," Nick said. He could tell Claire wanted to say something but he was proud of her for letting him handle this. "But he owns what he burned. No one else but an intruder who was trespassing was hurt, and he's not after insurance or involved in some sort of scam. Get him for not having a burn permit. If Marian James was trespassing again, her death was an accident and not first degree murder."

"So he says. But with the other murder charges pending, maybe he wanted to look like a hero, kind of like that Jace Britten who was at your reception and showed up in the newspaper as a valiant hurricane hunter."

Nick could tell Claire also wanted to respond to that too, but, thank heavens, she didn't. Headlights cut across them as the ME's van drove in, bouncing across the thick grass. As Jensen walked away to meet it, Nick pulled Claire back out of the glare of crisscrossed headlights.

"Are we leaving?" she asked.

"Strange as it sounds, I think we can see clearer here in the darkness. Don't turn on your light again."

"You want a glimpse of the body?"

"I do. Don't you look."

"Not so different maybe from studying those bog bodies. Method of death, yes, but all so wrenching, so tragic."

But the two men from the ME's office blocked their view when they bent over the thin, twisted and blackened form on the ground. Damn, but Nick had been hoping things would not

blow up, that Dale could ride it out so the Eva Braun connection wouldn't come to light. But it sure would now, under the
glare of publicity that could do nothing but hurt the case and
hurt the firm—and maybe cost Dale his life.

Every bone in Claire's body ached the next morning, and she
was certain she still smelled smoke in her hair, in the bedsheets.
She could not get the sight, even distant, of the charred corpse
of that woman out of her mind. Nick was gone already, heading for the station where Dale had been booked. They'd decided
late last night that they'd drop Lexi and Trey off at her sister's
for the day while Claire helped Nita and Bronco clean junk and
trash out of their new house, and Nick would be there as soon
as he could get Dale out on bail.

At least, Nick had said, the fire had happened late enough
last night that the local newspaper and other outlets probably
wouldn't report on it until later today when word got out about
the second woman's murder in that same neighborhood—with
the common denominator now under arrest.

Claire got up and dragged herself to the bathroom, took a
stimulant pill to battle her narcolepsy on top of her exhaustion.
Wait until Brad Vance heard or read about this latest publicity,
not that she would be named in it. But Markwood, Benton and
Chase probably would be, and that alone might be too much for
him. She did not want to be terminated from her work at Black
Bog. Would Andrea and Kris be on her side, or did they have
to side with Brad? The man seemed in control and yet ready to
explode sometimes.

And her own state of being? She'd have to try again to question Kris on Monday morning but keep from putting a damper
on her high spirits and excitement over her ice skating date with
Mitch Blakeman. Hopefully, she herself would not be skating
on thin ice with her friend to inquire about Brad and Andrea's
two antique and jewelry stores. She wished she had entered the

store as an anonymous special buyer, a cognoscente, as the shop staff called it.

Maybe if she drove across the state to Fort Lauderdale and went in their other store, she could start all over, learn more. Or maybe she could get someone to do it for her. But for now, she could only hope that Andrea and former Senator Brad Vance trusted her because she wanted desperately to prove herself to them, which she hoped to do tomorrow when she shared her initial theory on the buried trio.

Stifling a yawn and trying not to look at herself in the mirror, Claire jammed her feet into her slippers and went to check on Lexi and Trey.

"Where to start in this mess?" Nita said. "Okay, one room at a time, the master bedroom first, then the kitchen. Still can't picture me fixing food here where someone was put on ice. At least the guys from the police are ready to load up that freezer," she said with another glimpse out the living room window which Bronco was watching too.

The freezer which had been Cyndi's tomb sat in the driveway as the two men backed their truck closer to where they'd set it down. They had a lift on the back of the truck and had used a dolly to get it that far.

"Let's get busy," Claire suggested. "The sooner this place is emptied, then repainted and furnished, the better you'll feel about making it your own, though I don't mean you have to leave us right away."

Bronco was still watching the men with the truck. "This real nice neighborhood we picked, partly 'cause Dale gave us a good price for his Mom's place, is not looking so good right now," Bronco said. "Swear I can smell smoke hanging in the air."

"No more dragging your feet about this place," Claire said with a one-armed hug of Nita. "Come on, you two. Let's show Nick we got a lot done when he gets here."

"Right. Good riddance to that freezer," Bronco said and headed out the back door to the shed.

Inside, it was like a treasure hunt, but of worthless treasure. Though Claire supposed there was some sales value in stacks of old *Life Magazines*, and at least ten years of *People*, local newspapers, clay pots, some of which still held dead plants, and sacks of grocery sacks. They carted them outside to either Bronco's truck or the dumpster they had rented. "Let's keep these old 78 and 45 records, though," she told Nita when the two of them attacked that pile. "Collectors are really getting back into vinyl."

She wondered if people were really getting back into Victorian mourning jewelry—and if the so-called cognoscenti were actually buying jewelry inspired by the ancients. Maybe she could ask Jace and Brit to go over to Fort Lauderdale, in case Pippa Lee was over there for the day or she had to show ID and the staff there had heard about her visit.

She lugged out another load into the living room for Bronco to take to the dumpster when he finally finished cleaning out the backyard shed. She looked out a front window again to see if the freezer was gone. The two men hired by the police were surely taking their good old time, probably getting paid by the hour and not the job. They were just finishing cigarettes. At least they ground out the butts on the driveway instead of tossing them into the truck or dumpster. One lowered the lift, and they bent to slide the freezer onto it from the wheeled dolly.

Suddenly two other men appeared, both big bruisers. "That bastard Dale Braun trying to get rid of the coffin he put my sister in?" the one shouted. "He here? Heard he lives here'bouts."

Oh, no! Southern accent. Sounded slurred, maybe drunk. Fists clenched. One guy hit the truck driver on the shoulder, pushing him away from the freezer, while the other man opened it and peered in. Both Nick and Ken Jensen had described Cyndi's redneck brother and her first fiancé well enough to match what Claire had just heard and seen.

"Nita!" Claire called, lunging to lock the front door, then closing and locking the front window that was open. "Run out back and get Bronco. I'm sure the police are sick of us, but I'm calling them if those delivery men they sent aren't able to handle this. And I'm calling Nick."

In the background, on the street curb, she saw Betty Richards just watching, holding her little dog in her arms. Crazy thought, but it almost looked like she'd summoned the two loud louts and now was just watching, watching.

CHAPTER TWENTY-SIX

"Don't you go anywhere near those two," Nick insisted on the phone when she told him Tanner and his friend—she could not recall the other guy's name—were at the house.

"Nita went to get Bronco. Okay, he's out in front to talk to them," she said, still looking out the window. "The two guys picking up the freezer are not cops, but there is safety in numbers."

"Lie low. I'm halfway there. See you."

Nita ran in the back door and locked it behind her. She joined Claire in the living room, looking out the window. "Bronco and those two taking the freezer will make them leave," she said, out of breath.

The voices were so loud they had no trouble hearing the men.

"This here freezer was my sister's tomb!" Tanner repeated. Together, the two men slammed the lid on it. "Don't want it hid or made a sideshow. Gonna make that fancy lawyer bastard admit he kilt her, put him in here, show him what it's like. And hope they fingerprinted it already, 'cause ours is on there now, and you can tell the cops why."

"You'd better get off this private property," Bronco told them, not budging. At least, Claire thought, he was a physical match for Tanner—except that there were two of them, and the delivery guys were just staying out of the way, though one was on his phone.

"I heard Braun's out of jail, probably hiding out, lawyer fancied hisself up by hiring those other lawyers he works with. Get him out here so I can at least tell him what I think of his kind," Tanner insisted.

Claire told Nita, "At least Bronco didn't tell him he has the wrong house, Dale's mother's old place next door to Dale's." She shuddered. She dreaded Nick hearing this blame-the-lawyer talk. Here she was worried that he'd be upset that she'd called Jace to see if he and Brit would go over to the Vances' Fort Lauderdale shop to check it out for backroom buys. He would go ballistic if she went out there after he'd said not to, but she had to get these men calmed down or away before Nick arrived.

"Mr. Braun doesn't live here anymore!" Bronco insisted. "He sold me this house, and that's that."

"Well, won't trash it or burn it down then, like I was fixin' to do, like he deserves or worse!" Tanner shouted. "Where's he at then?"

Burn it down? Claire thought. Maybe these guys needed a closer look.

"Moved somewhere in the area," Bronco said. "Can't say I know."

Nita spoke again. "Good how he said that—not quite a lie." She was wringing her hands. "Hope those two don't have a gun."

"I think they would have pulled it by now. They were thinking of hurting the house—and that mention of wanting to burn it is interesting."

"Claire, you are not on this case. Nick will have your head."

"Not if I can get somewhere with them. Thank heavens we were here, but I can't have Nick charging in, even with Bronco to back him up, and those two workers are worthless. Besides, the neighbor lady is an eyewitness and the more people—maybe us so-called weaker sex—dealing with them, the better."

It seemed a momentary stalemate outside. Claire made a quick decision. She had to get rid of these two, and she'd handled worse before. Besides, how else was she going to assess whether they were sincere about losing Cyndi, or if they could have had something to do with her murder? Jensen had said they weren't accounted for when she died and that they hadn't been back to Zebulon when he was there. But would they have been stupid enough to come back here and make a ruckus if they were guilty? Over the years, she'd seen stupider moves by guilty parties.

"I'm going out," she told Nita, handing her the phone. "I'll talk them down and find out a few things. I'm not afraid with Bronco and those two others there—and Betty Richards and her tiny attack dog—ha."

"No, Claire, you can't," she said and started to cry.

"It's all right. The only problem I'll have is Nick will be livid, so I've got to hurry."

Ignoring Nita's protest, she opened the front door and went out.

"Hello," she called to them.

"You the missus?" Tanner, who seemed to be the spokes-man—the thinker of the two, if that was possible—called to her.

"No, just a friend of the couple who recently bought this house," she said, gesturing toward Bronco. Claire wasn't certain whether to identify herself as Nick's wife or not, but if he arrived, they'd figure it out. "We're inside cleaning it up, trying to move on from your poor sister being found here. We will always remember her.

"I didn't mean to eavesdrop," she went on, "but I take it you're Cyndi's brother and a friend of hers. I am so sorry for your loss." She dared to walk closer and extend her hand. The scent of alcohol hit her hard. Obviously surprised, Tanner shook her hand, his big paw engulfing hers. His fingers were dirty and calloused. Bronco edged along right beside her but at least he didn't interrupt.

"A damn tragedy," Tanner said, releasing her hand. "When I called the police station, I heard the guy's finally been arrested but got out on bail. Read in the paper he might of kilt some other woman too."

"That's all hearsay—just guessing at this point. Yet to be proved. But I'm sure whoever hurt your sister will be brought to justice."

The fiancé—why couldn't she think of his name?—stepped closer. *Always use the person's name*, she recited to herself from her hostile interview training years ago. She would have called Tanner by his name, but she didn't want to tip them off she knew much about them and, although she'd admitted she'd been listening, neither man had given his name. Could that mean they were hiding something?

"Bad enough she got killed," the former fiancé said. "But then to be put in that freezer like deer meat or somethin'."

"It's terrible. Where were you two when you heard what had happened?"

"On the road," Tanner said. "Truck drivers, work together sometimes. Got a call from home."

"Oh, what a sad way to hear about the passing of someone you loved and cared for. Have you been here in Naples for a while?"

"Truth is," he said, lowering his voice for the first time, "we been on a binge in Key West, tryin' to drink it all away, how she deserted both of us, took off with some cash she took from me, then paid the price."

Bingo! Claire thought. He had just given her at least the hint of a motive suggesting they might have met Cyndi here, argued with her about deserting them, perhaps stealing from them and maybe more than just argued.

"Well," Tanner said, frowning at the freezer again, "nothing else to do here. We're heading home but sure would like to give that Braun bastard a piece of my mind and a piece of this."

Claire gasped and Bronco pulled her back behind him as the man drew a hunting knife from his jacket pocket. "You ever see him, maybe he comes around for rent or whatever," he told Bronco, "tell him if he don't get life in prison for what he done, he's gonna get this!"

Thank God, he turned and walked away with his friend right behind.

"Get his license plate," Claire told Bronco, then turned to the workers. "And you two get that freezer out of here—please!"

To her amazement, Betty had not budged. Feeling she'd done something helpful—and Nick had not gotten here to blow up yet—Claire figured she was on a roll. The Georgia truck pulled away, and the two workers went back to their task just as a police car pulled up in front.

"Bronco," Claire whispered, "Nick should be here soon, so fill him and this officer in, but watch to be sure those two don't come back. I've been meaning to talk to Betty. And question number one is why would she be this nosy right now with two obvious brutes making a lot of noise."

Jace met Brit in Wynn's Market on the Trail. He hated not being open with her as much as he hated steering clear of Lexi lately. Mitch had managed some time with Kris, so he was just going to take Claire up on the idea she'd given him on the phone, partly because it would give him time with Brit.

"We've got to stop meeting like this," she told him with a little laugh. She was carrying an empty plastic grocery basket, but she reached out to squeeze his hand. She looked good. Either she was getting more sleep not being in his bed, or her natural resilience was back again.

"Hey, at least you're still speaking to me," he told her. "And smiling. And kidding around."

"This mess isn't your fault. You and Mitch were only trying to help crack down on drug czars."

"Want to head over to Lauderdale for a day? Get out of here?"

"Really? Just for a day?"

"Got meetings for the new job coming up in DC. Mitch and I are going to have to head there soon, where I know I'll be safe. But meanwhile, yeah, just for a day let's cross the state to Fort Lauderdale—I need to visit a really upscale jewelry and antiques store, and you could come along."

"Oh, I'm sure you'll be safe in DC. Nothing bad ever happens there," she added with a roll of her eyes and a wry smile.

For sure this woman had bounced back from her own tragedy, and he loved her for it. Fall down, get up. Get shot at, so to speak, hunker down and shoot back.

"So what's the Lauderdale deal?" she went on, as they strolled the aisles.

"It's actually a favor for Claire, though she couldn't tell me why. Says you should stop by the house, she'll fill you in, then you tell me. Man, I'm missing Lexi, so hug her for me."

"For Claire, for Lexi, will do. Claire almost lost her life helping me last year."

"Let's not think that. She needs someone who is not obviously tied to her to go into an arty store there and look at some pricey jewelry they might keep just for high rollers. Not buy it, just try to see it."

"Oh, yeah, that's us, high rollers. Meaning, I'll have to wear my one pair of designer jeans and Manolo Blahnik heels, and you can't just stroll in there in work jeans. Did she tell you more than that?"

"Yeah. She thinks the key word to get a look at the pricey stuff might be *cognoscente*."

"Key word? No kidding? Is she working on something to do with jewelry theft?"

"I think it's maybe tied somehow to knockoffs. You, know, copies of the real thing. Don't really know, and she wouldn't say."

"Maybe that's her consulting job," Brit mused as she put something in the plastic shopping basket on her arm. She took some smoked fish spread and cocktail crackers, then tossed in some granola bars. "You know," she went on, "maybe she's looking for people who are stealing old tribal jewelry, because there are all kinds of laws about returning Native American pieces, artifacts, even bones. I suppose a sting operation would be really hush-hush."

"That's my girl—you, I mean, up for a challenge. I love you," he said, planting a fast kiss on her mouth. "Believe me, I can do better than that. But here's the thing. I'm going to ask Mitch if he can fly us over in the chopper, then wait for us at the small airport I know just for a couple hours. We'd fly out of the Marco Island airport near here. The guy loves to fly what he calls helos, and this week's the last time he'll have access to a bird. We can take a taxi, have lunch, hit the jewelry store incognito."

"I'd like to see the Everglades from the air, and choppers fly pretty low. Maybe we'll spot a Florida panther. When?"

"Can you get off day after tomorrow—Tuesday? I know that's short notice."

"I think I can swing it. I've practically been living at the zoo, especially since I'm not living with you and have to move in with my second love."

"Yeah. Glad to know it's a tiger. Want to go out to my car and neck, like they used to call it in the old days? I'm really missing you, babe, but Mitch and I figure it won't be long before we can come out of hiding, so to speak. We really think that article in the newspaper about our new public government job seeking out hurricanes is insurance, instead of the undercover government job looking for drug runners and drug lords."

"Make out in a car in the store parking lot?" she said, much too loudly, so that two elderly shoppers looked their way.

"Well, I never," the man said to the woman as they turned away.

"Well, I never either," Jace said, so only she could hear, "but it seems like we're hitting parking lots for a lot of our special events lately."

"This isn't all an elaborate ruse to buy me a huge wedding ring in a chichi jewelry store in this so-fancy strip mall, is it?" she asked, elbowing him with a little laugh.

"Naw, I already bought the wedding ring and in a real nice store."

"Just promise me our ceremony and reception won't be in a parking lot," she teased.

"I thought maybe in a helo over the Glades."

"Over my—your—dead body."

"Don't kid about that, honey."

"We're a wacky pair, you know."

"Just as long as we're a pair. I repeat, I love you, Brit. What would I ever do without you?"

CHAPTER TWENTY-SEVEN

Nick still wasn't in sight when Claire walked up to Betty. She held her little dog in her arms. The dog looked scared, but the old lady only looked interested. Why hadn't she scurried inside when all this started?

"Betty, remember me? Nick Markwood's wife, Claire."

"Oh, yes, I recognized you. All that made me wish I had a German shepherd or a pit bull the way those two were acting."

"You seemed brave to stand there and listen. Let me walk you home. I know how hard all of this must be for you. Bronco, I'm going next door with Betty! Tell the police and Nick I'll be back soon," she called and steered the woman away.

She could see Nick's car turning onto the street and she didn't want him to stop her. No, this time, she was going to use her forensic psych skills to latch on to what Betty really knew.

"I'm sure it upset you to see the freezer in the yard. Those men were rude and crude, weren't they?" Claire asked, holding Betty's screen door open while she unlocked the inner one.

"Indeed they were, but you handled them. Dreadful to see that freezer out in the open like that and to realize what it held, and to think that poor girl was buried in frozen vegetables. Dreadful!"

Claire tried to recall if that detail had been released, but then Betty had viewed the picture of Cyndi in the freezer to ID her. Yet hadn't that photo just been of her face and not the surrounding bags of frozen veggies?

"So, did you ever see how packed that freezer was?" Claire asked as she followed her into a Colonial kitchen, which reminded her of her grandmother's whom she'd known so briefly. "I know Lucy was a hoarder, but even in her freezer?"

"Oh, I've seen it a time or two. Sit here at the kitchen table, and I'll get us lemonade. I'm not sure anyone's sat right there since Lucy died."

"I'm sorry your neighborhood keeps getting hit with tragedies. But you seem very brave and informed about them all."

"Including that dreadful fire on Saturday. I read all about it in the paper, but they didn't mention the smoke and drifting ashes, and they should have. Obviously that journalist wasn't up close and personal like some of us who live here. One had to be here to realize that old ruin was back there, you know."

Some of that seemed a mixed message. Was the subtext that Betty had been near the scene of the fire the night of the fire? But she didn't want to spook her or silence her, so she tried another tactic.

"Because knowing Lucy so well over the years, I'll bet you knew more than anyone else about that old ruined mansion, except for Dale."

Betty set the tall glasses of lemonade on the table. "Well, you know the name of that old TV show, *I Love Lucy*. I cared for my friend Lucy and she did me—before she lost her senses, we were best friends. That's why I could forgive her for treating Dale's so-called fiancée the way she did. I was her partner and backup in that," she said with a shake of her head and a strong sniff.

Claire saw her grip her lemonade so hard that her fingers went white against the icy glass. The way she'd said that—it was almost as if she meant she was Lucy's partner in crime. Backup in what?

"I suppose you also had words with Cyndi," she threw out another leading line.

"More than that."

Claire tried to keep her relaxed posture, elbows on the table, leaning slightly forward, but she was tempted to bolt out of her chair. "More than that?" Claire repeated when Betty said no more, but her lower lips trembled.

"I told her never to darken Lucy's door again or she'd regret it dearly. When I said that, the smart aleck bent over in the plants outside Lucy's door, grabbed a handful of dark mud and smeared it on the door to darken it, just to be cute—which she wasn't. Smarter than she looked, though, the snippy little tart."

"Did you see her again after that, and what did she say then?"

Betty shrugged, then looked down at her sweating glass. "I only saw her at a distance after that. When Dale was at work one day—unless he'd come home for lunch which he did sometimes, he drove right into his garage, so it was hard to tell—she and a woman drove back in toward the mansion."

"Do you know who the other woman was?"

"Didn't until I saw her picture in the paper today, the one died in the fire there, the historic committee woman."

Claire tried not to gasp. She had to go next door to tell Nick that he really should hire her as a junior partner. Since she'd seen him last, she'd collected eyewitness accounts and comments that indicated Cyndi's murderer could have been Tanner and her first fiancé. A longer shot, but even perhaps the Lucy-and-Betty duo had somehow done away with Cyndi. They both had access to the freezer. Maybe when Lucy died, Betty just figured there was no way to hide Cyndi's corpse elsewhere so she let it be found.

And then the ultimate gamble: If Marian and Cyndi had actually met, could something have gone wrong and Marian accidentally or intentionally harmed Cyndi? Dale had told Nick earlier that on her body Cyndi could well have had keys not only to Dale's place but his mother's—even on her very dead, soon to be frozen, body.

"I thought you'd be furious with me," Claire said as they finally drove away from Bronco and Nita's house after three more hours of hard work clearing out the clutter of over fifty years. She'd told him about what she'd learned from the Georgia duo and Betty. "Or were you just waiting until we were alone?"

"Oh, yes, Mrs. Markwood, I was scared and upset at first when Bronco said you'd talked to the Georgia boys. But he said you calmed them down, and he was right there with you. I wasn't crazy about the appearance of the knife, though."

"Which reminds me, I have to insist Brad Vance shows me the actual dagger buried with Hunter. It had some sort of crude carving on it, and that could be a clue to a lot of things. The Senator's close-up photos did not include pictures of the carvings for me to study."

"Nice try at diversion, but back to your taking over for Detective Jensen by questioning suspects," he told her as they turned out onto the busy Tamiami Trail and headed toward home.

"I was thinking I was taking over for you—to get more suspects than Dale, at least for Cyndi's murder, if not for Marian's," she explained, turning toward him. "I know it sounds crazy, but did you ever see the old Cary Grant movie *Arsenic and Old Lace*?"

"Claire, I don't have the benefit of your amateur English major degree from your mother."

"It wasn't based on a book, but a play. Anyway, two dotty old ladies have a body hidden in their house. And they are the murderers."

"You don't really think Dale's demented mother and that character next door to her—"

"I don't know what I think. Then too, about the Georgia crackers, Tanner said that Cyndi not only deserted both of them but stole cash from him and what's-his-name—"

"Will MacBride."

"That's it. Anyway, Tanner seemed righteously pleased to say that Cyndi paid the price for deserting them. So maybe they were the enforcers of revenge for her betrayal. Besides, you told me after you first met Tanner, he said he was at home and the coroner called him to say Cyndi was dead. But earlier today he told me he was on the road with Will driving a truck and relatives called them with the news. Nick, he's making things up as he goes."

"Or, like you said, he's blown what brains he had drinking in Key West for a week, and is just confused."

"I'm trying to help you!"

"And you are. All this is valuable for defending Dale."

"So maybe Tanner and Will then came here, met with Cyndi. Maybe it started out as an argument, she told them off, one of them in a fit of anger grabbed her around the throat. I don't know, but remember Dale told us early that Cyndi could well have had a key not only to his place but to his mother's. What if she had taken one to the Twisted Trees mansion too, and gave or sold it to Marian? Whoever killed Cyndi found the key on her and stashed her in the dead woman's freezer to make it look like Dale did it, or maybe they were planning to move her body after dark. The only flaw in that theory is that Betty would have seen something of that, though I suppose she has to leave her house sometimes."

"Then there's Marian James, since you said Betty claims she was heading with Cyndi toward the Twisted Trees property, so you could be right that Cyndi had a key to that too."

"That's what I mean. Maybe Cyndi also had or took a key which gave her access to the locked apartment above the garage. Maybe she even met with Marian and showed her around, or tried to assure her the place could be a historical site and she could act as its Realtor."

"I swear, sweetheart, I'm going to start taking you into court

with me. You impressed the hell out of me when you testified
to ruin my case the first time I saw you, and I'm glad you're on
my side now."

"Wish I could stay around to cash in on that," she said, smiling and stroking his thigh. "But I'm scheduled to present some
ideas to the powers-that-be at Black Bog tomorrow morning
and I've got to get some notes together. I can't just read them
my little essays as if I were channeling three dead, prehistoric
people. Oh, and Brit's stopping by tonight so I can fill her in on
her trip to Fort Lauderdale on Tuesday with Jace."

"Good thing Jace isn't coming. I still don't know if he's safe—
to be at our house in case he's being followed or targeted, I
mean."

They stopped at a red light. She reached for his hand, and he
held hers tight. "You're going to solve these two murders," she
said. "And I'm going to do everything I can to figure out who
killed two of my three Black Bog people, if it's the last thing I
do! Just a figure of speech," she added, realizing how that might
sound, as the light turned green.

That evening, since Bronco and Nita hadn't come back, Nick
put Trey to bed and read a story to Lexi while Claire talked
with Brit.

"I'm sorry I can't fill you in on more than these details I wrote
out for you," Claire told her, looking down again at the sheet
of paper. "I've signed a confidentiality clause with my current
employers, so I'm trying to honor that, even though I'm sending you and Jace on a cloak-and-dagger mission across the state."

She wished she hadn't put it that way—so much as mentioned
a dagger—but she said no more as Brit looked over her notes.

"Okay, got it," Brit said, frowning at the paper. "We need
to use an alias. We need to appear well-to-do and work in the
word *cognoscente*. Glad you spelled it out for me."

"If they show you any private stock, act interested, find out as much as you can about the original or the designer. The Naples shop has a jewelry designer, and she said there's a more veteran one in Lauderdale. I'm thinking there may be jewelry, maybe even an antique dagger so old it's made of stone, not metal."

"Really? Kind of prehistoric?"

"Antique. Very antique."

"So don't give the salesperson—or designer—info about how to contact us," Brit kept reading the notes. "We will discuss our finances, etcetera and contact him or her later."

"Right. And if you get the names of the shop owner, shopkeeper, salesperson, jewelry designer—anything like that—don't write it down until you get out of there so it doesn't look too suspicious. And, Brit," she added, reaching out to grasp her wrist, "if anything looks funny or, God forbid, dangerous, just leave calmly and quickly. I'm really grateful to both of you for doing this." She loosed Brit's wrist and sat back in the sofa with a sigh.

"I don't know what I would have done without your support when everything went so wrong at my beloved Backwoods Animal Adventure," Brit said, turning toward her. "And for supporting Jace with me—you know what I mean. Oh, I forgot that he asked me to hug Lexi for him, but I'm sure you can do that. I don't want to get her riled up if Nick's got her calmed down to go to sleep."

"Actually," Claire told her, "she has not been a happy camper about Jace not seeing her lately. I know he'll patch things up when he can. Soon, I hope."

"You know, we do plan to stay in this area, even if he has to report to or fly out of Washington, DC, for his new job. I'm sure he'll find something to do here when he's not on call, maybe teach flying at the little airport on Marco Island, something like that. That's where we're flying out of, you know—Mitch at the controls of a helicopter, no less. Then we'll land over there at a smaller executive airport, not the big busy one."

"It sounds like a good plan. I said I'd pay for the chopper gasoline and lunch and dinner for all, so here's an envelope with some cash, and don't say no. I consider the three of you are on assignment for me and please be careful above all." She gave Brit the envelope and, thankfully, she took it.

"Claire, whatever the point of this is, you be careful too. Jace said to tell you that you need to get out of your temp job or assignment if there's anything strange, illegal or dangerous—like maybe someone ripping off antiques or jewels or whatever. He said to tell you it isn't life and death."

"No, of course not. I understand that. Thank him for his concern."

But she couldn't help but think that her attempts to solve the dilemma of what happened to her beloved Bog People did hinge on their life and death; though, of course, she wasn't going to risk her own.

CHAPTER TWENTY-EIGHT

"I wish we had time to really enjoy the shops and a restaurant here," Brit told Jace as he parked their rental car down the street from the Art for Art's Sake shop in Fort Lauderdale about eleven o'clock on Tuesday morning. "It's a beautiful area."

"That it is, babe, but we're on assignment."

He thought things were going great so far. The heliport at the Executive Airport had been right on top of a parking garage, and they had easily rented a car. The airport was just five miles from downtown, and Brit was right—this neighborhood was great. Lots of restaurants, sidewalk cafés, art stores and shops. Not an area for carryout, but he'd find something to take back to Mitch, who had stayed at the airport.

"No time for a shopping spree, no matter how much cash Claire gave you," he said, taking her arm as they approached their target shop. "Okay, remember, you're using your mother's name, Ann Hoffman."

"All right, Ben Hoffman. And in case they ask where we live, we'll use Marco Island and just say we flew over for the day to give the impression we are rich. Best not to lie about too much, or we'll make a mistake."

The display windows were stunning—even Jace admitted that. Old-fashioned yet very elegant. Several antique swords, or maybe they were called sabers, and several knives from the Civil War era were displayed on dark blue velvet. They were shiny steel, heavily etched, hardly the stone primitive-looking daggers Claire had told Brit to be on the lookout for.

A bell jingled over their heads as they entered. A middle-aged woman with pink hair, no less, looked up with a smile. "Lovely day for strolling from shop to shop," she greeted them.

"Actually," Brit said, "we are fascinated by your display window. My father has a collection of old swords and daggers. He's kind of a connoisseur of those."

Where the hell did that father collection come from? Jace thought. They hadn't discussed that at all. Brit reminded him of Claire in some ways, which wasn't all bad. Bright, dedicated, clever on her feet, and sometimes too damn unafraid.

"Oh, is that right?" Pink Hair said with an obvious perusal of both of them. That made Jace nervous.

"We're looking for something very special for him for a birthday gift," he put in, trying to stay poker-faced. "He's been very good to us. We heard about your shop, so we flew over for the day from Marco Island. In her father's helicopter, no less."

The woman perked right up. "I always wanted a ride in one of those. Then have you visited our other store in Naples?" she asked.

"We've heard of it, but no," Brit put in. "We'll have to, though, if we don't find something here."

Man, Jace thought, she's good at this, barely hinting at the idea that something illegal might be for sale.

Pink Hair smiled. "Let me summon my associate in the back room—our master artisan, our jeweler—and I'm sure he'd be happy to show you what collector's pieces we have. Just a moment then."

"In like Flynn," Jace whispered, hardly moving his lips because

they'd talked about the possibility of security cameras monitor-
ing them.

"Yes," Pink Hair said, emerging from behind the curtain, "if
you wouldn't mind stepping back into our private showroom,
my associate Roger Bassett will discuss what might suit."

Jace took Brit's elbow as they went behind the curtain Pink
Hair held open for them. Brit's arm was shaking, but, damn,
his was too.

Claire actually had an extra day to prepare her initial theory about the possible relationships among the Black Bog trio
of Hunter, Reaching Woman and Leader, because the Monday
meeting had been canceled and moved to Tuesday late morning.
More than once she glanced at the clock on the meeting room
wall, one of those old schoolroom types with big numbers that
went *tick-tock* if there was a moment of silence.

Kris had said the reason for the rescheduling was that Andrea
and Brad were closing on the sale of their house on the beach,
one of the earliest mansions built in the upscale Port Royal
neighborhood, though they'd done much to renovate it. Today,
Yi Ling had left the bog site early because of terrible tooth pain.
Brad had said he'd called their dentist to take her in right away.
He himself looked the worse for wear. He said he'd cut his arm
and his cheek—Claire thought of Hunter's slashed face again—
on broken glass when he'd tried to change a window of their
new house here at the bog and had dropped it.

"Which just goes to show," Andrea had said, "he can fix most
of the problems around here, but he should leave the Mr. Fix-It
domestic work to someone we hire."

"Every dollar," Brad said, gingerly fingering the large bandage on his cheek which also showed the gauze wrap on his
arm, "needs to go to Black Bog. It's all input right now with no
profit, but just wait until we can sell magazine articles, book and
TV rights. We'll make it up."

"Speaking of making things up." Andrea smoothly took over the meeting again, "Claire says she has put together some possibilities of relationships among the bog trio—fiction based on fact."

"A good way to say that," Claire said. "In a way what I'm doing is what Alex Haley, the author of *Roots*, the groundbreaking book on African heritage, called *faction*. Much research but then some fictionalized accounts. I wasn't going to just read these three self-portraits of the trio, but I think I will start that way and then tie what I've written to the facts—and artifacts."

She looked across the table at Brad. He stared back, not budging, not commenting. Finally he said, "Slides will be available," as she lifted her paper to read the first person statement she'd written for Hunter.

"And, of course," Andrea put in, "the bodies themselves can be studied in more detail. And someday perhaps someone will find a way to download what's in those stored brains."

Claire thought of a smart remark about needing to use their own brains—by studying the artifacts themselves. And that she couldn't tell enough just from looking at the bodies. But, due to the sudden unspoken tension at the table, she said neither and started to read.

"So it went really smooth?" Mitch asked Jace and Brit as they walked the roof of the parking garage toward the chopper for the flight back. They'd be flying into a sinking sun so they wanted to head out as soon as possible.

"It seemed to," Brit said. "First we saw some chunky bead necklaces and a bracelet. And a dagger, which we'd kind of set up with the story about my father being a connoisseur of old swords and daggers. The so-called artisan jeweler called that the pièce de résistance. The dagger was kind of crude-looking but it had chiseled designs on it, strange ones. Animals and a woman holding up both hands like she was blessing them. At least that's what we thought it represented."

"So you sprang for how many hundred thousand dollars?" Mitch teased as they neared the chopper.

Jace saw a man had emerged onto the top floor of the heliport where they had landed the chopper, but he evidently knew to keep back from the wash or the rotor blades before Mitch started the engine. The man was covering his eyes with both hands in the sunlight. Mitch turned his head to look at Jace and Brit in the back seat.

"We told them we were going to think it over, maybe even ask my father and be back soon," Kris said. "Our supersalesman did leave us to make a phone call he had scheduled, but since we saw a camera and tiny microphone mounted in the room we made sure our conversation while he was gone was all about how Daddy would love to have that."

"Way to go," Mitch told them and gave both a fist bump. "And speaking of that, the helo's gassed up, so strap in and let's get going."

"I loved the view of the Glades from the air on the way over," Brit said.

It was a windy early evening, perfect for a flight into the sunset with the island hammocks and patches of water beneath them, the sight of gators catching the last of the sun, the flocks of ibis and egrets taking flight below—though the pilot had to watch out for those. Birds near airports in general were bad news.

Jace was content to be in the back with Brit, though he'd rather be at least in the copilot seat if she weren't here. Man, he missed flying, but jets, not helos. He couldn't wait to start training for the hurricane flights. The *whap-whap* of the rotor overhead became a blur of noise.

"Homeward bound," Jace told Brit and took her hand. He had to raise his voice. "And someday we'll say that about our own home, too. Soon. I promise."

* * *

As they flew westward from Big Cypress National Park, they could spot the Western Florida coastline with its mangrove islands of all sizes. The sun was sinking, throwing a blaze of crimson across the water. Mitch had notified Marco Executive Airport that they were coming in to be sure their landing would be clear of jets. He would put the chopper down near the hangar where they had left their car.

Mitch put the helo's lights on. As they sliced through the evening dusk, holding hands, Brit and Jace looked down at the jigsaw puzzle pieces of small islands and water. Some lights on heavily populated Marco Island were already lit. He spotted the bridge to the mainland. If she wasn't busy putting Lexi to bed, he would have insisted on stopping by Claire's to tell her about today.

"A small jet is going to land and gets precedence," Mitch told them, repeating what the airport control radioed back. "Going to go around, then put down."

"Ever heard about the sunset explosion?" Jace asked Brit, raising his voice over the sound of the rotor and rush of wind.

"Isn't that just a myth, a tourist look-for thing?"

"Absolutely not. When the sun sets over the Gulf of Mexico, if conditions are just right, there's a split second when the human eye sees what appears to be an explosion of extra color, sometimes even movement."

"Have you seen it?"

"Twice, but I think you have to be at beach level. Another exciting experience I promise to my beautiful fiancée."

Jace knew Brit wasn't a nervous flier as long as she had something to distract her, but she hadn't flown that much, except with him. He'd like to do more of that, fly them off into the sunset of happiness someday. He had to grin at that poetic thought. Should he tell her that too?

"Our turn to go in," Mitch said, maybe to himself.

Jace saw they were over either Addison Bay or East Marco Cove. The water here was darker, shadowed by the low mangrove islands as the bright ball of sun slanted even lower.

A jolt wracked the chopper. Brit screamed and grabbed his arm.

"Rotors!" Mitch shouted. "Bird strike? I saw something!"

Jace flashed back to the scene at the country club reception. Chaos. Cuts. Broken glass.

They tilted almost sideways. Despite his seat belt, Jace bumped into Brit.

"No control. Going down! Brace!" Mitch shouted. "Still got some gas on board, so pray for water instead of land!"

The chopper rotated, went into a spin. Jace was suddenly so dizzy he almost threw up.

"Brace," he told Brit, reaching for her arm. "Feet flat on floor! Head down! I'll get you out."

If I get out, he thought, as the impact of the water crashed into the side of the chopper and their spinning downward stopped.

The last horrible sounds stabbing his brain were *bird* and *brace* and Brit's endless scream.

CHAPTER TWENTY-NINE

Claire had just put Trey down and read a story to Lexi, who was a very good guess-some-words reader for her age and now wanted to help "read" her own big-girl books at night. Nita and Bronco were here for another day or two, until a still-shaky Nita could feel good about moving to their new house again. Every time they went there to clean the place out, something awful happened.

Claire sank on the couch, more than tired. Well, so what, because she had more Black Bog work to do. She was not allowed to bring any photos or detailed descriptions of bodies home with her but she was making some notes about the corpses she'd seen from earlier excavations. If she could see some sort of pattern, it might throw more light on her trio.

She'd just spend a few minutes on this, then check on Nick in his home office where he'd been making lists of assignments for himself and law firm associates in preparing Dale's defense. He was agonizing over whether to advise Dale to explain his Nazi connection to the police or just wait to see if it came up. Nick was also worried whether he, as lead lawyer, would be with-holding evidence on that, in which case he could face disciplinary hearings before the Bar Association. But wouldn't people sympathize with someone who wanted to obliterate his great-uncle's ties to Hitler and his horrible regime by destroying Nazi memorabilia on his own property?

Nick had also shared with her that he was wondering who else of Marian James's associates might have been told about Twisted Trees, even perhaps the Hitler connection. Could word of that leak to the media or the police through a source, a contact of Marian's, now that she was dead? Nick had said he was tempted to research the silent partners on her Endangered Properties Committee to interview people who knew her. Claire had told him she'd gladly help—but not tonight.

She kept her phone close by, waiting for Brit or even Jace to call with what they'd learned across the state today at the Vances' other Art for Art's Sake shop. Maybe Brit would even stop by, since both Jace and Heck were hoping the drone attack at the country club had been perpetrated by the wacko family in the dispute over the price of golf course land. That would mean it had nothing to do with them, and they were just innocent by-standers.

Nick came in stretching and yawning before she even started her project. "Not heard from them yet?" he asked. "It's dark. They won't just show up here, will they?"

"Brit said they'd call. I'd sure like to know what they found before I go to the bog tomorrow. I'm going to really press 'the Senator' for even brief looks at the artifacts I haven't seen, in-cluding one special item."

"Claire, if you're thinking he might be selling copies of—or the real—artifacts from those graves, be damn careful. I suppose it's partly finders keepers in the law, but I'd have to look into it—in my spare time," he said with a roll of his eyes.

"Remember, I didn't tell you any of that. I'm just fascinated by all this archaeology of the ancients. It is important, and I want to keep this job."

"Okay, I know." He yawned again and flopped down on the couch beside her. "Don't tell me any more so you don't have to shoot me, Mata Hari."

"Pick someone else to joke about," she said, leaning her shoulder against his. "She was shot to death by the French for being a German spy. I wish Brit and Jace would check in."

As if she'd willed it, her cell phone sounded. She reached for it and looked at the caller ID. Marco Island Fire and Rescue?

"Hello."

"I would like to speak with Alexandra Britten or Claire Markwood please."

"Alexandra's my six-year-old daughter. I'm Claire Markwood." Her voice trembled. She swallowed hard. Nick leaned closer, listening.

"This is the Marco Island airport patched through from our fire and rescue unit. A helicopter has gone down on approach to the Marco Island Executive Airport. I've called the contact name of Jason Britten left by the pilot Mitchell Blakeman, who filed a Fort Lauderdale flight plan, but Jason Britten doesn't answer, and from earlier flights from here we cross-referenced his contact number to this one."

Claire could tell by Nick's frown that he could hear.

The woman on the phone went on, "We know the approximate site from where the blips went off the radar screen. Help is on the way."

Claire's hand began to shake. She could hardly hold the phone. Couldn't breathe. That time they were in a plane that ditched near Cuba—raw nightmare.

"We know the people," she said, finally in full voice. "Three aboard. Went down where?"

Nick had put his arm hard around her and was leaning close to hear, maybe to prop her up. This was all her fault. She had sent them. How could this have happened with Mitch at the controls? Jace had said Mitch was a great helicopter and jet pilot.

"Our squad has gone out to search, and we've advised local Fire and Rescue also. We don't know their status at this time. We're sending another helicopter with search lights and the beach rescue patrol. We believe it was a water landing but—"

"If we come to the airport, can we get to the site from there?"

"Please don't come at this time. It may hamper the efforts of—"

Claire ended the call. "I'll tell Nita we're leaving," she told Nick, pulling from his embrace and springing to her feet. "You heard?"

"I'll get our jackets and flashlights, but we can't get in their way."

"It's my fault," she insisted, feeling sick to her stomach but also angry and energized. "I have to be there, have to help. If they are hurt or gone—any of them—I'll never forgive myself, and Lexi won't either."

Jace wasn't sure where he was. Swimming? No water near the base in Iraq. His head hurt, his soul hurt. Had he ditched his jet in the Persian Gulf?

Then reality returned. Chopper crash. Had to get out. Had to save Brit.

"Mitch? Mitch?"

Damn dark here, water rushing in through shattered Plexiglas. Not in the Gulf, but one of the waterways between the mangrove islands.

Brit. Where was Brit? Oh, strapped in right beside him. He unhooked his seat belt. The power of the water pouring in scared him. She was still in her seat belt, bent over in the brace position. Unconscious or dead? How long since they'd crashed? With this deluge, they were going under, going down to drown.

He unhooked her seat belt and hauled her up into his arms, sopping wet. She sucked in air, panting, clinging to him so hard her fingernails bit into his skin. Thank God, she was alive and conscious.

He tried to sound rational, calm. How large was this pocket of air? "Brit, we're going out through that hole in the dome, but it's sideways now."

"Can't see. Dark."

"Listen to me! We have to wait until the water comes up to a good level so we can swim out, hold our breath. Hang on here. Got to find Mitch."

He half swam, half dove toward the pilot's seat. Mitch must have hit his head bringing them down in a somewhat upright position. Thank God, his head was above water but he wasn't responding. Was he even breathing?

Jace unhooked his friend's seat belt, and, still fighting the driving force of fairly warm salt water, keeping his head above the rising level of it, he dragged Mitch into the back seat, nearer to the broken window. He was terrified at how limp he was.

"Mitch? Mitch!"

He shook him and hit his back between his shoulder blades as hard as he could manage in the water. If he stayed in here to give him breaths or CPR, the chopper would fill with too much water, and they'd all drown.

But Mitch spit out water and coughed. Two for two, Jace thought, but if they didn't move fast and just right, all three of them could be gone.

And then, made heavier with the air bubble gone, the entire chopper shifted and settled lower.

"Gotta go now!" Jace shouted but swallowed a mouthful of water.

He spit it out, grabbed Brit's arm and thrust her ahead of him, shoving her toward where he was certain the opening had been. Water wasn't pouring in anymore. He let go of Mitch and pushed ahead of Brit, feeling in the darkness for the jagged opening. If it had settled on the bottom of the bay, they were goners.

But no, there was a space, just at a different angle. He surfaced and told her, "There is an opening. Get a big breath. Go down my body, feel my leg. It's where my foot is. Go! I'll be right behind you! I love you. Go!"

She sucked in a breath and went under, grabbing his leg, kicking, fighting her way down. And then, thank God, she let go, must have gone out and surfaced. *Please, God, let her be all right. Let her make it, whatever happens to us.*

He could sense the tide or the moving water was going to shift this baby again. Glad he never flew these birds, only his beloved jets. Got to go now, drag Mitch out to fly another day.

He had trouble pulling Mitch under. Were his lungs full of air? They weren't going to make it, but he sure as hell wasn't leaving Mitch behind. Never leave a fellow soldier or pilot behind, not even their bodies.

His lungs were bursting as he held his breath to shove Mitch through the opening. His arm got cut along the edge of the shattered plastic bubble. So damn dark here. He wriggled through the opening after Mitch, still holding to him. His ankle snagged something hard—a broken rotor?—and he shot toward the surface with it clinging to him.

The first thing he heard and thought he must be imagining was the *whap-whap* of rotor blades. Was he remembering the wreck? But a blinding floodlight shot through the black sky to fix on them. A rescue chopper overhead?

"Jace! Jace! They've found us, they're all around!" a female voice screamed.

Brit. She'd made it. She must have seen or heard the rescue chopper, but who was all around? Mitch sucked in a breath, coughing, gagging, then another.

But in the reflected light of the search beam as the chopper circled overhead, Jace realized they likely hadn't been found by search and rescue. For in that beam, when it wasn't boring into his eyes, he saw pairs of glowing eyes, reflecting the light.

He'd been gator hunting with Bronco once, where they located their prey by shining lights into their eyes. He knew what those were.

"Claire, we can't get farther into this swampy area," Nick insisted, as he drove the unlit road near the small airport, following the big beam of light up ahead. That must be a second chopper, searching for the wreck. And it was circling one spot.

"Then we can go on foot," Claire insisted, leaning toward the dashboard and looking up.

"They have professionals out here searching," he told her, stopping their car but reaching over to be sure she didn't get out. "I know you're blaming yourself, but you couldn't know the chopper would go down."

"Poor Brit too! I asked her for this favor. What if some drug czar is still out to get Jace and Mitch? That picture in the paper may have been the wrong move. Nick, look, I see vehicle lights heading out there on the road."

"If it is criminals after them, we can't go closer. I'll call Jensen's police station, ask them to let him know. They may send help too."

"No, look! One of the vehicles out there is some sort of police car or rescue vehicle—a blinking light bar, see? Reminds me of when we got to Twisted Tree the night Marian died. Hope that's—that's not an omen," she added and burst into tears. "You know, with her body so charred from that fire that they're taking so long with the autopsy. Nick, please just go a little closer. If we can help… I've got to help, to know…for Lexi."

He heaved a sigh. "Yeah, for all of us. Jace is my friend too," he told her, regretting he'd not trusted him lately—or Claire's feelings for him.

He turned on the car's bright lights again and drove carefully down the bumpy road behind the lighted vehicles, toward the hovering helicopter which seemed balanced atop its light beam in the black sky.

★ ★ ★

"Brit, can you climb a tree?" Jace shouted. "There's gators!"

"I saw one. I am up a tree. But help on the ground must be coming!"

Damn, what a hell of a brave woman! But what if those gators came in the water after him and Mitch or tried to snatch them on the bank? He'd seen those prehistoric hangovers drag their prey into the water to drown and devour it.

"I can swim," Mitch gasped out. "Better off on the bank."

"I can hit them with something here caught on my foot," Jace said and reached down to free his ankle. He thought it was a piece of broken rotor blade at first, but it was something else. Shiny plastic. Black. It would have to do.

They both swam toward Brit's voice as she called encouragement. Jace crawled quickly up on the bank, then helped Mitch out. Though the chopper noise was still loud, Jace heard what he knew was a gator roar. Then, damn, here came Brit stumbling toward them to help drag Mitch to his feet.

A cluster of cabbage palms loomed before them. They'd get cut climbing those, but who cared? Better than a gator's teeth. He'd hit the gators right across the eyes if they attacked, or if these were hit men to try to finish them off. His thoughts—his ideas—foggy—floating…

Mosquitoes swarmed them, though that was nothing next to gators. Brit tried to swat the swarm of bugs away as men on foot with more lights burst into the area.

Gators or not, Jace was going to make them all hit the ground. If those men had guns, they were doomed.

"Airport search and rescue!" a man shouted. In the beam of the man's flashlight, for the first time, Jace could see they had missed the island, though this ground was swampy.

"Alligators here!" Jace shouted, but they could see and hear the beasts smacking into the water to get away from the noise and the men.

Brit burst into tears of relief. Jace sat Mitch on the ground where the guy looked dazed but at least conscious. In the looming lights he saw his friend had a big bruise blooming on his forehead. Hell, flying through hurricanes would be a snap after this.

Then—amazing—he heard Claire's voice. No, maybe he was hallucinating again. But there she was, crying, pushing closer, fighting her way along the narrow sandy bank on dry land that appeared to be across from a decent-sized mangrove island the chopper had just missed. Thank God, the gators had just vacated the area.

"Good landing, pal," Jace said to Mitch as his buddy shook his head, trying to clear it. "Is this real? Is she really here?"

"I'm so sorry I asked you to do this, Brit!" Claire cried, hugging Brit who hugged her back, before Claire embraced Jace too. Nick was here, right behind Claire, and he hugged Jace too.

They all huddled, Claire and Nick now holding up the two of them, sopping wet. "What's that you're holding, Jace?" Nick asked.

That's right, Jace thought. He'd hauled a weapon of sorts out of the water. He stared down in shock at the dark plastic piece of chopper blade under his left arm. No, not that. It was the chopped-up rotor of a drone.

CHAPTER THIRTY

Claire thought it was like a reunion at Naples Community Hospital that next afternoon—family and friends plus Ken Jensen visiting Jace and Mitch. The two friends were in the same hospital room, both under concussion protocol watch as well as being treated for cuts, contusions and some water intake, not to mention mosquito bites, which Claire and Nick had been scratching at too.

Mitch, who had some water still in his lungs, had been sedated since he'd been delirious with a fever, raving and trying to get out of bed, but by late afternoon the day after the crash, he had calmed down and his fever was gone.

Brit had been treated for bruises in the ER last night, but, amazingly, was in the best shape of the three of them. More power to women, Claire thought. The stubborn Brit had camped out next to Jace's bed last night.

Claire was so thankful the three of them were not seriously hurt. She'd promised Jace she'd bring Lexi to see him. After conferring with Detective Jensen, Nick had gone to pick Lexi up from school to bring her to see Jace. Claire had not gone to Black Bog as she'd planned, but had phoned to tell Andrea only that she had to visit a friend in the hospital. If the Vances could hold things back, she could too. But she had also called Kris to tell her what happened and that Mitch was going to be fine.

As Claire paced alone in the waiting room down the hall, Ken Jensen came in after interviewing both men and Brit.

"Nick's not back yet?" he asked, closing the door behind him.

"He should be soon. He's agreed to bring our daughter here for a short visit, because Jace and Mitch are going to disappear to Washington, DC, when they're released."

"So I hear. Hope that means they won't get targeted again. They said they needed to go there for training anyway."

"We're grateful for the officer you stationed outside their door. Washington won't be exactly the witness protection program, but they probably told you that Jace notified their new government flight boss what happened."

"Yeah. They told me. The two new hurricane hunters sound like they've been the hunted so far."

"Detective, the thing is, if this mess isn't solved, they may be too big of a risk for that new assignment they're so excited about. At least Jace considers a big busy hospital—with a police officer—safe for a little time with Lexi. Not seeing Lexi has been hard on him—on both of them."

"I can understand. Meanwhile, dealing with drug lords, if that's who's after them, is out of my element," Jensen admitted. "Except for an occasional low-level arrest, that is. Since there doesn't seem to be any reason Brittany Hoffman would have enemies, she may just have been in the wrong place at the wrong time."

"My fault, since I asked them to go across the state to do a favor for me."

"So you said—and that's all you're saying?" he asked, looking narrow-eyed at her. "None of the walking wounded are talking about where or why they went, and Nick said it's up to you to tell me. The thing is either someone's following them closely to know they took that helicopter, or else it was a random act by an idiot—not uncommon in this new world of drones. Everyone's on edge that a drone is going to bring down a passenger jet someday."

"Jace—my ex—used to fly those."

"Nice try at a topic change. So he told me. Fighter jets and travel jets, he called them. Look, Claire, there were no fingerprints on the drone, since it's been scoured by water and sand, but then there were none on the one at the country club either. By the way, no one in the helicopter blames you and they were glad to run the favor for you. That's all they'll say. I repeat, want to tell me more?"

"Not unless I have to. Nothing illegal, but my current assignment needs to remain private until—well, until the project is announced. I'm afraid I can't tell you more right now."

"I'll bet it's that you *won't* more than you *can't*. Let's sit down," he said gesturing to a round table with four chairs. He pulled out one for her and himself. He put his phone on the table, stared at something on it for a moment, then went on, "Claire, I suppose your favorite lawyer will have a fit I'm asking this without him here, but just answer this. Could the drone attack on their helicopter have anything to do with this little mission you sent them on?"

She startled. "I can't see how. No one but them knew about it. The drone—like you said, it must have been some idiot targeting a random helicopter or else the drug lords you mentioned. I'm sure Jace and Mitch told you there have been hits on Stingray pilots elsewhere."

"Yeah, and it needs to stay elsewhere. So this special advisory assignment you're on—no links to Marian James and pricy, historic real estate, right? I looked at your Clear Path website, and I see in the past you've advised various local companies about interviewing staff or vetting job applicants, even detecting fraud." He tapped his cell phone and her website came up on it. He lifted the phone and waved it at her, before tapping her homepage off. "Were your ex-husband and two friends over in Lauderdale on a fraud case, anything like that? I'm just groping in the dark on this."

"No one has hired me to look into fraud for several years," she protested, but her mind was racing. She had sent two men and a woman to check out the possible misuse of bog artifacts, so would that be considered fraud or theft? Had the ancient bog trio committed some similar crime and died for it?

She didn't want to lie to this man, but she could hardly confess her reasoning. Besides, just as with Dale's act of arson on his own land, the artifacts were found on private property. Even if the Vances had been told she'd been in their Naples shop asking about ancient artifacts, there was no way they could have known she was checking on them through friends across the state. She hadn't even told Kris about her suspicions.

"Did Nick have time to tell you the findings on Marian James's autopsy?" Jensen asked, surprising her at the sudden change in topic as he pocketed his cell phone.

"No," she said sitting forward, elbows on the table. "It must have just come out. Obviously, cause of death would be the fire. She must have been burned to death or died from smoke inhalation first."

"Neither, because the ME says she was dead by then. She had a high carbon monoxide level in her lungs. No throat damage because she wasn't breathing when the fire spread. She was choked to death—strangled. Her hyoid bone at the front of her throat was broken, just like Cyndi Lindley's."

"So, Lexi," Nick said once they were in his car, "I need to explain something to you."

It had taken him a lot longer to get her out of school than he'd planned. He understood safety protocol, but the secretary had to consult the assistant principal and he had to show ID because

Claire, Darcy and Jace were the only three people on the safe-
to-go list. That annoyed him. Sure, he was always at the firm
when Lexi was finished with school for the day, but Claire should
have thought to put his name on the permission list anyway.

"Okay, I'm listening," she said, sounding very adult, as if to
calm him. "You said Mommy's okay, but I heard you say we are
going to the hospital."

"Yes, Mommy's okay. Your dad is okay too"

"Remember, you're Dad and my real dad is Daddy."

"Right. The thing is your real father is just fine but he's in
the hospital because the helicopter he was in with Brit and his
friend Mitch had an accident. But no one is hurt bad."

"How bad, though?" she said, turning to him. "And Brit's
gonna be my stepmother. You sure she's all right?"

"Yes, honey, she's all right. Jace—your Daddy—just has some
cuts and bruises, but he wants to see you."

He saw out of the corner of his eye that she folded her arms
over her chest. "He didn't want to see me before."

"Yes, he really did, but he was afraid to. Darn it, Lexi, I'm
going to talk to you like an adult now, so I want you to act like
one, all right? Can you?"

"Was he flying the plane? He loves planes."

"No, he wasn't flying, his friend Mitch was. I'll let your Daddy
tell you. But the thing is, someone must have been angry with
him or his friend Mitch or even Brit. I know you've been angry
with him for staying away lately, but he wanted really badly to
see you and does now too."

"Somebody bad is after him?" she asked, frowning, almost
pouting.

"We—I—don't know. Maybe they are after Mitch, and your
Daddy was with him. You're going to see a policeman there
guarding them, so don't be afraid. Your Daddy needs you to
hug him and smile, not to be angry with him when it wasn't his

fault. You know adults and parents sometimes have hard times too, just like kids."

She heaved a huge sigh and reached over to touch his arm. "I love him, but I love you too, Dad, 'cause you love my Mommy and me too."

He had to blink back tears. "I sure do, Lexi. And I want to be not only your stepdad—your Dad—but your friend."

She patted his arm as if to reassure him. "Mommy loves you too, even if she worries about my real Daddy sometimes. I'll try to think like an adult—like you said—but don't tell her you said I'm grown up now, 'cause she might get upset. I want to take care of her but it's hard sometimes."

He was thinking *You got that right,* but he said only, "Then we agree on that. Good." Emotion swamped him so hard he almost lost his voice. He blinked back tears blurring his vision, so he wouldn't steer them off the road.

After Lexi hugged Claire, Claire took her in to see Jace. The dividing curtain was closed between his and Mitch's beds.

Across the curtain, Kris had just come with flowers for Mitch. "I should be sending you those!" Claire had heard Mitch tell Kris. "So glad to see you—and no ice skates this time."

Claire had noticed that Kris had hesitated at the door to the room for a moment, staring at a sleeping Jace, before Claire had pointed and whispered to her, "Mitch is in the bed by the window." With a nod and a squeeze of her arm, Kris had walked farther in. That face blindness, Claire thought. Could any man of a certain age in a hospital bed and a hospital gown pass for Mitch to Kris at first?

Just before Claire stepped out, she saw Lexi squeal and make a dash for Jace. He startled, opened his eyes and embraced her in a huge hug, then pulled her up to sit on his bed. He smiled at Claire over the child's head before Claire stepped out into the hall. Nick leaned there against the wall, looking tired and upset.

"The school didn't want me to take her at first," he said.

"Oh—sorry. I guess I forgot to put you on the list."

"Yeah, well, I'd like to be at the head of it."

"Let's go down the hall," she suggested, and they walked together. "You are at the head of *my* list, Nick. It's just that I overlooked it because you're always working when she gets out. I'll fix that right away." She linked her arm through his, and he pulled her closer to his side. "We've come through a lot. I thank God we have each other."

They sat on a sofa next to a potted palm and a window. They could see Jace's hospital door from there.

"Lexi's amazing," he told her. "She ended up comforting me in a way."

"She has her moments."

Still holding her hand, he leaned back and heaved a huge sigh. "Hopefully, all of us do. I see Jensen's gone but I'm agonizing over whether to level with him about Dale's Nazi connection, with Dale's permission, of course."

"Which he may not give you."

"I think I could convince him."

"And I'm agonizing about not telling him anything about what's going on at Black Bog. But what about the possible Cyndi–Marian James connection? Did our favorite detective tell you the results of Marian's autopsy, at least what the ME can tell so far? Are two strangulation deaths and two broken hyoid bones enough of a connection to assume they had the same killer?"

"Jensen thinks so. I do too. Is there any way you can do a little very private research for me into Marian's life—friends, enemies? Heck is too busy with this idea he has for an invention."

"You're thinking especially to look at people Marian worked with?"

"Jensen's pretty much eliminated family troubles as a reason for her death. There's an ex-husband she hasn't seen for years who lives in Hawaii. She lived alone, so that's a dead end—

Didn't mean it that way. Not funny. Damn, nothing's fun or funny right now."

She squeezed his hand tighter. "Yes, I'll check into Marian's Endangered Properties Committee, but I think she had some silent partners or investors, so I may run into a wall there."

"I know you're busy with your own bog business, so I appreciate that."

She nodded, wishing she could tell him even more than she had about her suspicions. Brit had filled her in on everything that had happened at the Lauderdale shop, so Claire felt she had something to hold over Brad Vance's head now, but to make him admit what? Was he so desperate for funding that he ignored the fact that someone could ask what inspired them to sell copies of ancient artifacts? Their work at the bog needed funding, which was why, she thought, the Vances had just sold a long-time home they loved.

So she was not going to confront either of them but just keep her eyes open—and view at least Brad's photos of those precious objects again. Brit had said the dagger they had seen in Fort Lauderdale had a woman with raised hands on the hilt, and Claire thought that figure might be Reaching Woman—or was she reaching for too much on that? And why hadn't she noted that in the detailed photos? Had he showed her all he had?

After a long pause, she told Nick, "Jensen tried to get me to explain why I sent Jace and Brit across the state, but I stonewalled him. I don't need him crashing in at the bog to question the Vances until I'm more sure what's really going on. So are we both holding out on him?"

"For now. I'll talk to Dale, and you just stick to keeping your eyes open, but no interrogations or confrontations."

"The truth is I don't want to get the Vances in trouble. I want to protect them and their work. It's important, far-reaching for historical knowledge, for mankind, really. And I want to be part of their continuing project."

But, she thought, wouldn't Brad's first sniff that she'd been checking up on his handling of artifacts mean that, no matter how badly Kris or even Andrea wanted her on the team, he'd terminate her?

CHAPTER THIRTY-ONE

That evening Nick was glad he'd phoned Dale. The guy sounded shaky. He said he was sitting at the end of the Naples pier just staring at the water, waiting for it to get dark and that he might stay there all night.

Nick explained to Claire, kissed her, Lexi and Trey and headed for the pier. He didn't like the idea of one of the firm's formerly competent lawyers, his client, out on bail but accused of a double homicide, sounding damned depressed out on the end of the pier as darkness fell.

He found a parking place and jogged toward the pier, then out onto it. The sun looked huge and crimson as it bled into the watery horizon. Not too many fishermen were out this late at this time of year like during the winter season. He was careful not to get hit when they flicked their line back over their shoulders to cast. When he was a kid, he'd gotten snagged by a hook on his ear, but his dad had rushed him to a doctor friend to tend to it.

How he still missed his dad who had been gone for years—his murder staged to look like suicide. Since then, Nick had helped numerous people prove cause of death with his South Shores side project, and he needed to help Dale now. But he didn't see him where he'd said he'd be.

His heartbeat kicked up. No—there he was, way over in the corner of the pier, as far out as he could go, leaning against the wooden railing, staring into the sliding depths of the breaking waves.

"Dale!" he called to him and joined him at the rail.

His former junior partner—relieved of his duties at the firm for now—turned toward him. Either the guy had been standing there so long that his face was streaked with salt water spray or he'd been crying. His usual suave and neat appearance had disintegrated to his wearing cut-offs and a ratty-looking sweatshirt.

"Thanks for coming out here," Dale said, his voice a monotone. "I figured we needed to talk. I suppose the office would be the best place, but if I can't be there as a partner, I'd rather not come in as a client. Everybody stares, pretending not to, no doubt thinking, 'Poor Dale. Law career over, might get disbarred. Maybe he even committed those murders, lots of proof against him.'"

Nick put a firm hand on Dale's shoulder. "We would all be behind you if you were just any client, but you're more than that. You're one of us, and we're going to fight for you."

He nodded, still looking out over the white-capped waves. The wind was increasing and so was Nick's unease about Dale's state of mind. But he had to pursue his plan.

"Dale, I was with Ken Jensen earlier today because he's investigating a plane crash three friends of ours were in—brought down by a drone right off Marco Island, though they all survived in pretty good shape."

Dale finally turned to look at him. "That's good news for them. And Jensen brought me up?"

"He was investigating the crash, but when I started to think about what we're holding back from him, I wanted to consult with you. You've got a good lawyer's brain. We don't want the

Nazi connection curse coming out at the trial. It needs to be eased out beforehand, common knowledge by then. The fact you wanted to burn Nazi memorabilia you detest and past ties to your family could get you sympathy, not blame, from a detective, a prosecutor and a jury."

"Except for that woman's burned body in the mix—like I was trying to stop her, as well as Cyndi, from dragging that out after all these years."

"Yeah, and one other problematic thing. Marian James was burned in that fire, but cause of death before that was strangulation with a broken hyoid bone—sound familiar?"

"Damn! And Jensen arrested me before he knew that, but now he'll have more evidence—so he thinks—to nail me for both murders. But I see what you mean. The Nazi connection needs to be communicated to the prosecutor before we go to trial. But we don't even have a date yet! That's way off in time, way off in thinking."

"Is it? As soon as that breaks from another source—"

"If it does."

"That would mean you could lose me and maybe the firm when we get slapped with professional misconduct for not admitting it earlier. And, yes, I'm worried about myself and the firm getting hit with fines or sanctions. We don't need that, but you need us!"

He looked away, squinting out over the waves again. Nick knew it would be so easy for him to jump from here, to hit his head on the huge wooden girders holding up the pier, especially with daylight fading where no one would see to help him.

"Nick," Dale said, still not looking at him, "I give you permission to tell Jensen about my great-uncle and the Nazi stuff I wanted to burn in that apartment. It gives me an even bigger—hopefully sympathetic—reason for the fire."

"That's brave of you and the right thing to do. Eva Braun's German diary suggests she was never pregnant—and of her desire to kill herself, which she must have done in the upper room of the apartment. Dale, suicide is always wrong, and your state of mind right now scares me. We're going to see this through together. And that diary is yours if you want it back for proof later, but how about I just keep it for now?"

"Yeah, that's best. So, Eva Braun speaks from the grave. Wonder where my great-uncle buried or burned her body. But for now, however damning it is to link my last name to Hitler's wife, I do need help," Dale whispered, pressing the palms of his hands over his eyes. "I have nightmares I'm burning up in that apartment I torched, that the woman burned there is Eva Braun, not Marian James. I've gotten to the point I can't stand to be closed in my apartment or at the house I want to sell. I keep thinking about prison, and I couldn't stand that, couldn't face being locked up or worse. Nick, I don't know how my life went so wrong so fast when all I wanted to do was get Cyndi out of my life."

Nick shuddered. Granted, Dale was the obvious candidate for the two murders. Other possibilities he'd checked into, as had Ken Jensen, came out in weak second place. And what Dale had just admitted sounded almost like a confession he'd hurt Cyndi, at least. This guy was really losing it. If he worded his desire to move on from Cyndi like that—"get her out of my life"—that could ruin him in a courtroom. Didn't he know that?

"Dale, let's get you to a psychiatrist. There's a good one the firm's used before. The doctor's trustworthy and discreet. It sounds like you're clinically depressed, maybe claustrophobic. Okay? You have your car near here?" he said, putting his hand on the man's elbow.

"I walked. Just wanted sky and sea."

"Sure, I can understand that. Let's take my car. If you don't want to come into the office as we put your defense together, we can meet outside somewhere, but you need to go home right now, see that doctor tomorrow. I'll set it up."

"Wish I could go home again," he said with a sigh as they

started back down the long pier. "Have my dad around, my mother in her right mind. That old Betty Richards next door has tried to mother me too, ever since her son hanged himself about twenty years ago, so maybe I wouldn't even mind her around. She used to be so possessive and protective of me after that. I hated it then, but could use some of that now."

Nick's mind seized on that latest bombshell as they walked off the windy, spray-spattered pier. Dale might be a flight risk, suicidal or even guilty. Betty Richards just had another motive hung around her neck for having at least killed Cyndi. And if Marian had been bothering Dale, maybe for killing her too. But could that old woman strangle someone? Betty had told Claire she'd seen the two murdered women together back when they were still alive. Could he trust that? Could he trust anyone but Claire?

Jolted awake, Claire sat straight up in bed. Nightmare! But at least one she hadn't gotten up to act out, though she wished she didn't recall it so clearly.

Beside her in bed, Nick slept on, snoring slightly. He'd come home late after getting a junior partner at the firm to stay with Dale in his apartment, then made sure he'd get him to a psychiatrist's office tomorrow for an appointment Nick had made.

She was too warm. She whipped the sheet off her side of the bed and got up carefully, quietly. She didn't have to have a psych degree to analyze where she'd cooked up that dream, at least some of it. She'd dreamed she'd crashed into the bog, going under, going down. She had fought her way upward through the black peat and mud and found Reaching Woman— Yes, reaching down to help her up so she wouldn't die.

But after Reaching Woman had pulled her up, Claire had seen she raised her arms the way Brit had described on that dagger in Fort Lauderdale, the way some people did in church when they were deeply moved. It was the way referees at a football game signaled a touchdown. Was Reaching Woman giving a blessing or a curse? Was she a religious figure, one who should be pure, but who had fallen for either Hunter or Leader and paid with her life?

Claire gasped. She envisioned the worst part of the nightmare, the part that had woken her up. She had seen again, just as when the dig team uncovered the woman's body, the dagger in her chest. And in the dream, Claire had clearly seen—knew for sure by the angle of the weapon—that the woman had stabbed herself.

Her knees went weak, and she knelt by the bed with her head on the sheet, using it to blot her silent tears. Could that be true? Or had she dreamed that because Nick had told her he thought Dale might be suicidal? That had set off his memories of his own father's death, and she had comforted him.

She knew she wouldn't sleep right now. Maybe she would go in Trey's room and watch him sleep innocently, no worries in the world.

She put on a robe and tiptoed out, checked on both children and went quietly past the guest room where Bronco and Nita slept. She sat at the dining room table where she'd left her laptop and turned it on. She'd just do a little work—that favor for Nick tracing Marian James's contacts—then go back to bed.

She turned a lamp on. First she searched for ancient artifacts for sale in the state of Florida. Nothing but some Seminole tribe souvenirs at their casinos, but then who would be stupid enough to advertise priceless, prehistoric artifacts online? Certainly not a former Florida senator or his savvy wife, who now owned and operated a historic dig that would rock the world when it was announced.

She turned to searching Marian James's Endangered Properties Committee. Bingo! A beautifully crafted, detailed website. Marian's name was still all over it, but no one else's except the committee's treasurer, Harmon Kingsdale, with his contact information and a plea to make a donation to the cause of preserving Florida history for future generations.

She wrote down that contact information. It wouldn't hurt to make a call or visit Mr. Kingsdale to see if she could dig up any other names for Nick's defense team to question. His name sounded familiar but she couldn't quite place it.

But now the hunt was on for any possible enemies Marian might have had. And her own hunt was on to study Hunter's dagger handle again so she could decide if Reaching Woman might have stabbed herself and why. Had one of the men she might have loved forced her to do it?

The next morning after Claire waited with Lexi until the school bus came and before Nick left for the office, they sat together for a cup of coffee. She held Trey in her arms. Nita was still in bed, and Bronco had headed for the law firm, since they were especially conscious of security lately with not being able to trust that Tanner and Will would be heading home as they'd said.

"Harmon Kingsdale," Nick said when she filled him in on her research last night. "No kidding? So there's probably big bucks behind Marian's committee."

"His name is familiar, but who is he?"

"The founder of Pine Ridge Luxury Homes. Big houses, some in Pelican Bay, some up by Estero."

"Well, I guess it makes sense a home builder would be interested in helping to save and preserve endangered lands or properties. Should one of us interview him?"

"We can hardly send Jensen. But I might make him nervous as he knows I'm a criminal lawyer. Dale would be persona non grata right now, though he needs something purposeful to do. You'd have to go with a fake name, and that's no good. Who's left that we can trust?"

"Lexi? Trey?" she said giving the baby a little bounce which he traded for a gurgling smile.

"Very funny."

"I don't want to ask anything else of Brit after I nearly got her killed."

"That wasn't your fault, unless you've been sneaking out to master using drones as a weapon. But without alarming Kingsdale that we're trying to learn more about Marian, how to approach him to get the names of others on their committee who might have had an argument with Marian, or at least know someone who did. Maybe we could have someone approach him for a donation. It's Gina's weekend to be off duty in the clinic in Miami, and she'll be here Friday afternoon, so how about we ask her to go see Kingsdale with Heck, maybe play up the donation angle, just something to get in the door with him and not tip him off as to why."

"Sounds good," she said and they clinked coffee mugs.

They were desperate for help. But what Claire didn't say again was that the last time she asked friends to do an errand for her to find out information, they were all nearly killed.

CHAPTER THIRTY-TWO

"Finally," Nick said, appearing from behind today's newspaper which he was reading at the breakfast table. "Marian James's funeral announcement is here. It's tomorrow afternoon at three, calling hours one until three. Her next of kin are evidently a niece and nephew from Pensacola. Not much time for people to plan to attend, but then the ME probably kept her body for a long time for a complicated autopsy. The testing for toxins would have dragged out the release of her body."

Claire shuddered. Although they hadn't seen the woman's corpse close-up, it had looked so dark and terribly twisted from the fire. At a distance, it had reminded her of the Black Bog corpses. And, though she tried to get it out of her mind, she kept remembering Cyndi's frozen body with that silent scream on her face. Had Marian's face—had Reaching Woman's face once—looked that way too?

"Maybe we should go and see who shows up," she said, trying to keep the tremor out of her voice. "I've heard of cases where the murderer attends a funeral out of curiosity or sick pride."

"For sure, Dale won't go. I wouldn't let him even if he wanted to."

"I didn't mean he'd go for that reason. Of course, he shouldn't go. But should we?"

"Let's. It's one of those long obits," he said, frowning at the paper he handed over. "She was altruistic…concerned about her community…trying to preserve Florida's history, especially around her beloved Naples…formed the Endangered Properties Committee."

"And then *she* ends up endangered. It's a good photograph of her."

"The two times I tangled with her, she hardly looked like that. Yes, let's go and keep our eyes open, not only for the committee treasurer Harmon Kingsdale we want to talk to, but any others who might show up we know."

"Going to brush my teeth and head out," he told her, popping up. "I'll kiss Lexi and Trey goodbye as well as my beautiful wife. Did you say Kris is dropping by early?"

"On her way out to the bog. I'm not going until I get my thoughts together on Monday, but remember I told you Heck is going to meet Kris here to advise him on his invention."

"Oh, yeah. I'm getting overprogrammed."

"Aren't we all and no wonder. I guess he wants to ask her style type questions."

"Style?" he asked, turning back in the kitchen doorway. "About an aid to help people with face recognition problems?"

She got up and started to clear dishes. "I think like whether to put the tiny computer camera in a sort of bulky necklace, some kind of pin or sunglasses, something like that."

"Oh, he did mention that on the phone. Got to get going, sweetheart. TGIF! Our private date night, even if we don't go out."

"Right—and tomorrow we have a date for a funeral. But remember, we promised Lexi a Saturday walk on the beach."

"When I say goodbye to her, I'll tell her we'll go midmorning tomorrow. Be right back."

At least there were several things to look forward to when they'd been through so much, Claire thought. She glanced down at the obituary on the table, then sat to read it carefully. You just never knew when someone who was so busy and full of life, maybe someone you needed and loved, wasn't coming home.

Heck asked Claire to sit in with him and Kris to give her opinion too. He showed them three computer-generated drawings of where he could secrete the camera lens so that when a person with face blindness was approached by someone who was not a stranger, but had his or her image already recorded and identified, a tiny, invisible device in one ear would give the person's name. If there was another short prompt needed, that would have been recorded along with the person's identity.

"Amazing," Kris said, beaming. "But can you make the camera micro-sized and make it work fast enough so there won't be a stupid pause, waiting for that message? That's the way I've always felt as I stand there like an idiot, trying to ID the person, looking for telltale signs, something familiar they might be wearing, hair color—like with Claire—anything."

"Got to admit size and speed will be the challenges," Heck said. "And finding a partner company to manufacture a good-looking necklace, large pin, glasses or sunglasses. But I've got to get this computerized camera and earpiece down first."

"Which means," Kris said, "you might not like my answer. I think it would be great if face blindness sufferers had a choice of devices to do this great spy work. Especially for a male to use this, the glasses would seem the best, but you know women like a variety of things. I suppose a chunky necklace would be my first choice, something ceramic, not a precious metal, to keep the price down, right?"

She looked at Claire, who nodded. Was Kris also picturing Reaching Woman's broken necklace? That reminded Claire that she wanted a moment alone with Kris before she left.

While Heck and Kris continued to confer, Claire went to get Trey up. The door to the guest room was open, and Nita was packing a suitcase on the bed. Claire gave a little *knock, knock* on the door frame, and Nita jumped.

"You're okay with moving into your house this weekend?" Claire asked, hovering in the doorway.

"Bronco says if it's too tough, I can't sleep or whatever, just stay two nights, then talk it over. I want it to work, Claire. But if there's one more thing that happens there, I got to say the house is cursed and we somehow got to find another."

Claire stepped in and hugged her. "It will all work out. I'm sure it will."

"I know you got guests. I heard Hector's voice. I was just going to get Trey up, change him and bring him down to all of you."

"I'd appreciate that. I'll see if Heck and Kris are done yet."

She stepped back and put her hands on Nita's shoulders. "You're a strong woman, Nita Gates. You are going to be more than okay."

Nita nodded, and as Claire went back out, she hoped that could be true for her too.

Still holding a very curious Trey, who seemed enamored of Kris, Claire walked her friend out to her Jeep.

"Kris, I wanted to ask you something before I ask Brad. Do you recall, either on Hunter's dagger or on Leader's staff, that there was a picture or carving of a woman with her hands up-lifted? You know, kind of like a ref signaling a touchdown in a football game?"

"Now there's a mixed message," Kris said with what Claire thought was a forced laugh. "But Andrea whisks the artifacts themselves away pretty fast for preservation and cleaning. Besides, since the Senator's claustrophobia bothers him if he comes out in the bog all hemmed in by those trees, he kind of panics. With my disability, I feel for him. So I get it that Andrea snatches the artifacts up and gets them to him so he can study them in his office or lab to feel part of a new discovery. That and fundraising are his part in all this."

"Wait. You said Brad has an office as well as that large lab with the screen to show the photos?"

"His office is behind the lab, through a door off it. Considering his problem with closed spaces, I don't think he uses it much. I only saw it once—desk, chairs, bookcase, locked drawers of relics, as he likes to call them, I think a safe with papers, contracts, stuff like that. Yi Ling helps him with his photography of items, so maybe you could ask her if she saw that raised-arms petroglyph too." She frowned and looked down at the ground. "But no, I don't recall that myself among all the other pictures or depictions."

"And it would have stood out. If it was a rendition of Reaching Woman, the upraised arms would mean something important. Maybe that she worshipped a higher being—some sort of creator or god, good or evil—or it could mean that she herself should be worshipped."

"What? I never thought of that. But she has a dagger in her!"

"I know what I'm going to say now sounds insane, but you're the only one I'm telling. I want you to promise you won't even tell Andrea or the dig team, let alone the senator, until I think this out to present to them."

"All right, I promise. But if you're on to a new theory—or some kind of suspicion—you are going to have to tell me that. Now you promise me!"

"When I can. I know we've been looking for a reason someone would have stabbed Reaching Woman. I have, anyway. But the angle of that dagger—kind of upward into her chest—and the feeling we have that something was wrong among the three of them... Kris, what if she stabbed herself? Decided to or was reared to be a sacrifice or was even made to because she broke some sort of rule about belonging to Leader but loving Hunter?"

"Claire," she said, hands on hips, "you're married to a criminal lawyer who gets people off from murder charges. Are you sure that isn't coloring your theory on this—I mean, like, you don't want her to have been murdered by one of the men? I know Nick's new client is up for murder—double murder now—and I know the two of you have been through tough times, but you're not transferring some of your past into this ancient death, are you?"

Claire bounced Trey in her arms. "I don't know. I don't think so. I'm going to ask Brad to let me see those items on Monday, and I hope you'll back me up on that."

"Andrea makes all those decisions, and I have to honor what she wants."

"Does Andrea make final decisions? Or does he?"

"They're a team. You know that. Like you and Nick. Like I hope to be someday with a man—maybe Mitch, though I don't know about falling for men with dangerous careers."

"Yeah. Been there, done that," Claire admitted, realizing Kris had shifted them off the subject of murder-suicide—murder-cide, Nick called it. "And who knows that Reaching Woman didn't share that fear with us? In her world, Hunter was living a dangerous life, but maybe that made him more appealing to her, more desirable."

"The price we pay for the exciting, macho guys, right?"

"Right. See you on Monday then since we're going to have a family weekend here. And let me know if you get any hint about what the Vances—all for one and one for all—might say about my looking at and handling the artifacts."

Kris nodded and patted Trey's back before she climbed in the Jeep. Claire lifted his little hand to wave goodbye as Kris pulled out.

She had learned a couple of interesting things. Brad probably kept the artifacts in his closed-in office he didn't like, so he wanted badly enough to hide them that he braved that room for storage. Yi Ling worked closely with him. And, although she hadn't heard this from him, he called the artifacts *relics*, which connoted they were especially dear and precious—almost sacred or holy—to him.

On the beach as they waded in the surf, the wash of waves felt so good around their bare legs. Claire and Nick held Lexi's hand for a while, then let her pick up shells. The water slid up the slick sand, depositing them and uncovering the tiny coquina, which then upended themselves and dug in again.

Lexi chattered on about everything she saw, but Claire was only half listening. "Mommy, those little shells! The ones that are open look like butterflies, see?" she said, extending an almost plaid coquina in her open palm.

"They sure do. Let Dad see them up close."

Claire was still floating on air, or maybe it was more like riding the waves, after Nick's lovemaking last night. Tender at first, almost teasing. She replayed some of it like a recorded favorite show. They danced, then kissed, then finally couldn't wait to love each other, and she was, as ever with him, swept away with passion and abandon...

"Oooh, what's that?" Lexi broke into her reverie, pointing at a blob in the sand that looked like a plastic bag full of air.

"Oh, oh," Nick said, tugging her back from it. "That's what they call a Portuguese man-of-war. It's an animal, and those purple cords are tentacles that can sting you really bad, so we have to walk way around."

"You can see inside of it. Ick!" Lexi said, but she let him lead them in a large path to avoid it. "I think it's dead!"

"It can still hurt you," he warned.

Claire noted a sign up on a grassy slope above the concrete breakwater: Sold. Pine Ridge Luxury Realty. While they avoided being stung, she remembered the for sale sign that Cyndi had posed with on her LinkedIn page.

"I'll watch out for more bad man-of-war tents," Lexi promised as she ran a bit ahead of them.

"Pretty close to man-o'-war tentacles," Nick said with a little laugh.

"Nick, this house—even though we're at the back of it—looks familiar," she told him, stopping to study the mansion with its fabulous view of the Gulf of Mexico. "It would face on Gordon Drive, right?"

"Sure. All these along here do. Why?"

"The Vances just sold a home along here, and this sign says sold."

"So, maybe it was their house. And?"

"And when we walk back to the car, can we drive by the front of it? There's a picture on Cyndi Lindley's LinkedIn page where she's standing in front of a house with a for sale sign as if she's the Realtor. That was either wishful thinking or a con job, which she was obviously capable of. Wouldn't that be something if the house she chose to take a fake picture in front of was the Vances' place—and being sold by that Harmon Kingsdale's company?"

"A spider's web of possibilities," he said as Lexi ran back to them with a piece of warped driftwood with some kind of small shells clinging to it. "But I've learned to honor what Ken Jensen likes to say: 'There are very few if any coincidences in detective work.' Sure, we can drive around."

"What are these?" Lexi asked, pointing to the piece of wood.

"I think they're called limpets," Nick told her. "They are a lot like little snails that just grab on with a sticky foot and won't let go."

Claire patted Lexi's back and nodded. Her suspicions about Cyndi and Marian—even Brad Vance—hung on, suspicions that clung like fears. Ones that just would not let go.

CHAPTER THIRTY-THREE

Marian James's funeral was held at the Saint Leo Catholic Church in Bonita Springs. It was a large lovely building of Spanish decor with a bronze statue of the Virgin Mary in front as if guarding the place.

Claire stared at the Madonna's slightly outstretched hands with her palms open. Were those hands supposed to be reaching out with a message of welcome? Of peace? Of help? This was another reaching woman from the past, one venerated and worshipped here. Claire could not shake the idea that Reaching Woman had been something like that to her people. She had to examine those hands-off relics Brad had evidently been hiding. Surely, he and Andrea wanted her to do what they'd hired her for.

They sat halfway back in the large sanctuary where they could watch people, since most sat closer to the front.

"There's Harmon Kingsdale," Nick whispered but he didn't point. "The one with the silver hair, mustache and light blue sport coat. Let's see who he sits with."

"That must be his wife. Really pretty. Younger."

Out of the side of his mouth, Nick whispered, "People are saying that about us."

She elbowed him and smiled. The glow of their lovemaking last night and their fun with Lexi earlier still warmed her.

They stood with everyone as the closed casket with an arrangement of roses and carnations was rolled down the aisle with the priest following. Boys with censers led the procession, their wisps of smoke a reminder to Claire of the terrible way Marian had perished. No, she was strangled first, Claire reminded herself. Two women dead, one frozen, one burned. And one—eons ago—stabbed to death by an enemy or by herself.

The priest's message praised all Marian had done for people, for her community. Still, Claire thought, it didn't seem that the priest had actually known her, as he offered no memories or comments of his own about her. Had she attended here, was she active in this parish? He hadn't said so. Maybe she'd been born and baptized Catholic but had fallen away and the church was being kind to bury her.

She drew her attention away from the service and admired the high wooden beams overhead with the stained-glass window of Noah and some animals from the ark just above the large statue of Christ on the cross. She skimmed the people gathered there again and jolted so hard she punched Nick with her elbow.

"What?"

"I didn't see him slip in. That's Brad Vance sitting with the Kingsdales."

"You're right. He hasn't changed much since he left office. But why are you surprised? You said Harmon must have sold their house—his company did, I mean."

"Or Brad was one of Marian's committee's silent partners, but I doubt it since money seems tight at the bog."

"Claire, Bradley Vance was a state senator for years. He probably knows most movers and shakers in the state, not just around here. Maybe Harmon Kingsdale was a big donor or the senator did some favor for him or for Marion too, if you must tie her in."

"Right. Right," she repeated.
But something just didn't feel right.

Monday morning as she drove toward Black Bog, Claire was still agonizing. In a reversal of her plans, she had given up involving Gina and Heck and had talked Nick out of their going to Harmon Kingsdale's office to see if they could get more information about Marian's silent partners and investors in the Endangered Properties Committee. If Kingsdale mentioned the Vances were on board with that, he might tell Brad or Andrea they had been asking and she didn't want to get any more friends in trouble. And so what if the Vances did contribute to Marian's work? Or perhaps they got some financial backing from her since they always seemed concerned for money. But how much had Marian known about the Vances' secret project, and had Cyndi just picked their house at random to lie about her real estate career on LinkedIn? Cyndi could have just stumbled on the house, walking the beach, as she and Nick had earlier today.

Claire waved to the guard at the gate. Of course, he took a salary too, a lot of outlay to run this operation and to keep it quiet. Her own salary was very generous; then there was Kris, the dig team, the office and labs they'd built. If Brad was trying to make extra money for their project by selling knockoff artifacts or things inspired by ancient designs, so what, the Vances would probably argue.

As she parked, she studied the Vances' new home they had built here. So modest compared to their mansion on the beach. And, although a few hours of sun hit it during midday, didn't all these ficus trees hanging over the bog make the claustrophobic former senator feel oppressed even in this house? Or was it just the bog itself here that disturbed him?

Though Brad's car was there, Andrea's was not. Nor was it in their short driveway or in their carport. Yes, even that was a real comedown from the three-car garage at their beachside home, but then, as she'd picked up more than once before, when the Vances were ready to go public and sell rights to things, all of that would change, because they'd be famous and rich.

Claire used her security card to get in the building. She turned on the lights in her and Kris's office, then put her purse in her desk drawer and took her two-way radio out. Kris must be out at the bog, unless she was in Andrea's or Brad's lab areas. Maybe she had asked him to see the artifacts or more complete photos, but if not, Claire was going to.

She headed for his lab. Andrea's door was closed. Claire knocked on that door then tried the knob. Locked. As for Brad's lab, the door was open as usual, but not wide, only slightly ajar. And someone was crying inside.

"I don't want to go back home. It's not really home anymore. A whole year?"

Yi Ling's distinctive voice.

"I just think it's best. You've been great, but we can't risk going on like this or someone might figure it out," Brad told her. "I'll pay for the round-trip ticket, of course, and your salary while you're away. We cannot have people finding out, questioning you, blaming you. We'll tell everyone your family asked you to come back for a while since your father is ill."

"I did it for this amazing project but for you too. Andrea still trusts me, and I've kept things secret like you said, so I'd like to stay."

Claire silently clapped her hand over her mouth. Brad and Yi Ling had been having an affair? Of course, the girl looked up to him, but he must have been the instigator, the seducer. Kris had said the young woman took his photographs for him, so this conversation couldn't be about that, could it? Maybe Yi Ling knew too much. After all, there were petroglyphs as Kris had called them on some artifacts which Yi Ling had perhaps photographed. Or maybe Yi Ling was in on the fake jewelry and ancient weapons being sold undercover, and he didn't want her questioned or caught.

Though she wanted to stay to hear more, Claire quickly did a U-turn and hurried back to her office. She hadn't told anyone on staff except Kris that she was coming in this morning. With Andrea away, and Kris evidently out at the bog, perhaps with the dig team, Brad and Yi Ling must have believed they were alone.

And, darn it, but she really felt for Yi Ling! A girl here on a green card who wanted to make good, but she had been brought here by the woman she was betraying—if she and Brad were lovers. Yet Brad Vance was the power partner in the affair, and she blamed him for this.

Still, she was going to calm down and put on a good front and face him about seeing those artifacts—at least a complete set of photos—today.

And here was her chance to face him alone, she thought, as Yi Ling raced past her office door, ebony hair flying. The poor girl looked distraught. Had she even stopped eating over this betrayal—this love affair? She looked almost gaunt.

When Claire thought she'd given her enough time to get outside, she went out of the office. If Brad was in a bad or sad mood, so be it. This couldn't wait. Maybe it would help to hit him when his defenses were down.

But there was Yi Ling, pressed into a corner inside the exit door to the bog, turned away, shuddering with now silent sobs.

Claire meant to leave her to grieve over the double hit of the end of a love affair and Brad's insistence she go back to China for a while. But the young woman must have heard her and turned her teary face away from the wall.

"Oh, sorry," Yi Ling said.

"Is there anything I can do to help? Are you ill?" First thought—*don't let her know I overheard her and Brad.*

"Just that I must go back to China for a bit," she said with single nod. She squared her thin shoulders. "My father—he is ill."

Claire darted back into her office and snatched two tissues from Kris's box on her desk. She hurried back and held them out to Yi Ling. "I'm sure with your experiences—all you have done here—you can work on a project there, or maybe go back to school for a year."

"If so, I must never tell—tell about this dig—until they are ready for the world to know."

"Secrecy is hard," Claire said. "Necessary at times, but sometimes not good."

The girl wiped under her eyes. "So very true. I will miss it much here," she whispered and blew her nose. "I am sorry."

It almost seemed the young woman was apologizing to her, but for what? She meant she regretted leaving.

"I'm sure you'll be able to come back."

"Thank you for those words—for your kindness," the slender young woman said as she opened the door to the bog. There was something familiar in the way she walked away before the door closed behind her. She seemed so defeated, but Claire was still angry at how Brad had treated the girl, used her, then planned to just send her away. But maybe that anger would help her to face him now.

Claire strode down the hall and called in his door, "Brad, excuse me."

"I didn't know you were here. No one except Kris and the dig team are around."

"I just got here. I may go out but wanted to ask you something first."

He sat on one of his stools and motioned her to step in. He looked totally calm, not like a man who had just broken someone's heart. And wouldn't Andrea be very upset when he or Yi Ling told her one of her dig team was leaving—for a year?

"To ask me what?" he said.

"It's come up that there was quite a unique petroglyph, perhaps on Hunter's dagger and perhaps on the staff or whatever that was that Leader had with him. One of a woman with her hands raised. Yet I did not see it on the photos you shared with me earlier and feel it could be key in my theory of their roles and relationships to each other."

"I can't imagine those weren't in the pictures you saw," he said, frowning and looking very concerned. "Yes, there was such a petroglyph on the artifacts of both men."

"I see now why you've called the artifacts relics."

"Did I? I try not to, though, to me, each thing we get from the bog is a relic—essential, almost sacred to understanding these ancient lives. Yi Ling took the photos, so perhaps she skipped or mislaid those of, not Reaching Woman per se, but Raised Arms Woman, almost as if she was under arrest, right?"

"That's another way of describing her positioning, perhaps better than my saying it was like a football ref calling a touchdown."

"Saying to whom?" he asked, frowning, though he didn't budge from his stool, nor she from just inside the doorway.

"Saying to myself as I try to figure out what that figure means."

"The woman with upraised arms may not even be Reaching Woman. But yes, let me go through the photos, because I'm sure I can find ones that showcase that figure."

She was surprised. So easily accomplished? "Brad, why not just let me look at the figure on the items—the relics—themselves? It would save you from going through the pictures."

She was trying to study his body language, but he seemed frozen in place. Yet his eyes darted toward the door at the back of the lab, no doubt the one Kris had said was his office.

"My rule from the first—Andrea's too, of course—is that we protect the bog bodies and their grave goods," he went on, sounding now in lecture mode. "The photographs will have to do. And, if the ones Yi Ling took do not have that raised hands figure, I must be certain she didn't pull them out for some reason."

"I'm sure she would have done exactly as you ordered."

He stared at her a bit too long, then said, "And I'm sure you have things to do while I check on this." He lifted his left arm and stared, frowning, overlong at his watch.

He went on, "I'll have them here for you to study to your heart's content in about an hour, because I have some other business. By the way, I've been glad to see you and your high-profile husband have managed to keep your names out of the news lately, because—I repeat—we like to keep a low profile here, to say the least."

"I understand," she said, deciding not to rush to Nick's defense but keep on track with the relics. "I'll be back in an hour, Brad. I really think that figure is important."

She went toward Kris's office, relieved no one knew of their ties to the helicopter wreck, which had received media coverage. Is that what Brad had been referring to? If so, Kris had probably told him about it, in connection with Mitch. But once Claire saw those petroglyphs, she would be clearer on her theories about the status of Reaching Woman and the men in her life. It was obsessing her, and that wasn't good.

And now, once again, Claire had seen that human nature had not changed over the centuries. A powerful man had seduced or coerced a younger woman, one in a weaker, dependent position, into a relationship with him. No doubt poor Yi Ling would have done anything to please him. If Andrea had known, would she have protected her and blamed Brad?

Claire jumped as the door to the outside banged open and Yi Ling strode in from the bog. "I don't want to leave," she told Claire, "but I must accept. My dig team friends and Kris, they are sad. I'll be gone tomorrow. I will pack my important things now," she added and went down the hall to the small room the dig team shared.

The door to the bog opened again. Kris, Doug and Andy stood there.

"Have you heard Yi Ling's leaving?" Kris asked, and Claire

nodded. "She's really torn up about it, but her father's very ill in Beijing. It's quite sudden, and she's flying out of Miami tomorrow."

"Wait until Andrea hears and has to replace her," Doug said, shaking his head.

"Anyhow," Kris said, "we're going to take her out to dinner to say goodbye for now, an early dinner since she has to pack. If you'd like to join us, that's great, but I suppose you'll want to head home to your family."

"Yes, and I have a meeting at four," she said, deciding not to tell Kris in front of the others that she'd gotten as far as Brad promising photos, at least.

"Do you know if Andrea will be here this afternoon?" Claire asked.

"Not sure," Kris said. "Doctor's appointment, I think. But, listen, if you have a second, could you help us with repositioning the platform and planks out in the bog? It helps to have four people, and Yi Ling's pretty upset. We've decided to branch out just a bit from the area where we found the trio to see if there are any artifacts we've missed before we move on."

Claire certainly didn't say so, but she felt there was something missing in understanding the living people here at Black Bog, not just the dead ones.

CHAPTER THIRTY-FOUR

Nick left work early, even though it was a Monday and he had a lot to do. Bronco had said he and Nita were doing okay in the house this weekend—which meant Nita had probably stopped crying—so he'd given Bronco today off.

The guy had stuck with him from the first case Nick had worked with Claire, when he'd almost lost her. He hated to be so possessive of her now, but he couldn't bear to ever be in a position like that again. She had always said if anything happened to her that her sister would raise Lexi, but now there was Trey too. And he wasn't sure he could go on if she was hurt or lost.

He'd like to check with her right now, he thought, as he turned into the housing division which had once all been Twisted Trees mansion grounds. But until she drove partway back toward town on the Trail, there were no cell towers to pick up a call, and the bog staff used walkie-talkies, no less. Claire had said the place was state-of-the-art, but that sort of communication—or lack thereof—to the outside world seemed as primitive as the people they were digging up. He wished too that he knew more about the culture Claire was studying, because "Stone Age" didn't really say much to him, but he honored her contract with its secrecy clauses and just accepted whatever she chose to tell him. After all, legal contracts helped to make his world go round.

He pulled up in front of Dale's mother's old house, next to Dale's own vacated one. He had to admit Bronco and Nita's place looked better than when he'd last seen it. Bronco had not only cut the grass but had trimmed the overgrown bright pink bougainvillea bushes. The windows sparkled in the late afternoon sun, and it looked like Nita had hung fresh curtains. Claire would be thrilled.

He got out and went up to the front porch, glad he didn't see Betty and her little dog spying on him. He heard the purr of the air-conditioning. Bronco must have gotten that repaired, because Dale's mother supposedly hadn't used it. But had she used the freezer for more than hoarding frozen food? Nick used to think perhaps the old lady had offed Cyndi Lindley, but evidently not, since Lucy Braun was dead by the time Marian was strangled— unless Mrs. Braun had come back as a ghost.

As he raised his hand to knock, Bronco opened the door.

"Hey, things are looking up!" Nick greeted him as Bronco unlocked the screen door and held it open.

"They were," he said, his voice quiet, which was unusual for the big guy. "Come on in. Finally got Nita to take a nap. She's been working hard."

"I'd say you both have. The front yard looks one hundred percent better. But what do you mean things *were* looking up?"

They sat in the front room, which also looked clean and re-arranged from when Nick had seen it last. Bronco hunched forward, hands on his knees.

"That old busybody next door stopped by with a welcome gift—pecan rolls."

"Sounds nice. And?"

"And in chatting with Nita when I was out in back finally

getting that shed cleaned out, the old lady evidently told her she always pictured her friend Lucy here—Dale's mother."

"They were friends for years. But that upset Nita?"

"When Nita asked her more about it, she said she'd seen her ghost here recently. For sure it was a woman, she said, maybe even Cyndi, all white, like covered with frost."

"What?"

"Lights at night. Shadows passing the windows in the day-time."

"Oh, hell. That's ridiculous and not what Nita needed to hear."

"No kidding, boss. I'm scared it will set her back about this place. I don't want to get off to a bad start in this neighborhood by telling the old lady to stay away—man, she walks by all the time—but she's really screwing things up."

"Crazy Betty has seemed to like me from the first, lucky me. I'll just stop next door on my way home and tell her that she needs to stop that kind of stuff. If she can't support her new neighbor, be upbeat, all that, she needs to stay away."

"She's creepy to say the least. Anything you can do—'preciate it, 'cause now I've got to settle Nita down again."

Claire knew she had to settle down. Finally, she was going to see missing photos of the petroglyph that must be key to her work here. Finally, Brad was going to trust her enough to share those with her, so she'd be fully informed in theorizing about the bog trio—and who knew what bodies they would dig up here after that? She hoped, as wary and difficult as he sometimes seemed, that she could establish a good working relationship with him the way she had with Andrea.

She didn't see him in his lab. She stood in the doorway, un-easy about going in if he'd stepped out for a moment. Or maybe he was in his office at the back. She glanced at her wristwatch. Exactly four o'clock.

"Brad? Senator Vance!"

Perhaps he'd just stepped out to the bathroom or to get some of that perpetual coffee and a BB frosted doughnut.

She saw a note on the stool where he'd sat last time she was here, and she stepped in to glance down at it. Yes. To her.

Her heart fell. What if he had left, made some excuse to put her off? But no, she thought, as she skimmed his angular hand-writing. *Be back soon. Pics in desk drawer.*

What a relief! She moved to the desk in the corner of the lab and tried the open the center drawer. It didn't budge. Locked?

She tried to slide out each drawer, but all held fast. Maybe he didn't mean this desk, but she could hardly just start open-ing drawers in here. She looked around for anything else that resembled a desk. His light table for viewing negatives. Shelves. Surely not that filing cabinet.

Could he have meant his desk in his office? Kris had seen it, described it. Well, if the door to that room was locked, she'd know that wasn't what he'd meant.

Just to be sure he wasn't coming down the hall, she stepped out and looked up and down the corridor. Then she punched in #1 on her handheld radio, his number. Andrea was #2, and Claire had recently peeked outside again to see her car wasn't back yet. Only Brad's and Claire's were there because Kris and the dig trio had gone out to a restaurant to say goodbye to Yi Ling. She could see that the gate guard's car was gone, so per-haps he'd been invited to Yi Ling's impromptu farewell dinner.

Brad didn't pick up on his radio. What if he'd fallen asleep or somehow hurt himself? Surely, he hadn't gone out to the bog, especially on his own. That was against Andrea's rules and any-way he feared the place that was the fierce focus of his attentions.

She went back into his lab, then to his office door. "Brad!" she shouted. "Are you in there? Are you okay?"

Feeling it would be locked, like so much around here, Claire knocked, then reached for the knob. It turned easily in her hand, and the door opened.

The light was on. Oh, whew, there was a note on the desk with an arrow and the word *pictures*.

Leaving the door ajar, she stepped into the room.

Nick knocked on Betty's door and heard her little dog start barking. At least she was home. He needed to get her to back off. Her snooping had gotten way out of line.

Wearing a pink housecoat, she opened the door, holding the dog.

"Oh, my favorite criminal lawyer has come calling," she said with an almost coquettish smile.

"Hi, Betty. Can you step out so we can talk for a second?"

"Any more trouble in this lunatic neighborhood?" she asked. He thought she might balk at coming out, but she didn't, and they sat in matching pink plastic molded chairs.

"I sure hope no more trouble," he told her. "I think you know that your new neighbors, the Gateses, are friends of mine."

"He works for you and you gave him the day off so he and Nita can finish tidying things up."

"Right. They will be good neighbors, but Nita's kind of shaky with all that's gone on here, so—"

"Aren't we all?"

"Yes, well, I'm hoping you won't scare her with ghost stories about her new house. It's hard enough that Cyndi's body was found there."

"Not to mention that not far away from here, another woman died—before a fire finished off the rest of that mansion. Talk about haunted. Besides, I think my dear friend Lucy—Dale's mother—probably does haunt her house. She loved living there all these years."

"I'd like to have your promise to be a good neighbor to—"

"I took them baked goods, pecan rolls, a touch of Southern hospitality. I have some left, if you'd like one."

Nick was starting to sweat. Not from the afternoon heat and

humidity, but from having to deal with this old woman, who seemed as sticky and nutty as pecan rolls. Besides, he kept recalling the story Claire had related to him in too damn much detail about how the old ladies in *Arsenic and Old Lace* had murdered people and hidden them around their house. Ridiculous, Nick scolded himself.

"Oh, by the way," she told him, popping up and holding the dog close, "I forgot to tell you I copied down the license plate numbers of everyone who doesn't live around here who parked on this street the evening of the fire. I could work for the police or a criminal lawyer like you, really I could. I'll get it for you—a pecan roll too."

Nick sighed as she disappeared into the house. That's all he needed, though maybe a list of cars could show others were around then, not just Dale. He needed everything he could get his hands on to get Dale's defense together now that he'd been indicted.

She came back out and handed him a paper plate with a roll and an index card—no, a recipe card. In large handwriting, she had indeed recorded a list of license plate numbers, nine of them. No doubt some would turn out to be curious onlookers who smelled the smoke, or TV or newspaper reporters, but he would give Jensen a call to run these numbers.

"I appreciate this, Betty. And I'd sure appreciate your building up Nita and not scaring her, okay? They're still kind of newly-weds and can use the time alone."

"All right, my favorite real-life Perry Mason. By the way, those reruns are on TV all afternoon—and, you know, that famous lawyer had a female helper named Della, his secretary, someone who knew how to dress, not like those girls in pants sitting at office desks today. Why, I told Cyndi she dressed like a tramp with those little shorts and bra-type things!"

"Did that start an argument?" Nick asked, still thinking that maybe there was a glimmer of a chance that this eccentric little sneak had gotten into a fight with the conniving Cyndi. He was grabbing at straws, but that's where he was at in preparing to defend Dale. And darned if he was going to eat this pecan roll since the title of that old movie had the word *arsenic* in it.

"Cyndi called me an old bat and used that other b-word right to my face!"

"She shouldn't have done that," he said as she kept nodding.

But, Nick thought, if Betty had somehow strangled and frozen Cyndi, no way she'd tell him all this—although he had seen some criminals who like to boast about what they'd done, loved telling it all to a cop or psychiatrist or lawyer. Yeah, it was kind of like those old Perry Mason reruns where the guilty party no one suspected stood up in court and shouted, "Yes, I did it! I killed so-and-so and here's how and why!"

With her heart beating hard, Claire stood still in Brad's office, holding her breath. She sucked in a huge gasp. A drone, so much like the piece of one Jace had pulled from the wreckage of the chopper, hung from the ceiling in the corner. Was it also like the drone that had exploded the glass window and ruined their reception? Of course, so what, lots of people had drones today, but—

"Find the photos?"

She spun to see Brad standing in the doorway. He seemed to fill it, block it.

"I— No. I looked out there. I thought you might mean this desk. I saw the sign," she said pointing.

"And, of course, saw my drone. Just a hobby. Or did Kris tell you I used to use a drone to view the excavations here since I couldn't stand the closed-in feeling the bog always gave me? But with the low-hanging trees, it got snagged and sank—down in the peaty depths forever, so I got a new one and don't use it for that anymore. Yi Ling borrows it sometimes."

"Sad she's leaving so suddenly."

"Some things, as sad as they are, are necessary. Well, confession time all around. Yi Ling has done several odd jobs for me."

For some reason, it was then that Claire's brain made the connection. That androgynous person who had followed her and Kris that time—so thin, face mostly covered, not a limp, but a hesitation with one leg. And the way Yi Ling had walked away out into the bog today... Could it have been?

"Confession time all around, for what?" she asked, edging toward the door. He did not budge.

"I hope the third time's a charm, but you do understand that this precious work for all mankind we are doing here must be protected at all costs."

"I've kept the secrecy agreement."

"It isn't enough. I was uneasy about having Andrea and Kris put you on the team, but I couldn't protest too much about your husband and your high media profile or they would have been upset. So I took a gamble, but you've rocked the boat, been in the wrong place too much, hanging out with the wrong people, lawyers, law officers. Getting in the newspapers. Damn, but people should have listened to me. Sad, but you'll be in the media this time too. Well, go ahead and open that drawer with the arrow pointing to it," he said.

"I'm leaving, Brad. Perhaps leaving for good."

"I'll second that."

He pulled a gun and pointed it toward her. Startled, she stepped back. The black end of the barrel loomed large.

"Open the drawer, then we'll discuss your leaving."

Starting to shake, she stepped back and pulled the drawer open, expecting to finally see a petroglyph of an ancient woman with her arms raised. But within it lay a folded faded flag, smudged with dirt or ashes, but she could see the swastika on it. And next to that was a photograph of Hitler with Eva Braun.

She gasped and looked at Brad. He was smiling.

"No, I'm not a neo-Nazi. But I am looking for things to sell on the international black market to help keep this place afloat, and I regret that you seem to be onto me for that, with your own visit to our antique shop in town and then sending someone across the state. I got a phone call from there while they were visiting, and it didn't take much to put two and two together. I regret the drone Yi Ling used only brought them down but didn't get rid of them. Now, don't you think I know you broke your contract to send them on that little dead end hunt?"

"There was nothing in the contract about that. Just let me out of here," she demanded. "My husband knows I'm here and so do your staff." She suddenly felt so nauseated she could have thrown up.

"Let you out of here?" he said. "Oh, I plan to. As much as I hate that bog, let's just go out there to see what we can find. This won't take long and then you—like two other smart-mouthed women who tried to pressure me and ruin this momentous work—will be on your way. This time, no strangulation needed at all. Now let's move."

CHAPTER THIRTY-FIVE

"Hey, Detective Jensen, Nick Markwood here," Nick said, glad he'd picked up on the call.

Nick was sitting in his car in the driveway of Claire's sister Darcy's house. Claire had said she'd meet him here around four. He glanced at his watch as he killed the engine: four fifteen. Darcy had picked up both Jilly and Lexi at their schools and had brought them here, so it was probably a noisy place inside.

"Counselor," Jensen said, "how goes your Monday? Got a dynamite case together to defend Mr. Braun?"

"Speaking of that, remember the old lady who lived next door to the house where we found the woman in the freezer, the one who ID'd the deceased from your photograph? The night of the fire and second murder, Betty Richards evidently went up and down their street with a flashlight, writing down license plate numbers of cars that didn't belong. I could probably find a way to have the owners identified, but I'd like to hand that over to you. We defense attorneys like to do everything on the up-and-up."

"Yeah, I hear you. And we detectives who work for prosecuting attorneys aren't supposed to make friends of defense attorneys and their wives. Okay, read me the list, and I'll check those out. Too many dead ends in this case, pardon the pun."

"And you'll get back to me with the names, in case anything clicks? I may have to share them with Dale to see if he can place any of them."

"Okay. Just don't rat me out so someone thinks I'm helping the opposition when we go to trial. Give Claire my best— and when she gets done with whatever private assignment she's on, I'm telling you, the department could use her for a forensic tech, part-time if she wants."

"You know, if it was just an office job, I'd say that sounds great—if she could work from home and not go out to inter-view possible would-be criminals."

"Dream on."

"Yeah. At least she has a temporary gig where she's only con-sulting. Thanks, Ken. I'll wait for your call back."

Taking his cell with him, Nick got out and walked toward the house. He could hear Jilly's and Lexi's voices from here. It was great being a dad as well as a husband of the woman he loved.

"I'm not going out to the bog," Claire insisted as Brad ges-tured with the gun that she should precede him out his office door. "I'm going to get my purse and leave. I'll keep this quiet, just as I have what's really going on here."

"Meaning what?" He moved aside for her to pass, but when she tried to squeeze through the doorway, he yanked her back against the open door. "I said there's something I want to show you outside. Move. Right ahead of me."

"No," she insisted, desperately trying to sound defiant and unafraid when she wanted to scream and explode in tears. This was so perfectly set up. No one was here. When would Andrea be back? But was she in on this too?

"Look, former state Senator Bradley Vance," she said, fight-ing to keep her voice from quavering. She had decided to try a different tack. "You have evidently murdered two women so you'd better take off before the police find you. My husband and his contacts will—"

"No way they can pin this on me. I have no obvious connection to Cyndi what's-her-name. Would you believe the little slut hung around our beach house, wanted to sell the place for us instead of our real estate rep, then she actually followed me here and threatened to blow the lid off this project? She went on and on about how she could get funding for the bog work by selling passes to a mansion with a Nazi connection, so I drove her to her friend's house and had to shut her up—stop her there before she went public with too damn much."

"I'd say strangling and freezing is one way to keep someone quiet."

As if he hadn't heard her, he went on, "I did have a business relationship with Marian James, though unlike Cindi, she had the moxie and power to expose everything here—take it from my control. Those two women could have blown everything, but I've covered my tracks. Haven't even tried to sell that Nazi stuff I took yet—and could have paid dearly for, since that idiot Braun started a fire when I was there meeting with Marian James."

She almost bluffed that her husband knew of the Marian–Nazi connection and would pursue him. But then—whether he killed her or not—would he go after Nick? And the children could be endangered. She had to stay calm. She had to find a way out of this. She feared he was going to try to stage a fatal accident.

"You know," he said, sounding almost wistful, "what really matters above all is eventually sharing my American Adam and Eve burial spot with all mankind. I'll get the rights to publicly and legally sell copies of the artifacts. As for you—I knew you were far too clever from the first. And now," he repeated as he shoved her out of the lab and down the hall with the gun barrel pressed between her shoulder blades, "our very own Over-

Reaching Woman Claire Markwood will get a close-up and personal experience of what our Black Bog people went through."

"Claire's late," Darcy told him, wiping her wet hands on a dish towel. "Probably got involved in something. I can't believe wherever she's working they don't have a phone."

"Too far from a cell tower," Nick told her, pushing Trey gently in the infant swing. "Traffic's probably bad. She'll be here, and if she's late, she'll call when she gets in tower range."

"I don't see why her work has to be such a big secret," Darcy groused. "You okay with Trey? I'm going to check on our angels—far too quiet in Jilly's bedroom."

"Sure," Nick said with a glance at his watch. Twenty-five after four. She'd be here soon.

Trey gurgled and cooed something when the music for Nick's phone went off. Hoping it was Claire, he checked the caller ID. Ken Jensen.

"Nick here."

"Fast work, huh? Listen, one of the plate numbers was of interest. You sitting down? Former longtime state senator Bradley J. Vance."

Nick jerked erect on the ottoman where he sat. His brain raced. His gut wrenched. He stopped swinging Trey, steadied him with one hand.

"Nick, I gotta tell you, he does have a connection to Marian James, but I can't say more."

"Was he one of the silent partners underwriting her Endangered Properties Committee? We thought maybe so but couldn't turn it up."

"All right. Yes. And he was at her funeral with another of her cronies—"

"Harmon Kingsdale. We saw them together."

"Damn, you and Claire have been overstepping again!"

"I hope not. Got to go."

"Nick, wait! Is there some connection now? I mean, Claire's been really secretive about who she's working for. If she was advising that committee in any way, she may be subpoenaed at the trial, and that won't look good with you as defense attorney. I need to talk to both of you—"

"I'll call you back soon."

Nick punched off his phone. Brad was near or at Twisted Trees the night of Marian's murder. So he knew the area, maybe had been there before. Dale may have set the place on fire, but someone had killed Marian first, just the way someone had killed Cyndi. Could the former senator have had any connection to Cyndi? No, too far out—unless, as Claire surmised, she had visited them at their beachside home to have that picture taken. No, he was thinking in circles.

Damn, he had to get to Claire, even if he got in trouble driving into Black Bog, if the guard she'd mentioned would let him in.

"Darcy!" he shouted, and Trey startled and fussed. Nick bent to hug and kiss him. "You need your mom and I do too," he told the baby.

"Nick, what?" she said, running in. "Was that Claire who called? Is she all right?"

"Of course she is, but I'm going to go check on why she's late. If she shows up here after I'm gone, call my cell."

He didn't say or do more, didn't even kiss Lexi. Something was so, so wrong.

"Are you really claustrophobic?" Claire was desperate for calm talk—for distractions. Maybe she could play on his phobia. Brad shoved her toward the door to the bog. Her pulse pounded, and her mind raced. She had to find a way to knock that gun out of his hand before they walked the planks over the bog. She could not go out there with him. Should she risk taking a bullet instead, so she could maybe fight back on dry land?

"Damn, I am paranoid about being shut in," he said, giving her a little shove again when she hesitated. "My older sister used to lock me in a big cedar chest when she had to stay home with me. Dark, hard to breathe. Everyone in the family thought she was Miss Perfect, pretty and blonde. But she was selfish and pushy."

Claire almost asked him if Cyndi had reminded him of his sister.

"But what must be done must be done," he added with an even more trembling voice.

"No one will believe I came out here alone, against the rules, when I should be heading home."

"Yeah, and no one will believe I finally came out here again."

"Andrea called and will be back soon. Is she in on all this too?"

"You've had too much contact with a lawyer. That's a lie about Andrea calling, because I talked to her on our house phone— the only outside line that works around here—just about when you went in my office. She's been diagnosed with breast cancer and is in the hospital for treatment. I'm going there when I close up—end things—here."

"I'm sorry for her. She didn't have any part in the murders, did she?"

"Just shut up. I said you're sounding like a lawyer."

"And they as well as the police will be all over this when I go missing," she insisted, then regretted bringing Nick into this. He would be insane with grief and rage, endangering himself to learn what happened to her. Then this warped bastard would get rid of him too. Somehow, she had to save herself, turn the tables here. She'd walked these planks recently and he had not. There must be a way to knock that gun into the bog, maybe to knock him in before he did her in.

Lexi's sweet face floated through her panicked brain. Trey's. Nick's. Barely minutes now until this monster made his move. She knew his plan now: he was going to bury her in the bog with the ancients, and maybe someday someone would find her deep in the muddy peat, reaching out for help.

★ ★ ★

Early rush hour traffic in Naples slowed Nick down. He'd taken back streets out of Darcy's neighborhood. At least she lived in the southeast part of town. Damn, but he wasn't even certain where to turn off the Trail to the bog. Claire had said it wasn't marked, but he knew about where it was and would look for an unpaved road. Hopefully Kris was with her, other members of the staff too. If Brad was a suspect in some way, was Andrea too?

He tried to settle his panic. Keep calm. So what if Senator Vance and his wife had hired Claire to keep their secret? They were public figures, dedicated, trustworthy, but who trusted politicians these days?

Still, Nick berated himself, he should have demanded to know more about Claire's work. But Kris was there, others too, he told himself again. So why did he feel she was in danger just became she was late? It seemed she attracted trouble. Hell, he had too over the years. At least the kids were safe, but what would he ever do without Claire?

"Steady," he told himself as he had to stop at another red light. "Steady." He hoped—he prayed—that it would turn out everything was fine, that he could give Claire the news that the senator knew Marian, had proximity, opportunity to harm her—but would a probably faked photo on LinkedIn taken in front of the Vances' former home be a possible connection to Cyndi Lindley?

Claire knew she was doomed and there was only one way to save herself—well, two. Talk Brad out of this or fight him somehow, and he outweighed her by far, not to mention he had the gun. But he was shaking, literally terrified.

"You do know that your little squeeze Yi Ling planned to tell the dig team and Kris about her affair with you—about the drones you've tried to kill people with."

"Nice try. Been eavesdropping?"

"No, Yi Ling was in tears and blurted it out, so I told the

team to be prepared for her confession. I think they'll take her
to the police to tell her story so she doesn't have to return to
China. At least, you didn't seem to be planning to plant her in
the bog—or were you hoping to bring down her international
flight with a drone?"

"Very funny. Just shut up! You know too damn much!"

"The police believe—and will prove," she went on, though
her voice was trembling, "that the person who killed Marian
also murdered Cyndi Lindley. They'll figure out it was you."
He shoved her with the gun again and she had no choice but to
start out on the plank walk over the bog,

"No, that would be Dale Braun," he insisted. His voice had
gone up to almost high-pitched. Somehow she had to use his
fear of this place with its hulking trees and growing darkness to
feed his fears, because hers were out of control.

"Were the two women working together to interest you in
buying or helping them get access to Twisted Trees with its Nazi
mini-museum? Not only to preserve historic property, but as a
source of money for the Black Bog project? Great name for this
place with its grasping, clinging peat and twisted trees. Everything seems to just close in here."

"I said shut up! Maybe Andrea and Kris were right to hire you
to get answers, so here's a couple. Like I said, Cyndi made the
big mistake of trying to push me around for support to set up a
real estate firm. She had followed Andrea here one day and figured out we were digging for something, said she was taking it to
the papers. She told me she had the keys to not only two Braun
houses, but the mansion. She had Marian on her side by then. I
met Marian at Twisted Trees, just like I'd met Cyndi—at her re-
quest—at the house next to Dale Braun's. The little blackmailer
threatened to go public about our project here—which Marian
had surmised and blabbed, though she had the details wrong—
and I had to stop Cyndi. Eventually, had to stop both of them."

"Why the freezer?" she asked, trying hard to keep ahead of

him and steady her feet on the slightly bouncing boards. "Why didn't you just get rid of Cyndi's body or put it in Dale's house?"

She had to keep talking and walking. Soon they'd be to the platform where the dig team worked, and there was no safety beyond that in the very center of the bog. If he pushed her in—he surely didn't want his bullet in her—could she grab a board or the platform to keep from sinking? But no one would be out here until maybe tomorrow, and she'd seen from buried bodies how the peat pulled a person down. And down.

"Ah, the freezer," he said finally. She could tell it was actually calming him down now to talk, maybe to keep his mind off the clasping, suffocating feeling here. She sensed it too.

He went on, "I needed to make it look like Dale Braun had stashed the body *not* in his house, but to keep it for now, move it later. The keys to both the house and the mansion's garage were in Cyndi's purse so I took them, being careful with fingerprints. I kind of liked the idea of preserving that poor, pushy little redneck in the freezer, though not the way my bog people were preserved. And Cyndi had told Marian about our bog work. Marian insisted that she and her committee come in on the action—use the profits and the precious information that should have been all mine—and Andrea's, of course."

She turned to face him at the end of the platform she had just helped to move earlier today. At least it was more stable than the pathway of planks. She had tried to keep control, but terror was taking over. She saw Nick's face and those of her beloved children, then the forms and faces of the dead—of Reaching Woman caught between the two men she loved.

But Brad looked terrified too. Ashen and trembling. He lifted his hand with the gun but did not shoot. "I'm sorry," he said, then lunged at her, shoved her.

She grabbed for his arm, seized it, trying to right herself, save herself. She went down, rear end first, into the muck.

She spread-eagled her legs and thrust out her arms, rather than letting herself be pulled down more easily by going feet first, but already she felt the pull of it. She took a huge breath, tried to blink mud from her eyes.

And then she saw he had toppled in too, panicked, thrashing, going down.

CHAPTER THIRTY-SIX

Claire realized her attempt to spread herself out horizontally wasn't working. Neither would trying to swim to stay afloat because that's what Brad was doing, and he was going down fast, maybe because he weighed more. She let her lower body sink so she was more upright to hold her head up longer.

If she wasn't so terrified, she would have laughed because the murderer thrashing next to her, trying to reach the platform, was screaming for help. His claustrophobia would make this the ultimate just death for him. One victim strangled, enclosed in a freezer, the other strangled, consumed by flames—and he would suffocate in the heavy grasp of the bog.

Dear God, what if they never found either of them—or when they did, far in the future, would they be just more bog bodies to study? Claire stopped trying to move, held her legs and torso steady. Her arms and shoulders were still above the dark surface. Her descent to death slowed a bit.

Her thoughts came scattered in her shock and panic. Surely, Reaching Woman, Hunter and Leader had been dead when they were interred. If only one of the dig team would come back.

Kris could save her. Andrea had cancer when her own husband had really been the cancer in her life.

She tried to stay very still. She panted, filling her lungs with air. Lexi's smiling face floated before her. How desperately she wanted to hold Trey again. What would their lives be like without her?

And her beloved Nick. Not enough time together. He was right to be possessive, want to keep her home… Darcy, their mother… And really, finally, no thought of Jace but that she hoped he would be happy with Brit.

Brad's cries had finally stopped, but he was sucking in huge sobs, nearly up to his chin in black muck.

She looked toward the heavens, praying wordlessly. The sky was blue but clouds were frowning. The trees leaned in, but much too far away to grasp.

Her chin hit the surface of the bog. She tipped her head up to keep her face free.

Brad screamed once, sobbed, then gurgled. She could not look at him, only at the sky as she tried to concentrate on those she loved.

Nick finally thought he was in the right place. An unpaved lane heading west—second one he'd tried just now—had a barrier and a little guard house, other buildings behind it in the growing shadows.

Yes! Claire's car was there. But why hadn't she headed home by now?

He jumped out, vaulted the barrier and ran up to the closest door of the sprawling building. Or should he try the house? One car was there. Kris's Jeep nowhere.

The door was locked. He saw an entry card slot.

He ran around the building toward a short boardwalk. So that was the bog beyond. It looked dark but placid and benign. Could she be out there?

"Claire!" he shouted, cupping his hands around his mouth. "Claire!"

★ ★ ★

Strange how she thought she heard Nick's voice. It echoed, echoed. It must be just that she was thinking of him, loving him at the last. Brad had disappeared, and she would too. She was dreaming she was on dry land, in their backyard, holding Trey with one arm around Lexi and Nick touching her... She gave a silent scream and then one that had her very soul in it.

Her feet hit something. Her eyes, nose and mouth were still above the surface. But surely the bottom of the bog was farther down. Brad was taller and he was gone.

She jerked alert. Had she hit bottom? She was standing on something. A bog body? It seemed to be something sturdy, something that did not suck her down, though she could feel the pull of the bog everywhere.

"Claire!"

Nick? Was she dreaming or was she dead? She felt then that Reaching Woman had once belonged to Hunter but loved Leader. In the end, had she chosen wrong and killed herself? Claire knew that ancient woman did not want to die. She did not want to die either.

"Claire! Claire, are you out here?"

She finally dared to turn her head, nearly slipped off whatever she was standing on.

It was Nick! Nick, really here, running on planks to the platform. Didn't he know to be careful? She tipped her head back farther to shout to him.

"Brad threw me in and he fell in! He's gone!"

"Never mind him. Can you raise an arm? I'm going to swing a board out to you. If you can't, I'll sit on planks and come in."

"No! It sucks you down! I'm standing on something solid! Brad killed them, both women!"

"Claire, shut up and reach for the board!"

She feared the effort would make her slip and pull her under, her last bit of air gone. But she couldn't have Nick in this deadly bog too. She sucked in a huge breath and tried to lift her arm closest to the heavy plank he extended. He was on his stomach on the platform, grunting, straining.

"Come on. Hold it," he shouted. "Now lift the other arm and grip it with that hand too!"

She tried hard. She had to or he'd come in. She knew Nick. He'd die for her, and she had to tell him not to, to live for Trey and Lexi. She gasped for air, trying so hard to get free of this drowning destroyer and preserver of people.

Her hands slipped off. Splinters in her palm. She grabbed at it again and tried to hold tight. Slippery grips. He pulled her closer, closer. Her feet left her platform. Slowly, heavily, she moved toward Nick. He was reaching out toward her because he loved her, because he wanted to save her, the way Reaching Woman had done for the ones she loved.

Nick had a fistful of her slick, slimy hair. Her scalp hurt, but she was so hysterically grateful for his touch she didn't care. He grabbed for her under one armpit. She slipped away, but he seized her again.

He grasped her muddy wrist so hard her hand went numb but he pulled her closer to him, closer. Finally, he had her by her T-shirt and a belt loop on her jeans. He half dragged, half lifted her onto the platform to her waist while her legs still dangled. Her chin scraped the wood. He reached down and yanked her up by her jeans, then laid her on her back like some slimy mermaid pulled from a prehistoric sea.

He laid beside her to embrace her as if they were in their very own bed, safe and so very much in love.

CHAPTER THIRTY-SEVEN

One Month Later:

Kris hugged Claire, then sat beside her on the couch in the Markwoods' crowded Florida room. They were hosting an open house for their friends with no worries that a drone would come smashing through the plate glass window.

Brad was dead, and Yi Ling had been charged with multiple counts of attempted murder for helping him to try to bring down the helicopter. A phone call from the manager of the Fort Lauderdale antique store had tipped Brad off that someone who flew in via helicopter from Marco Island knew too much about what to ask for. The man had followed Jace and Brit back to the executive airport. According to Yi Ling, who was even more terrified of being deported back to China than of being sent to prison here, Brad had thought the couple must be Claire and Nick—and he'd tried to stage an "accident" with a drone to eliminate them.

It turned out that Brad and Yi Ling had not been having an affair, though he'd convinced the girl that if she didn't go along with his plans, she could be deported. Andrea was insisting on testifying on Yi Ling's behalf, however weak she was from her radiation treatments for cancer. She had not been charged, as she could not be linked to Brad's actions or plans and insisted she knew nothing about anything beyond his having copies made of artifacts for sales to support their huge, important project.

"Claire found a unique way to discover more bog bodies," Kris announced to everyone. "Get thrown in by a murderer, then stand on one of their most precious relics, a 'Rosetta stone' to their ancient culture. She left not only no stone unturned but no bones unturned. We have finally recovered the stone and will begin to study it soon—with Claire's help. And former Senator Bradley Vance got a chance to rest in peat before his body was recovered—with difficulty—by the dig team while the police looked on. Sorry for the sick jokes, but Brad Vance was a very sick man."

Claire just shook her head at the gallows—that is, bog—humor. But Kris wasn't done yet.

"And here—Andrea said it's okay to show everyone—is the large artifact-relic we finally dug out that saved you from going all the way under, Claire. She wanted to show you she will totally share all artifacts with you to study." Kris motioned to Mitch and Jace, hovering in the doorway, to bring something in.

The two men, who had just finished early training in DC for flying into hurricanes, came in lugging what looked like a— Well, what was it?

Jace and Mitch put the stone carefully on the tile floor in front of the couch. It was about the size of a small bed pillow and covered with carvings. Claire leaned down and patted it. "Well, it did save my life—and of course Nick had a little something to do with that," she added, smiling up at him. "And I'm so glad to see we can now study these relics in person, so to speak."

Claire had been so busy working with the police and testifying that she hadn't heard what the new dig team had resurrected from the spot where she had almost drowned. She gasped when she saw what was carved on top.

Everyone came over, huddled, looking down at the stone, now cleaned of its mud and peat. It was covered with deep primitive carvings, including one which took Claire's breath away as she reached down to touch it. For there, in stark carved relief was a woman with her arms raised. It was as if Reaching Woman had reached out to save her, held her up when she could have been sucked down by the bog. And next to her were carved two men kneeling before her in obvious deference or even worship.

Claire held her breath for a moment. Her beloved Reaching Woman had lived a triumphant but tragic life. She could tell everyone was waiting for her to say something. She wanted to say *That stone was her gift to me.* But she said only, "They really weren't prehistoric if they worshipped a woman, now were they? That makes them sound pretty advanced to me."

Nick smiled but rolled his eyes as he leaned down to touch the stone. Jace elbowed Mitch. Nita and Gina grinned.

"Actually," Claire went on, her voice more quiet, "I believe the woman was some sort of goddess. I believe she belonged to both men—or they belonged to her somehow. I also theorize that Hunter was forbidden to her or beneath her, and that he paid for their love by being executed by his people. Not to go into the details with everyone here now," she said with a glance at Lexi, "let's just say, their form of justice was the price he paid. Yet, in more ways than one, Reaching Woman kept his heart. The tall man called Leader loved her too, and perhaps she loved him. I suppose he either died of a broken or weak heart but, when her people or herself saw her weakness and humanity, they let her do away with herself and buried her with both men—or she decreed it that way. In my own heart, I believe all that. But as for in my head—there's still much to be found and figured out at Black Bog."

Lexi broke into their huddle around the stone and got on her knees to study it. "This lady reminds me of you, Mommy. Like when I do things you don't like and you just raise your hands like you are really ticked off but don't know what to do."

"That's my girl," Jace said with a little laugh. "The small one, that is," he said and took Brit's hand to raise it to his lips, the hand with the diamond engagement ring.

"And my girl too," Nick said, and ruffled Lexi's hair. Everyone laughed, even Nita, who was living with a beaming Bronco in their new house and had finally learned to smile again. And to put up with Betty Richards who had followed every word of the national and worldwide news that she herself had helped to break by being nosy enough to read license plates at night.

It seemed the bog people had finally had their revenge for being disturbed and disinterred. Former and now deceased Senator Bradley J. Vance was guilty not only of selling ancient, protected items on the black market but of two murders and a third attempted one, besides his trying to eliminate those in the helicopter. Documents he had left behind indicated he felt vindicated to do anything to protect what he considered his great gift to mankind.

Nick had said earlier that it was a good thing Brad had died in Black Bog because that was far better than having to face the two revenge-bent hellions from small-town Georgia, let alone a lifetime in prison or even the death penalty—which Brad had managed to dole out to himself.

Andrea did have an aggressive form of breast cancer, but she had been cleared of any crime. It was punishment enough, Kris had said, not only that she'd lost her husband after learning of his terrible acts, but that the Black Bog project—the Vances' secret, private obsession—was now big news and in the government's domain. Kris had been named as head archaeologist, and Claire knew that she still kept Andrea up-to-date on everything they found. At least there had been only depositions and not a trial for Claire and Dale to go through in the witness box. Of course, it had helped Dale's reputation that he had donated Eva Braun's diary to the National WWII Museum in New Orleans instead of selling it to the highest bidder.

The double whammy of notoriety in this case was that Dale was so relieved to be exonerated that he had agreed to scores of interviews—at the law offices, with Nick present—about his great-uncle's ties to Hitler. Germany and Russia were calling the "Hitler's Wife Lived in South Florida" story an elaborate hoax, but the United States and the United Kingdom had the story splashed everywhere as real, not fake news.

At least all the publicity had made Ken Jensen lay off pushing for Claire to join the NPD as a forensic consultant. He hadn't been too pleased that Nick hadn't cued him in on Dale's Nazi connection or that Claire had not let him know about Brad Vance possibly selling knockoff jewelry and daggers. Ken had served a subpoena on both of the Vances' antiques stores and learned that several wealthy Europeans had recently contracted to receive stone statues or metal bangle bracelets and necklaces emblazoned with the image of an ancient woman with her arms raised in prayer.

What Nick was calling The Black Bog Case had also made Kris and Claire famous—though at least not infamous—as they gave interviews about what they knew of the ancient people's lives and artifacts.

Finally, when everyone had gone and Kris had left complete photos of all the latest finds for Claire to study before she could return to the bog and see the artifacts themselves, the Markwood family of four sat on the couch, Lexi holding Trey now, all quiet at last.

"Well," Nick said, "that's enough of special secret assignments."

"Not secret anymore," Claire said, leaning her head on his shoulder.

He sighed heavily. "And once you're finished with Black Bog, let's just move on to something light and lovely—and safe."

"Like pretty butterflies," Lexi said, "'cause they can't hurt anybody."

"Maybe," Claire said with a smile at Lexi, "we can plant some flowers and put in a feeder out by the pool to draw them here."

"Sounds good to me," Nick agreed, as he put his arm around her shoulders. "And, like Lexi says, *safe*. But I think I've stupidly said that before."

★ ★ ★ ★ ★

If you enjoyed Silent Scream,
don't miss the next suspenseful story in
Karen Harper's South Shores series,
Dark Storm
Coming soon from MIRA Books.

AUTHOR'S NOTE

Several books I've read on forensic psychology claim that "crime is character." Circumstances, motive, opportunity, proximity—it all boils down to the character of the criminal, and character is a central focus of suspense writing. I may start with a fascinating or frightening setting or plot, but above all character counts.

I also thought the claim that Sherlock Holmes created forensic analysis is fascinating. He solved crimes by psyching out what sort of person would murder someone and why. So the idea of studying possible "perps" to solve crimes came far before *CSI* and *Law & Order: Special Victims Unit* or some of the popular fiction about not only who-dunit but why-dunit.

I have read several articles about Nazi war criminals hiding in the United States, most recently the Minnesota arrest of Michael Karkoc, the "Nazi next door." One article, "There Could be 'Hundreds' of Nazi War Criminals Still Living in the United States" by Dan Amira appeared in *NY Magazine* on March 17, 2017, was especially helpful. Although war criminals would be in their eighties and nineties, we all must admit people are living longer these days. But I did make Dale's great-uncle dead for years so that Dale has to deal with that tragic heritage rather than the man himself.

The idea of having Eva Braun not die with Hitler, but flee to the United States, is an idea that occurred to me while reading a book about Hitler's fall in Germany. An author's imagination is always dealing with "what if."

Other somewhat unusual things mentioned in the book are fact, not fiction. It is difficult for most of us to understand that some people cannot recognize others' faces, even those close to them. The July 14, 2017, issue of *Time Magazine* had a fascinating article on this written by Kate Samuelson. An expert on face blindness, she believes that as many people as 1 in 50 have some degree of prosopagnosia. So I thought it might be interesting to link the big boom in facial recognition technology to that disability. Also, the fact that Claire suffers from narcolepsy bonds her with Kris even more.

As Kris mentions in this story, the prehistoric Windover Bog Culture, a 1982 archaeological discovery near Titusville, Florida, was a shock to the sedate, touristy south. It is now on the US National Register of Historic Places. Archaeologists used forensic psychologists to help them probe the ancient culture at that dig. Researching *Florida Bog Mummies* online will lead you to several articles about this site. NOVA has an official website about this on their PBS site under *Ancient America's Bog People*. There is also a video online entitled *Windover's Ancient "Bog People" Among Most Significant Archaeological Finds in North America*.

I hope you will watch for *Dark Storm*, the next book in the South Shores series. After all, Nick is finally convinced nothing bad or dangerous could possibly happen in connection with beautiful butterflies. He's been wrong before when he thought Claire's working with prehistoric dead bodies would not lead to danger. Stay tuned.

Special thanks to my great support team at MIRA Books, especially my editor, Emily Ohanjanians, and my agent, Annelise Robey. Thanks to my brother Tom in Atlanta for the information on Zebulon, Georgia. And, as ever, to my husband Don for proofreading my stories.

Karen Harper
February 2018

SUSPENSE IN REAL LIFE
BY KAREN HARPER

I didn't realize that, for years, my contemporary novels have been what's currently referred to as "domestic suspense" or "domestic thriller." To use several high-profile examples, think *Gone Girl* or *Girl on the Train*. (Hmm, should I start putting the word *girl* in my titles? *Girl Gives Silent Scream*?) Obviously readers love novels with marriage or family drama as well as the solve-this-scary-case stories.

Literary domestic dramas mixed with mayhem and murder are not new. The popular 1930s/1940s *Thin Man* series, featuring Nick and Nora Charles, became a television show. Also in that era on the brink of World War II, Dorothy L. Sayers wrote the delightful Lord Peter Whimsey/Harriet Vane series. Another domestic drama/suspense series with cozy and humorous touches were novels under the *Mr. and Mrs. North* umbrella which also was a television series. More recently Anne Perry's *Charlotte and Thomas Pitt* novels featuring a historic Victorian inspector and his wife are a continually fresh, charming and suspenseful blend of mystery and domestic drama.

I had written both stand–alone novels and an earlier series (The Queen Elizabeth I Mysteries) without categorizing them as domestic suspense. All I knew was I wanted to give my readers books with mystery, romance and complicated human relationships.

In my earlier stand-alone MIRA books, the two main characters fall in love while trying to solve a crime and stay alive. The romance evolves during the deadly suspense. The main characters have problems, but the stories end in commitment, usually an engagement or plans for a future wedding.

However, in this South Shores series, I stirred up this pattern by creating a very real heroine who has some modern "complications" she must work through in her domestic life as well as in her career: forensic psychologist Claire Markwood has narcolepsy, she is divorced with a child, and her ex-husband is one of the main viewpoint characters even as her new relationship with Nick, a criminal lawyer, develops. Lexi is a troubled child for reasons obvious in the first three books. Claire is trying to balance her career with family life; Nick is too. Their commitment to their work is admirable but is also a problem.

Does anything here sound familiar when we look at "real life" in today's demanding world? We have all observed stressed romantic relationships and marriages through media, family ties—hopefully not too close-up and personal. I know my silent study of such situations has helped me to create reality, tension and resolutions through my plots, characters and dialogue.

Perhaps how my main characters work through their problems now and in the future—as do the other secondary pairs of romantic characters in the series—will not only interest but also encourage readers in their own domestic dramas and suspenseful lives.